Colonel Hatch trotted forward and reined back in front of the Apache.

"Good day, Chief Victorio," Hatch said briskly.

Victorio never felt comfortable speaking with the White Eyes. A quick nod was all he got out before Hatch rambled on, as if long pleasantries had been exchanged instead of impolitely naming the Warm Springs chief in direct address.

"I'm disappointed to find that many of your people have left the reservation to ride with Juh. Nedhi and Chiricahua raiding must be stopped."

"Many ride with Geronimo," said Victorio.

"The raids must stop. These are more than annoying, they are very dangerous. Your people get shot at, some have been wounded."

"They are warriors." He saw no logic in the man's argument. Warriors fought and were rewarded with horses and cattle. That was the way it had always been. "Meat," Victorio said, "You promised us meat and gave us nothing. Why shouldn't we raid to get that which is ours by treaty?"

"You don't understand how it works," said Hatch. "Many of my forts aren't getting enough meat, either. It is expensive. Appropriations don't always make it this far west—"

"Meat," Victorio repeated. "We plan a peace treaty with Sonora so Juh and I can raid your settlements. Unless we get meat, this is the way it will be."

"Then it will be war!" raged Hatch. He turned red and struggled to control his anger. "You will be killed, every man among you, and the women and children will be taken to San Carlos where you belong!"

THE WARRIOR'S PATH

Karl Lassiter

P

Pinnacle Books
Kensington Publishing Corp.

http://www.pinnaclebooks.com

PINNACLE BOOKS are published by

Kensington Publishing Corp.
850 Third Avenue
New York, NY 10022

First Printing: July, 1998
10 9 8 7 6 5 4 3 2 1

Printed in the United States of America

The loveliest spring flower, the most delicate leaf,
The brightest plumed songbird,
All must fade in autumn and perish in winter's snow.

For Patty. Always.

The capture [of Victorio] is not very probable, but the killing (cruel as it will be) can, I suppose, be done in time.

General John Pope
Annual Report of the Secretary of War for the Year 1880,
I, Part 2, 88.

While it is based on actual events, this novel is a work of fiction.

PART I

Prologue to War

Seeds of War

"Kill them. Kill them all now." Victorio huddled near the guttering fire, his dark eyes fixed on the flames. What he saw were not the dancing sparks rising from the burning, popping fragrant green piñon log but vague, distant movement, encroachment on Apacheria, his homeland. He poked savagely at the fire with a smoldering stick. New sparks twisted into the cold New Mexico night air, turning and blazing like the hatred already within him for the *Indah*—the White Eyes—and their never-stopping slow theft of holy land. He straightened, his hand repositioning the emblem of the Warm Springs Apache, the buckskin band looped over his right shoulder and fastened at his left hip. The sacred *hoddentin* pollen from the tule cattails stained the leather a dull yellow, his badge of manhood, leadership, belonging. He had earned all this on the Sacred

Mountain, Salinas Peak, and had proven himself both a warrior and a chief repeatedly ever after.

"Enough of such talk! That is too dangerous a path to ride," Mangas Coloradas said quickly, contradicting his friend and ally. All sitting in council around the fire waited for the Eastern Chiricahua chief to continue his thought. Of those here, perhaps only Cuchillo Negro, seated at Mangas Coloradas's right hand, was as respected. "The White Eyes can be dealt with. Their distant war weakens them. We need not risk the death of our women and children when there are other ways to bring about peace."

"They fight themselves and still there are enough of them to dig our ground to steal away the yellow metal, *pesh-klitso,* and the white iron, *pesh-lickoyee,*" Victorio said hotly. "All along the Mogollón Rim they sneak like thieves and dig their tunnels into the body of the world, angering the Mountain Gods. They take away the *pesh-klitso* they find, and it brings more rushing in. They take the forbidden metal!" Victorio's breath came in heaving gusts now. His anger grew. "They might fight among themselves beyond the rising sun but they fill our land with their greed. You, of all here, ought to know their treachery!"

Before the Civil War, Mangas Coloradas had dealt with the Mexicans intruding on his land to mine copper. In the guise of friendship, the Mexicans had invited Mangas Coloradas and his people to a feast of corn and other food. A hidden howitzer fired into the group, killing many and scattering the survivors. Two of Mangas's wives had been killed and only after the massacre did the chief realize that the infant he had rescued from the chaos, clutched tightly to his breast and swaddled in a heavy blanket, was his own son, Mangus.

Treachery walked the land, and Victorio wondered why Mangas Coloradas did not recognize it. Even the fiercest storm lost its force if it blew too long. He snorted, thin plumes of exhalation freezing in feathery patterns before being swept away by the north wind. At times, Mangas was too trusting for his own good. Or the good of the Apache.

"There are honorable men among them. We can parley," insisted Mangas Coloradas. His frail form took on strength and dignity, and Victorio knew he could never deny the head chief, no matter how wrong he might be. Looking left and right, Victorio saw others shared his concern. He might challenge Mangas Coloradas now and win support from Cochise and Geronimo and Loco and Nana and even Cuchillo Negro. But he could not do it. He respected Mangas Coloradas too much.

"You are an old fool," Geronimo said, in his usual rude fashion. "They seek our death, both sides of their war. Did not General Baylor try to kill us all?"

"The Great Father Davis removed him," Mangas Coloradas said softly.

"And we deal now with Carleton, who wears blue and not gray. What will the Great *Nantan* of the bluecoats do with him?" Geronimo spat into the fire. Victorio joined him, as did Cochise to show their contempt for James Carleton. The old chief remained unmoved by this show of unity against his wish for a peaceable solution.

"We fought Carleton," said Cochise, "and you were gravely wounded. He used his cannon all too well against us at Apache Pass. Have your wounds healed so quickly?" Cochise tilted his head to the side, as if examining Mangas Coloradas. For months the old chief had recuperated at Ojo Caliente—and still he sought peace with Carleton.

Victorio looked around the circle at the other headmen, seeing how few believed in Mangas Coloradas's solution for their trouble with the Indah. He returned to poking the fire, stirring it to greater life until the heat burned at his face and arms. Only Mangas Coloradas thought the White Eyes could change their colors and become honorable. Cochise, Nana, who was older even than Mangas Coloradas, Geronimo, Loco, Delgadito, not one of those fierce and honorable warriors agreed. Victorio saw it in their eyes, the set of their shoulders, the way their hands moved restlessly on bone-handled knifes and fingered rifles resting in the crooks of their arms.

But Mangas Coloradas was a decent, intelligent, cunning man. Victorio respected him.

Victorio rose to his full five-foot-ten-inch height and looked down at the older man.

"Do what you will. The others are right. The White Eyes think only to steal from us, to move us from our hereditary lands. Talk to them, if there is any hope of peace. May Ussen give you strength and a clever tongue, but I will not be still long." Without waiting for a reply, Victorio vanished into the darkness, wrapped in his blanket and an icy cold that chilled more than his flesh.

Life was difficult, but Victorio knew it might be worse. His band of Warm Springs Mimbreño Apache ranged far and wide, successfully finding game in the Black Range. Twice he had even gone to the San Mateo Mountains on successful raids. His wife and their four children were content and well cared for. But the rumors always whispering in his ear from those traveling from the north told of bitter fighting between General Carleton's bluecoats and the Mescalero. Kit Carson, known as Red Clothes to the Navajo, knew Apache ways too well and tracked down even the wiliest of the Apache from his base at Fort Stanton.

Victorio sighted down the barrel of his rifle, flicking away a nonexistent speck of dirt. Coming suddenly into his iron sights was his sister, Lozen. He lowered the rifle.

"You are worried," he said. "Did you not steal enough horses from the White Eyes?" He tried to make a joke.

His sister was the equal of most warriors in his band and prided herself on always returning from a raid with at least one horse, usually the finest. This day, his bantering brought no smile to her grim face. Her clothing, a warrior's rather than that of a woman, was torn and filthy from her long ride. She wore a simple cloth headband holding her long hair from her dark eyes, a calico shirt, a breechclout supported by a belt with two sheathed knives, and buckskin leggings. Her moccasins showed holes from lack of time to repair them, another testament to her desperate travel. Unlike her brother and the others, she did not wear the symbol of fertility, the hoddentin-stained strip over her shoulder.

"I bring only sorrow, my brother," Lozen said. She hunkered down near him. He smelled gunpowder and blood on her, but she seemed unharmed. As was her habit, she had scouted alone, preferring to let the slower men blunder about by themselves. Victorio had often said—with no joke intended—the Apache would have nothing to fear if he had a dozen warriors as able as his sister. Even Nana, called Broken Foot, who had seen more summers than any of them, preferred her company to that of the young braves in his band in battle.

Victorio laid down his rifle and stood, face turned toward the brilliant blue cold afternoon sky. Above him, ice clouds like the skeletons of delicate birds fluttered across the sky. Victorio saw a huge crow wheeling high above their camp. A bad omen. From the black bird he turned slowly, hunting for other omens. None came, but the crow alone was enough. His heart knotted like a rope as he faced his sister.

"What word do you have of Mangas Coloradas?" he asked, instinctively knowing the source of her grief.

"Dead," she said, the word a burning bullet aimed for his heart. "He was tortured and murdered by the White Eyes."

"Who? Which ones?" Victorio wanted to scream and rant and tear at the heavens. He forced himself to calmness. Only after he learned who had killed his friend would the blood rage come upon him.

"A scout for Colonel West captured him. Joseph Walker, by name. Walker and those with him killed the three accompanying Mangas Coloradas, then took him to old Fort MacLane. Carleton ordered the death, calling Mangas Coloradas a robber and thief. But it was West who tortured him."

"They tortured him?" Victorio's heart threatened to explode from his chest.

"He tried to escape them three times, the soldiers said. They approached him at Pinos Altos under a white truce flag and they violated it!" Lozen's hands clenched and unclenched in fury as she spoke. She made no effort to hold back her anger, as did Victorio.

"What became of his body?"

"Buried by West. I know where it is. Conner told me everything, and he has no reason to lie. He did not know Joseph Walker. Conner volunteered everything I have told you, Brother. He is as outraged as any blooded warrior!"

Victorio knew Daniel Conner as an honest man and friend to both the Mescalero and Warm Springs Apache. Some, like the Indian agents, might stir up trouble with their greed and perfidy, but other Indah never gave reason to be doubted.

"You and I, Lozen. We will go to where they buried Mangas Coloradas. We owe him a decent burial so he can wander the Happy Place forever."

Lozen nodded once, spun, and lightly ran to her horse. She caught up the reins and vaulted onto its back and headed north even as Victorio chose a suitable mount and galloped after her. They rode all night and into the next day to reach the deserted fort, slowing only to rest and water their horses.

Victorio reined back and cocked his head to one side. As they rode, he had been especially watchful. If Colonel West had killed a warrior of Mangas Coloradas's stature, he would be boasting about it—and others would be seeking to give themselves names as heroes. Any who caught and killed Victorio would be equally honored by the slaughtering bluecoat commander.

Snowdrifts in the shade of tall pine and blue spruce reminded Victorio of the recent storm, but the sight of a mound of fresh earth told of a different tempest. He circled the clearing in front of the deserted fort, noting an abandoned iron kettle beside ashes from a recent fire, perhaps three days old. Had the bluecoats warmed themselves on this fire as they tortured Mangas Coloradas?

Victorio never tortured his prisoners. The Apache showed no mercy, but few warriors would bear up well under the sight of a helpless man dying by inches. He had noticed among the White Eyes the streak of cruelty that brought only suffering to the innocent.

Mangas Coloradas should have died as a warrior, with knife drawn and fighting.

"No one is near," Lozen said, and Victorio believed her. She had an uncanny knack for scouting, although this was not her real enemies-against Power. Whenever she wished to know where the enemy hid, Lozen would stand with arms outstretched, palms up to the sky, and pray to Ussen. Following the path of the sun, she would turn slowly until her palms tingled and her flesh changed color, sometimes changing to a deep purple. The intensity of the sensation told how far the enemy was, the closer the foe the more obvious the tingling.

Victorio slid from horseback and walked to the grave. Kneeling, he began digging, slowly at first and then faster and faster as bile rose in his throat. Using hands and knife blade, he tore at the soft dirt until the body of his friend lay revealed to the open sky and Ussen's gaze.

Victorio recoiled, rocking back and coming to his feet. Tears came to his eyes and rage unlike any he had ever felt seized him.

"They cut off his head!" Victorio cried.

"I think they must have boiled off the flesh in the iron kettle," Lozen said, her own voice choked with fury. Her moccasined foot kicked hard at the kettle, sending it spinning away. "He will wander the Happy Place without a head, lost and shunned forever!"

Victorio's back arched as he turned his face to the sky. A wordless cry of rage ripped from his throat. He slashed at the world with his knife and knew there could never be peace with monsters who committed such vile acts.

Relocation

Fall, 1865
Pinos Altos

"Another is dead?" Victorio's shoulders slumped when he heard his scout's report. After Mangas Coloradas's death, Delgadito had become chief of the Eastern Chiricahua Apache. Then *he* had simply . . . vanished. No one, not even Lozen, who had gone to track down the errant leader, had found so much as a footprint in the sand. That left the Warm Springs band without a leader until Victorio had slowly worked his way into command.

With that came the sorry task of hearing of every death in his band.

"Cuentas Azules was lost in a skirmish with the buffalo soldiers two days ago," Kayawa said, shuffling his feet and wishing he could be anywhere else. "He did not steal even a single horse. He was shot from ambush as he rode in to raid a new settlement near Ojo Caliente."

"They kill our women and children, too," Victorio said angrily. "Our horses are scrawny, and the settlers on our land have too few cattle to bother stealing." He shrugged this off. He never stole an entire herd, always leaving a few for the White Eyes settlers to breed back. This tactic worked well with the Mexicans on his raids south of the border into Mexico. His ally, Chief Juh of the Nedhni, from his fastness in the Blue Mountains between Sonora and Chihuahua, often commented on this skill for keeping the Warm Springs people fed.

The truth was upon him, though. Victorio had to admit his battle plan had failed because of Carleton's orders. The fanatical bluecoat commander scorched the earth and killed any brave found alone. Never would he engage directly. Always his soldiers sniped and took the coward's way in a battle, attacking women and children when the warriors were raiding. Worst of all, this worked.

Their ancestral land was slipping away, as sand slipped through his open fingers. He missed Mangas and his wise counsel, even if the old chief had foolishly trusted the truce flag. Victorio closed his eyes and pictured Apacheria as it once was, in his younger days. He had endured forty summers, heat and cold, starvation and enemies. How he longed for a decent enemy! To chase after the Comanche again, the wind whipping at his graying hair, the smell of blood and victory in his nostrils, the feel of a powerful stallion striving beneath him as he loosed arrow after arrow—those had been good days.

The sacred lands had been the domain of the Mountain Gods alone, not defiled by the settlers and miners hunting gold and silver. But there had been good times, and those he missed the most.

"I understand now," he said, revelation washing over him like a wave of putrescence.

"What is that?" asked Kayawa. The scout turned and

cocked his head to one side, listening to the distant thunder of approaching hooves.

Victorio did not hear the horses; he heard only his own thoughts. "Mangas was tired. That is why he sought peace with the Indah. And that is why I will follow Loco's wise counsel and do the same."

"Soldier!" cried Kayawa, jerking up his rifle from where he had leaned it against a scrub oak.

"Many soldiers," Victorio said wearily, knowing what had to be done and not looking forward to it with any joy. "Colonel Davis asked to parley, and I sent Lozen to arrange this meeting."

"Where are your guards! Remember what happened to Mangas Coloradas!"

"There is no need. I understand Mangas more than any other now, even Nana. He was a wise man. I can only hope I follow the path he would choose now." Victorio sucked on his teeth, knowing he would never have made such a declaration in January when he found the headless body of his friend. Eight months of sporadic battle had left him tired and his people impoverished. He trusted Lozen to be certain he did not come to the same sorry end that Mangas Coloradas had. These soldiers were under strict orders to put an end to the sporadic clashes between bluecoat patrols and Apache raiders. Lozen said Colonel Davis was an honorable man, even if he took orders from Carleton.

"Why here?" demanded Kayawa. "It is here that they murdered Mangas Coloradas!"

"I chose this sorry place to remind me of the folly of too much trust," Victorio said. But he was tired. "I also think the spirit of Mangas will guide me here, if it can find me."

He hefted his rifle, then mounted. Kayawa looked uneasy about accompanying his chief, yet would not remain behind. That would show cowardice in the face of the enemy. Victorio waved the scout into the forest a mile away.

"There are others waiting out of sight. Find Lozen in the forest. If anything happens to me, she will exact vengeance. But I do not expect trouble. Not this time. When Colonel Davis leaves, follow him and his soldiers without them seeing. I want to know what they plan that they aren't telling me."

Kayawa thrust his rifle skyward in a defiant gesture, then raced off. Victorio wished others could be with him as he spoke with the bluecoat officer, but he knew this had to be his decision alone. He carried the burden of command and the others would listen to him, as he had to Mangas Coloradas.

Victorio rode slowly from the hilltop down to the Pinos Altos ruins. He could not remember what had happened to this outpost. Had Apache burned it or had the bluecoats destroyed their own fort? He had seen how, as they withdrew from useless sites, they left nothing behind that might aid their enemy. A slow smile crawled onto his lips. It felt good to be known as their enemy. Chief Nana, wise in his old age, often said that life without decent enemies led to a worthless existence. Defeat a praiseworthy foe and honor came to the victor. If only Carleton and his black-faced buffalo soldiers would fight rather than destroying everything around them like a plague of locusts before fading away into the dark. They were nothing more than a shadow cast by a guttering campfire. But what shadow left behind death and starvation? Victorio knew he could become the most renowned warrior ever to ride through Apacheria opposing them and their murdering ways.

His broad chest expanded as he took a deep breath, then let it out slowly. What might have been fought with what must be in Victorio's mind. The decision had been made some time ago, on a lonely mountain peak after three days of fasting. The vision had confirmed what Victorio already knew. Mangas Coloradas had been right. A treaty with the White Eyes was the only way for the Apache to survive on their ancestral lands.

He sat on his pony, waiting patiently for the approaching cavalry column. He saw the sergeant motion, splitting the double line so they could flank him. Twenty men against a solitary brave. The odds were lopsided—in his favor. Victorio wanted to laugh again. They treated him as if he might charge their rank and slaughter them all.

In his day he had killed far more than this patrol.

"Chief Victorio?" called the one with gold braid gleaming in the autumn sun. "I am Colonel Davis, sent by General Carleton to accept your surrender."

"I would talk first," Victorio said. The White Eyes did nothing but talk. This appeal ought to be accepted readily. He barely restrained his sardonic laughter when it was. Davis swung from the saddle and walked forward, his sword clanking at his side. He rested his hand on the hilt, as if considering how he might charge Victorio and slice off his ears for a trophy.

Again the Warm Springs chief felt a glow of pride. How they feared him! He stood alone, and still they feared him! His delight faded when he remembered soldiers such as these had tortured and mutilated Mangas Coloradas. If the summer raiding had gone differently, they would have been begging *him* for mercy.

"General Carleton is adamant on one point: your total surrender. You will be relocated from the land around Ojo Caliente to Bosque Redondo."

"Bosque Redondo? Where you take the Navajo?" Victorio considered this. Many of his Mescalero brothers had been removed to this prison without walls along the Pecos River. They told of moldy food and no game to hunt.

Comanches raided with impunity, and there were few horses to steal on this reservation. But there might be compensation. The Apache could kill their enemy, the Navajo.

Victorio considered this lure, then worried that the soldiers would prevent the Apache from going south into the San Andres Mountains for religious ceremonies. Bosque Redondo, under the guns of White Eyes soldiers at Fort Sumner, did not sound like the kind of future he sought for his people.

"We will give your tribe food and guarantee peace. In return, you will leave immediately for Bosque Redondo and promise to cease all raiding. Never again will you steal horses and cattle or endanger the settlers."

"What of the Navajo? They raid us even as we speak," Victorio said. He *would* enjoy fighting the Diné. At times they met in peace. More often, Apache and Navajo fought. They were worthy enemies, and having them on the same stretch of land would give them the opportunity for good fights. Victorio had heard of the Mescalero raids on the Navajo already moved to Bosque Redondo. Many warriors came away with herds of cattle and many horses.

"We will protect you from them," Davis said, clearing his throat. "And we will defend them from any raiding you might feel obligated to launch."

Victorio considered what the Indah officer said. The chief's belly rumbled from lack of food. He had ridden hard and fast these past days, but the hunger among the women and children in his band near Ojo Caliente came not from rapid travel but from soul-grinding deprivation. The soldiers destroyed everything and made life disagreeable at every turn. Always they followed like curs hunting for scraps of food, sniffing and nipping, but never fighting.

"I would see Bosque Redondo before I lead my people there," Victorio said carefully.

"Agreed. In one week, I shall personally show you how life will be different—and better—when the Mimbreño Apache are situated at Fair Carletonia."

Colonel Davis saluted smartly, executed an about-face, and marched to his mount. How silly he looked, but Victorio barely noticed. In one week he would study this place on the distant Pecos River where the Indah would feed, clothe, and protect his people.

It was what Mangas Coloradas would have wanted.

Death to the Apache

Late Fall, 1865
Ojo Caliente

For two days Victorio had outrun the cavalry patrol, and his feet were weary. He sank down in the nest of jagged-edged red granite boulders, holding his rifle in the crook of his arm as he tore off a piece of jerky and gnawed on it. He had stolen the salty meat from a trooper he had silently killed yesterday just after sunset. This was his first chance to eat. If he had been able to take the soldier's horse, swaybacked and broke down though it was, he could have outdistanced Colonel Davis's entire company.

He spat, then drank sparingly from the canteen he had also stolen. The metallic taste caused him to spit again, this time wasting precious liquid. He was miles from the nearest safe water. The area around Warm Springs hid many sweet water places in addition to the more obvious sulfur-laden springs, but he was not near any of them.

A clank of metal and the creaking of men shifting in their uncomfortable McClellan saddles alerted him to the nearness of the bluecoats. Victorio hastily put away his sparse food, slung it over his back in a rolled-up blanket, and prepared for battle. Again. As he had over the past weeks.

Dropping to his belly atop the waist-high sun-warmed rock, he sighted along the barrel of his Sharps. The rifle needed cleaning, but he had no time to do it. Davis's buffalo soldiers had kept him on the run, and he respected their tracking and fighting abilities too much to dally. Victorio waited patiently as the first rider showed himself not twenty yards away, his black face shining in the sun. Sergeant's stripes on his arms told Victorio to bide his time, although the buffalo soldier reined back, head up, and turned slowly as if sniffing him out.

Victorio knew the black soldiers were good fighters, but they weren't *that* good to find him like a dog hunting fresh meat. He was downwind and they were not endowed with the Powers like his people. Not one, either Indah or buffalo soldier, had a Power capable of unerringly finding the enemy, as did his sister Lozen. Not one located ammunition as easily as Nana simply by praying to Ussen, then turning slowly until the god told him where to find the supplies needed most by the Apache.

"Cap'n!" shouted the Negro noncom. "He's been this way. I know he has."

Victorio began to doubt his own belief about the soldiers. Perhaps this one had a Power. His finger tightened on the trigger, choosing to take out the sergeant rather than wait for the white officer to move into clear view. Better to remove immediate danger than to be dogged for the next dozen miles back to his band at Ojo Caliente.

"Is the red bastard still on foot?"

"Reckon so, sir," the sergeant said. "Not been any sign of horse's hooves."

"Why'd he choose to go it on foot?" mused the officer, riding forward to stop beside his sergeant. His gold braid gleamed in the warm afternoon sun, and his saber clanked as he shifted his weight in the saddle. "Can't rightly make sense of that." He shucked off a canvas glove and used his yellow bandanna to wipe sweat from his face. The sergeant's dark eyes continued to dart here and there, seeking his quarry. Victorio appreciated the way he did not waste time sopping up the sweat on his face. Like an Apache, he was single-minded in his hunt.

For Victorio.

Victorio wavered, the buffalo soldier resting in the precise spot in his sights for a clean kill, then moved a fraction of an inch to sight in on the officer. A fight with the squad of black troopers might be more difficult, but the death of their officer would throw them into disarray. His finger came back smoothly, and the heavy rifle bucked hard against his shoulder. A puff of white smoke from the muzzle filled the air, then drifted away on the soft afternoon breeze. Victorio saw the Indah captain stiffen in the saddle, start to reach for the small red spot growing on his chest, then slump and fall to the side. A clean hit.

Any hope he had that the buffalo soldiers would be confused or frightened evaporated like water splashed on a rock in the desert sun. The sergeant located him quickly and bellowed for his men to charge. Victorio had no time to reload. He slid back into the protection of the rock, wishing he had his bow and arrows. He had left his wolf-hide quiver in camp, along with his arrows poisoned with deer spleen mixed with the leaves of nettles and lichen scraped from rock. A single scratch would kill.

Slinging the rifle over his shoulder, he settled into a distance-devouring stride that took him away from the attacking soldiers and into a small stand of pines a quarter mile away.

The tree limbs were too high for him to use. He sought out a cottonwood a few hundred yards on the other side of the pines, downhill and near an alkali pond. Underfoot, he felt the vibration of the bluecoats' horses galloping behind as he swerved from the game trail he followed, found a tree, and swung into the low, rough-barked branch overhanging the path. Heart pounding like a war drum and sweat soaking his headband, Victorio drew his knife and waited, this time with no patience at all.

He wanted to make another kill. He had tasted the blood of the White Eyes captain and now wanted black blood spilled. They had pursued him when there was no reason. Now it was time to gain revenge for the past days of dodging and dangerous evasion.

The first trooper thundered by not two feet below, never seeing him. Then came the sergeant and a half dozen more. Victorio counted softly, launching himself like a cougar as the final trooper passed beneath him. His knife flashed out in a shining silver arc, caught the man on the shoulder rather than across the neck, and caused a yelp of pain instead of instant and silent death.

Victorio bounced off the horse's rump and fell heavily into the undergrowth beside the trail, momentarily stunned.

"Sarge, back here. He tried to stab me!"

Victorio scrambled to get his feet under him. He slipped and fell heavily again, off balance because of the heavy firearm slung across his shoulder. He rolled and came to his hands and knees like a hunting cat, then bolted for the thicket to the side of the trail. Bullets tore at his back and shoulder, knocking him down. More slugs ripped through the leaves around him, seeking his body with their leaden promises of death.

"Surrender, damn you!" shouted the sergeant. "We got orders. You either go back alive or you go back dead. It don't matter, as long as you go back!"

A fallen log provided a little cover for Victorio. It had rotted through, and the whistling bullets disturbed termites inside the decomposing wood. He might be killed here, but he would never be captured. The knife clutched firmly in his hand, he looked left and right for any refuge. He saw nothing. Ahead, coming at him on foot in a broken line, were the buffalo soldiers. He saw the frightened expressions on their faces—and his own death.

They wanted him dead, not alive.

"Another death for you, Mangas Coloradas!" he shouted, rearing up and brandishing his knife. He started to attack when a volley of shots rang out. For an instant, Victorio stood stock-still, wondering if this was what it felt like to have his life ripped from his body. The Ghost Pony had not come to take him away. And it felt no different being in the Happy Place than it did in the world where he must endure so much hardship. Then he realized he had not been shot—it was the buffalo soldiers who had taken the deadly fusillade. Three were down, wounded and cursing. One had been killed. The sergeant tried vainly to get order back into his ragged line of frightened troopers.

A second volley ripped through the woods, wounding another buffalo soldier. This was more than the sergeant could tolerate.

"Retreat! It's an ambush! He led us into an ambush!"

Victorio whooped and vaulted over the log, making his way through the ankle-twisting detritus on the ground to reach the nearest fallen soldier. The man jabbed weakly at him with a shiny bayonet. Victorio sidestepped easily and dispatched the trooper with a single thrust to the heart. He spun, hoping to get another.

The skirmish was over.

Shadows firmed and a dozen Apache emerged from hiding. Behind them came another ten. Victorio recognized their paint. Mescalero.

"We heard the soldiers and came," said the one in the lead. He dropped to one knee and rummaged through a fallen buffalo soldier's belt to retrieve a few cartridges. The Mescalero hefted the rifle but threw away the bayonet. It had broken off at the hilt when the buffalo soldier fell on it.

"Why do you come to Warm Springs territory?" demanded Victorio. He was thankful for their help but knew their aid had less to do with him than with the simple pleasure of killing the bluecoats.

"We were looking for you," came the surprising answer. "When you did not come to Bosque Redondo, the bluecoat colonel was furious."

"My horses were stolen," Victorio said. "I tried to find more but could not, so I did not go to the Pecos River."

The Mescalero spat. "Bosque Redondo is a prison. They starve us. They let the Comanche and Navajo kill us. We fight back, we take their horses, the bluecoats punish us! We have come to join you."

Victorio's mind turned over all this new information. If the Mescalero had left General Carleton's prison without walls, bluecoats all over the territory would come hunting for them. He had heard how the Navajo were being starved and killed by inches. No food, no blankets, their lands— their precious peach trees—burned until nothing would grow.

The Apache could not be corralled so easily. Victorio had considered going south to join with Juh in raids against the Mexicans. The bluecoats would never follow into another country. He shook his head as he pondered this. There was no fence keeping them out of Mexico. They simply agreed not to pursue the Apache into Mexico by crossing an invisible line. It made no sense. Victorio roamed where he chose, and he could lead his band of Mimbreño there for the winter where game was plentiful and *los ricos* had cattle and horses to steal.

"What of your own chiefs?" Victorio asked.

"They are old women. They would stay and be fed the garbage from Fort Sumner. They let the bluecoats kick them and spit on them and treat them like dogs."

"Is there more?"

"When you did not come to Bosque Redondo, Carleton repeated his order, 'Death to the Apache, and peace and prosperity to this land!' I spit on him and the way he forces everyone at Bosque Redondo to bend to his religion. He denies Ussen!"

Victorio had already heard how Carleton had ordered Kit Carson to kill every Apache warrior outside Bosque Redondo. The soldiers, in their zeal, more often killed women and children because the men were out raiding. How long would Carleton allow the Warm Springs Apache to remain on their ancestral land? Not long, Victorio suspected.

"What of Bosque Redondo?" he asked. "If there is no game and the Comanche rob you, can crops be grown there?"

"In rock? In sand?" The Mescalero warrior spat again. "Easier to leave than to watch the insects chew up what little does grow."

Victorio reached a decision that had been growing daily but only now came to full realization. He would lead his band south. If these Mescalero and others from Bosque Redondo wished to join him, he would lead them also.

"*Enjuh!* Good!" he cried, his voice ringing loud and clear. "Death to the White Eyes!"

And so began the war.

Truce

"Five children," Loco said to Victorio, hitting the Mimbreño chief at his most vulnerable spot. "You have five children and a wife. All are starving. They will give us money—$2800 for the Mimbreño and all those who still ride with you, no matter if they are Mescalero, Chiricahua, or Chihuahua Apache." Chief Loco pulled the threadbare blanket closer around his shoulders. He looked up and then turned slowly, surveying the area where they huddled next to the small fire. "This is good land." His gaze skipped across the snowy terrain. "But the winter has come early. Again. Crops are sparse, but there might be enough to get through to the spring, if the cavalry ceased their constant raids."

Loco fell silent and let Victorio stew for a while on all he said—and hinted at. Victorio hated having to make such a decision. He felt as if he betrayed not only his own honor but that of his people.

"I am a warrior," Victorio said. "You are, also. Let the women scratch at the ground and bring forth their few crops. We can hunt and bring back enough to feed them all! We are mighty raiders!"

"The bluecoats would buy us food and clothing," Loco went on inexorably, as if he had not heard Victorio.

"Are we so easily bought to stop the fight?" Victorio shot back. He drew his knife and stabbed it repeatedly into the hard ground, hardly aware he did so. Each thrust was into the belly of a soldier. The past years had been hard ones, but he remained near his ancestral land, no matter that settlers circled all around and slowly moved in on it. Cañada Alamosa was not Warm Springs, but it was better than Bosque Redondo.

"Fight," scoffed Loco. "The Navajo. Remember what Carleton has done to even mighty Manuelito. His sons go to the White Eyes' school far to the east in the place they call Pennsylvania." The alien word twisted strangely on his tongue. Loco paused, as if trying to imagine such a thing, then continued. "Manuelito is a great fighter, a great chief. He now serves as tribal policeman, they call it, for the White Eyes."

"Carleton bought him," Victorio said bitterly. "Would *you* enforce *their* laws on *our* people?"

"Do we have a choice? Four years you have fought them and are you living happily at Warm Springs? No. They are like the wind. Slash and cut and what good does it do? Always they are there, nipping at your nose and tearing at your ankles with their cold teeth."

"Cañada Alamosa is not so bad." Victorio sounded sullen and hated the way it came out. He was like a small child, pretending his toy was as good as another's when he knew it was not so. His resolve to remain free wavered.

In spite of the White Eyes' treachery and all they had done to other Apache at Bosque Redondo, he wavered. "Will they let us return to Warm Springs?"

Loco shrugged. A white scar ran across his shoulder and down his chest, mostly hidden by the blanket. It seemed to move like a snake with his gesture. He pulled the blanket closer when a cold wind began whipping from the north off the snow-capped San Mateo Mountains.

"We can still fight. We are close to our homes, our real homes," Victorio insisted.

"Your rumbling belly drowns out your words. Five children," Loco reminded him. "Five little bellies and a wife to feed. The bluecoats are everywhere now that the Navajo are at peace."

"They have returned to their own land, to Dinetah," Victorio said. "If Carleton allows them this return, he can let us go to Warm Springs without constant fighting." Victorio shook as if he had a fever. He was light-headed from lack of food and had been living on the trail for almost a week, dogged by the cavalry patrols from Fort Bayard. The buffalo soldiers proved more tenacious than even Carson and his troopers. They were able to stay in the saddle as long as any Apache—almost.

Worse, there seemed to be an endless supply of the black soldiers and their white commanders. Kill one and two rushed in to replace the fallen. Where did they come from? The lands ravaged by the war between the blue and the gray-uniformed Indah? Victorio did not know.

"Many whites have settled at Warm Springs," Loco said, "but I shall ask Carleton's messenger about this. If we promise to stop raiding, perhaps we can return to Ojo Caliente."

"Why raid if we have all that we need?" asked Victorio, agreeing with Loco in a backhanded way. Loco rose and walked off proudly. Victorio wanted to call to him, to tell him he would agree to anything in return for feeding his family. Loco's words belied his name. In battle he was ferocious, crazy, a warrior to be reckoned with. But now he spoke the messages of others.

The words of the White Eyes dripped from his tongue.

Victorio slid his knife into its sheath and waited, the wind sighing softly in his ear. He listened for a hushed word, a hint of what Ussen might choose for him. The Mountain Gods did not speak. He needed to go on a retreat to the sacred mountain, to Salinas Peak in the San Andres Mountains to receive true word from Ussen.

"Ussen will not speak to you," came a grating voice. "Ussen has already let it be known what we should do."

Victorio nodded, not bothering to face his sister. Lozen always drove her arguments knifelike into the heart of any doubt. Ussen had not spoken to him in some time.

"What of you, Sister?" Victorio heard her moccasins crunching on the patches of snow. "What does your Power reveal?"

"I have looked for enemies in all directions," she said, coming around and squatting beside him. She shook her head. "I am not sure what Ussen tells me. I see enemies everywhere—and nowhere."

"Loco would deal with the White Eyes. He goes to Fort Bayard to speak with the new Indian Agent, the one he calls Drew."

"Drew is an honest man. The Great Nantan in Washington is an honest man, also," Lozen said. "The others, the ones in New Mexico, are not. They have visions of their own glory."

"Carleton," Victorio said tiredly. "So there are enemies and not enemies to deal with among the Indah. What am I to do? We might never return to our land at Ojo Caliente, but is it so bad here at Cañada Alamosa?"

"Not if the bluecoats stop their skirmishes," she said.

Victorio fell silent, thinking of a dozen things that had nothing to do with the problem of the Warm Springs band he led. Loco held an equal position among their people, but he was older and always ready to parley. Victorio could not forget the death of Mangas Coloradas. To roam forever without a head!

The White Eyes did not even know where the head had been sent after Orson Squire Fowler took it to examine the lumps. Victorio shook his head in wonder at the odd things the intruders into Apacheria did.

From the corner of his eye, he looked at Lozen. A handsome woman, his sister. Without her he would have failed a dozen times over. He admired her strength but wished for her only peace, a husband and family, although that might be impossible. When she was a young girl she had met a traveler, the Gray Ghost he was called, who rode alone on a magnificent black stallion. A warrior of great stature and power, he was nevertheless trapped by cavalry. Victorio had silently pointed out a hiding place to him, where he stayed until the bluecoat patrol had passed. The Gray Ghost had come to their camp and remained for several weeks.

A nantan from far toward the rising sun, he had told Victorio, and Victorio had believed him. Victorio had been reluctant to see the Gray Ghost leave when a wagon escorted by twelve guards rattled into their camp. In addition to the guards and driver there had been an old woman, all of whom spoke the language of Mexico but were not Mexicans. And inside the wagon rode a young woman of unsurpassed beauty.

When they left, so did the Gray Ghost, following them westward. Lozen had been too young for marriage then but vowed, after seeing this strange, elusive chief, that no other man would ever interest her. Many fine warriors had tried to appeal to her, but none matched the mystery or allure of the Gray Ghost.

She rode as a warrior and an equal to any in the Warm Springs band, and for that Victorio was glad.

"You do not trust them," Lozen said.

"Loco is an honorable man. He seeks peace."

"As you once tried. Because your horses were stolen and you could not ride to Bosque Redondo, they attacked you!" protested Lozen. "For four years we have fought them, and they have fought us. Not once would they listen. Carleton's ears are closed to anything he does not wish to hear."

Victorio stared across the gently sloping land toward the distant mountains. Distance obscured the taller peaks as a storm bulled its way down from the land of the Navajo. But the river carried clear water and the land would produce decent crops, under proper urging. The mountains provided refuge and game, and this place was not far from the sacred places.

"Cañada Alamosa is not such a bad place," he said softly, thinking of his wife and children, and Lozen, and all the others in his band of Mimbreño. Then he added, "Warm Springs is better."

San Carlos

Spring, 1876
Warm Springs Reservation

Victorio honed his knife, then turned his attention to his bow and arrows. He made his arrows from the wood of the desert broom, with no hardwood foreshaft so he could affix metal arrowheads more easily. Quail feathers were all he had for fletching, after he painted the area beneath the red of hematite and the black of charcoal. He refused to use the cane growing along the Gila River for his shafts, because their enemy the Coyotero were living there.

He polished shafts using rock from distant Bear Canyon, keeping a lookout for any bluecoat who might object even to this primitive weapon. The White Eyes did not like it when their wards worked openly on rifles, although Victorio had a box laden with Winchester carbines hidden nearby. He had stolen many rifles, but needed ammunition for them and, if the rumors were true, he would need much. The weather warmed, crops went into the ground and burst out, green stalks reaching for the brilliant blue sky. Snow melted in the mountains and swelled the rivers with clear, clean water, and it was time to find more horses.

"They know you were raiding again," Lozen said. She stared at him, her expression unreadable. Victorio could not tell if she approved of the occasional forays or simply stated the truth. She had stayed in the confines of the reservation all winter, never venturing out as he had done.

"Colonel Hatch is coming to inspect the reservation himself."

"He is coming to remove us," Victorio said bitterly. "Cochise is dying, and the soldiers no longer fear the Apache. They think they can do whatever they want to us, now that they have us all safely locked up on our own land." He drew back his deer-sinew bowstring, the familiar tension against his fingers. Hardened skin told of long hours of practice—and use. He need not work hard to imagine a bluecoat on the far side of the arrow. Or only the feathered end sticking out of a trooper's chest.

"Be glad General Crook is chasing Juh in Arizona," Lozen said. "If *he* came, he would kill us all."

Victorio snorted in contempt. They had been given their lands back at Warm Springs, but the very act rankled. *Given* land that was theirs!

"Crook has wanted us off our land for some time. Have you forgotten how he tried to keep us at Tularosa like whipped dogs?" Crook had prevailed, but only for a short time. None of the Warm Springs Apache had been content on those desolate lands, after Cañada Alamosa had been pledged to white settlers. Superintendent of Indian Affairs Dudley had authorized the Warm Springs Reservation, but Victorio knew his band had little time left here. More settlers poured into the area, flowing like a river of ants finding honey.

The settlers were a mixed blessing. They yielded their cattle and horses quickly to lightning raids, but Victorio would have preferred them to live at a greater distance. Getting his booty back proved increasingly difficult, since more than two thousand Apache now called the Warm Springs Reservation their home.

"You would raid with Juh?" Lozen asked. This time Victorio heard a note of longing in her voice. She railed against the muzzles of the rifles circling them as much as he did. The buffalo soldiers from the New Mexico forts to the south swept through constantly and chased back any Apache they found off their reservation. Victorio had heard that the Mescalero were increasingly active, causing trouble for the bluecoat soldiers everywhere.

"Colonel Hatch comes to remove us," Victorio said. "This new reservation, this San Carlos on the Gila River. It is as bad as Bosque Redondo!"

"San Carlos is nothing but desert," Lozen agreed, "but how do you know they want any of us to go there? We are peaceful enough here." She left it unsaid: "Except for your raiding."

"They covet our lands," Victorio said. He stood, thrust his knife into its sheath, and grabbed a wolf-skin quiver for his arrows. The metal arrowheads were easier to fasten onto the shafts, but he needed to kill a few dove or quail for more fletching. "They want us to stay peaceable so they can steal from us without any danger."

"The Mescalero are leaving their reservation to join Juh," Lozen said. "I have heard of many of them. Perhaps Hatch only wants to be sure we do not join, also."

"Land," Victorio insisted. "They give us back our own land, then want to steal it again." His eyes drifted toward the cache of rifles. "They promised meat, and they have not given it to us. Would they starve us? The settlers on our land and *los ricos* farther south all have cattle. It is only right we get all the Great Nantan in Washington has promised.''

A bugle blast brought him up, fingers curling around the deer-gut bowstring. In the bright sunlight flashed gold braid and brass. Along with the eye-dazzling brilliance came a double column of troopers, Colonel Edward Hatch at their lead. Victorio fought a combination of envy at such fine horses and anger at all the broken promises when he saw the cavalry soldiers. Juh might be right. Raid constantly, then melt into shadow and let the White Eyes gallop past, never knowing where their enemy hid.

"Troop, halt!" came the command from the sergeant riding just behind Hatch. The line came to a ragged halt, the soldiers looking uneasily at the large number of warriors slowly massing around them. Victorio had not called these warriors here for a council. They had trickled in over the past few hours in anticipation of the noisy, showy colonel's arrival. Like their chief, they had listened to the whispered rumors of being moved from Warm Springs to San Carlos.

Hatch trotted forward and reined back in front of Victorio. His horse reared, but he controlled it expertly. The soldier dismounted, marched over, his mirror-polished boots kicking up dust with every measured step, and gave a precise salute.

"Good day, Chief Victorio," Hatch said briskly. Behind him trailed a half dozen others, some anxious officers, others from the Indian Agent's office, looking arrogant and superior to their heathen wards. Those Victorio recognized. Not a one would he trust not to steal maggoty meat, should it be left in the hot noonday sun where they could find it.

Victorio never felt comfortable speaking with the White

Eyes. He wished Loco were here to speak for them. It never seemed any but Loco—and before him, Mangas Coloradas—had the knack for piling their words up in such a way that the Indah understood and granted their wishes.

A quick nod was all he got out before Hatch rambled on, as if long and detailed pleasantries had been exchanged instead of impolitely naming the Warm Springs chief in direct address.

"I am disappointed to find that many of your people have left the reservation to ride with Juh. Nedhni and Chiricahua raiding must be stopped. We have even heard of Mescalero going south to join Juh."

"Many ride with Geronimo," said Victorio. He had no liking for the abrasive Chiricahua, but Geronimo rode with the wind and had no shackles on him. He raided where he chose, and the bluecoats sought him in vain.

"Another matter to be discussed at length," Hatch said crisply. "You have spoken with Geronimo recently. My scouts report this is true, so do not lie about it."

"I do not lie," Victorio said, offended but trying not to show it. For some reason, Hatch wanted him to lose his temper. Would an outburst be reason enough for the White Eyes to move them from Warm Springs to San Carlos? "Unlike you."

"You insult me, sir!" bellowed Hatch.

"What of San Carlos? You want to move us there!"

"Too many of your people are crowded on this reservation. It's no longer safe or healthy. Ojo Caliente is a growing community and—"

"Crowded with white settlers," Victorio interrupted rudely.

"Sir, allow me," said a middle-aged man Victorio had seen at the agent's office. The man smiled insincerely and spoke directly to Victorio. "The raids must stop. These are more than annoying, they are very dangerous. Your people get shot at, some have been wounded."

"They are warriors," Victorio said. He saw no logic in the man's argument. Warriors fought and were rewarded with horses and cattle. That was the way it had always been. Like too many of them, this White Eyes Indian Agent fought with words, and the penalty for failure was not death or injury but imprisonment. Resentment mounted over the short time he had spent on the Tularosa Reservation.

It had been bad. San Carlos would be worse, far worse.

"Yes, of course, but Geronimo and his Chiricahua are uncontrollable. We would settle them peacefully. And Juh," hastily added the agent.

"Meat," Victorio blurted. "You promised us meat and gave us nothing. Why shouldn't we raid to get that which is ours by treaty?"

"You don't understand how it works," said Hatch. "Many of my forts aren't getting enough meat, either. It is expensive. Appropriations don't always make it this far west, especially now that the South is being drawn back into the Union and—"

"Meat," Victorio repeated. "We plan a peace treaty with Sonora so Juh and I can raid your settlements. Unless we get meat, this is the way it will be."

"Then it will be war!" raged Hatch. He turned red in the face, then struggled to contain his anger. "You will be killed, every man among you, and the women and children will be taken to San Carlos, where you belong!"

Lozen moved to her brother's elbow and said quickly in a low voice, "They do not understand what you meant. They think you are declaring war to get meat."

Victorio was confused. An alliance with Juh against the settlers meant only that they would receive all they had been promised. General Crook was eager to fight them in the field but not to supply them with what they needed, should they start taking it in the name of peace.

"We will remain here in peace," Victorio said, "if you honor your promise. But we will never go to San Carlos. I have seen those barren lands. They are not fit even for a Comanche."

"Fort Davis is dealing adequately with the Comanches," Hatch said, frowning, "and they are also going after renegade Mescalero raiding down in West Texas."

It was Victorio's turn to ponder all the Army colonel said. He had no reason to care about Comanche or even Mescalero raiders in Texas. He cared little for Geronimo and his abrupt manner or what he and his Chiricahua did. The more Victorio spoke with Hatch, the less he understood. Except that he would not allow his band to be relocated to San Carlos.

"We will wait," Victorio said, "before making any treaty with Juh. We will wait for your meat."

"Rest assured we will fulfill the treaty to the letter," Colonel Hatch said. "We will defend you—and we expect you to remain on the reservation."

"Meat," insisted Victorio. "And we will never go to San Carlos."

Hatch's parting salute was sloppier than the one in greeting. The Indian Agents murmured among themselves. The one who had spoken to Victorio flashed a quick, wan smile and then rushed to join the others. They chattered like women.

"What do you see?" Victorio asked his sister. "Are we surrounded by enemies—or those who are not?"

She frowned and turned in a full circle. She lifted her hands to the sky and chanted a prayer to Ussen. Victorio wondered if she would get an answer. So many times he had prayed, and every time he had been denied a response. It was confusing.

"My hands burn," she said, facing him again.

"The colonel? He lies! I knew it!"

"Wait, Brother," she cautioned. "Although Colonel Hatch might be less than an honorable man, he is not the threat I have been told about. Ussen warns me of an enemy—there!" She pointed to the south and west, in the direction of the Black Range. "Many enemies, many, many. Send a messenger to tell the colonel. He promised protection."

"Never will I let another fight my battles," Victorio said. "Who is this enemy? Can you tell?"

Lozen stared at her reddened palms. Already the heat faded visibly, replaced by the warmth of a spring sun and no more. She looked up at her brother, desolation in her dark eyes.

"I cannot tell, but there are many of them. Like grains of sand in the desert, there are many."

"Gather the others," Victorio said. "We ride to defend what is ours." He ran his finger up and down the taut bowstring, then bent the strong, flexible bow to pull off the string. There would be time later to refit it. For battle.

The darkness made Victorio uneasy. In the night crawled snakes, the natural enemy of the Apache. The faint light of a false dawn told him it would soon be time to move and the heat of the day would drive the snakes into their holes. The war party had ridden all afternoon the day before and had wound their way through canyons and down valleys known well only by the Mimbreño. And in their ride they had found evidence of a raiding party. Bits of war feathers, scraps of leather and cloth, a broken shaft from a Chiricahua arrow, spent cartridge casings, a horse stolen from the Warm Springs Apache and ridden to death, then butchered for food.

Geronimo.

Victorio seethed with anger at the raiding Chiricahua and their chief. Never had he liked Geronimo, but the unbending nantan had withstood the onslaught of the White Eyes, and for this Victorio admired him. However caustic he was in speech, Geronimo was a wily foe and a fighter to be reckoned with. Moreover, his sister Dahteste had married Juh, forging a stronger bond between Nedhni and Chiricahua.

Still, Geronimo made a good enemy.

"They are close," Lozen said, returning from her communion with the gods. "Ussen has told me they are in that direction." She pointed into the dark distance beyond Loco's encampment.

"No one riding with Geronimo has your Power," Victorio said. "We will attack at dawn." He assembled his warriors and saw they were ready for battle. All carried rifles, twins to the stolen Winchesters he had cached. Too few had enough ammunition for a real fight. How Victorio wished Nana rode at his other elbow! Lozen located the enemy with unerring skill and Broken Foot found ammunition using his enemies-against Power. The rifles might as well be used as war clubs without ammunition.

He mounted his pony and circled the gathered fighters, assessing their strengths and weaknesses. He found more strength than fault. They had painted their faces with white, red, or black stripes under the eyes. All had their hair tied into a topknot, bound by a red cloth. Around the mouths, like Victorio, many had painted white dots. Their bodies were in red and all carried buckskin coated with mescal, ground corn, and ground berries.

All the omens pleased him. They had raced here, arriving to attack on the day preceding a full moon. Victory would be theirs this day, and tonight would have them performing a victory dance.

"Enjuh!" he cried. They were ready for the fight.

Following a narrow trail led them to a wide valley, verdant and alive in the new spring. Dotted here and there were campgrounds for Loco's band. In too many places smoldered fires that left only burned tipis. Worse were the bodies of men, women, and even children.

Faster, Victorio urged his warriors to ride through the valley. He frequently glanced in Lozen's direction. Dexterous Horse Thief she was known as in warpath language. Her healing skills would soon be needed. Victorio had often been patched up by his sister and her clever use of nopal to heal dangerous wounds. She held her head up, the pine-fragrant wind catching her long hair and pulling it back from her head like a battle pennon. A red cloth headband held the black hair from her eyes—and those eyes were fixed intently on the far end of the valley, where Loco's band had been slaughtered.

Victorio's breath came faster when he saw the fleeing Chiricahua scouts. Lozen had been accurate locating them—and he had been right placing the blame. Geronimo. Why the Chiricahua chose to raid his Warm Springs brothers was something only he could answer. And answer he would—at the point of a war arrow!

"Loco, there is Loco," called Lozen. She pointed to a tight knot of men and women at the far side of the valley. A dozen Chiricahua fired arrows at them, but Loco had chosen his spot well to make his defense. Rocky terrain prevented a full assault without exposing the attackers to accurate fire from above. This strategic advantage did not keep the Chiricahua from pressing their attack.

"Is Geronimo there?" asked Victorio of his sister, now using Apache warpath language. All the war taboos were now in effect. Lozen shook her head. Racing with the other warriors, she was unable to give the proper prayers to Ussen to get such a divine revelation. Victorio split his party to attack the Chiricahua from the flanks. The Chiricahua could rush Loco in his stony fastness and be cut down from three sides or retreat back down the valley.

If the raiders chose that course, Victorio would have the high ground along one flank. Lozen waved to get his attention. He knew what boiled in her mind, and made a sign for her to take a half dozen warriors to the far side of the valley. In this way, they would catch any Chiricahua in the valley from high ground on both sides. As much as he would miss her skill in battle, he would appreciate it more when they went to kill all the fleeing dogs who foolishly followed Geronimo and attacked the Mimbreño.

Loco might be named Crazy One because he trusted the White Eyes as he did, but he was a brother and a Mimbreño. No Chiricahua would kill any Warm Springs Apache!

A slug ripped past Victorio's head, whistling hotly back up the valley. He had ducked and the slug sailed past without drawing blood. He never flinched in the face of possible death as he galloped forward, his stallion straining to maintain the breakneck pace that would ensure victory. Victorio lifted his rifle and fired until the magazine emptied. He sheathed the rifle behind him and then drew his bow and arrow. Racing along, he neared a Chiricahua brave on foot. The brave's rifle jammed. He died with Victorio's arrow buried in his chest.

The flight of the arrow and the Apache's death had taken but a second. Victorio raced on, nocked another arrow, and sought a new target, only to find himself shot at from left and right. Turning, strong legs holding him upright on the straining horse's lathered flanks, he loosed another arrow. This one missed its target.

Victorio never hesitated. He launched himself from horseback and crashed into the man he had missed with his arrow. Mimbreño and Chiricahua rolled over and over,

struggling for supremacy. Victorio won. His knife traced
a thin line from ear to ear along the pinned man's throat,
but the Warm Springs chief got no pleasure from watching
another Apache die under his knife.

A heavy war club smashed into the back of his head,
sending him rolling. Stunned, staring up into the rapidly
brightening blue sky of a new day, Victorio found himself
unable to move. His legs twitched, but his fingers refused
to grip the knife hilt. He saw his attacker rise up in his
field of vision, rawhide war club ready to finish the job it
had started.

A shot echoed in his ears, and the warrior intent on
bashing his brains out vanished from his narrow field of
vision. Victorio struggled and managed to regain his senses
enough to sit up.

A dozen paces away stood Loco, a smoking rifle in his
hands. In warpath language, Loco called, "Death to them
all!"

"Death to them all!" Victorio grated out. He wasn't sure
if he meant only Geronimo's band of Chiricahua or any
who sought to drive the Mimbreño from Warm Springs.

Whichever it was, Victorio knew the true battle had just
begun.

PART II

The Tenth Cavalry

Far Afield

"We've found their camp, Captain Boynton," reported the scout. "Leastwise, we think it is." The man dusted off his floppy black felt hat, sending up a tiny cloud of grit that irritated the officer more than it ought to have. He stepped back, knowing he showed weakness in the face of this obnoxious scout. The man refused to follow any military discipline, much less hygiene, such as it was on the trail.

"You don't *know?*" Lester Boynton made no effort to keep the disgust from his face. He was saddled with incompetents, and those that weren't spent most of their time figuring ways to get out of patrol. He resented being sent to Fort Davis to command Company N when he might have had a real post in Colorado. The dust and heat wore on him, like a grindstone working on steel. Boynton wiped sweat from his face and wished he could reach for his canteen. He knew better. There had not been a decent watering hole in the past three days, and the way the scouts worked, it might be that much longer before they found any fresh water.

Worse than all this, he missed his wife. He ought to be at Fort Davis waiting for her to arrive from back East instead of chasing around the country hunting down Geronimo. Every time on this, his first patrol, Boynton reached out to grab the elusive Chiricahua, he found the chief had slipped away. And now the scout said he *thought* he had found the renegade's camp. For the tenth time.

"Hell, Captain, all them Injuns look alike. How we supposed to know if this is Geronimo's camp or not?"

"He was reported coming back into the U.S. from Mexico. We've been on a trail for over three weeks. We followed that trail from Fort Davis, along the Rio Grande, and into New Mexico Territory. What do you mean you don't know if it's Geronimo! You said—" He bit off his angry denunciation. The scout was not in the Army, not technically. If he took it into his head, he'd simply leave one day and Boynton's company would be without any scout.

Boynton weighed sending one of the buffalo soldiers out as a scout against letting this incompetent continue to guide them into increasingly dangerous terrain. The best he could figure, they were intruding on the Ninth Cavalry's territory, but he could not be sure. He had not brought a map of this part of the country. After leaving Fort Quitman, he had thought to capture Geronimo easily and return to Fort Davis for a well-deserved rest. The success and accolades attached to stopping the renegade would give Sarah an added cachet among the other wives. It was a long, hazardous trip, even if the Comanche had quieted down, and half of Boynton's thoughts were hundreds of miles off with her and their two children, Thomas and Peter.

Instead of being there for her as a hero, he would have to explain to his commander why all his horses were broke down, the ones that hadn't simply up and died, and why he had no captives to show for a three-week-long foray. Boynton was thirsty and bone tired and wanted to kill something. He considered dragging the scout behind his horse for a few miles but knew he could never do that. His horse would falter and die, too, under the additional load.

"There *is* an Apache encampment ahead?" Boynton asked sarcastically.

"Reckon so. Don't think the settlers in these parts live in hide tipis. Know they don't—"

"Enough," Boynton snapped. "You don't know if it is Geronimo. Can you tell me if it appears to be a simple encampment or if there are warriors?"

"Warriors all over the damn place, yes, sir," the scout said. He scratched at a flea working its way across his chest. "You surely are gettin' mighty touchy, Captain. Why not pay me my due, and I'll just ride on out of here. Make us both a mite easier to get along with. You're turning into one edgy galoot."

"Very well," Boynton said firmly. "Return to Fort Davis and tell the paymaster I have released you from duty."

"Fort Davis! That's a hard ten days from here."

"Indeed, is it? If you don't get lost—again—you might make it in a week."

"You mangy cayuse," the scout growled. He subsided, then spat a gob of tobacco. "Reckon we ought to get on with this here fight. When you want to get to the camp?"

This sudden change of attitude took Boynton by surprise. He glanced around and saw two of his noncoms watching curiously. How he hated being in charge of darkies! Always spying, always sitting around gossiping. The only good thing he could say about Company N was that drunkenness was not the problem with them it had been with other commands. At Fort Riley, he had twice court-martialed his top sergeants for being drunk on duty.

"I have never seen the Apache fight after sunset. There must be some religious fear in them that prevents it," he said, talking more to himself than to the scout or his sergeants.

"They don't much like snakes. That's why they don't get out much," the scout said.

"We ride so that we attack just after midnight," Boynton said.

"A night attack's mighty dangerous, Captain," the scout opined, stroking over his bearded chin. "Your boys yonder might get confused and shoot one another. Hard to see 'em when the sun goes down."

Boynton drew himself up to his full five-foot-eight height and peered down into the scout's weather-beaten face. Cold gray eyes turned colder as he found an outlet for his anger.

"My troopers are the best in the Tenth. They are seasoned soldiers and neither their ability nor their courage will *ever* be questioned by the likes of you!"

"Don't get your dander up. I was just pointin' out the trouble you're askin' for," the scout said.

"Sergeant Kingman, assemble your men. We have an Apache outlaw to capture!" Boynton shot a quick look in the direction of the hulking, slow-moving sergeant. The man was three inches taller and his hair was shot with gray. Hands like smoked hams clutched his musket, well tended and as trustworthy as any weapon was likely to be in this dust and heat. Kingman lifted his heavy rifle with easy grace, waved it in a silent circle, and brought his troopers on the run.

"Listen up," Kingman said in his baritone. "We're goin' after Geronimo." He silenced the whispers before they got out of hand. "Captain Boynton wants a night attack, so we's got to be plannin' and doin' just right."

"Thank you, Sergeant," Boynton said briskly. He hated his assignment, but the scout had touched a sore point with him. He commanded these men, and only he would ever say anything disparaging them. That was his right as their commanding officer.

He looked around the circle of dark faces and wide white-rimmed eyes staring at him. For a moment, Boynton lost his confidence. They trusted him. He was their commander, and he was getting ready to lead them into battle for the first time, where casualties might be high. It was up to him to keep them from getting killed. He took a deep breath, and refocused himself on his target of capturing Geronimo.

If it even was Geronimo.

"We will approach slowly until sundown, then advance with greater speed when the Apache are less likely to counter an attack should we be seen. Circle the camp, swoop down here and here," Boynton said, getting into the tactics of the fight, using the scout's rough sketch on the ground of Geronimo's encampment. "We drive them toward this small stream and force them to cross it, slowing them."

"We pick off the stragglers?" asked Sergeant Kingman.

"Later, after we have secured their camp. Burn supplies, capture horses, find Geronimo, and take him prisoner. If possible." Boynton let the words hang in the air. They had been on the trail of the elusive Chiricahua chief for three weeks and all knew the real meaning of the orders—Take Geronimo prisoner, if possible. If not, kill him.

"And," Boynton said, turning to look squarely at the scout, "I do not tolerate scalping in my command."

The scout spat, took another bite off a plug of tobacco he had been hoarding, then snorted in disgust.

"We need to chow down, check our weapons, and then leave in one hour," Boynton said decisively. "Sergeant, carry out your orders!"

"Sir!" Kingman snapped to attention, saluted, then got to the chore of preparing his men for the battle. Boynton wasn't sure who was more apprehensive, the buffalo soldiers in his command, or him.

"Don't rightly know what that means, Captain," said the scout, frowning and shaking his shaggy head. "She's standin' on a rise, hands up like she's makin' an offering to her gods. Every time she turns, she stops, facin' us smack on."

"She can't see us," Boynton said, wondering if this tall tale was a way for the scout to get out of a fight. He had never heard of a woman warrior, much less one who stood guard. "What's the problem?"

"No way she can see us, but it's as if she don't need eyes." The scout hitched up the heavy leather belt cinched around his waist. With real disgust, Boynton stared at the three scalps hanging there. If necessary, he would shoot the scout to prevent this practice from being performed under his command.

How was Sarah going to react to uncouth men like this? She had been raised in Boston and had never been exposed to anything on the frontier more uncivilized than her sister's house in St. Louis. It would take considerable time for her to work into the society of the other officers' wives, but Boynton knew she could do it. Sarah was committed to him and his ambition to be a career officer. And the boys? They would take immediately to Fort Davis and the freedom it offered youngsters.

Boynton smiled slightly at this thought. He would have to be careful not to give them *too* much freedom. Discipline had to be maintained, even as they explored and learned to adapt to this wilderness.

"One woman means there might be more," the scout said. "That don't matter to me, but this one is like a compass needle as she follows us around."

The woman had been silhouetted against the setting sun. Now only the empty hilltop remained to taunt Boynton.

"Now," he said, "we attack now. She's warning those in the camp. There's no other explanation!" Boynton mounted, wheeled his balking mount around, whipped out his saber, and held it high to catch Sergeant Kingman's attention. "To the camp, Sergeant. We attack now!"

Boynton noted how the slow-moving sergeant jumped to obey. Kingman's swaybacked horse protested the weight on its back, then settled down as the sergeant rallied the troopers into an attack formation. Boynton wheeled back, saw the scout had vanished, felt a moment of dread, then forgot it all in the heat of the attack.

"Column forward!" Saber lifted high, Boynton took off at a gallop. He wanted to cover the ground between his position and Geronimo's camp as quickly as possible to keep the Apache from putting up a decent defense.

Hooves thundering, he rode down a sunbaked trail and into the copse of cottonwoods a few hundred yards from the small river, as was Apache practice. He licked his lips, knowing how good the water would be after the attack. Then Boynton forgot all about cool, clear water, and swung his saber in a wide arc that ended on a warrior's shoulder. The Apache yelped and fell back, dropping a six-shooter.

Boynton had no time to see what happened to the man he had wounded. His horse, although slowing, still hurtled forward. From the corners of his eyes, Boynton saw the Apache camp stirring and the warriors grabbing for rifles and bows and arrows. He hoped Kingman had properly deployed the twin column, one to either side of the camp. If not, there would soon be a dead cavalry captain.

The ragged volley that ripped into the Apache on his left told Boynton half the attack had formed. Then came distant gunfire signaling the right flank had found Apache targets. Boynton yelled a rallying cry, only to gasp when an arrow ripped along his right arm. The saber slid from his fingers, slippery with his own blood.

"Damnation," he said, seeing how his uniform had been ripped away. The arrowhead had cut a groove next to a long pink scar he had received during saber practice at West Point during his senior year. The pain rattling up his arm brought him out of his shock in time to dodge an arrow aimed for his chest.

Fumbling with his pistol, he clumsily drew it and fired. His fingers refused to close; he dropped his reins and switched the pistol to his left hand. Firing awkwardly, he shot a young boy in the face. The boy staggered back, arms outstretched. For a brief instant, Boynton was horrified at what he had done. Then he saw the war club in the boy's outflung hand. Even their children fought like devils.

"Get them, get them!" he shouted. But the rifle fire had died down and those surviving the sudden attack high-tailed it for the river.

"Captain," shouted Kingman. "Don't go after 'em. They know the country and we don't."

"Did we get Geronimo?" he demanded. Boynton looked around, a curious mixture of panic and determination alternating in him. He wanted to run and hide as much as he wanted to prosecute the battle. It had gone well so far.

He glanced back at the boy he had shot, and shuddered. It had gone well enough.

"Where's Geronimo?" he demanded. Boynton spun

around, his horse almost stumbling under his powerful knee commands. He slid from the saddle and wandered around the camp, stepping over bodies. Too many of those fallen were women, but Boynton remembered the reports he had read concerning Geronimo's raids in Mexico and Texas. If he had been peaceably sequestered on a reservation, as Crook wanted, this would never have happened. It was all the Chiricahua's fault.

"Captain," came the scout's gravelly voice. "Come on over here. Got someone who wants to talk to you real bad." The scout held a man's head by his hair and shook. Blood trickled down the Apache's chin, possibly from a bitten lip. As Boynton approached, he saw three bullet holes in the man's chest. The Indian bled from the inside and out through his mouth. From the bloody pink froth spewing out now, Boynton knew the Indian wouldn't last long.

"Tell 'im," the scout said, shaking the man's head. Dark eyes fixed on the scout, and Boynton saw the lips curl for a contemptuous spit. The scout did not allow it.

"What is it?" Boynton asked. "I don't think he's going to answer any questions. Where's Geronimo?"

As Boynton said the Chiricahua chief's name, the injured Apache's eyes widened. He rattled out in his own language, then collapsed.

"What did he say?"

"I was afeared of this, Captain. Look at his paint. This ain't a Chiricahua. Mimbreño, unless I miss my guess. And what he said was real disturbin'." The scout spat, then dropped the Apache to the ground. The brave had died.

"Are you telling me we attacked the wrong band?" Boynton felt a cold knot tighten in the pit of his belly.

"Might be, since this one said we're in the middle of Victorio's camp. He's a Mimbreño chief, not a Chiricahua. From all I've heard, him and Geronimo are enemies."

"We attacked the wrong camp," Boynton said numbly.

He slumped, then looked around. "They were painted up and ready for battle. How was I to know?" He clutched his injured arm to his side, oblivious to the blood soaking his uniform jacket. A new one would be needed after he returned to Fort Davis, no matter how he cared for this one.

"They was huntin' for Geronimo, too, is my guess."

"Which one is Victorio?" Boynton saw that the buffalo soldiers were laying out the dead in neat rows for counting. Sergeant Kingman personally supervised tending to the wounded.

Kingman came over, took off his garrison cap, and rubbed his head. It took him several seconds before he spoke in his slow Southern drawl. "Seems Victorio and his sister, along with most of the warriors, got plumb away. One of the women, that one yonder, goes on and on about how Victorio's sister, Lozen by name, knowed we was comin'."

Boynton remembered the woman on the hill, always turning to face them like a compass needle finding north. He shook off the notion that she had some special sense for locating them.

"Do what you can for them, Sergeant," he ordered. "Then we're going back to Fort Davis. It is obvious we have been following the wrong trail."

Lester Boynton slept poorly that night, visions of the boy he had killed mingling with a woman dressed in warrior's garb pointing accusingly at him.

A New Commander

"You're one of the damnedest, luckiest sons of bitches I ever saw," Captain Evan Larkin said, his feet hiked up on the railing. Tugging at his collar and working down the front, he pulled open the brass buttons to let out the heat building under the wool uniform. He smoked the cigarette he had just rolled with some appreciation. With an indolent motion, he flicked the ash inches away from Boynton's shining boots. The man smirked at Boynton's discomfort at both this bullying and the way his uniform flopped open in a decidedly unmilitary fashion, and took another long, deep puff of smoke. He held it in his lungs until Boynton wondered if he had swallowed it. Then, in a slow stream, it came from both the post quartermaster's nostrils, making him look like a locomotive building steam to pull out of the station.

"Because the commander got transferred?" Boynton asked, as uneasy at how accurate this was as he was at Larkin's slovenly appearance and manner. He had returned to Fort Davis expecting a reprimand for the unprovoked attack on Victorio's camp at the edge of the Warm Springs Reservation only to find the post in turmoil because of sudden transfers. Half the company had been moved south, with new troopers—and camp commander—due in soon.

"From what the lavishly flowing bugle oil says, you got on the wrong reservation, attacked the wrong Indians, then just packed up and came home without ever even *seeing* Geronimo." Larkin laughed in delight. "We got a telegraph wire that Indian Agent Clum thinks he knows where Geronimo is—and it sure as hell isn't in New Mexico Territory. Geronimo is farther west, kicking up sand over in Sonora."

Boynton did not need his fellow officer's smugness, though he had to admit the colonel's transfer had saved him a dressing-down. If no one reported the attack officially, this might never be entered on his service record. If it ever was, he might be reduced in rank or even court-martialed. The wrong Indians had died by him blindly following the damnfool scout's information, even if this Victorio was something of a firebrand himself, resisting relocation to a reservation in Arizona.

Boynton closed his eyes and pictured the boy with the war club—and the boy's body sprawled lifelessly on the ground after he had shot him.

"I want to ride patrol with you, Les, I do. Anyone with your luck has to be living a charmed life."

Boynton said nothing. He leaned back against the barracks wall, staring up the canyon behind Fort Davis. Through heat shimmers came the occasional glint of sunlight off rifle barrels. Sentries posted on the towering rock walls, waiting and watching for sneak attack made no attempt to conceal their positions. From any direction, those at Fort Davis could see the enemy coming for miles. He wondered if he ought to tell the lieutenant in charge of post security to have all brass and shining metal parts darkened before sentries were sent out.

"You reckon your wife's gonna be ridin' in with the new commander?" Larkin's words brought Boynton back from his mental wandering.

"Sarah and the boys ought to be here," Boynton said, his mind turning to more pleasant things. He missed her terribly and needed someone to confide in. Too many of the other officers were like Larkin, willing to criticize and possibly to dip into post accounts but never to drill their troops or look in the least like proper officers.

"She might get to know the colonel's wife real good, if she is coming in. That'd be a step up for you. There's going to be a major's position open, now that O'Malley got transferred. Imagine that, *Major* Boynton, you leading two, three companies into the field. And attacking peaceable Indians in their sleep!" Larkin laughed uproariously.

Boynton started to retort about missing post supplies and Larkin's ability to lose incredible amounts of money in weekly poker games. Then, instead, Boynton shot to his feet and stalked off, hardly noting the hot sun burning down on him. Sweat stained his uniform but he never noticed as he strode east across the parade ground. Waiting for the new commander was as nerve-racking as wanting to see his wife and family again. Boynton considered going into the commander's empty office and idly looking through the stack of reports the post adjutant had left there. Was a wire from Agent Clum there telling how one of the Tenth's captains had raided a peaceable encampment?

"The wicked flee when no man pursueth," he decided. Still, he paused on the boardwalk outside the empty commander's office and peered through into the dim interior, trying to make out what might be on the simple desk set with a kerosene lamp. His spying was interrupted by the bugler sounding assembly.

Boynton ran back to the parade ground and looked up at the bugler, now pointing east in the direction of the road.

"Sergeant!" barked Boynton. "What's he see?"

Sergeant Kingman ambled out, cocked his head to one side enough to make it seem as if his garrison cap was put on straight, then turned to his company commander.

"Sir, seems to be some big commotion. Might be Colonel Magee and his party comin' in."

This was the first time Boynton had heard the new commander's name. He cursed himself for being so caught up in his own thoughts. Every detail of the new officer's life ought to be his to make polite conversation, to properly welcome him to a hostile West Texas environment, to make certain discipline was maintained at Fort Davis.

To be sure he got the best possible quarters assigned, so Sarah and the boys would be comfortable.

"Why the bugle?"

"Looks to be trouble, sir," was all Kingman said.

Lieutenant Benneton's squad had already saddled and mounted. Boynton hurried to the young shavetail's side as he started to climb into the saddle to join his men.

"Lieutenant, escort him in with some dignity. Don't repeat your performance from last review."

The ruddy-faced young officer looked upset that Boynton had alluded to the incident with the loose saddle cinch. In front of the entire post, Benneton had fallen off his horse, saluting their commander the entire way to the ground.

"Sir, you might consider getting the entire company ready. The colonel's party was attacked."

Lieutenant Benneton swung into the saddle and got his column moving. Boynton stepped back, fear raking at his guts. "Sarah," he cried. He ran to the stables, out of breath from the exertion in the hammering Texas sun. Fumbling in his haste, Boynton saddled his horse and swung up.

At the stable entrance stood Sergeant Kingman.

"Sergeant," Boynton called, "assemble the men. Wait for my orders. Lieutenant Benneton's squad will provide immediate support for the colonel, if it is needed. But be ready to respond if we need reinforcements!" He snapped his noncom a hasty salute and galloped off, not waiting for the slow-moving man to respond. Horse straining under him in the heat, he continued the gallop for almost a half mile until it became obvious the animal would die under him unless he slowed.

Alternating between a canter and a walk, Boynton stewed over the uncertain fate of his family. Benneton's column had already reached the lead element of Colonel Magee's wagon train, if two freighters could be called a train. Ought he to have ordered out the rest of his company? No, no, he decided, arguing with himself. That was foolish until he determined the extent of the problem, if there was any. It would show Colonel Magee his clarity of thought and ability to position troops for maximum effect.

He reined back when he saw a tired-looking old man with a filthy beard and mustache with colonel's insignia on his shoulders standing beside the lead wagon. He jumped to the ground and hurried over.

"Colonel Magee? Captain Lester Boynton, at your command."

"At ease, Captain," said Magee, making a vague gesture rather than returning the smart salute. "As you might have guessed, we were attacked a few hours ago." Magee's vision hardened and for a moment Boynton saw the steel behind the man's will. "Boynton? Your wife and sons were on their way to Fort Davis?"

"Yes, sir. Are they with you?"

"Son," Magee said, putting his hand on Boynton's arm and steering him away from the wagons. "Life on the frontier is harsh, especially for womenfolk and young 'uns."

"What happened to them?"

"Can't say. We were attacked. Apache, I'd say. Might be Geronimo, since he was specifically mentioned in my orders."

"He's in Arizona Territory, sir, hundreds of miles from here."

"Then it was another of those red devils. We had a train of eight wagons. Your family was in the middle wagon. The attack cut the train smack down the center. We fought and lost two more wagons."

"Sir, what of Sarah and my boys? Thomas and—"

"Peter," Magee finished. "A stout lad, that one." Magee looked more military than at any time since Boynton had set eyes on him. "I don't know, son. You'd best prepare yourself for the worst. They might be dead."

"You don't know? You said they—"

"Get your company together, go find those murdering bastards. And I hope you find your family." Magee pushed Boynton gently in the direction of his horse.

"Sir, will you be all right? Lieutenant Benneton is a good man. He can tend you, but if you need—"

"Draw rations for a two-week scout, sir," Magee said. "Get on it right away. We weren't attacked ten miles outside Alpine. It's taken us the better part of the day getting this far with so few mules. With hard riding and good soldiering you can get there by dawn."

"Yes, sir!" Boynton sent a messenger to Fort Davis to order out Kingman, then set off on his own as fast as he could, forgetting to salute as he left his new commander. He could do nothing by himself against an Apache raiding party, but waiting for Company N would have driven him insane with inactivity. Sergeant Kingman and the rest would overtake him, he knew, but he had to be first on the scene of the attack to find out what had happened.

Thoughts of his wife and family burned too brightly for him to give coherent orders, but Sergeant Kingman had done all that was necessary for the patrol.

As he rode back down the road in the direction of the attack, all Boynton could see was a dead Mimbreño boy with a bullet in him and a war club beside his lifeless hand. Was he going to find his own son dead, killed in the same way?

Family

Lester Boynton saw the razor-edged morning sunlight glinting off the spent brass cartridges ahead on the ground before any of his troopers. He tried to force his exhausted horse forward but the stalwart beast refused after riding hard all night, stumbling and almost throwing him.

"We are close. There, there!" he shouted, pointing out what he had found to Sergeant Kingman. The noncom nodded slowly, his brown eyes finally fixed on the same spoor Boynton had already seen.

"Reckon you might be onto something, Captain," the sergeant said carefully. "You want to circle the spot and be sure we're not ridin' into a trap? We got the sun to our back right now."

Boynton blinked. He had missed the obvious. He was in such haste to find his family he had forgotten simple tactics. Many was the patrol that had rushed to the rescue, only to find Comanche or Apache warriors remaining, waiting for new victims. If the rescuers were too numerous, the raiders simply slipped away. If there was only a handful, they would be massacred, too.

"Send out scouts," Boynton decided. "While they are seeing what we're riding into, rest the remainder of the men and horses and have them prepare for combat."

"Yes, sir," said Kingman, obviously relieved some sense had returned to his captain. He went to dispatch the scouts, two of the men Boynton had his eye on for promotion to corporal, and then set to getting the troopers settled for battle. Boynton could not rest. He fumbled out a small spyglass and began scanning the desert.

New heat shimmers intensified through the magnifying lens and hampered his vision more than simple naked eyes. He ignored this and kept looking at the terrain, vainly searching for any hint to the fate of his family. The crepuscular animals were still stirring, causing him to jump every time he spotted a rabbit dashing for its burrow or a coyote hungrily stalking breakfast.

"Sarah, I should never have let you come out here," he muttered under his breath. He covered the same barren desert over and over, trying to resurrect the attack. The wagon train had driven down into a small ravine, their flanks hidden by the rising banks of the arroyo and the huge expanses of waist-high grass and clumps of prickly pear. Over the top on both sides of the sandy gulch had swarmed the Indians, splitting the train down the middle. The back four wagons had tried to escape to the northwest. The remainder, with Colonel Magee and his family, had fled southeast, gotten free of the encumbering arroyo banks, then curled around through the sandy terrain and hurried directly west to Fort Davis, losing two wagons en route.

This was the spot where the attack had occurred. It had to be, from the evidence. How long had the fight continued? Boynton could not tell. Not from here. He stuck his spyglass back into his saddlebags, waiting impatiently for the scouts to return.

"You might want to rest your mount, Captain," suggested Kingman. Boynton looked down at the black man, trying to read his words and expression. He could not. There might be a hint of condescension or even pity. Or only acceptance of his lot as a noncommissioned officer. Boynton was a captain; Kingman never would be. Some men had the aptitude and discipline to command, but these weren't all that would hold back George Kingman. In the history of the U.S. Army there had been only one black officer graduated from West Point, Henry Flipper. Boynton had heard he was stationed somewhere in Texas, perhaps at Fort Quitman or Fort Concho. But Kingman? He would never rise in rank.

"Yes, of course," Boynton said, slipping from the saddle. It had been so long since he had touched ground, his legs almost failed him. The horse snorted in gratitude and then shivered in relief at losing the weight on its back. Boynton let one of the troopers lead his horse away to graze the best it could along the arroyo banks in the sere blue grama.

"What we gettin' ourselves into, Captain?" asked Kingman. "We takin' on a whole slew of Apache, or is this mission something else?"

"Rescue," Boynton said without hesitation. "My family, and four other wagons in the train were driven away at that point." He stared into the increasingly heat-racked distance, trying to imagine Sarah standing up valiantly to her attackers, and Thomas and Peter helping the wagon driver get to safety.

"Sir, we don't know what went on over there, but if

you're expectin' to *rescue* them . . ." Kingman's drawling voice trailed off.

"I refuse to believe they are dead."

"Might be for the best if they are, sir," Kingman said, his dark brown eyes fixed on Boynton. "You heard the stories 'bout folks taken by the Indians."

"The Apache are cruel, but they would not torture women and children," Boynton said hotly.

"Not what I was gettin' to, Captain. I was thinkin' more of them bein' taken as slaves."

"A war party? No, they wouldn't take prisoners. They'd be on the move, traveling fast, and wouldn't want—" Boynton bit off his words, the horror of what he had just said hitting him.

"Sir, think on the best. Might be they holed up somewhere. Four wagons filled with guards and drivers can deliver a considerable amount of firepower." Kingman silently returned to his squad, leaving Boynton to suffer in silence.

No matter how he argued, the death of Sarah and his sons seemed the only outcome for the Apache raid. Even deciding to wait until he had more information did nothing to hold at bay the numbness settling over him.

A half hour later, the scouts returned with their report. Five minutes after that, Boynton had the company in the saddle and trotting toward the battle site.

"How long do you reckon we're goin' be on this trail, Captain?" Kingman asked. For two days they had followed the trail left by the fleeing raiders. All four freight wagons had been located, along with six men—all dead. Of Boynton's family there was no trace.

"Until we find them," the officer said grimly. The only hope he held out was the lack of dead horses. Sarah and the boys might have taken horses from the overturned wagons and ridden away, even if he had found no trace of them racing away from the main body of Apache. He had ordered Kingman to have six scouts on either flank hunting for any trace of them, but so far not a single scout had noticed any deviation from the trail they now followed so tenaciously.

"Are you the proper one for this here mission, Captain?"

"What do you mean by that?" Boynton snapped. "Are you impugning my abilities as a field officer?"

"Don't know exactly what you're saying, but I meant no disrespect, sir. All I was sayin' was you got a personal interest that might not make you the best choice to make the hard decisions, if they're needed."

"I want them back, Sergeant, and I want the murdering Apache who did this." Boynton reined back and glared at his sergeant. For the first time, he had the feeling Kingman withheld something from him. "What aren't you telling me?" Boynton's heart ran away with itself. "If you found their bodies and did not tell me, I swear I'll—"

"Nothin' like that, Captain," Kingman said. The uneasy look on his usually impassive face told Boynton the sergeant knew something.

"What is it you have not told me? I'm ordering you to tell me, Sergeant."

"A few of the men and me, well, we think this band of Indians might belong to the same ones we raided back in New Mexico."

"Mimbreño?"

Kingman nodded, but did not look his commander in the eye.

"The same band? The very same?"

"Heard tell they left the Warm Springs Reservation after our raid. It was mixed in with all the reports on Geronimo.

Nobody made much mention of it, 'cept to wonder if Victorio had left to join forces with the Chiricahua.''

"The scout said Victorio and Geronimo were enemies. That wasn't likely to happen. Even if they both hated us, that wouldn't make them allies.''

Kingman remained silent.

Boynton sucked in rapidly cooling air. The sun slid behind Sierra Diablo, and the temperature in the West Texas desert dropped fast. He considered pushing his column for another hour, even in the twilight, then decided against it. Rattlers came out and a horse could more easily step into a prairie dog hole. Boynton wanted every trooper in the saddle and able to move fast and fight hard.

"Have the scouts range forward a few miles, then come back. Rest of the troopers, pitch camp for the night. Post sentries, Sergeant.''

"Yes, sir.''

Kingman waved his arm and got two corporals to pass along the orders. Boynton watched them vanish into the dusk, only occasional glints off their brass buttons giving any hint to their location. He wished he had a lieutenant to share the load, but Fort Davis had been stripped of so many officers recently. Worse, few officers wanted to be stationed with black troopers. Those that could, got out for more prestigious posts. Being saddled with inexperienced officers of Benneton's ilk made him feel more like a school-marm than a cavalry officer. He was just as happy the lieutenant had remained behind to escort Colonel Magee to Fort Davis.

"So many are like Custer," Boynton muttered to himself. The Boy General had moved heaven and earth to avoid assignment to the Ninth, being rewarded for turning down the position with the same rank and command of the newly formed Seventh Cavalry. Some officers had the knack of turning adversity into glory.

"Sir," called Kingman, "Come on over here. Right away!"

Boynton's hand flew to his side arm, but he did not draw. He hurried in the direction of the sergeant's voice, finding the man huddled with a scout who had just returned. Both horse and scout were out of breath.

"What is it?"

"Not a half mile ahead, Captain," panted out the scout. "Looks like the Apache left behind their dead. Must know we're hot in pursuit to lighten their burden like that, otherwise they'd take 'em back to their holy land in New Mexico Territory. They got rigid ways of makin' sure their dead don't get lost before reaching the Happy Hunting Ground."

"Show me," Boynton ordered. He, Kingman, and the scout retraced the path and came on a depression in the gently rolling terrain. Huge mounds of prickly pear cactus obscured many of the bodies, but not even the distant howling of a coyote or the whistling wind could mask the low moans of pain.

"Wounded, too. Careful, sir. They'll be snappish like a mad dog," warned Kingman.

"Get a dozen soldiers," Boynton ordered the scout. "You and I, Sergeant, will see how hydrophobic this group is." He drew his side arm and cocked it. The sound caused a sudden diminution in the wails of agony, then they returned. Boynton started down the slope on foot, picking his way carefully, although he wanted to rush forward yelling Sarah's name.

Boynton passed three dead braves. They had come this far before wounds received in battle with Colonel Magee's wagon train guards had felled them. Another pair had been dead much longer. Boynton's nose wrinkled as he moved on. Kingman paused beside one of the injured warriors, but Boynton was driven to find his family.

Scattered around were bits of booty stolen from the wagon train and unwanted by the rest of the band. And dead horses and mules. Boynton saw a half dozen dead animals around, ridden into the ground, abandoned where they'd fallen. He picked his way through this improvised burial ground until he came to a small body off to one side.

Boynton stood slowly and stared, feeling nothing inside. He had gone past emotion.

Kingman came up and stood at his captain's shoulder. Then his huge black hand closed on Boynton's shoulder and pushed him away gently.

"I'll take care of it, if you like, Captain. Or would you want to take your boy's body back to the fort?"

Boynton opened his mouth to answer, then clamped it shut. He had no way of knowing what he wanted. And it got worse when the squad of buffalo soldiers arrived and found his other son and wife.

Seeds of Hatred

Summer, 1879
Fort Davis

Colonel Amos Magee sat behind the small wooden desk and shuffled papers nervously. He looked up, adjusted his wire-rim half glasses until his watery eyes looked as big as saucers, then licked his cracked lips as he hunted for the right words. Lester Boynton stood locked at rigid attention before his new commander.

"I am sorry my arrival at Fort Davis has not been more, uh, sanguine," Colonel Magee said wistfully. "I wish events had proceeded more happily. A parade would have been nice." He shuffled the papers some more and looked away from Boynton, staring out a small window in the log wall to his right, as if he could conjure up marching troopers on parade and a full band playing jaunty military marches. "I've never been good at such things as what's facing us now, Captain. I've read your performance reports. You are a good soldier. As such, you know the danger of our profession."

"Yes, sir," Boynton said in a clipped tone. His mind wandered back to the desolate stretch of desert where he had found his Sarah and his two boys. Dead. All three had been killed quickly, no suffering, they were nothing but trouble for their captors, slowing their escape. They had been murdered because they could not keep up rather than out of malice or cruelty.

His fists tightened until his rough fingernails cut into his flesh. A single drop of blood from his left palm trickled over his index finger to fall to the floor. Magee never noticed. He continued to stare outside into the noonday heat.

"In this life, sooner or later, we all lose those we love. I can promise you a funeral with full acknowledgement of their importance to our cause on the frontier. I had come to know Mrs. Boynton and your boys on the trip from Fort Griffin, at least a little. She was a good, decent woman, and I know you will miss her."

"Yes, sir." Boynton tried to call up the image of his wife as he had left her in St. Louis. He found the mental portrait curiously distorted. Her hair. Sarah had such pleasing, long fine hair. She always combed it with one hundred strokes every night before going to bed. As vivid as this memory was, Boynton could not exactly remember the chestnut hue, not on the day he had ridden out after his brief leave before coming to Fort Davis. And his sons. Thomas with the quick, mischievous smile and serious Peter. Which one had glued shut the pages of the family Bible? He had always thought Thomas, but suspected Peter. Neither had confessed and neither had implicated the other. He had appreciated their loyalty. They had been brothers dedicated to each other. They would have grown up to be fine men.

All gone now, and he could not remember them. Everything jumbled in his head. He squeezed harder until new trickles of blood dripped from his self-tortured hands.

"Yes, full honors will, uh, be accorded them. And I do not approve your resignation, Captain. We need officers of your caliber. Your record at Fort Riley was outstanding. Since coming here, you have not been involved in any skirmish of note, but because of transfers, I find you are one of my senior officers. The death of your family ought to bring your duty to the forefront. While we will not tolerate revenge for personal reasons, we do need officers able to understand the woe of those settlers who, uh, who are alone as they try to tame this barren land." Magee shuffled the papers some more, then decisively shoved them aside.

"That will be all, Captain."

"If you cannot approve my resignation, then I want to be on patrol to capture the savages who did this."

"Well, uh, yes, that is possible. My orders call for renewed importance at Fort Davis, more activity on our part in the region. The Tenth will gain another company."

"Buffalo soldiers, sir?"

"What? Oh, yes, Negroes. A newly formed company. More officers will be transferred here to fill the gaps in the table of command. We must deal with Geronimo and the, uh, one responsible for this deplorable raid."

"Victorio, sir?"

"You know him? Good, you are well informed, as I knew you would be, being such a good officer and all," Magee said, his voice trailing off. "Seems this chief came from the Warm Springs Reservation—something about moving the lot of heathens to San Carlos in Arizona he did not like—to cause us trouble. Ranging throughout the Southwest. Some reports, more rumor, although from credible sources, of course, but your Sergeant Kingman found evidence this Victorio led the renegades responsible for ambushing our wagon train and killing your family. Victorio, Geronimo, any other war chief, it does not matter to me, we will stop them all!"

"Yes, sir," Boynton said. He began to wobble slightly from strain. He kept his knees locked like a raw recruit, however. He hardly knew what amount of pain it would take to drive out the guilt he felt over his loss. He should have been there for Sarah.

"I am glad you understand our mission, Captain." Magee paused, as if considering adding something more, then said, "Dismissed."

Boynton saluted his new commander, did an about-face, and marched from the cool room into the stifling heat outside. Even under the porch roof outside the colonel's office, Boynton felt as if the sun cooked his head directly. He put on his cap and started down the boardwalk, not sure where he went.

"Captain, Captain!" came an insistent call.

"Yes." Boynton held back a flash of resentment when he saw Ruth Magee beckoning to him. She was alive, and his Sarah had died. He held his anger in check, realizing it was not this woman's fault she had survived. He stooped to keep from banging his head on the lintel as he entered the small supply room where she rummaged through goods to replace the belongings lost in the raid. She was much younger than her husband, perhaps twenty years younger. Her long brown hair fell in tangles, needing washing. Boynton squeezed his eyes shut for a moment to quell the tears forming there.

Ruth Magee's hair looked so much like Sarah's. But there the resemblance ended between the two women. Mrs. Magee was three inches taller, matching his own height of five-foot-eight, and heavier boned. She was nowhere near as lovely as Sarah, though there was a comeliness to her that came through enduring hardship and triumphing.

"I wanted to tell you how sorry I am for your loss, Captain Boynton."

"Thank you, ma'am."

"I know Amos does not handle some details well, and he might have left you with the impression he did not care."

"He was quite sympathetic, ma'am," Boynton said.

"Then you were not speaking with your new commanding officer,' " she said sharply. "Your loss is great, Captain, greater than you understand at this moment. Do not try to keep your grief hidden or it will curl within your gut like some poisonous snake. I know. I've had my share of loss, too."

"Colonel Magee was not injured—"

"Captain Boynton, he is not my first husband. I've been married to Amos only six years. My first husband died in combat against the Sioux. I *know* heartache. I am just sorry you must know it also."

"I apologize, Mrs. Magee."

"No need to. You are troubled now. Don't let your sorrow get you into a plight you will come to regret. More than your own life is at stake out here. Your men depend on you and your rational thought."

Boynton thought it curious to be getting this speech from her, but said nothing.

She heaved a deep sigh. "I am no stranger to posts such as Fort Davis, Captain. We are here to quell insurrection and bring justice to the frontier. We are here to *civilize*, Captain."

"Are you settling in well, ma'am?"

A flash of anger crossed the woman's face, then she subsided. "I am, thank you. Captain Larkin has arranged for a striker for us, and has reallocated families to make room for us until the commander's quarters are refurbished. It is nice to find a quartermaster so competent, after some of those on posts I have been."

Boynton knew that seniority of the husband meant everything among the families. If there were not adequate quarters, the most junior officer's family often slept in hallways. Sarah would not have had to endure such ignominy. He looked squarely at Ruth Magee and wondered if she ever had. Possibly, from the way she spoke of getting a striker, a black enlisted man to do all the small chores that usually fell most heavily on the women.

"Captain Larkin is an accomplished officer," he said.

"But you don't like him, do you? Or is it that you don't like anything having to do with Fort Davis and those stationed here?"

Boynton held down his anger at her insight. He wanted to be alone, and she engaged him in needless conversation.

"We are getting by, Captain Boynton," she said suddenly. "Thank you."

He read dismissal in her voice, the snap of command a good leader used. In spite of the obvious desire to end the exchange, he paused, not knowing exactly why.

"Mrs. Magee, do you have any children?"

"Yes, Captain, a son. He is one year older than your oldest, I think. He's eleven." She smiled at this. "His name's Caleb. I am sure they would have become fast friends." Ruth Magee's smile faded, and she looked around at the chore ahead of her, finding what she needed in her temporary quarters. "Now I must get to work. If you see Private Kingman, please send him over, will you?"

"Charles Kingman, my sergeant's brother?" Boynton raised an eyebrow in surprise. From all he knew of George Kingman, he would never have thought the man would allow any of his family to act as a servant, even to the post commander.

"I believe so." Ruth Magee stared at him with her wide-spaced brown eyes. He failed to read the questions he saw there. He nodded, turned, and ducked under the low lintel, then went into the heat of the day. He intended to ride over to Limpia Creek and find a quiet spot to think.

"Think," he snorted. "I want to be alone to feel sorry for myself."

Boynton mounted and rode slowly from the post, heading north, stopping only when he saw Charles Kingman working in the hot sun, stripped to the waist.

"Private," he said, "Colonel Magee's wife requires your assistance."

"Yes, sir," the man said, taking the break to wipe sweat from his face.

"What are you doing?" Boynton frowned. Kingman was loading supplies onto an outbound wagon when the fort needed them.

"Captain Larkin, sir, he said this is to help some folk down to the south what need big help."

"Carry on. And don't forget Mrs. Magee."

"No, sir, I wouldn't do a thing like that." Charles Kingman returned to single-handedly loading the wagon. Boynton wondered where the driver was and why Larkin had given in to such a charitable impulse. It must have been the first the young officer had ever felt.

Then Boynton was swallowed by the stark landscape, away from the post and the soldiers and, for a while, the constant reminder of his wife and sons' impending funeral.

Death to Victorio

Late Summer, 1879
On the Banks of the Rio Grande

"Why would Victorio come back into the U.S. now that
he is safe over in Mexico?" asked Lieutenant William Quinlan. The young officer looked around uneasily, as if he
would see the Mimbreño chief pop up from behind a
scrubby creosote bush or sneak out from behind the wiry,
spiny clumps of ocotillo whips. The sandy-haired shavetail
had been assigned to Fort Davis less than a week before
Boynton had begun this patrol, sweeping from Fort Quitman south along the river. The terrain grew increasingly
rugged, with higher jagged rock walls rising to create the
twisting canyon that was Big Bend. If they rode much
farther south, Boynton would have to cope with the threat
of Victorio sitting fat and sassy on the lip of the canyon,
tossing heavy rocks down on their heads. Too many patrols

from the feckless Ninth Cavalry had run afoul of this tactic in Dog Canyon, north of Fort Bliss.

If their information held even a shred of truth, Victorio was here, possibly having already passed down along the opposite bank of the Rio Grande, staying in Mexico. Boynton sucked in the air, as if he could scent the wily Apache. He shifted in the saddle, wondering if he would ever set foot on the ground again and not hurt. But such concerns were minor. He would push his buffalo soldiers—and himself—day and night if it meant engaging the Apache who had killed his family.

He had simmered while enduring meaningless patrols under Colonel Magee for the past three months. Every field mission had shown the older officer's incompetence. How Magee had achieved his rank lay beyond Boynton's understanding. Rumors of a brilliant counterattack on a weakly held Confederate position at the Battle of Pea Ridge had made its round of the officers' mess, but no details were attached.

As far as Boynton could tell, the brains of the family rested with Ruth Magee. He had spoken to her briefly at several of the post social gatherings, but the gaiety of those gatherings told him he did not fit in any longer. Only she seemed to understand, and often came to draw him into the dances or simply to talk with him.

"He is looking for rifles," Boynton said, shaking out of his reverie. "Rifles, ammunition, cattle, horses. If he can steal them, he will." Squinting, the captain slowly studied the terrain, taking in every detail of the rocky Rio Grande banks on both sides. "If we go downriver we run a risk of being ambushed," Boynton said, pointing out the increasingly steep canyon walls that climbed a full hundred feet to contain the churning river. "Where did the colonel say he would be patrolling?" He fumbled out his tattered field map, trying to locate his company's position and figure out where Victorio might attempt to cross the Rio Grande. If he anticipated the Mimbreño chief's move, he could trap him and put a dangerous foe to rest—permanently. The rising canyon walls told Boynton Victorio would have no escape route, unless he remained in Mexico, technically out of reach for the U.S. Cavalry. Unfortunately, the military scouts had failed to find any spoor showing the Apache were within his jurisdiction.

"Can't blame the Injun too much," Quinlan said. "I mean, him getting cheated out of the Warm Springs Reservation and shipped to San Carlos. That's enough to make anyone kick up some dust and do some shooting."

"There's nothing wrong with the San Carlos," Boynton said, distracted. What would he do if Victorio remained across the river in Mexico? A rifle shot would not be enough to flush him from the tangled growth along the river, much less do anything to bring about his death if Victorio headed back into Mexico. The Apache had thumbed his nose at them long enough. It was time for action.

"Nothing wrong?" Quinlan snorted. "Captain, I heard about that place. It's near Camp Goodwin, on the Gila River."

"Sounds promising. There was never enough water at Bosque Redondo on the Pecos, or so I'm told. The Gila is a big river, with enough water for all of them and their crops."

"You ever *see* that place, Captain? It's a hellhole. Malaria wiped out the garrison, so it was abandoned. That's where they want to move the Mimbreño."

"You sound like you consider their raiding and killing a natural, acceptable course of action. Is that so, Lieutenant?"

"Don't go putting words in my mouth, Captain. I lived over there. My pa was an agent for the Tonto Apache, leastwise for a spell. There's nothing to do but die at the San Carlos."

"Good. Then it is incumbent upon us to be sure Victorio is returned as quickly as possible." He folded his map and tucked it into the front of his uniform jacket.

"Didn't think I'd hear you saying that, Captain," the lieutenant said.

"What do you mean?" Boynton turned about in the saddle and glared at his junior officer.

"It's no secret what happened. You want nothing more than to get Victorio in your sights—then squeeze the trigger slow-like."

"I would squeeze the trigger slowly only in that it would not take my weapon off-target," Boynton said. "I will see him dead. I *will.*" In spite of the cooler breezes blowing across West Texas and off the river, Boynton was drenched in sweat. The heat from the rocks did it. Or was it the passion of his hatred for Victorio?

"Didn't mean anything by it, Captain Boynton," Quinlan said hastily. "I just want to be sure you're not riding us into a trap because of your hatred."

"You've lived among the Apache too long, sir," Boynton said coldly. "You have adopted an attitude that there is something noble about them. There is not. They are murderous savages. While General Carleton went too far in his Christianization attempts, he did not go far enough in putting them on reservations where they can be watched—and guarded like the criminals they are."

Quinlan started to reply, then bit back the words. He was a junior officer and had no place contradicting his superior, no matter how outrageous he might be.

"Understood, sir."

"Good," Boynton said. "Our intelligence reports Victorio has hidden in Mexico, allying himself with Juh. They occasionally do battle with the Coyotero Apache, in a kind

of red man's civil war. Their primary opposition seems to
be Geronimo and his band. Victorio has his entire band
with him in Mexico, numbering as many as two hundred
and fifty men, women, and children. Perhaps fifty are warriors."

Boynton held his breath for a moment as a ghost image
flickered in front of him. A boy rose, spiked war club
swinging. Boynton's hand flashed to his revolver, then he
relaxed when he realized he saw only shadows cast by
windblown mesquite limbs.

"See something, Captain?"

"Nothing," he said too quickly. "As I was saying, Victorio's group of Warm Springs Apache are on the move.
With him are some able leaders—Nana, Loco." Boynton
frowned. "There is even talk of a woman, perhaps his
sister, who fights alongside them as an equal."

"I doubt that, sir," said Quinlan. "I never heard of
an Apache woman fighting with them. They *can* fight, of
course, and I'd rather not tangle with any of them, but
accepted as an equal? I doubt it, sir."

Memory of the lone woman on the hill slowly turning,
always pointing at him while he and the scout were hidden,
taunted Boynton. He was beginning to think anything was
possible with the Mimbreño, led by Victorio.

"If Victorio is heading this direction, he will enter Texas
along this stretch. Farther north and he runs the risk of
being seen by a patrol from Fort Quitman. To the south,
he has to make a long loop through hostile country to
return to New Mexico."

"You reckon he's heading back to his ancestral lands,
Captain? Going back to Ojo Caliente north of Fort Bayard
or thereabouts?"

Boynton shrugged. He doubted Victorio wanted anything more than to raid settlements, steal cattle, steal
horses, kill settlers. Whatever Victorio's motives he would

find himself staring down the barrel of a good cavalry carbine.

"Captain," came Sergeant Kingman's deep drawl, "we got ourselves lined up, ready to go on down the river."

"What are the scouting reports?" asked Boynton. "We ought to contact the colonel before entering the canyon."

"Behind us, maybe an hour's ride," Kingman said. "If we bivouac and wait, then come sunup we kin—"

"No," decided Boynton. "We need to know if Victorio is even nearby." He shielded his eyes with his hand, looking across the river. Shallows here meant a scout might make it across.

"Sir, look!" cried Quinlan. The lieutenant pointed a quarter mile farther down the river. The two braves astride their horses wheeled around and raced off. The echoes from their hooves caught the edge of the canyon walls and drew Boynton's attention.

"After them!" he called to Sergeant Kingman. "Get the column moving. They're on this side of the river. After them!"

Boynton put his blunt spurs to his horse's flanks. The pony snorted, tried to rear, and then set off at a gallop over the uneven ground. Boynton slowed his attack, knowing his horse would turn a hoof on the rocky ground if he kept up this pace. Moreover, he wanted the rest of his soldiers behind him. If two Apache scouts showed themselves, the main body would not be far away.

If he hit them hard and with his full troop, he could put an end to their predation.

He might even put an end to Victorio.

Glancing over his shoulder, he saw Kingman had gotten the black troopers moving in a ragged attack pattern. From the broken ground and the way the canyon walls squeezed down, this was the best he could hope for. He had nothing critical to say about any of the soldiers in his command.

They were seasoned veterans, and he had come to trust them more than he'd thought possible even a few months earlier. Still, they were Negroes, and needed constant supervision.

"There, there they go!" Ahead the two Apache scouts splashed through the river, on their way back into Mexico. "Don't let them get away. After them!"

"Sir," called Lieutenant Quinlan. "We can't go over there. Orders!"

"To hell with orders. We dare not lose them now. Victorio's entire war party is nearby. I know it!" Boynton reined back for a moment, studying the river. It flowed more sluggishly here than in deeper areas. In places he saw stones glistening just beneath the surface. This was a perfect ford—and the Apache already knew about it.

Boynton impatiently waited for Quinlan and the others to catch up with him.

"You need not accompany me, Lieutenant. That is your prerogative."

"Sir, this isn't right."

An arrow arched high in the air, caught sunlight off its metal arrowhead, then sank into the gravelly bank of the Rio Grande not ten yards away.

"We have been fired on," Boynton said. "Under our standing orders, we can defend ourselves. Sergeant?"

"You're the captain, Captain," said Kingman. "But you might think a bit more on what Lieutenant Quinlan is sayin'. That's not our country on yonder side."

A half dozen arrows streaked through the air, but Boynton and his troopers were still out of range. If they attacked, they would have to ford the river, then regroup for an attack. If he did nothing, Victorio and his renegades would be free to continue their raiding.

"Sergeant, have two squads cover the rest of us as we

cross. When we reach the other bank, join us. We will provide support.''

"Yes, sir," said the black sergeant, his eyes wide. "If that's what you want."

Boynton had already splashed into the river. Behind him came a dozen of the stalwart buffalo soldiers, with Lieutenant Quinlan close behind them. Rifles began crashing, sending their .50 caliber slugs ripping through undergrowth on the far side of the river. It took Boynton longer than he anticipated to reach the Mexican side of the Rio. He quickly deployed those troopers with him to lay down a covering fire so Sergeant Kingman and the rest of the column could join them. A few arrows came their way, but mostly his troopers' fire kept the Apache under cover.

"Ahead," Boynton said as Kingman joined him. "We have only a narrow stretch of shoreline to approach along, but when we do, we can overrun their position."

"Why they holdin' the line, Captain?" wondered Kingman. "If it was me and I saw an entire company sloshin' toward me, I'd be long gone."

"They might be giving their main force time to escape. This might be a holding action to hide their true movement." Boynton drew his pistol, cocked it, then lifted it high above his head.

"Forward! For God and glory!"

His pony died under him within twenty yards, a lead slug through the lungs. Boynton pitched to the ground, luckily avoiding the fusillade that cut through his troopers. The Apache had lured them on with a few arrows, then used their rifles to deadly effect in an attack that left at least two of the soldiers dead and a dozen more wounded.

Boynton came up to his knees, saw a brave, and fired. The gun twisted in his grip so his first bullet missed. Getting a better grip on the butt of his pistol, his second caught the Apache on the side of the head, jerking the man's face around. The warrior slumped to the ground. Boynton would have rushed over to be sure the brave was dead, but he found himself the focal point for half a dozen snipers.

"Get back, Captain!" shouted Lieutenant Quinlan. The young officer rushed out, his pistol barking out lead in all directions.

"No!" The word had hardly left Boynton's lips when he saw the arrow bury itself deep in Quinlan's chest. The man staggered, then fell face-forward. The arrow was driven entirely through his body by the force of the fall, the bloody metal arrowhead sticking up out of his back.

Boynton made his way to the fallen officer's side, bullets and arrows filling the air all around him.

"Quinlan, come on. Lieutenant!" He shook the man, in spite of the hot stings running across his face and back and hands. In a daze, he tried to roll over the fallen lieutenant, only to have black hands grabbing at him and pulling him away.

"Nothin' you gonna do for that one, Captain," came Sergeant Kingman's voice. This time the words were hurried, run together in a blur. Boynton looked down and saw blood all over his uniform. Scratches on his hands and arms accounted for some of it, but not all.

"Quinlan," he said numbly.

"Dead, sir. Very, very dead, like we gonna be if we don't move our asses out of here and get back 'cross the damn river."

They were pinned against the face of a cliff, no way to get across the river without being slaughtered. The Apache held the high ground and fired down on them. Retreating upriver exposed them, and downriver lay the ambush that had already stolen away William Quinlan's life.

"What are we gonna do?" demanded Kingman. "They got us good and proper."

Boynton winced as he moved. An arrow had raked across

his back and he had not known it until now. The shock wore off enough to let the pain tear at his brain. In a way, this helped him fight off the desperation and concentrate on what had to be done if any of his company would ride away.

"They'll cut us down if we try crossing back to the U.S.," Boynton said, craning his neck. He caught the glint of sunlight off no fewer than three rifle barrels. "There's no way we are going to outwait them."

"Supplies are running a mite low," admitted Kingman. He scratched his head, then put his garrison cap back on. "Not much in the way of ammunition, either. We rushed into a fight we can't finish."

This gentle admonition was as critical as the slow-moving sergeant was ever going to get. Boynton felt the sting more than any of his wounds, though. He had not thought through a decent plan, and now he stood to lose his entire command, along with his own miserable life.

"Any way of knowing if that's Victorio we face?" he asked.

"Don't matter much," spoke up a corporal. Boynton was embarrassed that he did not know the man's name. They were going to die together and he didn't know who would be laid alongside him on the riverbank. "Victorio's bullet is as like to snuff us out as Loco or Nana's."

"Can't stay, can't retreat. That leaves only one direction to go," Boynton said. "Sergeant, get the men together. We're going to charge smack down their throats."

"Don't you figure that's what they're waitin' for, Captain? Those rocks and the undergrowth behind it might hide a hundred Apache."

"Victorio's only got fifty warriors with him," Boynton said. He heaved a deep sigh. "Unless he's got some of Juh's braves with him. We *might* be facing a small army."

Boynton hated to admit it, but Victorio had outmaneuvered him. Now all he had to do was die.

"I'll wait until sundown, then sneak out and see what I can do. Might take a few with me, create a diversion so the rest of you can escape back across the river. Mark the spot where the ford is so you'll be able to find it in the dark."

"That's mighty poor thinkin', sir," spoke up the corporal. "We need you to lead us. If you wind up dead . . ."

"Might as well. If I get out of this, I'd be court-martialed for incompetence."

"Even so, sir," Kingman started. He turned and looked back across the river where Colonel Magee and a handful of soldiers gathered.

Boynton shot to his feet and tried to wave off his senior officer, only to be driven back by rifle fire from downriver.

"Colonel! We're pinned down. Get the rest of the company!"

Magee did not answer. Boynton could not even tell if the man had heard him, but the colonel issued orders to the half dozen soldiers accompanying him. They drew their carbines and dismounted. As they did, the snipers on top of the cliff above the remnants of Boynton's trapped company opened fire. Three of the troopers with Magee died in the first fusillade.

Boynton's mind raced. He might lead his men in a frontal assault downriver, but if he did, the narrow space between river and canyon wall would funnel his soldiers directly into the muzzles of dozens of Apache rifles. He dared not stay, he dared not attack. And Colonel Magee's squad was getting cut down one by one.

"Sergeant Kingman, mount the men. We're going back across the river right *now!*"

"Yes, sir!"

Boynton reloaded his pistol and went through the ranks

of his men with words of encouragement, instilling in them what confidence he could and the need to hurry once they got mounted. Only Magee and one soldier remained to lay down any covering fire.

"Sergeant, lead the way across the river."

"Here, Captain, take my carbine," Kingman said, handing over his rifle. "You're gonna need this more'n me. Leastwise, for a few minutes."

"I'll be sure you get it back," Boynton said, knowing that wasn't likely to happen. He had to stay to fire at anything moving in the tangled brush. Without it, the Apache downriver would rush forward and shoot every one in the middle of the Rio Grande. He cursed his impetuosity in rushing after Victorio without considering the situation more thoroughly.

"Captain, get back," came Colonel Magee's command.

"Go, Sergeant, ride like you mean it!" With those words, Boynton rushed out to the bank of the river and began firing up at the top of the cliff. His shots drove back the snipers there. The buffalo soldier on the far bank saw what Boynton did and added his firepower. As soon as the soldier sent chips of rock flying in front of the Apache riflemen, Boynton whirled about and fired into the thicket where so much death had been spawned. His first shots produced a cry of rage and pain.

Ten warriors boiled out of hiding and ran toward him. He dropped two before the carbine magazine emptied. Then he fired with his six-shooter. His hammer fell on a spent chamber when all the remaining Apache turned tail and dived for cover again.

Boynton had only a split second to make his decision. He vaulted into the saddle and urged the horse he had inherited from some nameless fallen trooper across the river. Shots plinked into the water around him, splashing water knee-high.

"Ride, Captain, ride!" shouted Magee. "You can make it!"

Boynton bent over, head next to the horse's neck to provide as small a target as possible. Halfway. He heard war shouts on the Mexican side of the river. His horse let out a cry that was almost human and toppled to one side, its leg shattered by a bullet. Boynton crashed into the waist-deep water and sputtered to get half the river from his mouth. Tiny fountains of water rose around him, each marking a bullet narrowly missing his head.

Boynton plowed on, the current tugging at him and threatening to carry him away. Boynton was tired past exhaustion, his wounds drained him of energy, and simply giving up would be easy, so easy.

Hatred drove him on. Victorio had killed Sarah and Peter and Thomas and had not paid for it yet. If he simply gave up now, the Mimbreño chief never would be brought to justice.

"Captain, get under cover," urged Colonel Magee. The older man reached out to help Boynton, then he stiffened and fell to one side. He tried to wiggle about, then stopped.

"I can make it, sir," Boynton said. He stopped where Magee lay, eyes staring. It took Boynton a second to realize the colonel had died without even knowing it. The bullet had caught him in the temple. A dark hole bled very little. The rifle slug had not exited the other side of the colonel's head.

"Git on back, sir," came Kingman's urgent words. "The corporal's found a crevice in that there canyon wall where we can hide. Nobody's gonna reach us if we all git into it." Kingman's Southern accent deepened as strain mounted.

He stumbled and staggered and finally reached sanctuary. Sitting heavily with his back securely against a granite wall, he stared back across the Rio Grande into Mexico, where the Apache fighters danced around, waving their rifles in the air and hooting derisively. The setting sun caught the white war paint on their faces and the red on their bodies, turning them into exotic devils.

"Colonel Magee," Boynton said, staring at the body of his commanding officer in dumb amazement. The man had gone through the Civil War, had fought Indians at a half dozen posts and had finally come to the banks of the Rio Grande to die in an Apache ambush.

Lester Boynton had thrust him into that trap as surely as if he had marched him in at gunpoint.

PART III

Victorio's War

Pursuit and Capture

March, 1879
San Carlos Reservation

"The black soldiers follow us everywhere," Victorio said, eyes fixed on the clouds moving into a delicate white wreath around the summit of Standing Mountain. The late winter storm had stranded Victorio and his followers just inside the U.S., only a few miles from Fort Cummings at the base of Cooke's Peak. He sighed in resignation. Another holy mountain desecrated by the incursion of the Indah, the White Eyes. "When will we again hear the music of the crops growing? Must we always watch our backs, listen for their heavy feet thudding on the land? Is there no rest?"

"We have fought them well," Loco said. "We need to surrender to their power. We live on nothing. Our families need more and more supplies. When the Indah bring the food and ammunition and rifles and horses, we take them and prosper."

"There are more dangerous paths to follow than constant raiding," spoke up Nana. "Giving in and being hidden away in the White Eyes' prisons without walls is surely the worst." The old warrior drew his thin blanket closer but did not shift his weight toward the fire. It gave little enough light and almost no warmth now. The small circle where the feeble campfire heat had melted the snow barely allowed the three chiefs to sit on bare ground. Nana thrust out his crippled foot to warm it near the embers.

If only his luck had continued favorably. Victorio's band had starved for the better part of the winter, dogged constantly by the Ninth Cavalry when they ventured into New Mexico Territory, and even the decimated bluecoats of the Tenth posed some small nuisance, black dogs whining and barking whenever they moved. Victorio wished the Comanche were less of a danger around Fort Davis. He might enjoy Texas raiding some more. It was so easy.

"Brother," came Lozen's soft voice. "A rider comes. It is one of the Indah settlers."

Victorio motioned his sister back into hiding. He considered telling both Nana and Loco to similarly hide, then decided against it. He had protected the settlers around Ojo Caliente in return for occasional meals, cattle, even horses. The agreement had worked well for both, he protecting them from bands of raiding Chiricahua and Coyotero Apache and they giving him what his people needed most to continue their fight to remain free of San Carlos.

"Victorio," called the rider, jumping to the ground. He limped over. Victorio remembered this one. He had fought in the White Eyes' war far to the east and still carried a bullet in his leg. As with all Indah, he was rude, but Victorio ignored it.

"Sit, enjoy the warmth of the fire," Victorio said.

"No time for that," he said, looking around uneasily, unsure of his welcome in the circle of Mimbreño. "We done called on them buffalo soldiers over at Fort Bayard, and they cain't hep us one little bit. Apache raiders took or kilt all my cattle. *All* of them," the settler emphasized.

Victorio nodded. He never raided a settlement to take all the cattle or horses. It was best to leave some behind to renew the herd for future raids. Whoever stole from this man did not understand the ways of the Warm Springs Apache.

"How do you know them to be Apache?" asked Nana.

"I seen 'em. They didn't wear those yellow buckskin bandoliers you do, but otherwise they didn't look much diff'rent."

Victorio nodded again, coming to a decision. They had stayed in this encampment long enough. It was time to move on. It was time for battle again. "We will take care of this." He paused, mind racing. "There is danger to us."

"From them soldiers? I heard. They want to move you and yer families on over to San Carlos. Don't want to see you folks go. You give more protection than a dozen forts filled with them Negro cavalry troopers."

Victorio said nothing, waiting for the settler to say his piece. The man finally understood the silence. "We kin scare up a few cows to leave out for you. Murchison, he's got some left. And Bitterman on the other side of Ojo Caliente might be willin' to put up a cow or two if it means no more raidin'. But we don't have no ammunition."

"We will find these raiders. They might be Chiricahua riding with Geronimo." Victorio spat, in spite of the sour look he received from Nana. The old chief did not share Victorio's dislike for the Chiricahua leader.

"Thank you muchly," the settler said, getting back onto his swaybacked horse. He rode quickly from the camp, going faster than he had come. Victorio reflected on this.

In spite of their beneficial dealings over the past two years, the settler still feared him. Slow to approach out of fear, quick to retreat, again from fear.

Somehow, this pleased Victorio.

"What do we do?" asked Loco. "He has been truthful with us before, but now?" He shook his head. "We starve and the bluecoats work hard to move us to San Carlos."

"This is our land. Warm Springs cradles our families and our souls. We will not leave,' " said Victorio. But he felt so tired. Had Mangas carried such a load? Victorio slumped, then straightened, considering how best to track down the renegades. "They will go west, into the Mogollóns. They think to find refuge with the Coyotero rather than the Mescalero. We can stop them."

Lozen returned slowly and hunkered down beside her brother. She looked at him sideways, her eyes limitless pools in her wide face. It took several minutes before she spoke, her words formed perfectly to be in harmony with her thoughts.

"Brother, you ride into great danger following these Apache. I see only enemies around us. Everywhere, enemies—black, white, red."

"Then go to my wife and family and prepare them to move on. We cannot be pinned down any longer. Get them and the others to safety, with the Mescalero, if necessary."

"I understand. I shall not fail you."

"With a hundred like you, we would not be driven like dogs from one camp to another," Victorio said. In the distance came the voice of *tzoe*, the coyote. A bad omen. Victorio turned from his sister and plotted out the best way of overtaking the raiders. Lozen would take the cattle from the Indah settlers and keep his people from starvation for another week. With Ussen's aid, the raiders would be killed and some of what they had stolen recovered. There was no reason to return it to the settlers. They no longer had their cattle and horses. It would be added payment for the pleasure of tracking down renegade raiders.

Again in the distance, the coyote gave voice to its frustration. Victorio tried to ignore the bad omen. He failed.

"They follow closely," Nana said. "The bluecoats are behind us. Less than a day's ride."

"We outride them," Victorio said, but he wished Lozen had come with them. It was nice to think his wife and six children were safe with her, on the move, getting away from those that would pen them up on worthless desert land at San Carlos. Still, her Power would have been so useful, determining which trail to follow now.

Try as he might, Victorio could not decide which fork to take, the one leading to the northwest or the one going due south. He wanted to turn south, to return to Mexico and Juh's stronghold in the Sierra Madres. He felt safe there. But instinct told him the Apache raiders he sought had ridden to the northwest.

To the northwest, in the direction of San Carlos. It was as if he was nothing more than a maverick being herded toward a corral he tried vainly to avoid. He stopped, closed his eyes, and inhaled deeply, trying to seize the scent of the wind. Other omens had been confusing, as if Ussen tested him like a young brave. He had climbed the sacred mountain, Say-a-Chee, and had received a clear vision of his life. Since then he had come to believe truly that the present was evil and the only good lay in the future.

To go south and raid or to go toward San Carlos and capture the renegades? One lone consideration decided him. Lozen would have taken the Indah's cattle by now. A deal had been struck, and he must honor it.

"This way," he said, taking the trail he had vowed never to follow. At least he was not alone. Old Nana rode close beside him. Nana's brother, Blanco, laid back to watch their trail and alert them if the cavalry got too close. And with him, giving him the power to deal with any trouble, scattered around the trail, were two dozen stalwart warriors.

Less than an hour along the faint track, Victorio slowed, his keen ears picking up noises ahead. He switched to warpath language as he gave orders to Nana and Loco.

"Ahead, circle to north and around to cut off escape," he said to Nana. "To south with a dozen warriors," he told Loco. Victorio waited with the few remaining braves until he was sure the two stalwarts had found their positions. Then Victorio rode boldly into the renegades' camp.

The nine braves, all Chiricahua, as he had suspected, jumped to their feet. One leveled a rifle, then stopped when Victorio made no move to attack.

"Brothers," Victorio called. "Why do you dishonor us?"

"We ride with Geronimo. He is our war chief!" cried the one with the rifle. "Who cares if shame is heaped on the heads of Mimbreño?"

Victorio's hand tightened on his rifle. He longed to squeeze off a round and end this miserable snake's life. Looking around, Victorio assured himself no one would escape the camp should he start the fight. Yet he wanted to know more. Geronimo was no one's friend, but all Apache were being ridden into the ground by the White Eyes. Better to ally with the snake than to die at the end of a bluecoat's bayonet.

"I would speak with Geronimo. Is he riding with Juh now?" Victorio felt a moment of irritation with Juh, who rode with any Apache seeking sanctuary. There ought to have been more loyalty. Yet, Victorio reflected, what was he doing now? Did he not seek out Geronimo to forge a peace?

As Mangas Coloradas would have counseled.

The braves huddled together like conspirators, whispering among themselves. Victorio saw a young boy to the side, securely tied up and obviously a prisoner. The boy might be Mescalero or Tonto. It was hard to tell through the layers of dirt, and because he had been stripped naked, except for a breechclout, any other hint from clothing had been removed. His body was covered with deep cuts, as if his captors had been whipping him, but his wide eyes showed no fear, only alertness and the sudden recognition that deliverance was at hand.

"Aieee!" The sudden war cry caught Victorio by surprise. He lifted his rifle and fired, hitting one Chiricahua in the leg, sending him tumbling down into a ravine. The others began firing wildly, thinking only to escape.

The sharp snap of rifles farther away told Victorio that Loco had stopped some of the fleeing Chiricahua. He rode over, easing his horse down the bank of the arroyo and over to the wounded brave. Rifle aimed, he prepared to kill the man.

"Wait! We are witches!" the warrior cried. "Kill us, and it will bring only evil on your heads!"

"It is true!" shouted the young boy. "They *are* witches."

Victorio's finger came back. His rifle bucked and sent the fallen man to the Happy Place. Considering burying the man without any belongings appealed to Victorio. These Chiricahua had brought only disgrace to him by violating the covenant he had with the Indah settlers near Ojo Caliente. Still, he put the boy to digging a grave and allowed those killed to be buried with only moccasins and their knives in the graves.

"It is more than they deserved," Victorio said after seeing the Chiricahua laid to rest in their shallow, sandy graves. Let them wander forever with only a knife and moccasins with holes in the soles, spurned by true warriors in the Happy Place.

Loco seemed uneasy, staring at the graves in the sandy

arroyo bottom. "They were witches. I believe we have brought great harm to ourselves by killing them."

"Boy," called Victorio to the youngster struggling into the threadbare cavalry jacket taken from a fallen warrior. "You will stay with Loco."

"And y'all are gonna stay with us—right after you toss down them rifles," came the drawled command.

Victorio whipped around, then froze. Completely circling them was a squad of the Ninth Cavalry. He recognized the man who had spoken fluent Apache as a scout, Al Siebert, the one called Man of Iron. Although not Apache, he was as good as any warrior in hunting and fighting. This explained how he had brought the buffalo soldiers into a ring around them without any Mimbreño noticing. A bluecoat standing back a ways held a pistol to Blanco's head to insure his silence. Nana's brother stared straight ahead, aware of the harm his capture had brought to the Warm Springs Apache.

"Yes, sir, you're gonna go right along with us this very minute. To San Carlos!"

Escape

Victorio rode slowly, sickened by what he saw. The Mimbreño died around him, as surely as if a heated knife had been thrust into their bellies and then twisted slowly. At his side rode Loco, the man's body racked by the persistent cough that threatened to shake him loose from his life.

"The boy was right," Loco said glumly. "They were witches. We are cursed and there is no way to regain harmony. Ussen will never smile on us again. I am thinking of going to an Indah doctor, perhaps at Camp Grant."

"Witches," scoffed Victorio. "Those Chiricahua were not witches. They were frightened. They wanted only to save their own lives."

"How can you explain all this?" demanded Loco, fire in his eyes. The fire died quickly as coughing again shook him. When they had been captured and brought here a month earlier by Man of Iron and the buffalo soldiers, he had been a strong, commanding warrior. Now he wobbled as he rode, starving and sick.

"They put us into an old fort where their ghosts roam to taunt our lives," Victorio said. "Malaria, they call it. Bad air." He wondered how the air could be bad, but the Indah medicine man had called it that. Then he had left after doing nothing for them or to them. Victorio's band had sickened and died at ever increasing rates after the doctor returned to Fort Apache.

"The crops die. They barely poke their stalks above this miserable alkali dirt, then they die as we watch. The water is never enough." Loco's finger stabbed in the direction of the Gila River. All summer it had flowed sluggishly, mud and silt in every drop. "They do not give us cattle, as they promised. They do not give us any meat. We would have been better off to die fighting rather than let Man of Iron capture us."

"Our families," Victorio said distantly, thinking of his long-suffering wife and their children. His eyes skipped over the desolation of San Carlos Reservation and went toward the Mogollón Rim to the east. If he could only find a way of getting his family away from this hellhole and over the mountains! Warm Springs was not that far off.

It might as well have been on the other side of a vast canyon.

A week's travel, no more, kept the Warm Springs Apache from their hereditary land. Except the bluecoats would kill them if they tried to leave this arid, plague-racked desert. The women and children would slow them if they ran and present easy targets for the black soldiers and their white leaders.

"We cannot live here any longer," Victorio said, knowing action had to follow his decision. Mangas would have debated with the Indian Agent. Loco thought John Clum was a well-meaning man, as so many of the White Eyes were, and agreed with him often. Victorio hoped to never again fall under the power of such men, for they were worse than the soldiers with their fine carbines. The well-meaning lacked power but made hollow promises that dripped like honey into the ears of those wanting to believe. Like Loco.

In his way, Victorio felt sorry for the Indian Agents like Clum. They knew the proper things to do—and could not do them.

They could not because the evil ones in power would not let them. The Great Nantan in far-off Washington changed often, also. Each new Indah chief had a different notion of how to deal with his Apache brothers.

Victorio would have spat, had there been enough saliva in his mouth. He dared not drink from the Gila, and this was the only water available. He reached into his medicine pouch, fumbled around with the magical pollens and herbs, then put a small smooth pebble he found there into his mouth, rolling it about to dampen his tongue. On the warpath, an Apache warrior could fight and ride for days without food and water. Why should he and his family be forced to endure such hardship when they were not at war?

He reconsidered. They were not at war because he and Nana and Loco and the others had been captured. Without realizing it, they had surrendered when they ought to have fought, to the death, if it had been necessary.

"Agent Clum would not allow women and children to be harmed," Victorio said. "If we left to go raiding, he would not permit the soldiers, even General Crook, to hurt them."

"Where would we go? The cavalry patrols constantly along the border between Arizona and Mexico. Geronimo and Juh raid endlessly." Loco started to cough and held back the reflex.

"North," Victorio decided. "The Hopi and Zuñi and Navajo have not felt the force of our raiding in some time."

"Nana will ride with us," Loco said, more animated than he had been in weeks. "We will return to our own land!"

"Warm Springs," Victorio said, memories of the pleasant land coming back. He blinked, the good land replaced by this barren desert where he was penned like an animal. Rage mounted in him. They had few rifles and almost no ammunition, but when did an Apache warrior need that to raid? Cunning and skill, those were all any Apache needed.

"To raid!" Loco cried. He put his heels to the flanks of his scrawny horse and trotted off, happier than he had been since coming to San Carlos.

Victorio shared the energy. The decision had come slowly, but now that it was made, he knew his destiny.

"They follow like buzzards, that squad of black soldiers," Nana said. The old warrior poked a stick in the ground to show the best spot for an ambush. "We can take their horses."

"As if we would want such broke-down nags," said Loco. He coughed, the sound almost delicate compared to his earlier chest-deep cough. "They are not worth the knife slash it would take to open their throats."

"We will take the horses, ride them into the ground, and then go back to our own mounts," Victorio decided. "I am more interested in the guns we might take."

"And ammunition," Nana reminded the war chief. "I have asked Ussen, and he has told me. They carry much ammunition with them."

Victorio was pleased. They had ridden from San Carlos

without any trouble, and within days the entire Ninth Cavalry in New Mexico Territory knew their knife. Three times in one week they had raided and come away without any losses. Horses, a cow, some rifles—they had grown stronger every time they raided. Loco no longer coughed the way he did, now that they were away from San Carlos. And Nana, hunched over with age on the reservation, rode his pony like a young buck as he used his war lance on soldier and settler alike.

"Let us fight," Victorio said. He paused when the boy taken from the Chiricahua renegades moved to one side. He distrusted the boy, and he could not say why. Loco claimed the boy was Tonto Apache, but Victorio thought he might be Jicarillo or even Mescalero. Why would the boy lie about his clan?

"Nana, Loco," he said suddenly. "Mount up but do not attack there."

"What? Why not?" demanded Nana. The old man's face hardened into a mask of anger at being denied. He was a master tactician and Victorio seemed to be flaunting his position as war chief for no reason.

"We fight here. We have been betrayed," Victorio said. "By the boy!" Victorio motioned the others to their horses.

The young boy took off like a frightened rabbit. Barely had he crashed into the undergrowth when the snorting of horses and the sounds of cavalry moving on them came skipping along on the gentle morning wind. Victorio levered a round into the chamber of the rifle he had taken from a dead soldier three days earlier, and fired blindly. The slug ripped off a limb from a creosote bush, but the response was more than he had anticipated.

A dozen rifles spat lead in his direction. His horse reared and threw him. Victorio hit the ground hard, momentarily stunned. All around him responded his comrades. Nana and Loco returned fire and so did the two dozen warriors riding with them, although slower than their leaders. Victorio rolled to hands and knees and forced himself to stand.

A bullet passed across the top of his head, not breaking the skin but taking off a piece of long black hair as a trophy.

"Aieee!" He let out a war whoop and charged. This focused those in his war party. They crashed through the brush and overran the bluecoats' position, bursting out of the ring drawn tightly around their camp. When his rifle magazine came up empty, Victorio fought on, using knife and club and thrown stone and his fists and feet. Like a demon he fought until he stood alone in a clearing, bloodied and barely able to keep from falling over from exhaustion.

"They are all dead," came Nana's report. The old chief rode up on a new pony, a paint that shied and tried to bolt every time its rider moved. "We have one prisoner."

Victorio wiped blood from his face—and it was not his own that had been spilled. The only wounds he had sustained were minor scratches from thorn bushes.

He turned and saw Loco leading the boy out of the shadows, a rope around his neck. The boy's eyes were wide with fear. A jerk on the lariat sent him to his knees in front of Victorio.

"We saved you from the Chiricahua. We fed you and treated you as one of our own, and you repay our kindness with treachery," Victorio said.

"I'm not Apache!" the boy cried. "I was taken when I was a baby. By the Mescalero! I'm white, and I *hate* you!"

"My nephew was killed by the White Eyes soldiers, for no reason," Victorio said. He looked down at the boy, who now grew defiant. "I do not kill, except with reason."

A quick movement drew his knife across the boy's throat.

Blood spurted out as the boy kicked and thrashed, trying to stanch the flow of blood. In minutes, he lay still.

"Gather all their ammunition and weapons," Victorio called out. "We have much more to do!"

To the north they rode and raided for two months.

Return to Peace

Summer 1879
Warm Springs

"We can return to Mexico, raiding along the way," Nana said. The old warrior worked to keep his pony from rearing. He had stolen the horse only a day before, and the animal had not accustomed itself to his style of riding yet. It had been broken as a cavalry mount and hardly suited the old chief.

"I prefer to go into Texas," Victorio said, heaving a sigh as he thought on the good land in West Texas and the herds of mustangs still roaming there. The settlers had more cattle than they could use, especially around Fort Davis. Limpia Creek provided sweet, clear water and territory to enjoy it in.

But he could not ride back, no matter how good the raiding was. His forays into the rolling land east of Fort Davis had been good. He smiled crookedly as he remembered the wagon train he had raided there. It had come on the heels of cavalry raids on his encampment. A somber mood settled on him as he pictured his dead nephew. Lozen had warned of the cavalry raid and allowed the warriors to slip away, but never had Victorio thought the bluecoats would kill women and children. Not then.

He had taken no pleasure in killing the women and children in the wagon train. Rather, the loads of food and weapons had supplied his band for months, and in that he took real satisfaction. The horses from the wagon train had afforded them the chance to range as widely as the hard-riding Comanche, and they had had enough ammunition, something that had occurred too seldom in the years since. Even Lozen's Power had been unable to find that which was not present.

"We might go to Mexico," Victorio said slowly. "We might return to Texas. But we cannot. We must talk."

"Loco was a fool to let himself be captured so easily," spoke up Cuchillo Negro. "We are Apache. We know the danger of the battle."

"Would you be the one to let the Indah keep him in their stinking prison?" demanded Nana. The old warrior's wrinkled face looked like leather crumpled into a tight ball. He squinted at the younger, hotheaded Cuchillo Negro. "Would you rot away in filth?"

"I am Mimbreño!" cried Cuchillo Negro. "They can kill my body, but my spirit will return to haunt them!"

"Fine words," Victorio said, "but misplaced courage serves no one now. Again, we need more than a quick knife and a fast horse." He turned slowly, scanning the distant hills for movement. Against a patch bare of grass he saw the blue and gold of a cavalry uniform. Then he saw a second trooper followed by a third and a fourth. Boldly, a dozen soldiers rode exposed to his keen vision.

The approaching officer at the head of his squad made no effort to conceal himself.

In that lay the Apache's problem. The cavalry fought year-round now, with growing expertise. The buffalo soldiers were veteran fighters and the officers showed ever more determination to put an end to Apache raids. Damn Colonel Hatch!

"Loco is one man. We are fifty!"

Lozen trotted up, her face a mask. She turned slowly, eyeing Cuchillo Negro—and then staring through him. Expertly controlling her horse, she waited until Victorio tilted his head slightly in her direction.

"Only those few come," she said. "They show no fear."

"Why should they?" demanded Nana. "They hold Loco captive."

"They hold more," Victorio said. "Our families are hostage at San Carlos. Their patrols are a noose around our necks. We must deal with them now, or they will gain even more power."

"We meekly hang our heads and return to San Carlos like whipped dogs?" Cuchillo Negro's outrage caused other nearby warriors to reach for their rifles, wary of his temper.

"You do not trust your chief?" asked Nana. "Then leave us!"

Victorio held his rage in check through force of will. He dared not fight Cuchillo Negro now. The younger braves would follow Cuchillo, splitting their force when he needed the largest show of force possible. But how could he tell the younger warriors of his need to hold his wife, rather than leave her on a disease-riddled reservation even the White Eyes shunned? And his sons. They deserved guidance in so many things. They, too, were prisoners to the cavalry.

All because the Great Nantan wanted the Apache kept

on worthless land that would kill them when traditional land around Ojo Caliente was theirs for the taking.

"Chief Victorio?" called the officer, a captain by his insignia. Victorio had worn a captain's jacket for a few weeks until he had lost it in a race with one of Juh's braves.

Such it was with others things, as well.

"I am chief of the Warm Springs Apache," Victorio said in English.

"I am Captain Andrew Bennett, Ninth Cavalry, Company I, out of Fort Wingate and under orders from Colonel P. T. Swain. We have much to discuss." The captain showed a little uneasiness until Victorio slid from horseback and walked forward, leaving his rifle behind with Lozen. This seemed to relieve the officer's worries. Victorio almost laughed. Lozen was a better shot than most of the warriors and, at this range, she might be able to outshoot even the weapon's owner.

"We will never return to San Carlos," Victorio said rudely. For some reason, this put the officer at ease.

"I'm glad you are not going to dance around what are the most pertinent points," he said. He cleared his throat. "We captured another of your chiefs. Loco."

Victorio remained impassive, though he seethed. The boy they had taken with the witches had been nothing but a curse to them. They ought to have let the Mescalero boy go rather than trying to bring him into their band. Victorio let Bennett talk, hardly listening, as he considered his options.

The sun began to set and both parties retired for their meals. Then Bennett returned and continued the negotiations. Victorio and Nana finally got a promise of transfer from San Carlos to Warm Springs.

"We will remain in peace at Warm Springs," Victorio said with feeling. "What of Loco?"

"He will be there before you go. Lieutenant Colonel

Merritt will personally oversee your families' return—and Loco's release."

Victorio glanced at Cuchillo Negro and saw disbelief on the young warrior's face. It was unseemly to show such a reaction during negotiations.

"Food?" asked Nana. "What of food?"

"We'll see what can be done," the officer promised.

Victorio listened to Captain Bennett's words and heard hesitation, something held back. But the words dealing with Loco's release and the Mimbreños' return to their hereditary lands at Warm Springs were genuine. Any other obstacles could be dealt with after Victorio's people were again settled.

The Judge and the Chief

Late Summer, 1879
Warm Springs

"This is not a good thing," Victorio said. He stood on the gently sloping hill, staring down past the grama grass and clumps of prickly pear to the valley where 150 warriors gambled, rode endlessly in and out of trees shouting insults at each other, practiced their war skills, lived without families. "They will become restless and turn on each other soon, unless there is an enemy. We do not even have ceremonial dances any more."

"You learned much from Mangas Coloradas," Nana said. "Perhaps too much. How do you keep them together until their families arrive to keep them out of trouble?" Nana lifted a leathery hand and swept it across the valley, indicating those who had faithfully followed Victorio for so long and now fell to fighting among themselves.

"Some are not even Mimbreño," Victorio said. "A few are Mescalero and others . . ." He shook his head. "Who knows what clan they claim as their own—or which claims them?"

"The weather is good now," Nana said, his face turning to the sun and his eyes closing, "but it is too late to plant crops and harvest them before the autumn brings frost. What will we do for food then?"

"What, indeed?" Victorio paced the hilltop, his eyes seeing the land of his people. Warm Springs—Warm Springs Reservation—was his clan's once more. There ought to be crops thrusting up waist-high to furnish grain in a month. Cattle ought to be grazing on the juicy grass. And horses? There should be remuda of horses everywhere he looked, the sign of wealth of any decent band of Apache.

Even Colonel Hatch agreed this was Mimbreño land. Since coming here almost two months earlier, they had been given food enough by the bluecoats, but Victorio realized this was not enough. Their families had not been removed from San Carlos, and Hatch had refused to allow any Mimbreño to travel to the hellhole on the Gila to fetch kith and kin.

"Have I done what Mangas counseled but without the wisdom to understand other problems caused in that solving? Have I led my band into new captivity? We will starve, as we did in the San Mateo Mountains last year, unless there is ample food." Victorio tried not to think about the way the Indah always looked with narrowed eyes at any Apache carrying a rifle. It was as if every warrior was a potential killer, in spite of the honeyed words of peace Hatch and the others let flow from their mouths. They spoke of peace but prepared for war constantly—against the Apache.

"The settlers close in around us, taking the best farmland for their own. Our crops will be on ever smaller patches of land if this continues,'' Nana said. ''How can our women hope to grow enough if the White Eyes settlers complain? We have not even planted and already they run to their bluecoats with complaints.''

''Not all,'' Victorio said. Those settlers around Ojo Caliente still received his protection, even if that security had caused him and his warriors to kill witches and bring evil down on their heads. The boy was better off dead, being hexed too.

''The only thing that is as Captain Bennett promised is Loco's release,' '' said Nana, ''but he remains drunk most of the time on their firewater. It was never this way when all we had was *tiswin*. They give us plenty of liquor but deny us our women and children. There is much to this I do not like,'' Nana said. ''Was it only a ruse to trap us?''

Victorio did not answer. The warm summer day soothed his body, yet he felt at war with himself. Everything Nana said was true. They camped on land that was theirs but did not truly live on it. Victorio had seen war camps with a greater feeling of permanence than the valley filled with his band.

War. Peace. He balanced them in his mind. ''There is much honor to be gained in raiding,'' he said finally. ''We will never see our families unless we agree to remain on the reservation they set aside for us.'' Even as he spoke, the words disturbed him. Colonel Hatch promised them settlement at Warm Springs, but had done nothing more. Worse, scouts working for the bluecoats out of Fort Stanton had told him of possible relocation to Mescalero.

Even this would be acceptable. Mimbreño meshed well with Mescalero. And Fort Stanton was not San Carlos.

He twisted slightly, head cocked to the side as the low chant of prayer to Ussen reached him. Nana had already pinpointed the source of the invocation to higher powers and stared uphill to where Victorio's sister was silhouetted against a darkening sky. Behind her billowed thunderheads laced with occasional lightning, not a good omen.

"Lozen feels danger," Nana said simply.

Victorio sucked in a deep breath, his chest expanding until it felt as if it would burst. Only then did he let out the breath. His sister never gave her prayers up to the sky unless an inner need prodded her.

"Have any of the braves been raiding?" asked Victorio.

"None, though—" Nana bit off his words. He turned from Victorio to stare at Lozen.

"What have you heard?" Victorio demanded.

Nana did not speak, and Victorio stewed in his need to know. Forcing himself to patience required a wait of almost an hour, until after Lozen had finished her prayers. She came to him slowly, her face dour.

"Brother, you must leave immediately. They come for you!"

"Who is coming? Geronimo? I will fight him! He has—"

"Go, Brother, now," she urged. "I will ride at your side. The White Eyes settlers come for you."

"Why?" Victorio was confused. "Colonel Hatch said this was our land. They cannot throw us off without the cavalry approving."

"I have heard rumors, the whispers of squaws at Ojo Caliente," Nana said carefully. "They say their nantan wants you for killing and stealing."

"I have not raided for weeks," Victorio protested.

"Judge Bristol," Nana said, "and the one they call the prosecutor, are not your friends."

"Colonel Hatch said we have nothing to fear from them," Victorio said, but his conviction began to fade.

"They are close, my brother. Please go!" Lozen pulled her rifle from a shoulder sling and stuffed rounds into the magazine. *"U-ka-ski!* Go away now!"

Victorio laughed scornfully. He would not leave when his wife and children would be here soon. Depending on the bluecoats for food galled him, but he would refrain from raiding as long as the Mimbreño stayed at Warm Springs. He shrugged his shoulders. Even sharing the land with the Mescalero was not too outrageous an accommodation in exchange for a more peaceful life without the black soldiers constantly nipping at his heels like hungry dogs.

He strode down the hill in the direction of his camp. A small fire had burned to embers. He kicked at it, then added a few branches of dried pine that flared into sudden fire. He looked around for the remainder of the deer Cuchillo Negro had killed the day before. He frowned when he did not see it. He stalked off toward a stand of trees to see if Cuchillo Negro had strung up the carcass there to keep it away from the packs of dogs roving up and down the valley. As he ducked under a low limb of a partially uprooted cottonwood, he heard a commotion behind him. Victorio turned, then froze.

A dozen settlers galloped up, spreading out to circle his camp. One man he recognized as the county prosecutor—Albert Fountain, he was called—rode straight through the fire, his horse's hooves kicking flaming wood in all directions. The horse reared, but Fountain kept it under control.

"Where is he?" demanded a stocky man with a long mustache, dressed in black, his cloth coat buttoned in spite of the day's warmth.

"Can't rightly say, Judge," Fountain said. "We were told he'd be here." Albert Fountain wheeled his horse around and rode to another man in their party.

"You said Victorio was going to be here," Fountain accused. "You're Grant County sheriff."

The man wearing a star pinned on his vest glared at Fountain, then spoke instead to the black-dressed man.

"Judge Bristol, these savages all look alike. But I reckon we spooked him gallopin' up like Prosecutor Fountain wanted."

"Don't bicker," Judge Bristol snapped. "The murdering heathen is here somewhere, unless he is out raiding in plain daylight. I swear, he will be brought to justice. I will not tolerate murder and horse stealing!"

"We'll get him, if we have to kill the lot of 'em," the sheriff promised.

"Brother, this way," came a low whisper in warpath language. From behind him crept Lozen, moving as quietly as a shadow drifting across another shadow. "Your horse is ready. Nana and I will go with you, to escape their so-called justice."

"They want to put me in their jail!" Victorio was astounded. "Colonel Hatch promised sanctuary here! Warm Springs is our land!"

"They would hang you. Ussen warned me of their coming. You must not fight them. Too many in their posse range through our camp even as they steal your belongings." Lozen pointed in the direction of the deputies ripping apart all that Victorio had carried with him these past months, taking what they wanted and destroying the rest. "We would lose both land and life if we fight them now, while they are strong and we are weak."

"My sons, my wife," growled Victorio, seeing his sister was right. To fight Judge Bristol and Fountain and the sheriff and those riding with them was sure death, as was allowing them to pass judgment on him. He had stolen horses. Perhaps he had even killed in that theft, but it had been months earlier, before Colonel Hatch offered them sanctuary at Warm Springs Reservation.

"You will never see them again unless you ride away," said Lozen. She grabbed her brother's arm and tugged insistently. Her fingernails dug into his flesh. The pain focused his thoughts as she said with great feeling, "Now, now!"

He allowed her to pull him deeper into the copse of low-branched, fragrant juniper. Every step he took carried him away from his land and family, as surely as if he climbed the steps of the White Eyes' execution gallows. The settlers would never allow the Warm Springs Apache to stay here, he realized with sudden clarity. The Mimbreño would be hunted one by one, killed by laws and customs not their own.

"Mangas never faced such a situation. There can be only war," he said, swinging up onto the back of the powerful stallion Lozen had brought for him.

"Then let there be war!" Lozen said, her dark eyes shining.

Together they raced the wind over the hills. Nana joined them before they reached the boundary of the reservation. And Loco, barely able to stay on his horse, caught up with them the following day. Others came, slowly, slowly, and then in increasing numbers until Victorio's cry of *War!* echoed across the land.

PART IV

Boynton's War

Transfer Denied

Early Fall, 1879
Fort Davis

"Why haven't you reported it?" asked Lester Boynton. His sergeant shifted from one heavily booted foot to the other, uneasy with the question. Sergeant Kingman chewed on a splinter held in the corner of his mouth, then spat, tossing the gnawed toothpick after the dark gob before speaking.

"Well," he drawled, "you aren't the best commander I ever had, but then again, you're not the worst, either."

"You know what happened," Boynton said, his face flushing in anger. "I was responsible. Because of me, Colonel Magee is dead!"

"You been workin' on this a long time, haven't you, Captain?" Kingman wiped his mouth, then reached for a canteen on the barracks common table. He held it out for Boynton, who impatiently dismissed it, before the sergeant took a long drink of the tepid water. "Been stationed at places with real awful water. Not here. Good water, in spite of the post bein' in the middle of such godforsaken land, excuse my blasphemy, Captain."

"You could have reported that I risked my command, that I stupidly crossed the Rio Grande in violation of direct orders from Magee, you could have—"

"Captain, I coulda done a whole lot of things in my life. I grew up a slave."

"Yes, but—"

"Please, Captain, let me say my piece since you upped and asked. I sneaked around a mite when I was younger. Learned to read, I did." Kingman smiled a little as he remembered how this had happened. "I'd fetch the master's chillun from school every day in a buggy, so's they wouldn't have to walk the five miles. On the way I always asked them what they'd learned. They tole me, and I learned along with them, them thinkin' I was just bein' polite."

"I don't see what this has to do with anything." Boynton calmed down, then said, "I wasn't aware you could read and write."

"That's part of your problem, Captain, if you'll excuse me sayin' this. There's a whale of a lot you don't understand 'cuz you don't pay any attention to what goes on around you. Right now, nothin' but your wife and chilluns' passin' is on your mind."

George Kingman took another drink, then set the battered canteen down carefully. It made no sound. All Boynton could hear was the buzzing of flies in the room and the sharp commands of a corporal marching a squad of soldiers on punishment duty out on the parade ground under the burning sun. He grew increasingly uneasy, wanting to shout and pace and strike out, but Kingman remained calm and set on his course, undeterred by his superior officer's anxiety.

"I took it slow and easy and learned to read and write and even cipher. Nothin' to hurry about. I had all my life. But my master didn't want me doin' none of this. Felt a touch of guilt now and then 'bout sneakin' 'round behind his back, but the pangs went away the more I thought on it."

"I don't see what this has to do with my dereliction."

"Folks knew what I was up to. I was the only black boy sneakin' a look at books. They didn't turn me in 'cuz they knew I'd be whupped—or worse."

"They were loyal," Boynton said, struggling to figure out what his sergeant meant.

"They wasn't. For an extra piece of chicken they'd've turned me over to the supervisor. No, I was useful to them since none of them could read and write, and I knew things. Whenever somethin' happened they couldn't figure out, they came to me."

"The men in our company still go to you," Boynton said, knowing how few discipline problems he had to contend with because of Kingman's expert control. In other companies he had commanded, there had been continual problems with drunkenness, fighting, and even outright desertion. Nothing of the sort happened at Fort Davis, with Kingman intercepting the worst of the problems and taking care of them before they blew into a real storm.

"I was told not to learn to read, and I did. When the war came, I run away, followed the Big Muddy till I got to free land, then joined up in the Union Army. Never saw much in the way of fightin', but that didn't matter much. The Army and me, well, we fit together real good."

"Why shouldn't I feel guilty about disobeying orders? This is not a plantation. It is the Army! I disobeyed!" Boynton's heart raced. He swiped at sweat on his forehead.

It had been eating away at him for weeks that he had not been brought to justice for his foolish mistake in the field. The very authorities he ought to have reported to were dead. Because of him. It hardly seemed enough to have wired his resignation to district headquarters.

Worst of all was trying to face Colonel Magee's widow. She had lost her husband because of Lester Boynton, fool. He had not gotten over the passing of his own family, and now he was responsible for the death of his commander. Boynton had avoided her at every turn, in as cowardly an act as it had been foolish when he had gotten her husband killed by the devastating Apache cross fire.

"You don't think you'd go and do anything like that again, do you, Captain?"

"I . . . I don't know. If there were a chance of getting Victorio, I might."

"But you'd think a tad more on it, wouldn't you? Victorio making a fool of you's not what you want."

"I want him dead for what he's done," Boynton said, "but if that is not possible, then I want him brought up on charges."

"What you got out there in the Rio Bravo is a hard lesson in command. Man, am I glad I don't have to haul that about, weighin' me down like a big ole bale of cotton. Bein' a sergeant is easier."

Bugles sounded, swinging Boynton and Kingman around. The sergeant sauntered to the door and peered out, squinting against the hot sun.

"Reckon that's our new commander."

"Colonel Grierson," said Boynton. "Don't know much about him. He was post commander over at Fort Concho."

"Don't know anyone who served under him, either," said Kingman. "Reckon we ought to hie on out and greet him proper-like."

Boynton settled his uniform, soaking with sweat. He

settled his cap on his head and marched out, ready to do what had to be done. The dry grass crunched under his boots as he made his way across the broad parade ground. He felt as if every eye at Fort Davis was fixed on him. With military precision, he halted, saluted, and said, "Welcome to Fort Davis, sir."

"You're Boynton," the slender, sharp-eyed colonel said. "I want to speak with you." Benjamin Grierson snapped a quick salute at the other officers who had rushed out to welcome him. To them he said, "Gentlemen, you will present your troops in parade one hour before dinner. Have a decent band playing. I like a good, lively tune. It makes the foot step a little livelier. I will speak with each of you in turn, afterward. Dismissed."

Grierson squinted slightly at Boynton. "You look like you got a ramrod crammed up your ass. Must irritate bloody hell out of your horse, you ridin' all stiff like that. Come on."

"Sir, I—"

"That's my office?" Grierson pointed at the small office Amos Magee had used only a few short weeks earlier. "Used to bigger rooms. The whole of Fort Davis stretches out and no walls around it makes me a mite uneasy. I'll get used to it."

"Sir, I tendered my resignation."

"Get in there, Captain." Grierson stopped outside the door and looked around the post. "I'm going to like it here. I can tell. And I intend to bring the wrath of God down on the Apache."

"Sir," Boynton said, growing antsy.

"Son," said Grierson, settling into the chair. It creaked slightly although he was not a big man. He rocked back and forth, testing its mettle. Then he dropped his hat on the desk and drew his saber, placing it next to his hat. "Son, I saw your report on Magee's death and your request for termination. What do you intend to do if I accept your resignation?"

"Sir, I—" Boynton stuttered. He had no idea.

"That's about what I thought. I read your record. You're not an exceptionally good soldier, but then again, I've served with worse. Hell, I've shot worse in the field for dereliction of duty." Grierson fixed Boynton with his steely eyes.

"Colonel Magee died because I—"

"He was a soldier. He knew the risk of going into the field against the Apache. I've fought the Comanche for years, and they're like trying to grab a handful of water. First they're there, then they're gone. More 'n twenty years I've been out on the frontier and never once have I seen a man die for any good reason—only bad ones."

Boynton fumed at the way Grierson danced all around accepting his resignation.

"I can't make you stay, Captain," Grierson said finally, seeing his subordinate's impatience. "I wouldn't want you here unless you could do the job—unless I *thought* you could do the job. If you resign, there's no way you will ever stop Victorio. Are you content to let the murdering savage get away with killing your wife and sons?"

"No, sir. I—"

"Shut your mouth and let me talk. I don't appreciate sass from anyone, especially officers who are too loco to know what they want."

Boynton swallowed hard. He had not thought about life after the Army. It had been his career, but without Sarah and the boys, what was he to do? He was lost.

"The way I see it, you'll do the job of ten men to stop Victorio. I need that devotion to duty in my troops. Now, I'm sorry you lost your wife and sons, but that doesn't stop the raids from the Apache. We're at war with them."

"I am resp—" Boynton started to blurt out his guilt, his

defiance of Magee's orders and how it had gotten the colonel killed trying to pull his fat out of the fire. Colonel Grierson cut him off with a sharp rap on the desk. The echo startled the orderly just outside the door and brought the young man in, hand on his pistol. Grierson shooed him away.

"You will be responsible for clearing all intelligence dealing with Victorio," Grierson said. "You will keep me apprised of his movement, who rides with him, scouting reports, and rumors. Your company, Company N, I think it is, will be at the forefront of any attack against Victorio. You will be the one who brings him to justice, sir. Do I make myself clear?"

"You are not accepting my resignation?" No one would punish him for his disobedience and foolish disregard for his command. Sergeant Kingman had refused to turn in a report condemning him, apparently because of loyalty and the thought that he might have learned from it. And now Grierson. He had said much the same thing, that Boynton had the potential to be a better officer.

Boynton wondered what the truth was. It might be as simple as many of the experienced officers being transferred. Who wanted to serve in the Tenth, out in godforsaken desert with only Negro soldiers?

"You been out in the sun too long? Does it sound like it? I *need* you. I need an officer who can learn and be even more devious than that goldarned raiding Apache. I see that man standing in front of me. No one's ever accused me of wasting material. 'Course they *do* accuse me of going on too long. When you muster your troops for inspection, Captain, warn them I am likely to go on overlong."

Grierson's eyes fixed on Boynton.

"Yes, sir, I will tell them."

"Good. Now get out of here and let me settle in. And remember, Captain. This is *war.*"

"Yes, sir," the captain said. He saluted and did an about-face. His guilt at Magee's death burned in him, especially when he saw the colonel's widow under the porch, approaching to pay her respects to the new post commander. But something else seized him, something that overshadowed the disgrace of responsibility for his commander's death.

War, Colonel Grierson had said. War against Victorio. Boynton's war.

Striking Lightning

September 4, 1879
Ojo Caliente

"My son is dead?" Victorio went cold inside when he heard the dreaded words. He wanted to shriek and cry out in anguish, but he held it inside. He was an Apache, and warriors accepted death. But his son!

"He fought well," Loco said, eyes averted. "He will ride always in our memory as a true Apache. He had stolen three horses and returned for two more when the Indah soldier shot him in the back. He turned and fought, killing the soldier. Two buffalo soldiers came then and sent him on the path to the Happy Place. He never stopped fighting."

"I am proud of him," Victorio said, a catch in his throat. "What of the others? My wife?" It rankled him that he could do nothing about the women and children stranded at San Carlos, prisoners as surely as any of those the White

Eyes held at the dismal gray penitentiary at Yuma, overlooking the confluence of the Gila and Colorado Rivers.

"She is well, though mourning for her son," Loco said, "but San Carlos is a constant test of endurance, even for us Mimbreño. Your son, Istee, wants to join you, as do your other two sons."

"No! He is my youngest and only nine. The others would do well defending those who cannot leave San Carlos. There are enough warriors riding with me. Almost sixty." Victorio closed his eyes and let the vision wash across him like a black cloud pouring down burning rain. In a crazy, dizzying vision he saw his entire family dying. Rage mounted within him. He had raided well and stolen dozens of horses. Nana had located enough ammunition for them to fight on through the winter. Here and there along the path from their brief encampment at Warm Springs he had cached weapons and ammunition for the Warm Springs raiders. Food was no problem, not now, not for raiders. But his family? Victorio worried that they starved at San Carlos. There was always so little. And the disease that crept on the night wind. *Bad air,* the White Eyes medicine men called it.

Slow death, Victorio called it, a slow death that could not be seen or fought.

"He will be a man soon enough," Loco said. He rubbed his lips and moved with a jerkiness that told Victorio of the need for firewater. "But there are few enough left to train our boys. We need to return to the sacred mountains to test them."

"We will," Victorio promised. "The White Eyes kill us like snakes. They hold our women and children hostage. But we will drive them all from our land, white and black alike."

Victorio turned and stared at Loco. He had never liked the older, more volatile chief, but Loco was a good fighter if he stayed sober. He was loyal to his two wives and cared for others in his clan. Victorio thought he talked too much and often showed disregard in his dealings with the Indah, if for nothing else but to get more whiskey. But Loco was an Apache, a Mimbreño of the Warm Springs clan, and his influence rivaled Victorio's.

"Return to San Carlos," Victorio said. "Give them the benefit of your strong arm and quick knife. You can rally support and lead them wisely."

"I would raid with you!" For once, Victorio felt a bond with Loco.

"Do as you will on the way back to San Carlos. We must be a thorn under their rumps. The more thorns, the more likely they are to leave our land."

"They will do it on foot," said Loco, smiling broadly, "because I will steal all their horses!"

Victorio had to smile also. "Do it. Now go and see your daughter, Siki. Take care of your wives. Major Morrow follows us closely, and we have raiding of our own to do."

"I'll lay false trails. It will take their buffalo soldiers days to find your trail—and mine!" Loco went off, back straighter and with more purpose in his words than Victorio had seen for months. Loco had fallen prey to the lure of the potent liquor offered by the White Eyes settlers. Now he had returned to the way of the warrior, and would dance in victory many times.

"Keep my family safe," Victorio said softly to Loco's departing figure. He knew that the new commander of the Ninth Cavalry, General Pope, wanted to draw him back into Arizona and trap him there. Victorio would never be caught so easily, even by the clever Albert Morrow. His ranging would draw the cavalry supply lines thin—then he would snap them and cut off the soldiers from their precious food and water. The best of the soldiers could not rival the meanest of Apache fighters when it came to sheer endurance and surviving in this often cruel land. They did not know the hidden water sources the way even small Apache children and women did, nor could they find their way through the rugged canyons and broad deserts.

"I will see you all dead," Victorio promised the unknown soldiers who had killed his son, turning somber again. Unlike many of the chiefs, he had only one wife, but she had given him four sons and two daughters. Now his family was diminished. *He* was diminished.

"Nana!" he called, swinging into action. "Lozen! Are the warriors ready for the raid?"

"They are," Lozen said, riding over to him. "We have fifteen warriors on either side of the canyon, high on the walls. The soldiers will chase us when we steal their mules and supplies. Then—" She made a chopping motion with her hand, showing how the cavalry would ride into a bear trap, only to find its steely sharp jaws snapping shut on their necks.

"Enjuh!" He was ready. Lifting his arm high, rifle clutched in his hand, he waved to those who would accompany him into the soldiers' camp. Victorio, Lozen, and Nana, with twenty others, went to the raid.

"Who commands them?" asked Victorio, hoping to find information about the night-crawling snake who had killed his son.

"He is named Hooker," Lozen said. "I crept within ten yards and listened to his sentries. They are all indolent. We can strike and get their horses before they know our bullets have robbed them of their lives."

"We want them to pursue," Victorio said, reminding his sister of their great plan. "Sanchez and Raton are able leaders. They will cut down any soldiers pursuing us."

"We are not far from Ojo Caliente," she said, reaching into her medicine pouch, dipping her finger in sacred corn pollen, and carefully drawing a line under each eye. Lozen was prepared for the skirmish.

"Morrow will follow us," Victorio said. "We will draw out his troops into a long, thin line and remove even more of them!"

Victorio signaled to Nana and those with him. Nana, though old and hindered by a bad foot, was agile and moved like a summer breeze to the far side of the corral, where fifty horses began stirring uneasily at the approach of their new owners. With Lozen at his side, Victorio dropped to the ground and moved like a spider, taking full advantage of shrubs and rocks for cover. Only when he was within a few yards of two guards did he rise up and charge. His moccasined feet pounded on the sunbaked dirt and his knife gleamed in the bright sun.

Even so, he reached the first guard before being discovered. Victorio stood two inches taller than his victim. His strong hand threaded through the buffalo soldier's black hair and yanked his head back. A single swift jerk of his knife over the suddenly taut throat brought forth a fountain of blood. Victorio let the dying man drop and spun, kicking out to knock the rifle from the other surprised soldier's grip.

Before Victorio could recover his balance, Lozen ended the disarmed trooper's life with her own knife thrust. Then ragged fire started, signaling that Nana's warriors had been detected. Another volley echoed across the corral, spooking the horses. Then only a few sporadic shots sounded, flat and distant.

"The horses," Victorio said, breathing hard. He took the rifles from the fallen soldiers and searched them for ammunition. They had none. Lozen had already grabbed at a hackamore to put on the horse nearest her in the corral.

"Forty-eight, Brother! We have forty-eight new horses!" she cried. "Let us ride!"

"Did any soldiers escape?" he asked. Lozen shrugged. Victorio jumped onto the back of a sturdy gelding, rode to the far side of the corral, and repeated the question to Nana.

"None, but the shots will bring Morrow like flies to carrion," Nana said, working to bridle the horse he had chosen as his own booty.

"What of this Hooker?"

"He is nothing. See how poorly this new captain placed his guards?" Nana spat. Reaching out, he tossed a loop of rope around the neck of a swaybacked mare. "See how poorly he keeps his horses!"

With that, Nana led the way to the south, herding the horses that had not been roped. Victorio followed, using a short rope quirt to whack the rumps of the horses, to keep them bunched together. The raid had been successful. Eight soldiers had died quickly. More would follow.

"They track us as you said, Brother," Lozen declared, shaking her head. "Will they ever learn?"

"They think their cannon will always blow us out of the hills," Victorio said. He did not fear their mountain howitzers, though he had a healthy respect for them. The artillery gave the cavalry an advantage which was erased by the Apaches staying always on the move. Ahead of them, Sanchez and Raton laid the trap in the canyon for Lieutenant Colonel Dudley, who had taken up the hunt for the raiders.

"Dudley strings out his men. Without horses, he marches

his troopers on foot, day and night. They will be exhausted if they ever catch us."

"They will reach us, Sister. Soon," Victorio said, picturing the battle in his mind. "He is a foolish officer, unlike Morrow, and he can never defeat us no matter how he tries."

Victorio had run for almost a week after the raid outside Ojo Caliente. Some of the horses had died under the fleeing Apache, but they still had more than forty horses to show for their efforts. He rode slowly down the high-walled canyon, seeing how the two groups of Apache had arrayed themselves along the rim. Here and there a careless glint off a rifle barrel showed. Victorio signaled, and even this small trace vanished. Loopholes had been formed in the rocks along the walls at ground level and just above, but from the rim would come the worst destruction, raining down in a leaden storm on Dudley's head.

"There we will make our camp. Put the horses into a corral over there." Victorio pointed out a sand spit.

"He will know it is a trap. We would never corral horses where they have nothing to eat or drink," protested Lozen.

"From there we can herd the horses down the side canyon and be away." Victorio looked up at the canyon rim again, worrying that the sun was setting. He did not like to fight after dark. Snakes came out then.

"It is the one called Dudley, who leads his troops," Nana said, riding up. "He will be here within an hour."

"Then we can rest," Victorio said. "Get the horses into the arroyo where the bluecoat scouts can see them. And we can eat."

For all his words about relaxation, Victorio worried until the leading element of Dudley's force appeared. Then he knew the soldiers were going to be cut to bloody ribbons. Everything went exactly according to his plan.

Victorio shouted and got his small band on horseback, then had Lozen herd their captured horses down the branching canyon. He wheeled around once she got the scrawny horses moving, ready for a fight.

The first bluecoats spotted him and opened fire, their muskets banging loudly and white puffs of smoke rising in the still air. Heavy .50 caliber lead musket balls whined off into the distance, none seriously threatening Victorio or his warriors. He motioned left and right, forming a single line with his braves to make it appear there were more of them than there really were. Then he let out a throat-ripping yell that echoed down the canyon. The screech grew softer, more distant, but never any less chilling.

The buffalo soldiers recoiled at the sound, then were reinforced with others from Dudley's second company, working their way from the protection of the base of the canyon wall to the undefendable center.

Again Victorio loosed his bloodcurdling shout. Then he fired deliberately into the troopers. He was on horseback, and his skittish mount prevented accurate shooting. But he signaled his warriors high above. Sanchez and Raton passed the command along, and the Apache snipers lying in ambush opened a withering fire into the entire length of Dudley's column. Two companies of troopers panicked, were wounded and killed, routed and driven to hiding, by that accurate, well-placed fusillade.

Victorio wanted to rush forward to avenge his son, but knew he was not needed here. There would be other days for revenge. He recalled the few warriors with him, falling back, hopefully to draw even more of the soldiers to their deaths. He trotted along the narrow game trail Lozen had already traveled, slowing only when he heard the thunder of hooves ahead of him.

"Wait here," he told those with him. He and Nana galloped ahead, meeting Lozen less than a mile into the branching canyon. She was flushed, and her eyes wide.

"Cavalry," she gasped out. "They came up the canyon, and we ran directly into them. They killed two. The rest are bringing the horses."

"Who is it?" demanded Victorio. "Can we fight our way through?"

"It is Major Morrow," Lozen said, recovering her breath. "I recognized him at the head of his column. They are mounted and fresh, unlike Dudley's troopers. An entire company, Brother."

"We cannot fight them," Victorio said, realizing Morrow had cut off escape down this canyon. But he would have no problem retracing his path to the main canyon and going down it away from Dudley's doomed command until they came to a secret exit through the high wall that would lead them south. Let Major Morrow follow, eating their dust all the way to Texas. Let him drive his Ninth Cavalry into one trap after another along that death trail.

Victorio relished the challenge. And this change in his plans allowed him to see Juh again and raid into West Texas. He liked that land—horses were plentiful, and the cattle fat. Even more exciting, he anticipated killing more of the Tenth's troopers, as he had done so easily before.

Untenable Position

September 14, 1879
Fort Davis

"What else? Has anything more come in?" Lester Boynton hovered over the cowering private like a vulture waiting for dinner to die. He pawed through the stack of telegrams that had come in, all packaged neatly for inclusion with the weekly dispatches from Fort Concho.

"Sir, that all's not supposed to be seen by anyone but the colonel. I ain't so sure you oughta be—"

"This is my job, Private," Boynton said sternly. "Colonel Grierson ordered me to keep track of Victorio and his movement. I need the latest intelligence reports. Is there anything in here about his escape from New Mexico Territory?"

"Captain, I want to give this to you, but it's supposed to go straightaway to the colonel, not you." The private screwed his leathery face up in a frown that made him look like an accordion, working hard to figure it all out and failing.

"Private, allow me to carry the missives to the colonel. I will personally deliver them. That would give you a few minutes free time to do as you please."

"He never said nuthin' about me handin' it all over personally," the private said. With some reluctance, he pushed over the flimsy sheets that the messenger had brought. Some letters were still sealed, but most were single pages without envelopes, the entire pile held together with red ribbon. All those were official communiqués with the hidden tidbits Boynton wanted to ferret out.

"That's all, Private," Boynton said, taking the stack. He left the small office and was hit in the face by the noonday heat. He shielded his face with the wad of papers, then walked slowly by the post adjutant's office and stopped outside Colonel Grierson's silent door. He knew his commanding officer was not inside. Grierson worked at his desk, grumbling constantly and often profanely at the paperwork. Often, he sang to himself as he worked, able to carry a tune surprisingly well. But only when he was astride a horse and in the field did he stop the incessant complaining.

Boynton leafed through the sheets as he stepped into the cooler office. With no wind blowing, even inside and away from the sun was hardly any better than outside. Still, the harsh sun did not cook his brains directly. Boynton flipped through the stack, dropping the sealed envelopes onto Grierson's desk and scanning the rest. A slow smile crossed his lips.

With some anticipation, Boynton had been following Victorio's departure from Warm Springs after his refusal to return to San Carlos Reservation. Initial reports from Major Morrow's command at Fort Bayard hinted at incompetence on the part of Lieutenant Colonel Dudley. Victorio had ambushed that officer's entire command, costing him most of two companies. It had been a crushing defeat, saved only when Morrow rode to the rescue. Boynton's enthusiasm faded when he realized Morrow had had to rescue Dudley to keep the entire command from dying— and this rescue had allowed Victorio's escape.

But Colonel Hatch and General Pope had finally done something worthwhile, transferring Dudley to another command where he could do no more damage to his own troops. Reading between the lines, Boynton guessed Morrow was the new commander, with eighty buffalo soldiers and eighteen Indian scouts. He had never met the man, but considered Morrow a decent field officer who would dog Victorio's footsteps. Or at least this was his reading of the reports he had bullied from the private.

"What do you think Victorio is doing?" came Grierson's razor-sharp voice. Boynton jumped, like a child caught stealing candy. Guiltily, he turned to face his commander, outlined in the door, the dazzling sunlight obliterating any chance to see the colonel's expression.

"Major Morrow is after Victorio. I think the Warm Springs Apache will be moving in our direction as Morrow continues his campaign. Victorio will never stand and fight, not against mountain howitzers."

"Overrated," Grierson said gruffly, coming in and dropping his gold braid–bedecked hat onto his desk. He sank into the rickety wooden chair, grabbed the edge of the desk to steady himself, and then made sure the chair would not collapse beneath him before reaching for the sealed letters Boynton had neglected. Grierson did not immediately ask for the sheaf of papers Boynton still clutched. The captain shuffled through the sheets he had not had time to read, then reluctantly placed the pile on the edge of his commander's desk.

"Is that why you don't deploy our cannon, sir?"

"Ride fast, ride hard, fight harder. Man to man. That's the way you win a battle against the Indians. Worked for me time and again during my time out West." Grierson ripped open an official document from the pile, read it slowly, then tossed it onto the desk before going to the next letter. It twisted around as it landed so Boynton could read the neat lines from the secretary of war. His eyebrows rose, though he was not sure Grierson intended for him to see it.

Grierson had been given a field promotion to brevet major general, and placed in command of the Tenth Cavalry and all Army campaigns in West Texas.

"Should I order out patrols, up the Rio Grande and from Fort Quitman, to intercept Victorio?" asked Boynton.

"You got a bug up your ass, boy. Let me see some evidence he's coming, and then you can run our men into the ground chasing him. Till then, keep those boys honed like a knife, ready for action. Don't use too much of a whetstone on them, though. Turns 'em brittle. They'll break when you go to use 'em. What I'm saying is that there's no sense in dulling the cutting edge till necessary with endless, unnecessary patrols."

"Major Morrow is now in command of Fort Bayard," Boynton said. "Do you know him, sir?"

"Know of him. Hatch thinks well of him, and I think well of Hatch. Think well of John Pope, for all that. Think well of everyone—and never underestimate your enemy." Grierson growled deep in his throat as he read another of the letters directed to him. He crumpled this one and tossed it into the corner of the room for his orderly to clean later. Boynton had no idea as to the contents, but whatever had been inside clearly annoyed Grierson.

"Yes, sir," Boynton said, not sure where Grierson was leading.

"Never underestimate him," Grierson said, chewing on

his lower lip. "No patrols, not yet, Captain. But no one leaves the fort. Double the guards on all supply trains coming this way. Write it up, put my name on it, send it off to Fort Concho and Fort Griffin. I won't lose another month's supplies."

"No one leaves, sir? But Colonel Magee's wife was supposed to return to Kansas City this week."

"It'll be more pleasant for her to stay here another few weeks than to hit the road. Dusty out there. Dirty and . . . dangerous. Go inform her of my decision. Allow her to remain in her temporary quarters, though I am sure the junior officers, wives will find this a nuisance. That is a matter they must work out among themselves. Never meddle in the fort's social structure, Captain. Do what you can about accommodations for all of them, will you? But do it gently."

"Right away, sir," Boynton said, cold inside. He had moved from his quarters when Sarah and his boys had been murdered by Victorio's band, giving up the small cabin to Evan Larkin and his wife, although they had no children. The officers' barracks was enough for him, and the resulting shifting had allowed the most senior second lieutenant's wife to move from the corridor in the post hospital where she had slept on a doubled-over blanket. The second lieutenant's entire family still camped out at the other end of that corridor, eager to get their own housing. Grierson's arrival, and the need for quarters for his family, had sent ripples down the chain of command. Ruth Magee was not entitled to quarters any longer, although Grierson permitted it. This decision created more than a ripple, it started a tidal wave that would bounce from one side of the post to the other until the situation was resolved—by her departure.

Every time a senior officer passed by, the second lieutenant's wife glared at them as if they were personally responsible for her plight. Boynton wanted to tell her it was better here than at other frontier posts. But he did not, already knowing the advice Grierson had given him about meddling in the social organization that kept the fort functioning, if not smoothly then without too much friction.

Boynton could deal with the complaints from the junior officers. Facing Mrs. Magee was the chore he dreaded most.

He considered all the times he had faced enemies in the field and decided this might be worse. How could he possibly confess to her that he had been responsible for her husband's death? The answer was simple. He could not.

"Captain Boynton!" The voice drove a spike into his heart. Ruth Magee.

"Ma'am," he said turning from his path and angling toward the adjutant's office where she stood. "I'm afraid I have some bad news for you."

"I am aware of it, sir," she said, almost primly. Her lips were drawn into a thin line and the dark circles under her eyes made her look a dozen years older. The weight of Amos Magee's death had taken its toll on her. Still, her long brown hair was neatly tied back and her gingham dress was spotlessly clean. Boynton sucked in a deep breath, then let it out. He had been under the same strain, and shared some of her agitation. Victorio was responsible for the deaths of both their families.

If only . . .

"Colonel Grierson said the increased Indian activity makes travel too dangerous for you, at least for the moment. I am tracking Victorio's path the best I can. He bolted from San Carlos and was temporarily housed at the Warm Springs Reservation, but he went on a killing spree from there."

"I know all that," she said tiredly. A flush came to her

cheeks, giving her a more animated look. And increased beauty. She almost smiled as she looked sideways at him. Boynton couldn't help comparing her to a bud that blossomed in the spring, turning from a closed bunch of inhibited petals to a fully open beautiful flower. But she was no tender flower that grew in a soft, grassy meadow. Rather, she was a sturdy flower blooming in the desert and daring the elements to deny her.

"The post rumors continue to churn, no matter what else is happening in the world," she said. "The other ladies know my concern about Victorio and pass along all they hear."

"He's a vicious one, ma'am," Boynton said. The hot sun worked on his head and made him sweat. Or was it the sun? "When he escaped custody at Warm Springs he killed eight troopers from Fort Bayard, stole a corral full of horses, then went on a real tear. Colonel Hatch reports nine settlers killed."

"Then there was the military disaster," the woman said.

"Disaster? You mean—?" Boynton almost choked on the words. How could she know? Kingman! Or his brother. Kingman's brother, Charles, had been striker for Amos Magee.

"I do not predict much of a future for an officer who allows his men to be killed in such great numbers."

Boynton felt faint as the blood drained from his face.

"Oh, I am sorry. Is this supposed to be a military secret? The other women do gossip so. That Lieutenant Colonel Dudley is not much of an officer. How he was ever promoted to such a position of authority is beyond me. Amos used to say . . ." Ruth Magee's voice trailed off as she stared at Boynton.

"What is wrong, Captain?" She stepped from the shade and put a hand on his quivering arm. He let her pull him into the shade of the porch. Boynton did not even protest when she fetched a cup of water from inside the adjutant's office.

"You must be exhausted to have the sun affect you so," she said. She pressed her hand against his forehead. Her fingers were cool. Somehow Boynton felt as if she poked him with a branding iron, though. He pulled back.

"Haven't eaten today and turned a bit faint. That's all."

"Sit a moment. It won't hurt you none," Ruth said. She pointed to a chair beside the adjutant's door. Boynton considered the propriety of it, then sank down. Grierson had ordered him to inform her that she and her son were stranded here for another few weeks, and this was a public place. Still, if he spoke overlong to her, there would be flapping tongues. From the corner of his eye he saw two wives, their husbands both second lieutenants, watching intently, ready to launch a new rumor the instant they found someone to listen.

"Are you doing well?" he asked, not sure what else to say.

"Yes, thank you," Ruth answered. "Caleb still misses his stepfather, of course, but that is to be expected. I miss Amos, also, but perhaps not as much."

Again the difference in their ages struck Boynton, but he made no comment on it. That wasn't his place.

"Colonel Grierson fears Victorio might again raid over here since the last foray was so successful. We have scouts ranging out, but no patrols, not yet. The colonel wants to hold the men in readiness so we can react quickly when Victorio is sighted."

"Then everything I'd heard is right. I must stay here another week?"

"More than that, I fear, ma'am," Boynton said.

"I hope Victorio is caught quickly. Major Morrow is a capable officer."

"Capable, yes, but his command is not well supplied. Not like the Tenth."

"Yes, Fort Davis is lucky in that regard." Ruth sighed. She brushed away nonexistent wrinkles in her blue and gray–checked gingham dress. "I am such a burden."

"No!" Boynton sat straighter at his vehement—and unexpected—contradiction. "I mean, your presence can only enhance the social condition of the fort. You are most gracious and . . ." Boynton let his words trail off, realizing he was beginning to babble. This was unmilitary, and he hated himself for it.

"Thank you, Lester," she said softly. "I knew you were different from the others here. So many say such odious things, just loud enough for me to overhear."

"When it is safe for you and your boy to leave, I'll see to it personally."

"Thank you," she said. Her smile was brighter than before. Then she dropped her head and walked away, again dejected.

In that, Lester Boynton shared her sentiment. Then he heaved himself to his feet and marched across the hot parade ground to his barracks to study the field map and try to guess where Victorio would run next.

Victory

"We lost ten warriors," Lozen said grimly. "Morrow will not stop. He comes after us like he is glued to our heels."

"Ten dead," agreed Victorio, "but we have killed more of them. Their horses fall from under their riders. When the soldiers go to ground and walk, their boots wear out. They are not like Apache, carrying three spare sets of moccasins and a way to repair their soles." Victorio sat cross-legged on the ground, using a needle to pull the long strand of yucca cord through a piece of cowhide, cinching it tightly to the sole of his moccasins. In the past week he had spent as much time on foot as he had on horseback. The buffalo soldiers with their Indian scouts had given them no chance to rest.

"We have killed more of them and stolen many of their

horses and mules," Lozen said with wolfish satisfaction. "We can string them out throughout the territory and—"

"And nothing," Victorio said, finishing his moccasin. He slid it onto his foot and knew it would take a day or more of wear before it molded properly to his foot. Still, some of his one hundred warriors went barefoot, their moccasins holed beyond repair. "Morrow relies heavily on his scouts. Many are Apache, Coyotero," he said with some disgust. "They would kill us and consider it a good day. We cannot outrun them. We must outfight them."

"Morrow has fewer soldiers," Lozen said. "He would lose an all-out battle." She looked out into the mountains, as if hunting the proper place to set a trap. The churn of Las Animas River nearby muffled low sounds, making this an ideal spot to camp—or to be ambushed.

"You have seen the buffalo soldiers fight. They will not easily be defeated," Victorio said. He appreciated their endurance and valor. It puzzled him that there were no black officers, though he found it hard to believe he would ever find as tenacious and bold an officer as Morrow. With only three companies from Fort Bayard, he had kept on their trail with the skill of an Apache.

"I hate them," Victorio said suddenly. "The Apache scouts he uses. They turn against their own people." Victorio fumbled under his blanket and found the colonel's insignia he had taken as a trophy. The officer's jacket had lasted halfway through winter, wearing out eventually. Best of all were the weapons Victorio had earned. They had taken twenty rifles and ten pistols from the fallen patrol. The long saber carried by the colonel had been broken; Victorio had left it on the riverbank. Yes, it had been a good fight when the colonel rode the Ghost Pony.

"They have no love of the Mimbreño or Chiricahua or even Mescalero," said Lozen. "Some are Coyotero, others Tonto." She spat.

"Geronimo is partly responsible for cementing this unholy alliance," Victorio said. "If he had not raided the Tonto as he did, they would not have forged such a bond with the White Eyes."

"Indeh," said Lozen coldly. "They are dead men. We will capture them and put them to death."

Victorio had other concerns weighing him down. Supplying so many warriors was hard enough in the best of times. Doing it while fighting rearguard actions and trying to raid for more horses and ammunition as they swept across the land was even more difficult. Nana scouted ahead, along the Mogollón Rim for allies and possible sanctuary. If necessary, they could always cross the Mexican border and seek out Juh.

Juh was a staunch ally, but Victorio missed his wife and children.

If only he could move them from San Carlos!

"We cannot continue to run," he said. "We must stand and fight. Those rocks might give decent enough shelter for our warriors."

"We go to ground and shoot them as they ride past? Dudley lost most of his command that way. You do not think Morrow will repeat that mistake, do you, Brother?"

"No. And we haven't enough rise on either side of this valley for the kind of marksmanship our braves showed then. We scatter throughout the tumble of rocks, then let Morrow ride past. We fight until we kill them or begin running low on ammunition, then we ride off, down that arroyo."

"Where does it lead? We do not want to find ourselves trapped in a box," Lozen said.

"The river is fed from a stream running from that canyon. There must be a way out of it. Go see," he told his sister, "but return before dark. Even without your Power I feel Morrow approaching. He is not far." Victorio turned and lifted his chin, as if sniffing the air for his bluecoat enemy. Morrow and his buffalo soldiers would be hours away, but Victorio wondered if he might detect one of the officer's scouts. He *felt* their presence, even if he could not see them.

"Do not kill any of them without me," Lozen said. She grinned, then vaulted onto her pony and rode off. Victorio only glanced after her, his attention fixed in another direction. Would it matter if his attack was discovered by Morrow's scouts? Morrow had to engage. He had no other choice, not after the hardship he had endured for the past week and a half. Victorio went to position his best marksman in the rocks to await the cavalry's approach.

By midday, the battle had begun.

Victorio sighted along his rifle, slowly tracking the blue-uniformed rider. As he swung his rifle in a smooth arc, he squeezed off a shot. The soldier fell from the saddle, as limp as if every bone in his body had turned to mush. Frightened, the trooper's horse bolted and raced off. Victorio knew one of his warriors would capture it before it ran itself to death.

He ducked back, reloaded his magazine, then poked his head above the sheltering rock again. Morrow stretched out his soldiers in a ragged line to face the tumble of boulders where Victorio and his comrades hid. Many Apache horses had been killed, putting some of them on foot. This bothered Victorio, knowing a speedy escape might be necessary if Morrow got reinforcements from Fort Bayard. Without knowing the depth of that possible support, Victorio wanted to take no chances.

The ambush had started successfully, then ammunition began running low. Somehow, Morrow had rallied his troops and they had attacked, forcing Victorio's warriors from their original secure positions. The inexorable blue tide washing against the rocks pushed the Mimbreño back, along the route Lozen had scouted for their escape.

"Three dead," Lozen reported to him. "We have killed only two of them."

Victorio realized their position was becoming more perilous with every passing minute. Without enough horses, they could not outride their enemy. Worse, if they tried to retreat on foot, they would get bullets in their back for their effort. It was fight or die.

"We need more horses. How many does Morrow have?"

"Enough," was Lozen's answer.

Chips of rock flew like tiny birds just above her head. She hardly cringed from the flying shards. Brushing the dust off her broad, impassive face, she stayed low and moved away from Victorio. Her brother knew she would not fail to find more horses—and that Morrow's command would be completely afoot soon.

Victorio saw how the rifle fire pushed his warriors back. The buffalo soldiers seemed to have a limitless supply of ammunition. Through the afternoon and into the evening the fight raged. Victorio's braves fired less often now, taking shots only when they had a clear target. The troopers, however, fired relentlessly, preventing Victorio from escaping along his chosen route.

Long after sunset, the cavalry stopped their attack. Victorio considered creeping away, then knew he could not get far enough in the dark to make the retreat worthwhile. He slipped from position to position, seeing how his warriors had fared. A slow smile remained on his lips as he saw he had not lost any more of his valiant men.

Lozen rejoined him.

"How many horses?" he asked. Although her face was hidden in shadow, he knew she grinned.

"Two dozen," she said. "Enough to replace those we

lost. The bluecoats rest now, cooling their rifle barrels. Some were beginning to warp from rapid fire."

"Any chance of escaping now?"

She shook her head. "With the horses we have, only in the daylight will it be possible to get away. We must reduce their rank," she said jerking her thumb in the direction of Morrow's troops. "Kill more of their horses, and they must get new mounts. Kill a few more of their fighters, and Morrow will need reinforcements."

"Tell Nana to put the best marksman close to the bluecoats' camp. At dawn, pick off as many sentries as possible. Create a diversion so their horses are once more ours for the taking. *Then* we will leave."

"Enjuh!" With this she vanished into the shadows to pass along Victorio's orders. The weary chief settled down, pulled his blanket closer around his shoulders, and in minutes fell asleep, his dreams of victory and many horses.

Victorio lay alongside Blue Pony, a Mescalero from the southern Sacramento Mountain region. The young brave balanced his rifle against a stack of stones as he picked out his target in the Ninth Cavalry's camp. Victorio chose a different sentry, one higher in the rocks. The buffalo soldiers stirred in their camp, preparing a cold breakfast. The sounds were deliberate, purposeful, and told Victorio that the skirmish would begin when their quartermaster passed out new boxes of ammunition.

Victorio would see to it the soldiers had no chance to begin sending out a constant hail of bullets, as they had the day before.

Blue Pony fired. The sentry stiffened, then dropped to one knee. The buffalo soldier clutched his side and started to call out. Blue Pony's second shot took off the man's head. And with that shot, the soldier disappeared. Victorio was not sure if Blue Pony had killed the sentry or merely wounded him. It did not matter. Sporadic shots from all around Morrow's camp told of Victorio's sharpshooters. He squeezed off a shot of his own, missing his target. For several minutes the sniping took its toll on the cavalry camp, then it stopped when Morrow and his officers regained control and began putting up an unrelenting return fire.

Victorio signaled, and his warriors moved away. Lozen had been successful a second time in stealing cavalry horses. All but a handful of Victorio's band mounted and rode away, singly and in twos and threes, to prevent the thunder of hooves from alerting Morrow to their retreat.

"He will follow,'" Lozen said. "Major Morrow is not the kind to give up easily."

"Let him try to stop us," Victorio said. "We head toward the Mogollón Rim."

"They know we will try to free those at San Carlos," Lozen pointed out. "Better to go south and circle."

"The Mogollóns," Victorio insisted.

For six days Major Morrow struggled after the swiftly riding Apache, then was forced to give up the chase when most of his cavalry troopers ended up as foot soldiers through the attrition of his mounts and the lack of supplies.

On Patrol

"He did it, he did it!" chortled Boynton as he slammed the dispatch down on the desk so hard it made the private jump. "Morrow ran him out of New Mexico Territory and down south into Mexico!"

"Sir, I don't know that much, but all this said was how Morrow engaged Victorio and pursued him west."

"Where else could Victorio head after Morrow gave chase?" demanded Boynton. His mind raced. Victorio would be blocked from going west by Morrow's vigorous campaign. The Apache might turn north, but if he did he chanced meeting enemy Pima or Navajo. East brought Victorio back into the jaws of the rest of the Ninth Cavalry from Fort Cummings and Fort Craig. Everything Colonel Hatch relayed showed that Morrow held sway in the field. That meant Victorio's only escape lay to the south. And if the renegade Apache went into Mexico, he would eventually cross the Rio Grande to raid again in West Texas, in the Tenth Cavalry's bailiwick. There simply was not enough booty for the Mimbreño to survive on across the river.

Boynton would again have a chance to engage and destroy Victorio and his entire Warm Springs band. This time he would not fail. This time he had a real commander backing him. Benjamin Grierson was a dedicated, war-trained soldier, not a fool like Amos Magee.

As this thought flashed across his mind, Boynton felt a pang of guilt. Magee might have been a nincompoop to try to rescue his troops the way he did, but he had left a widow and orphaned a son. Boynton looked out the small window of the dispatcher's office and saw a half dozen children playing baseball. The spindly one, the one with a shock of unruly brown hair that rose like a cock's comb in front, was Magee's stepson, Caleb.

A lump formed in Boynton's throat. His own children ought to be there playing.

"You want to send a reply or ask for more information like you usually do, Captain?"

"No, Private, not this time. I have all I need." Boynton clutched the flimsy yellow sheet of foolscap and rushed out, trying to ignore the children's cries as one of them— Lieutenant Kincaid's boy—hit a cowhide ball just beyond the reach of young Caleb Magee. The others jeered as Caleb struggled after it, dodging through a patch of spiny Spanish bayonet. His own boys could have given Caleb a pointer or two about fielding and throwing.

If they had not been killed.

Boynton's stride lengthened, and he ducked into Grierson's office. The post commander sat at his rickety chair, mumbling to himself. He looked up, relief on his face at the diversion Boynton presented to the mountain of paperwork that always avalanched onto his desk when the

weekly supplies arrived with all the dispatches from Fort
Concho.

"What put the burr under your blanket, Captain?"
Grierson's eyes gleamed at the prospect of something more
interesting than dealing with inventory reports.

"Morrow routed Victorio," Boynton said without preamble. "He is circling and coming in our direction. He must
be! Sir, I request a company to patrol along the Rio Grande
and intercept him when he comes into the U.S. from
Mexico."

Grierson took the dispatch and scanned it quickly. He
dropped it onto a small clear spot on his desk, leaned back,
and tented his fingers under his chin. Boynton started to
speak, then bit back the words. He had to let Grierson
come to his own conclusion, no matter how much he
longed to *do* something. Sitting in the post, watching the
children play baseball and the men drill, was tearing away
at him.

As Grierson thought, Boynton heard the click of heels
on the walk outside. He cast a sidelong glance at Ruth
Magee and immediately pulled his eyes back to his commander. Too many confusing emotions rolled through
him when he saw her. She was such a pleasant person and
endured her loss well, befitting a colonel's wife. Being
stranded at Fort Davis put an additional strain on her.
There had been talk of moving her into town, away from
the post until she could safely return to her family in Kansas
City. Boynton had spoken persuasively against tossing Ruth
and her son out of her quarters, and could not figure out
his real intentions.

Guilt? Yes. He had been the reason her husband had
risked life and command. More? He wasn't sure.

". . . right away, Captain," Grierson was saying. Boynton
blinked as he tried to pick up the sense of what the colonel
said.

"Does this surprise you, Boynton?"

"Why, uh, yes, sir, it does. Could you be more, uh, precise?" Boynton struggled to recover his poise. He felt pulled in too many ways and knew he had to concentrate on only one thing: Victorio.

Victorio and revenge.

"Two squads only, get them out on a weeklong patrol. Use it as a training mission. Get your men into fighting trim. Victorio might come this way, but if he does not, I don't want my troops needlessly consuming supplies. I have trouble enough getting a reasonable allotment for a fort populated with . . . Negroes." Grierson snorted. "If they had a dozen regiments half as good as our boys, the U.S. Army would have no Indian problem anywhere in the West."

"Yes, sir, a patrol along the Rio Grande!"

Boynton saluted, did a smart about-face, then left quickly, politely touching the bill of his garrison cap as he passed Ruth Magee. She gave him a slight, enigmatic smile that bothered him—until he got to the barracks and gave Sergeant Kingman orders for two squads to leave at dawn the next day. Then he had something more than his own insecurities to deal with. He was going after Victorio!

"We oughta be headin' back, Captain," said George Kingman. The burly sergeant kicked at a rock, sending it skittering over the edge of the cliff and down a slope to the Rio Grande. The rock failed to get into the water by several feet. Somehow, Boynton felt like that rock. So near its target, yet missing by inches.

"Victorio is out there. I feel it, Sergeant."

"Sir, he might be out there, but finding him is gonna be too hard for us. We've got men to defend a wagon train. We've got enough to even give pursuit if we happen on him, but that's not gonna happen 'less *he* wants it.''

"What are you saying? That you are incompetent to find a savage?" Boynton's words came out harsh and biting, and he did not care. They had spent a week in the field, and he was tired. Worse than that, he was frustrated at the lack of action. His two squads had patrolled and drilled and engaged in mock attacks. And that was all. They had passed near the edge of Fort Quitman's patrol duty, then gone south along the Rio Grande.

Not once had they seen another living soul, American, Mexican, or Indian. The only thing Boynton had seen large enough to shoot was a stray cow on the Mexican side of the river.

"He's a wily one, Captain, that's all I was sayin'," Kingman said.

"You were saying I am incompetent to lead, weren't you, Sergeant?" Boynton's face flushed, and his anger mounted. "Get your men back into the saddle. We will ride all night and see if that doesn't get us to his camp."

"All right, sir," said Kingman, his usual drawl erased by the sharpness in his reply. "Which way? Which way you wantin' us to ride to find Injuns that aren't even out there?"

"You are insubordinate, Sergeant! I will not have this!"

Boynton struggled to keep his rage in check. He stepped past Kingman and looked at the men stretched out on the rocks, resting.

"To your feet!" he ordered. They jumped to, their carbines coming to rest butt-down on the ground, their backs straight and eyes ahead, at attention. "You men are lazy, shiftless, and are shirking your duty. We were sent to track down a renegade. You have failed to find him in the week we have been in the field."

"Sir," cut in Kingman.

"Silence, Sergeant." Kingman stepped back and took his place in the ragged line of buffalo soldiers standing at attention while Boynton dressed them down. The captain paced back and forth, eyeing them and seething at how they had failed.

Morrow had run Victorio to ground. The Mimbreño chief must have gone south and east through Mexico. By now he must have crossed the Rio Grande, yet they had found no trace of him in a week of patrol. That meant the soldiers were slacking off. If they returned empty-handed now, some other company might be sent out. Boynton could not bear to think of that popinjay Evan Larkin leaving Fort Davis on a scout and running into Victorio's main body. Boynton was not certain, but he thought the other captain spent far too much time in the supply warehouse with the two sergeants responsible for rations and ammunition. Rumors hinted at Larkin diverting the supplies for his own end, but Boynton could not believe that.

Everyone at Fort Davis knew the importance of stopping Victorio. Stealing government supplies was treasonous, and gave aid and comfort to the enemy. What galled Boynton most was the that braggart would have the pleasure, the honor, of stopping the renegade Apache if he was sent out now after this abject failure.

"You will fan out, get out of the strict column formation, and look to the ground for any sign of Mimbreño passage through this terrain," Boynton said.

"Sir, I must protest. Spreading out the men like this makes 'em targets. They can get picked off one by one. Sir."

"Sergeant Kingman, I am in command. Now, spread out and not a peep out of any of you unless you find enemy spoor!"

"Sir, I hope your anger isn't gettin' the better of you."

The final word *again* hung unspoken in the air between them.

For the rest of the day, the only sounds reaching Lester Boynton were the occasional click of shod hoof against stone, the soft hot wind whistling in his ears, and the distant gurgle of the Rio Grande.

And at the campfire that night, there was none of the usual geniality of his men. They ate, eyes down, words swallowed with the canned rations. Even on the return to Fort Davis, no one spoke unless he directed a question or an order.

Lester Boynton found this to be just fine as he stewed in his own juices, angry that he had failed to find Victorio. But next time would be different. He would see to that, even if he had to push his troopers harder and demand even more from them. Next time!

Escape

October 22, 1879
Mogollón Mountains

"More horses?" asked Victorio, seeing the herd Nana and his small band moved along the mountain path. He counted quickly and stopped when he got to forty.

"The soldiers are careless and never learn," Nana said, laughing. "I walked into their corral and chose the ones I wanted. No one noticed. Of course, I had killed two guards!"

Victorio joined Nana laughing at the ease with which they stole supplies from the cavalry. Morrow was a good commander, putting his troopers into the proper positions for battle. Every commander under him seemed to be as inept as he was expert.

"I prayed to Ussen for an hour," Nana said, "and my head hurt. Every direction I turned I felt ammunition." He held out his hands. The leathery palms were rosy. "Like your sister, my flesh burns when I use my Power. It gets stronger—or there is just more to steal!''

Victorio had to agree. They had fought Morrow several times, each battle pitched. Over the last week, Victorio had lost only two warriors, and Morrow had seen five of his buffalo soldiers die. But Victorio did not have to live off the land. Instead, he lived off the supplies sent to support Major Morrow.

And horses? Victorio had lost count of the number they had stolen. His warriors rode their horses until they collapsed under them, then they shot and ate them. They had ammunition enough for this simple act of mercy. He remembered times when it had been necessary to slit the animals' throats, no one having a bullet to spare. But now? They stole whatever they needed from the cavalry and then rode off, leaving behind only wounded and dying bluecoats.

"We can be over the mountains and down to the Gila River in another few days," Victorio said. "If only Morrow would retreat. What does it take to run him off? We take his food and weapons and horses. We kill his black soldiers. And still he comes after us."

"Their boots have holes in the soles," Nana said. "They walk more than they ride now, because of our raiding. But you are right. They are like us. They never give up."

"A week," Victorio said. "A week is all we need to find our families and get into Mexico, where we can live with Juh until the spring, when we can return to Warm Springs."

Nana said nothing, but the expression on his face told Victorio this was a spirit dream and nothing more. In spite of what Nana thought, Victorio would never stop until they were once again settled on their ancestral lands around Ojo Caliente. They were Mimbreño Apache of the Warm Springs clan, and he would not give up his people's heritage easily.

Even Colonel Hatch had said they ought to be settled there instead of San Carlos. The promise had been made, no matter what the Great Nantan in Washington said.

"We can ambush them again," Nana said. "Perhaps this time we can eliminate all of them." The old man's bloodthirsty cackling pleased Victorio. Nothing would stop them in their quest to get their families free of San Carlos and into Mexico. Along the way they would kill many enemies.

"Morrow commands them too well," Victorio said, suddenly despondent as other facts tormented him. How long they had fought and still had not triumphed! "If we kill enough of them, they will have to retreat. There cannot be an endless supply of the buffalo soldiers."

"I do not understand what their war was about," Nana said, "but it might have given them as many black soldiers are there are grains of sand in the Sonora Desert."

"They do not feed them well," said Victorio. "Even before we take their food, they do not get fed well. The horses we steal are broke down. Only their ammunition is plentiful. That and the black fingers curled around their carbine triggers."

A new wave of dejection washed over his head. The white officers threw their black soldiers into battle with abandon. Did they care if any of them died—or all? It did not seem so. How could anyone fight that, especially when the buffalo soldiers fought so well?

"Your sister will return from scouting soon," Nana said. "You brood too much. This will be a good fight. We will win again, as we have won before."

"Not all the fights have given us a clear victory," said Victorio, remembering the clash at Las Animas River. Morrow had most of his horses and mules stolen, but he fought long into the night, until his soldiers' rifle barrels glowed dull red in the darkness. Only when those barrels had turned soft did he halt the fight. Such determination!

"We need only live to fight on other ground, in ways they do not understand."

"They understand," said Victorio. "It's just that they choose to take their losses so they can continue with their battle plans. Morrow is a good field commander, but what does General Pope tell him from Fort Union? What can he know of us that Morrow does not?" He vaguely understood that the officers like Morrow chasing about from their forts had been ordered to do so by superior officers. Victorio barely understood the idea of a nantan greater than himself. He was nantan of the Warm Springs Apache, as well as war chief. Nana and Loco and the others who served so nobly were chiefs of their own clans, but they were not war chiefs. But at any time, if his warriors lost confidence, Victorio knew he would no longer ride as war chief.

Were the Indah the same? He wondered how it could be when there were no black officers. It seemed as if only the Great Nantan in Washington could remove the incompetent officers, rather than letting the men he commanded choose their own leader.

"They take too long for the Great Nantan to tell them what he wants," Nana said. "We will stop them!"

"Then let's prepare," Victorio said. He laid out his two rifles, both recently stolen, with a half dozen boxes of ammunition. With great deliberation he loaded the weapons, wiped his fingers clean of the grease used on the cartridges, then sat and stared into the distance, eyes seeing not the pine trees and steep slopes of the Mogollóns but the fight that would come and turn the serenity into a bloody hell.

He did not feel good about this fight. The Apache had won repeated victories because they chose their battles carefully, but this one? He prayed to Ussen for guidance and did not receive it before Morrow's troopers came over the crest of the hill behind the Mimbreño camp. Victorio heaved a sigh, got to his feet, and let out an undulating war cry that rallied his fighters. He heard their response, not with other cries, but with the whinnying of horses suddenly carrying riders, the snap of rifles cocking, the silence where once there was a soft susurration of prayers to Ussen and quiet conversation.

There had not been time for a proper war ceremony. All his warriors would have to rely on their own enemies-against Power.

"What do we do?" Nana asked, anxious to get to battle. Victorio knew, if they failed this day, it would not be from lack of courage.

"Attack. Straight down their throats. We split them into tiny groups, circle, then kill anyone in the smaller groups."

Nana nodded briskly, wheeled his horse, and raced off, the wind tugging at his long hair, now mostly white, like one of the cavalry's fluttering battle pennants. Victorio looked around, saw that the line of bluecoats had finished crossing the ridge, outlined against the sky for a brief moment, and knew Morrow had no reinforcements. If he did, they laid in wait just over the hill. It would take precious minutes for the word to get to any such reserves to counter an all-out attack.

"Aieee!" Victorio's throat strained with the intensity of his battle cry as he galloped forward. Time and again, Morrow had found his men attacked from ambush. He had no reason to believe Victorio would change successful tactics.

Which was why Victorio did.

Panting harshly, lips pulled back in a thin line, Victorio lifted his rifle and fired. The shot went wild but startled the black trooper with the nearness. The man fumbled to get his own musket raised, eyes wide with fear. He died as Victorio rode past, this time firing point-blank into his enemy's chest. Then Victorio blazed past and plunged into the middle of Major Morrow's lead column.

To his right, Victorio saw old Nana lose his rifle as a buffalo soldier reached up and clutched fiercely at the hot barrel. Nana refused to be unseated. He released his rifle, kicked with a moccasined foot, and drew a pistol taken a week earlier from an officer. Three shots removed the threat.

And then he was off to find new enemies to vanquish.

Victorio let out another ululating cry, wheeled his attacking warriors to the left, and charged straight up the hill. If Morrow had hidden reserves, they would find themselves instantly plunged into the fray. When Victorio got to the top of the hill, he saw Morrow was alone. He had foolishly blundered along, never once thinking a savage could change tactics.

Downslope, Victorio saw blood being let. Most of it was from cavalry troopers. One or two warriors fell, wounded, but were quickly rescued by others in their clan. By ones and twos the warriors made their way through the main body of Morrow's buffalo soldiers and formed a line beside their chief.

"Back!" cried Blue Pony, ever anxious to spill White Eyes blood. "We can kill them all!"

Victorio saw this was not to be. Morrow was a capable officer. He rallied his stunned soldiers and formed effective defensive positions. An attack downhill would be easier than coming uphill, but the element of surprise was gone. Victorio had lost a few warriors, very few compared with the losses the cavalry sustained.

"How many horses?" Victorio asked.

Lozen trotted up, the grin giving Victorio his answer.

Her hands were sticky with blood, none of it hers. "We got six horses!"

"Do they have any left?" Victorio saw the cavalry now relied on boot soles for their transportation. Morrow was no longer a factor.

Or was he?

"They saved most of their supplies," reported Nana. "I could not shoot their pack mules fast enough!"

"They are afoot," Victorio said. "To attack them again means too many of us will die." His mind raced. There was so much to do. But if he tried to go directly to San Carlos Reservation for his family, he would draw fresh troops from Fort Apache and Fort Wingate. Better to let Loco try to spirit them out so they could be reunited later. Victorio had led the buffalo soldiers on a wild ride and had put them afoot.

That would do for the time being.

"No more horses, nothing to gain by killing them," he said to Nana and Lozen.

"But we can kill them all!" protested Blue Pony.

"At what cost? They will not follow." Victorio raised his rifle high, fired three times and got the attention of the warriors along the ridge line. He motioned for them to turn south. It was time to let Loco do what he could. And it was time for the Mimbreño to vanish. For a while.

Blue Pony and a few of the younger braves railed against his decision, but Victorio's commanding presence was such that they sullenly joined the line of warriors heading south into Mexico for a well-deserved rest.

Social

October 22, 1879
Fort Davis

"Cheer up, Les," Evan Larkin said in his irritatingly lighthearted way. "You spent a week camping under the stars. A grand adventure. Away from dreary garrison duty and being under Grierson's thumb all the time. So what if you never found Victorio? He's a ghost, I tell you truly. Reach out and he fades into the darkness. Be glad you *didn't* find him. Look at all the trouble he's caused already." Larkin turned back to making careful notations in his small diary, a stack of crumpled greenbacks on the barracks table in front of him.

"Victorio killed my family," Boynton said angrily. He hated Larkin for his lack of concern. All he ever did was copy his long lines of numbers into that diary and count money. Larkin was the quartermaster, but always seemed occupied with more than his duties. Just once Boynton

wished he could get the young officer into the field and
show him how serious their duty at Fort Davis was.

"And he killed Colonel Magee," Larkin said. "That
looks to be a mixed blessing." He turned somber for a
moment, or as doleful as he ever did. "Colonel Grierson
runs a tighter mess than Magee ever did, but then Colonel
Magee didn't get much of a chance to do anything, now
did he?"

Boynton held down his anger. He wanted to strike out,
but hitting another officer meant court-martial. Grierson
had set precise limits when it came to conduct for his
officers. He tolerated not one whit of variance.

If only his patrol had found Victorio—or even Victorio's
trail. Boynton would have felt better.

How was he to know that Morrow had not routed the
wary, devious savage? The report had hinted that the Ninth
had run the Mimbreño from the territory. Later reports
proved this to be far too boastful—or optimistic. Boynton
haunted the private in charge of receiving the dispatches
until the man thought he had an extra shadow, always
reaching around to snatch away the flimsy sheets sent from
Fort Concho.

"Victorio's in Mexico by now. Count on it."

"Why would he be?" demanded Boynton. "Morrow
hasn't enough horses to pursue."

"He's got Coyotero Apache scouts. They have no love for
Victorio. They'll chase him out of New Mexico Territory."

"If Victorio goes into Mexico, there's no way to know
if he will turn east and into our patrol region," complained
Boynton. He wanted Victorio. He wanted Victorio's *blood*
on his hands.

"Patience, my good man, patience. That's what it takes.
Your problem is letting your emotions run away from your
common sense." Larkin closed his diary and stuffed the
wad of bills into the front of his uniform jacket. He frowned

for a moment, then added, "Don't go telling the others about my money, will you?"

"Your money?" Boynton was confused.

"You always seem to be around while I'm doing my, uh, accounts," Larkin said, a trifle uneasy. "You ever need a few extra dollars, let me know. Or maybe I can do something to help out Mrs. Magee."

"What do you mean by that?" Boynton said, irritated at the turn in conversation. Larkin had no call to even mention Ruth Magee. And when it came to money, Larkin was far more serious than when it came to their duty to protect the settlers in West Texas from the threat of Indian attack.

From Victorio.

"Are you going to the social tonight?"

"The colonel requested all officers to be present," Boynton said. "I have no reason to go, but since it was as close to an order as he can give, I'll go."

"You'll go, determined not to have any fun." Larkin smiled his exasperating grin. "Force yourself to get into the swing of things, Les. The colonel is quite the musician, after all. It's been a while since your wife was, uh, since she died. Mourning period is past."

"I promised to honor her 'till death do us part,' " Boynton said.

"Of course you did, but she *is* dead."

"She is," Boynton said, "but I'm not."

Larkin shrugged. "See you at the hoedown. Try not to be too much of a wet blanket. Your gloomy mood casts a shadow a mile long." With that, the younger captain stepped outside, pulled his cap down to shade his eyes just a mite, and headed across the parade ground to the supply warehouses. As Larkin went he whistled "Lorena" and seemed not to have a care in the world.

Boynton went to the table and spread out his campaign map, tracing Morrow's route and all the reported sightings of the Warm Springs Apache. The Ninth had been ill-equipped to pursue such a fast-moving force, Boynton saw. They were luckier in the Tenth. Grierson kept them supplied well when other posts struggled for even basic equipment.

Boynton heaved a sigh. Even this long after the war, having black soldiers caused unwanted ripples back in Washington. He leaned forward, elbows on the table, staring at the map and not seeing it. He remembered his upbringing in Indiana, the autumn at Turkey Run when he had spent the entire day with a black boy, the son of a slave who had taken the Underground Railroad north from Alabama. They had never been friends, he and Jacob, but that had been as much a matter of difference in age as anything. Boynton had been twelve and Jacob only eight.

Boynton hoped that was the reason he had never befriended Jacob more than the few excursions to the mill where cornmeal was ground. They had floated leaves down the river, watching their green boats fall over the wheel and be carried away in the frantic, frothy millrace. Even then he had been drawn to far-off places, wondering where the stream went, leaving Jacob far behind.

Jacob had told him of life in the South and it had startled him, it was so different from how he and his family lived. But even if he had not become a real friend to Jacob, his notions about the world and the tight agricultural community of central Indiana had changed. Boynton had vowed then to see more of the world. The Army had been that ticket away from bad crops and insects and dawn-till-dusk backbreaking labor in the cornfields.

The Army. West Point. Sarah, lovely Sarah and her shy looks at the handsome cadet in his dress uniform and the social where he had asked her to dance, outwardly bold and commanding as a cadet officer had to be, but trembling inside like a small child. It had surprised him when she had so eagerly agreed not only to that dance but every one after. Boynton had to smile, remembering the shocked expression on her aunt's face. A chaperon ought to have been more in control, but Sarah Laurel Smith had her own ideas.

Those had meshed so well with Boynton's, it seemed a fever dream now. A chance meeting, since she was only visiting from Boston. But he had courted her, and they had been married when he graduated, much to her aunt's chagrin, and her mother's. Boynton had never gotten along with the other women in Sarah's family, but her father had a touch of the wildness and wanderlust in him, the knowledge that a man had to seek adventure to be fulfilled—although he never had. A staid banker rather than an explorer, Marchant Smith had traveled widely through the scouting reports of John Frémont, his account of the bee, and finding the tallest peak on the continent. Smith had contented himself with vicarious thrills in his son-in-law's assignments, relayed by Sarah in glowing terms, even when the adventures had been more tedious than daring.

If only Sarah had married a banker and remained in Boston. He would have lost the best woman any man could want, but she would not have died at the point of a savage's knife. Her children would have grown up, prosperous and respected, and safe. Boynton swallowed hard and stared at the map where he plotted his vengeance. Somehow, he could not focus his eyes through the tears.

The band kicked up a lively tune and officers offered their arms to the ladies and were soon dancing under the stars. The faint warmth of day had faded quickly and left a chill known only in the desert, yet no one took notice. They were having too much fun.

Boynton stood and watched the gaiety, emptiness swallowing him. How Sarah had loved to dance.

"Amos never appreciated a good dance," came a soft voice from behind. Boynton spun, startled from his self-pity. Ruth Magee came up, her son beside her.

"Ma, can I go find the other kids? Andy said we could, well, we could be, uh, together and—" Caleb looked guilty at the anticipated devilment he would get into, rather than being contrite for something he had already done. How Boynton wished Peter and Thomas were here to get into trouble.

"Go on, but behave yourself," Ruth said.

"Thanks!" Caleb ran off, his gangly, loose-jointed frame almost like a small stick man scratched carelessly in the dust by an inattentive artist. In a flash Caleb vanished behind the hospital to join the other boys in whatever mischief they had already plotted.

"How are you going to punish him?" Boynton asked.

"For what? Oh," Ruth said, smiling when she understood what he meant, as only a parent could. "You mean when he *does* get into trouble? I haven't any idea. It will depend on how serious it is."

"Firecrackers left over from the Fourth of July have been appearing all around the post," Boynton said. He suspected Evan Larkin had a secret cache and doled them out to the boys—for a price. For all that, he suspected Larkin illegally sold other things, mostly from company stores. That explained both his eternal record-keeping in a private diary and the stacks of greenbacks he counted endlessly.

"That might put a damper on the festivities," Ruth said, moving closer. She stood only a foot from him, yet he could feel the heat from her body. The night was cold.

They fell silent, listening to the post band playing and watching the dance in progress. Boynton fought the urge to turn and walk away. The music brought back too many painful memories.

"Did your wife like to dance?" asked Ruth.

"What? Oh, yes, Sarah did. She was quite light on her feet. I am afraid I blundered about, but she never complained." Boynton smiled wryly. "In fact, she never seemed to notice. It was a sprite dancing with a plow horse."

"You exaggerate, sir. I've watched you. You move lightly and would no doubt dance divinely."

This startled him. He turned and saw she was not mocking him.

"As I said, Amos never enjoyed a dance. Certainly never as much as I." She looked at the dancers, now twirling about in a waltz. "I remember when I first met Amos. He was a major then. My father was a supplier for the post Amos commanded in Missouri. I am not quite sure what it was that struck me most about Amos."

"You loved him," Boynton said, wondering at how this could be. He and Sarah had been a match made in heaven. However had an old man like Amos Magee attracted a younger woman like Ruth?

"I did," she said. "But there was so much I found disagreeable about him also. My first husband—Caleb's father—was so different. A second lieutenant with so much energy! But cholera is no respecter of youth or goodness."

Ruth sighed and moved a little closer to Boynton. Their arms brushed. "Perhaps I was tired of living with my family and again wanted to be on my own. It is difficult finding a man who will accept a boy into his life the way Amos did."

Boynton had nothing to say to this. The waltz ended and a Virginia reel began. He had to fight to keep his feet from moving with the beat, even though he had not lied when he said he moved poorly at dance.

"You must find it difficult remaining at the fort because of the constant Indian raids," he said.

"Two months back I ought to have gone," she said, sighing. He watched the rise and fall of her firm breasts under her dress. The firelight from the large bonfire cast shadows on her face, turning her into an exotic creature. Not beautiful, not in the way Sarah had been, but alluring. Ruth had bigger bones and was sturdier, but she seemed as determined as Sarah ever had been.

"You miss your family. In Kansas City, is it?"

"My mother lives there, with two of my aunts. My father died soon after I married."

"I am sorry."

"Death seems so much a part of the world, more than life itself, at times." She sighed again. "I thank my lucky stars every day for Caleb. While my people are in Kansas City, I feel distant from them in ways more than miles. Caleb is my family."

"You are lucky to have your son," Boynton said, a knot in his throat.

Another brisk tune started.

"Sir, we can stand here and chill our bones or we can go join the dance. For my part, I would prefer to be moving and warm than standing and freezing."

Her forwardness took Boynton by surprise again. If he danced with her, tongues would wag. Already the gossip was that Ruth Magee sought ways to keep from leaving the post. Boynton doubted that, knowing full well that the reports on Indian activity precluded departure. Although it had not been Victorio or his band of Warm Springs Apache, every wagon train into Fort Davis over the past three months had been attacked. Some evidence showed Juh had ventured over from his Blue Mountain citadel in Mexico. Other evidence hinted at Geronimo, though this could never be confirmed.

Not a single supply train had arrived without at least one casualty. For a woman and her son to venture back to Fort Concho was out of the question unless Grierson wanted to send along a column in support. Boynton knew why the colonel did not want to commit that many soldiers now.

Victorio might be back. If the Mimbreño chief did come into Texas again, every trooper at Fort Davis would be needed to prevent new depredations against settler and soldier alike.

"I would be honored if you would allow me this dance," Boynton heard himself saying.

The next thing he knew, he was swirling around, Ruth Magee in the circle of his arms. Even more amazingly, he was oblivious to the buzz of gossip all around them as they danced out the rest of the night.

Apache Scouts

November 2, 1879
Pelonsilla Mountains

"He has to be Apache," Vlctorio said, more in disgust than in praise. Lozen and Nana crouched nearby, warming their hands at the small campfire. It was an hour past sundown and the frigid wind whipped through the canyons, hinting at snow on the higher peaks before daybreak. For all that, it had been a warm winter so far and one that favored them and their raiding. "How else can Morrow stay in the field and come after us as he does? He has no more horses. His buffalo soldiers carry everything on their backs like beasts of burden. And they do not stop. They come on and on and on!"

"I counted eighty-one soldiers," Lozen said. "They have only two mules. I could kill them, but what is the point?" She thrust out a green stick where a piece of rabbit had been impaled. Thrusting it into the fire where it crackled and popped as fat dripped off, Lozen watched it cook. When it was done, she handed it to her brother and started another hunk taken from the rabbit she had clubbed just before it had ducked back into its warren an hour earlier.

"None," Victorio said, thinking hard. Major Morrow had been defeated soundly ten days earlier. His command had been reduced in number, his horses and mules killed or stolen, and still he followed. He was a nit refusing to stop biting the dog on whose back he clung with mindless ferocity.

"We can outrun them," said Nana. "We head for Mexico. We will cross the border before his men can march on us, if that pleases us, but we have enough horses for our men and the White Eyes major has none. Why not attack? We can remove them as a threat for all time!"

"We have more horses now than when we last fought Morrow," mused Victorio. Over 150 warriors rallied behind him now, with more joining his band every day as they poured like floodwater from the reservations and followed his trail of dead and injured cavalry soldiers. All the Apache rode horses and many had a string of two or three trotting behind them. Never had Victorio led such a well-equipped band. Nana found them ammunition, and Lozen failed to find many soldiers to fight. All he needed to do was keep going and Morrow would fight only the night breeze, dueling with ghosts.

"What of the scouts with him?" Nana asked. "Gatewood commands eighteen traitors. They should be punished for fighting Mimbreño. They were never good for anything but target practice before the Indah came. They are worth no more now."

"All of them are Coyotero," Lozen said. "But Morrow's chief of scouts is better than any of those Coyotero. I have watched him follow a game trail. He is good, very good."

"Those Apache can keep up with us, no matter how fast

we travel. They are, after all, Apache, no matter what we think of their allegiance to the Indah. We need to stop them. Or we can ignore them and let them nibble at us as we go."

"Brother, we will be in the Candelaria Mountains soon. They will not pursue. Their bluecoat masters will tug on their leashes and pull them back." Lozen stood and turned slowly, staring into the crisp darkness enveloping their camp. Victorio wondered if she intended to search for enemy troops now or if she merely scented the evening air in an attempt to find bad omens. He had heard a mournful coyote earlier, and an owl hooting gave him bad feelings. Again.

Victorio closed his eyes and tried to force away the feelings of impending doom that threatened to overwhelm him. He had chosen the proper path every time. Morrow was no longer a factor, even if Lieutenant Charles Gatewood and his scouts might still chevy them. Time and again, fight after fight, the Warm Springs Apache had defeated the bluecoats, and still he experienced a chill that ran up and down his spine as he considered their future away from the hated reservations. A definite warning. Of what? He had no enemies-against Power, not like Lozen or Nana.

Why, then, did he win and win and win and still feel as if disaster loomed?

"Gatewood will not push his scouts to travel at night," said Victorio. "He could never do that. However, the buffalo soldiers will."

"No, no, you misjudge them. Morrow will order them back to Fort Bayard where he can rest them, outfit them, find new horses," insisted Nana.

Victorio valued the old man's opinion, but this time Nana was wrong. They discovered this a half hour after dawn, when Lieutenant Gatewood and his scouts attacked.

* * *

"We outnumber then ten to one," insisted Nana. "Why not fight them? Attack, as you attacked Morrow. They will disappear and show their cowardly ways."

"We would lose many warriors," Victorio said. Gatewood's Coyotero Apache had positioned themselves so they controlled the escape routes through the mountain pass leading to the south and safety. If Victorio ordered his warriors to retreat, many would be killed. But if he ordered an attack, many of his braves would die. He might kill all the scouts, but they might take two or three Mimbreño with them. Victorio did not wish to see that many of his warriors ride the Ghost Pony.

What was he to do?

If they stayed in their camp and did nothing, they might outwait Gatewood. From the way he had positioned his scouts, they had no way of attacking those Mimbreño who simply sat and did nothing, fat with their booty. Gatewood needed food and supplies. That told Victorio that Gatewood wanted to play a waiting game because Morrow was moving his buffalo soldiers in a forced march toward them. From his superior position, Gatewood might chance a battle, even when his commander was outnumbered two to one and his exhausted, on-foot soldiers fought mounted, rested Apache.

"We are trapped," Victorio declared. "The hand squeezes down around us without touching us—unless we move."

"Then attack!" urged Nana.

"Retreat," Lozen said. "My brother, all we need do is slip past a dozen of the Coyotero snipers."

"We can send our men up after them," Nana went on. "We can kill one or two at a time. There is no need for a frontal attack such as you launched on Morrow. Stealth will be our ally."

Victorio saw merit in both courses of action—and action was dictated. Remaining safe for the moment spelled death in a day or two when Morrow and his troopers arrived. And he had no doubt they would. He had seen a rabid wolf clamp its jaws on a bear and refuse to release, although it meant certain death. The bear always killed the wolf, but the cost!

He was the bear and Morrow the wolf.

Victorio had no desire to lose his leg or endure the mouth-frothing sickness. That would be his fate if he simply waited.

"We retreat," he said to Nana. "My sister is right. There is no advantage in wiping out Gatewood and his scouts, much as revenge on such traitors appeals to me."

"But to run!" protested Nana. "We will be disgraced."

Victorio shrugged. "What do we care what is said about us? Those who know us will know the truth, no matter what is said. Those who want to think ill of us will never be swayed, no matter how much truth is heaped on their heads."

"Is it honorable to run in the face of a lesser enemy? We can kill them all!"

"We will," Victorio said. "Later. We will escape into Mexico again. Then, later, we will take our vengeance on them for all they have done to us. And after our families have joined us. Do not forget Loco and his mission."

"A diversion is needed," Lozen said. She faced a tumble of rocks uphill from them and pointed to it. "There is Gatewood's main force. If I feint with a half dozen warriors toward them, firing and making great noise, we can draw their attention and let the rest of our band slip away to the south."

Victorio studied the lay of the land and wondered how

he had allowed a camp to be pitched where such a trap was possible. None of the warriors leading such a diversion was likely to escape injury—or even death.

"I would not lose my sister. I will lead the party. When they see me, they will think it is an all-out attack. Escape for the rest of you will be all that much easier."

"I want to fight. Let me," insisted Nana.

"Go. Protect the flanks as you go. I will join you before you reach the border into Mexico."

"If Gatewood is not killed, he will set his tame Apache dogs on you," said Nana.

"Let him. I eat dogs."

With that, Victorio found a half dozen young warriors willing to fight, among them Blue Pony and his brother. Victorio waited until Nana and Lozen rallied the full band and got them mounted before shrieking and shooting his rifle as if he intended to ride down the Apache scouts' throats.

Victorio galloped headlong, rifle firing and sending bits of rock and dirt sailing through the air. He reined back and raced parallel to Gatewood's position until his rifle was empty, then he switched to his other rifle, a Winchester he had taken from a dead settler.

Blue Pony shouted and whooped and hollered, covered with blood from several minor wounds. The blood flowing over his torso and mingling with dirt there to form crimson mud gave him a wild, savage look that had to give even the Coyotero scouts a moment's pause. This bloody aspect allowed Blue Pony the chance to ride closer and fire point-blank into one startled scout, who must have thought he had killed Blue Pony a half dozen times over. Victorio saw that Blue Pony had only wounded the Coyotero, but the effect was to cause their rank to fade back, to retreat just enough as they scrambled for new positions.

"Away!" Victorio shouted in Mimbreño warpath language. "Enjuh!"

Blue Pony and one other rode with Victorio down the path into the pass and down the mountain behind. The other three, including Blue Pony's brother, had died. Another debt Victorio would collect when the time came. If Blue Pony did not take his own revenge first.

They reached the El Paso–Chihuahua City road the next day and in three days were secure in the Candelaria Mountains deep in Mexico.

PART V

Mexico and Texas

Feast

November 7, 1879
Carrizal, Mexico

"What of Morrow?" Victorio asked his sister. Lozen dropped to the ground, grateful for the respite after three days of hard riding. She brushed off dust from the long trail, shook loose a long mane of dark black hair, and smiled slowly. This gave Victorio the answer he needed before she put her report into words.

"Gatewood wanted to continue after us, but Morrow appealed to Colonel Hatch for more troops and was denied. For all the buffalo soldiers in New Mexico Territory, fewer than three hundred are able to fight. Their command is in shambles. They starve inside their own forts, the settlers cheating them mercilessly. They get broke-down horses and mules that refuse to carry loads. Morrow might be determined, but he has met his match."

"We can return and get our families from San Carlos,"

said Nana, coming up to hear what Lozen had to say. He chewed thoughtfully on a flour tortilla, folded over twice and laden with butter. Wiping his lips, he looked almost content.

"Yes, Loco will be able to bring them," said Victorio, feeling as if the weight of a thousand pounds had lifted from him. "But now we rest. We can spend the winter here, then return in early spring. General Pope will not have changed anything. They starve their own soldiers because of their skin color," Victorio said, astounded at the notion. The buffalo soldiers fought well and yet the White Eyes' nantans refused to keep them in the field. He understood taking slaves; all the tribes did. *Los ricos* were infamous for their cruel treatment of captured Apache, which did nothing to endear them to Victorio. But the bluecoats put only whites in charge, while the blacks fought the real battles.

The blacks and Lieutenant Gatewood's traitorous Coyotero scouts.

"You want to raid into Texas again," chided Lozen. "What is it about their fat cattle that draws you so?"

"I enjoy riding the land that once belonged to the Comanche," Victorio admitted. "They are gone. We can raid at will in Texas as easily as in New Mexico—and Texas is closer. Just across the Rio Grande."

"Think on this," cautioned Nana. "Why does that land no longer belong to the Comanche? The bluecoats have chased them away."

"They are no better equipped in Texas than in New Mexico," said Victorio, making a motion like swatting a fly. "We can get horses, cattle, rifles from their settlers. We can bring honor on ourselves with daring raids. Let no one say we turned our back on easy raiding."

Nana grumbled. "We run from Gatewood but attack

settlers. You grow old and soft. War, not raiding, brings us honor."

"Horses and cattle for our families when they arrive bring us honor, not dying in futile battle," countered Victorio. He missed his family and wondered constantly at Loco's success. The other chief ought to have sent word by now of the rescue from San Carlos, but he had not. Victorio imagined his wife and family back on their hereditary land at Warm Springs. If the Indah had allowed them to remain there so many years ago, untold death and destruction could have been avoided. But they had allowed settlers to sneak onto their land and slowly push the Mimbreño away. Those settlers at Ojo Caliente were not the problem, as Victorio saw it. He got along well with them. They allowed him to raid and he always left cattle and horses for them to continue. Rather, the trouble came from the huge numbers of newcomers from the east, chased from their own land by the strange war the White Eyes had fought fifteen years earlier.

But from all Lozen said, Loco would come with the women and children soon enough.

"It is pleasant here," Victorio said, looking around. The small town of Carrizal nestled at the base of a tall mountain, surrounded by fields with good earth in them, now fallow until the spring. From all Victorio could tell, the harvest had been good for these people. They had plenty of corn, looked healthy and friendly, if wary, and even shared their firewater with those in his band. This Victorio did not countenance, but he had no say over what a warrior did when he was not out raiding. He had warned many of the younger braves that tequila and pulque were stronger than tiswin, but they did not listen.

Too many of them staggered back into camp before sunrise, daring to be out all night. The liquor made their fears ease and whetted their thirst for even more potent beverages.

"It is pleasant,' " he said, "but we need to prepare for our raids into Texas."

"They will be warned we have left New Mexico," said Lozen. "I feel so many enemy in that direction." She pointed toward the rising sun.

"We raided the supply trains to Fort Davis and Fort Quitman before. We can do it again. And the settlers with their cattle!" Victorio's mouth watered at the thought of so much beef waiting to be eaten. And while his warriors had ample horses now, more would only enhance their wealth. When Loco told them where their families had settled, they would return like conquerors, rich beyond the dream of most Apache.

A dozen horses. A hundred! It was possible, and all theirs if they raided wisely.

Victorio had never seen Fort Davis, but wondered how easy it would be to steal a corral filled with their horses. A slow smile crept onto his lips. The Tenth Cavalry's insignia was a crest with a buffalo. Let them ride the woolly beasts. He and his Warm Springs band would ride horses like rich men!

"Look," said Lozen. "A peasant from the village." She spat. Lozen cared little for the Mexicans.

"*¡Hola!*" the small, dark-skinned man called. He made furtive motions, rubbing his hands together as if he came to steal. Victorio strutted out, chest thrust forward, to meet him.

"You are the alcalde of Carrizal?" asked Victorio.

"*Sí*, I am. We saw your group ride up yesterday. Some of your warriors came into town and stayed in our cantinas last night. It is only natural that we wondered who you were, since your warriors said little but drank much." He was several inches smaller than Victorio's five-foot-ten height and cocked his head to one side, as if listening for an answer other than that he was likely to hear. A thin mustache rippled like a drunken caterpillar on his quivering upper lip. Victorio knew he could reach out and crush this insignificant bug whenever he wanted. He decided not to dirty his fingers.

"We are Mimbreño, Warm Springs Apache, allies of Juh and here to bask in your warm sun."

"You are peaceful?"

Lozen spat. Nana made a rude noise. Victorio smiled, the corner of his mouth turning up into what became more of a sneer.

"We are Apache. We are warriors who have defeated the U.S. Army. But we mean you no harm."

Relief flooded over the small man's features. "I am so glad, I am, I am. Since you are camping here on the edge of our poor village, we would ask you to join us this evening at our fiesta. We celebrate our great good fortune and the hard work that brought us an excellent crop."

From the corners of his eyes Victorio saw both Lozen and Nana react to this. Some braves had drunk too much the night before, and now they were all invited to a fiesta where more would drown in the swiftly flowing river of tequila. Victorio saw the problems, yet he was being honored for the great war chief he was.

"How can I turn down such a gracious invitation?" he said.

"*Bueno*, good, come to the village this evening. The feast will be simple but abundant." The *alcalde* of Carrizal bowed, bobbing up and down like a leaf in a fast running stream, then turned and almost ran away. Victorio had to laugh.

"What a strange little man. But aren't they all?"

"They feed us to keep us from stealing what is theirs," said Nana. "That is good."

Victorio passed the remainder of the day mending his moccasins, cleaning his rifles and sorting through the ammunition he carried in a big burlap bag, discarding rounds of the wrong caliber and letting others in his band paw through the rejects to supply their own diverse weapons. Satisfied, Victorio ate a light noonday meal and slept until commotion in the Apache camp awakened him just before sunset.

"Everyone is excited about the fiesta," Lozen said. "They eye the village women. There will be trouble."

Victorio shrugged it off. They only passed through this part of Mexico. In a few days they would be raiding across the river in Texas again. With enough horses, they could go to Juh with an offering even the jaded Apache chief would appreciate.

Music from the village drew Victorio. He had fought long and hard. It was time to enjoy the festivities offered by Carrizal. Swaggering down the road, the others in his band joined him. Only Lozen remained in their camp, choosing not to indulge in the revelry.

Barely had Victorio reached the outermost adobe house in Carrizal when he slowed, suddenly cautious. He had feared the worst when he had fought Morrow, but no disaster came to pass. Even their last fight where he had allowed Gatewood and his scouts to gain position on him and those riding with him had not been a calamity. With the death of only three, they had escaped.

But now? Victorio felt a cold chill the length of his spine. His hand dropped to the sheathed knife at his hip as the first shots rang out. From deep ditches on either side of the road rose villagers, firing shotguns, ancient muskets, pistols that smoked as they belched their load of lead. The guns were deadly, but the murderous expression on the faces of the peasants convinced Victorio to retreat.

"Back to camp! They are trying to kill us all!" As he

cried out his command to the others, he found himself
ducking and dodging hot bullets singing past his head.
The villagers were terrible shots; only one Apache was
wounded before they retraced their steps to camp.

"What happened? So soon you enraged them?" asked
Lozen, almost at the point of laughing. Then she sobered
when she saw the expression on her brother's face. "They
ambushed you," she said in a flat voice. "They lured you
into Carrizal, and they ambushed you!"

"Mount. Get away from here," Victorio said angrily.
Even as he saw that the other Warm Springs Apache in
his band were struggling to get on horseback, he considered what might be done. As he swung onto his pony and
caught up the reins of a half dozen other horses he had
captured, the plan took shape in his mind.

"There, that way," Victorio called, leading the way.
"Ride as if your lives depended on it!"

"But they are only peasants!" protested Nana. "We can
beat them!"

Victorio glared at the feisty old warrior until Nana subsided and obeyed. They were equal in rank, but Nana—
again—followed Victorio's orders. So far, his instincts had
been good in battle, and Nana saw no reason to counter
him now.

"Stop!" called Victorio after they had ridden less than
a mile. "You, you, you—all over there." He pointed to a
few scrubby jacaranda trees. "Into the branches and get
ready for an ambush. The rest of you, deeper into this
canyon, then half of you dismount. The rest of you, remain
mounted where they can see you. The others, come with
me."

Victorio led a quarter of his warriors to the side of the
canyon and scattered them around to command the trail.
Then he loaded his rifles and laid them on a rock where
he could reach them quickly. In less than fifteen minutes,

the exultant villagers charged down the throat of the canyon. Victorio wasted no time giving the order to open fire. These were not trained soldiers, and he knew the first round of deadly fire would rout them.

He wanted as many dead as he could before the survivors regained their wits and scrambled for cover. Victorio got his wish.

Withering fire ripped through the gaudily dressed peasants, turning their fiesta into *deqüello*. No quarter. Victorio snatched up a rifle and fired steadily, taking care to aim every round into the body of a villager. He longed to find the treacherous alcalde, but the man was nowhere to be seen.

He contented himself with killing two villagers. When the last echo died away and the cold wind blowing through the canyon ripped away the cloying haze of gunsmoke, no Mexican stirred. A few moans of pain reached Victorio's ears. He dropped his rifle and drew his knife. The piteous cries stopped abruptly as he swept through the battlefield, an angel of death come to earth.

On the Trail

November 12, 1879
Along the Rio Grande

"I want to cross," Lester Boynton said. He jerked at the reins until his horse reared. It took several seconds to get the horse gentled again, time he did not want to spend and an action he did not want to take. Three days earlier he had been alerted to Victorio's presence across the river in Carrizal. It was a long, hard day's ride from the river, but he could do it. "To hell with the Mexicans!" he said.

"Captain, you should think on this some more. Nobody's invited us over there. All Colonel Grierson told us to do was tie up with the Rangers." Sergeant Kingman looked worried, as worried as he ever was over his captain's wild ventures to capture Victorio.

"Texas Rangers," Boynton said, still fuming. With a company of soldiers he could run down Victorio before the renegade got twenty miles. If he had left Fort Davis immediately and ridden like the wind, he could have been in Carrizal by now. But Grierson had other ideas. For some reason, Lieutenant Baylor and a company of Texas Rangers had been alerted. They were riding down from El Paso, or so Boynton had been told.

The river bubbled and boiled, sending white froth up against the rocks. In places, the Rio Grande was only hip-deep, in spite of the rapids directly in front of Boynton's position. He had strung out his first squad along the banks, covering any approach from the other side, should Victorio try to come this way. He had pored over maps of the area until choosing this particular ford. It was the best location for a raider to use. To the north lay Fort Quitman and to the south the treacherous canyons of Big Bend. Plunging straight into the heart of Texas gave Victorio the chance to raid both settlement and army post, should he want to do either.

More significant to Boynton's way of thinking, Victorio could cross here and ride due east and cut off the supply trains bringing weekly rations and supplies to Fort Davis. This was the tactic the Warm Springs Apache had used before. When he had so brutally killed Sarah and Peter and Thomas Boynton.

His other squad Boynton had cast out on constant patrol, scouting for any hint the Apache were sneaking across the river in some other spot. He controlled a length of Rio Grande almost twenty miles from north to south. It left him woefully weak, should a scout find Victorio crossing, but the scout had explicit orders to report, not engage.

Boynton could throw his entire company against Victorio in a matter of a day. And he would. Oh, he would! Given the chance.

"The colonel wants us to report, not fight," Sergeant Kingman said in his slow speech. "Reckon he wants to see some of us return to the fort after the patrol."

"You are not in command, Sergeant," Boynton said coldly. He itched to ride into the fray against Victorio. He would finish the chore Major Morrow had started. Victorio would be returned to the San Carlos Reservation—or killed. Without realizing it, Boynton had clenched his hands into tight fists. When he forced himself to relax, the muscles in his forearms began to protest. He needed to get better control if he wanted to beat Victorio in battle. Any mistake now meant lives lost.

Ghosts of memory fluttered through his mind as he remembered Magee's death. The colonel had ridden to his rescue after his junior officer had stupidly crossed the river and sprung Victorio's trap. But Colonel Magee had been an Army officer and knew the risks.

Boynton kept telling himself it was as much the higher ranking Magee's fault as his own—but Ruth. . . . Ruth kept haunting him, so young and lovely and open with her friendship. He had been responsible for her husband's death and . . .

"Captain, got a flash signal from north. A dozen riders comin' this way mighty fast." Kingman shielded his eyes and watched as the distant scout signaled using a mirror. Boynton tried to read the code but missed too many words.

"The Rangers?" he asked, although Kingman still watched the quick flashes of the incoming message.

"Reckon it is. Can't rightly identify 'em, but they're not Apache. Riding using fancy-ass saddles with silver all over 'em. No Apache except for a squaw would use a saddle."

"A dozen?" Boynton had forty men. Another dozen gave him a force more than adequate to take on Victorio and his band. His troopers were rested and had plenty of ammo. A quick ride into Mexico, acquisition of Victorio's trail, a fight, and he could be back on the Texas side of the Rio Grande before the Mexican authorities even knew they had been invaded.

"Reckless, those Rangers," Kingman said. "They might even violate international treaty and go after Victorio without bein' asked by the Mexican army. What would the colonel think of that?"

Boynton shot his sergeant a cold stare. In his way, Kingman warned him again that Grierson would not tolerate any violation of the border. The captain sagged a little. He had done it once with ill result. He needed more information about Victorio and his whereabouts before he committed his men willy-nilly.

"Yep, it's that Lieutenant Baylor and his boys," Kingman said. "I can tell by their white faces and red necks."

For a moment Boynton was startled by the observation. Then he had to remind himself there were no black Rangers—or none he had ever heard of. Commanding a company of buffalo soldiers had changed his outlook on what enlisted men ought to look like. It might take him a while to readjust when he transferred back east and had a regular command again.

After he brought Victorio to justice.

Boynton adjusted his uniform, then wheeled his horse around and walked over to a sandy spit where he waited with Kingman for the Rangers. It seemed an eternity as he watched them pick their way along the rocky bank of the river, but he knew he was only anxious to get on with the hunt. Grierson had told him to coordinate with Baylor, and he would. But he was not under the Ranger's command.

"Captain Boynton," a sandy-haired young man called, throwing a sloppy salute ln his direction. "I'm Lieutenant G. W. Baylor, Company C, Texas Rangers out of Ysleta. The Mexicans contacted General Jones down Austin way and requested our presence over in Carrizal. Seems they've had a run-in with an Apache by the name of—"

"Victorio," finished Boynton. "I am aware of his presence. What can you tell me of his attack and where he is likely to have holed up?"

Baylor took off his tall Stetson, knocked trail dust from the black floppy brim, used his bandanna to wipe sweat from his face, and only then did he answer.

"Don't know as much as I'd like, but it sounds like I know more 'n you. A Tarahumara Indian seems to have riled up the local alcalde with tales of how nasty Victorio could be. The townsfolk lured him and his boys down to the town on pretext of some fiesta, they're always throwin' fiestas, you know, and then the peones botched an ambush. Bad choice of victim. Victorio's fresh out of New Mexico Territory, where he whupped up on the entire Ninth Cavalry." Baylor's pale eyes worked down the defense line Boynton had posted. "You got anythin' but them black boys?"

"You can tell by their unit insignia they are all soldiers of the Tenth Cavalry," Boynton said stiffly. "All are under my command."

"Reckon that's so, if you say," Lieutenant Baylor said. "Well, I got orders to go on over and see if I can bring this fellow Victorio to justice."

"Why'd the Mexicans contact you? Ysleta is a far ways off."

"Well, Captain, it's like this. Me and some of the boys wander down that way now and again and have decent relations with the folks in Carrizal and other villages. Now, they don't have such good relations with their own army, made up of a bunch of thieves and bandits no better than the ones they're supposed to be out catchin'."

"I am ready to go after Victorio," Boynton said, disliking Baylor more by the minute.

"Can't say I got any orders about you and your men, Captain," Baylor said. "A company of Rangers is more 'n enough to deal with any Injun threat. But if you want to ride along—just you—there's no reason you can't come as official observer."

"You are saying my men must remain here?" Boynton was shocked.

"That's it in a nutshell. Things are mighty quiet along the border right now. Want to keep 'em that way. We was asked over, you weren't. Can't say what a Mexican Army general might think if he found a company of bluecoats sashayin' through his country. Now us, we were asked all official-like."

Boynton looked from Kingman to his men and back at Baylor. "What if I ordered my men across the river?"

"Got orders, Captain," Baylor said. "Don't cotton much to fightin' the U.S. Army, but others in my family have done worse than that not that many years back. Texas means to preserve the integrity of the border, and that means keepin' you and yours on this side just like it means keepin' greedy rascals like General Treviño on his side."

"But you will go after Victorio on Mexican soil," Boynton said darkly.

"You figured it all out. Good for you, Captain. See, he's a threat to both sides—and the Mexican authorities asked for our help."

"Sergeant Kingman, remain in position and wait for my return," Boynton said. He caught the drift of Lieutenant Baylor's veiled threat. The Rangers would willingly fight the troopers and then cross to fight Victorio. Boynton had heard all the boasts about Rangers and their fighting prowess. But he doubted a dozen of them could come out on top of any battle with *his* company. Still, he sought something more than fighting his own side, if the Rangers could be placed on the same level as the U.S. Army.

Stopping Victorio was paramount.

"Let's ride," Baylor called. His ragtag band of Rangers, all looking more like road agents than lawmen, but each with a Ranger's small star pinned on his vest, took off with a whoop and a holler and splashed across the Rio Grande at the spot Boynton had identified as the most likely ford.

"This isn't such a good idea, Captain," Kingman warned.

"Signal Lieutenant Kincaid to come in from patrol and reform this unit. I want both squads looking for hostile activity."

"You're placin' him in command?" Sergeant Kingman sounded skeptical.

"He is wet behind the ears, but he has the makings of a good officer." Boynton glanced over his shoulder. Lieutenant Baylor and the Rangers had reached the far side. They took a minute to shake off the river water and be sure their braces of six-shooters were in good condition, but Boynton knew they would not wait for him.

"Get him here on the double. Until he arrives, maintain this position, Sergeant."

"Yes, sir."

Boynton put his spurs to his horse's flanks and entered the rapidly flowing river. He felt the horse stumble when they got to mid river, but the animal kept on and soon they were standing alongside Baylor.

"Glad to have you along as observer, Captain." Baylor started out without further words. And that suited Boynton just fine.

"Carrizal ain't much of a town, even as sleepy Mexican villages go," Baylor said. "But now it's likely to blow away if what they say is true."

"Twenty-six men dead?" Boynton shook his head. "That must be most of the men in town." A flock of women gathered around them, all chattering Spanish in shrill voices. Boynton could not understand the language, but from their expressions he knew they were distraught over what had happened. More than one young girl had tear-tracked dusty cheeks.

"Reckon so," said the Ranger. He palavered with an old man for a few more minutes, then shook his head and rocked back on the saddle. He brought up his leg and curled it around the pommel, almost as if he were riding English style.

"Hard to figure the villain in this piece. The alcalde got all spooked and attacked Victorio and his braves without provocation. But there's no telling if Victorio would have swooped down on the village once he and his boys got liquored up after the fiesta."

"He has killed enough. It wouldn't have mattered," Boynton said, trying to hold his hatred in check and keep a level voice. From the way Baylor looked curiously at him, he knew he had failed. And he did not care. He would have Victorio in his sights, either in Mexico or across the border in Texas. It did not matter as long as the outlaw Apache was caught or killed.

For a moment, Boynton wondered if he would prefer seeing a noose dropped over the war chief's neck or if he would garner more revenge by simply drawing back on his own trigger and doing the deed himself. He did not know.

"Let's go find your old chum Victorio," Baylor said, prodding Boynton. The captain refused to rise to the taunt. He did not like the Ranger, and the less he had to do with him, the better. But Baylor was in the catbird seat, officially in Mexico while he was not.

For the privilege of riding along with the Rangers, Boynton was willing to swallow a bellyful of bile if it meant putting an end to Victorio's raiding and killing.

"There wasn't much cunning about the way they rode," called out a scout, kneeling beside the dusty road. "Wind's erased most of the trail, but they rode off the road here and left deep hoofprints." He reached down, his finger gently tracing out the deep impressions in the earth. "They was runnin' hard down that way," he said, pointing into a canyon with high walls.

For a moment Boynton fought the fear clutching at his throat like a gripping hand. The high walls along the Rio Grande where he had crossed and been trapped were like this. Except there was no river. And he did not have to worry about his men. Lieutenant Kincaid had returned to take command by now, if Sergeant Kingman had done his duty. What worried at Boynton's mind like a cocklebur was the similarity of the terrain to where he had been ambushed.

"He likes canyons for his ambushes," Boynton said. "He defeated Morrow in country like this."

"We'll keep an eye out for him," Baylor said in an almost offhanded manner. "I don't figure to find him. He's long gone." Riding slowly, letting the scout work on the spoor left by Victorio and his band, Boynton held his fear in check. He could not shake the sensation that he'd repeated the same mistake he had made before. Colonel Grierson did not know he had an officer across the Rio Grande in Mexico, sticking his nose where it did not belong—and where he had specifically ordered Boynton not to go.

"You look a mite pale, Captain," said Baylor. "This your first time in pursuit of an Injun?"

"No," was all Boynton said. The canyon walls rose on either side, crushing him. Sweat began to bead on his forehead, although the weather was turning colder by the minute. A storm with big black billowy clouds brewed in the mountains and promised a dusting of snow before morning. Boynton swiveled about, looking every which way, hoping to see Victorio or the ambush he knew was being laid for them.

The Ranger rode on, oblivious to the danger.

"Hey G. W. come on over here and take a look," came

the call from deeper in the canyon. Baylor exchanged a quick look with Boynton, then trotted forward. Boynton followed more reluctantly, fearing what they would find.

"Scattered all over the damn place, they are," said the scout. "These poor Mexican sons a bitches never had a prayer. Way it seems to me, the Apache hit them from both sides and maybe even from deeper in the canyon."

"A three-sided attack. The alcalde might have retreated, but on foot, there wasn't much hope of getting far." Baylor roved aimlessly around the site of the carnage. Boynton stared at the bodies. Most had been stripped of anything useful, but a few still sported colorful ribbons or white linen shirts. All weapons were gone, as was any ammunition the villagers might have carried.

"They thought he was gonna be easy pickin's," said the scout. "Fooled them. How many you count, G. W.?"

"Twenty-six," Baylor said.

"Same. From here they rode on through the canyon. We're days and days behind them." The scout climbed into the saddle, fumbled out a plug of tobacco from his shirt pocket under the Ranger's badge, and bit off a thick brown piece of the ropy chaw. He worked on the tobacco a few minutes, then spat.

All the while no one said a word. The Rangers milled around as their lieutenant had, gathering whatever intelligence they could about the attack.

"We go on back to Carrizal," Baylor decided. "Tracking Victorio through these hills is a fool's errand."

"You're not giving up!" protested Boynton.

"Didn't say that. Need to get someone who can tell us where the bastard's most likely gone. He's not ridin' into the mountains for his health. Heard tell Juh and Geronimo are raiding around here. Like as not, he'll join with them, then we'll have one hellacious fight on our hands."

Lieutenant Baylor turned and the company of Rangers

started back in the direction of Carrizal. Boynton considered tracking down the Apache himself, then discarded the notion. He was a soldier, not a scout. Watching Kingman and some of the others pick out a faint trail was worlds different from doing it himself. One small mistake, a missed clue, and he would be lost. Worse, he might fall into another trap if he did not carefully consider what he did. Boynton turned his horse's face and trotted after Baylor.

They had barely reached the road leading to Carrizal when Baylor let out a sound like a leaking steam engine. The air had turned cold enough to form silvery, feathery icicles as he exhaled.

"What's wrong?" asked Boynton. Then he saw what the Ranger already had. A long column of Mexican troopers marched into Carrizal.

"General Treviño," said Baylor. "Don't know if he'd cotton much to you bein' over here, Captain. Might I suggest you hightail it back across the Rio and let me deal with him?"

"I can—"

"Captain," Baylor said sternly, "he is one mean son of a bitch. Might be just the man to set on Victorio's tail, but only if he's not distracted. You catch my meaning?" Baylor's eyebrows raised.

"I'll continue my patrol," Boynton said with suppressed anger, "on the other side of the Rio Grande. Victorio won't get by me when you flush him out."

"I'm counting on it," Baylor said, already turning to the challenge of dealing with the corrupt Mexican general. Boynton heard him mutter something about "nigger soldiers" and then was gone.

Lester Boynton thought it was a thousand miles back across the Rio Grande and a million years of endless patrol after he reassumed command of his company from Kincaid. The worst part of it was that he never saw hide nor hair of Victorio or his Warm Springs Apache band.

Into Texas

January 6, 1880
Along the Rio Grande

The nipping desert wind kept tearing at the corners of Boynton's heat-yellowed survey map. He knelt on one tattered corner and used red rocks to hold the other three as he drew his finger along the meandering blue line that represented the Rio Grande. Finally coming to a stop at a worn spot on a crease, Boynton stabbed down hard. The paper crinkled and threatened to puncture under the pressure.

"Here. He will come across here."

"What makes you think the savage will do any such thing, Captain?" asked Lieutenant Kincaid. The young officer had aged years in the month they had been in the field. Weather had been a factor, with biting winter wind and more snow than usual falling, from all the stories the settlers told. But being away from his family had told the most on Kincaid.

Boynton understood—and did not care. He was so close to catching Victorio that nothing else mattered.

"I've received dispatches from Baylor. He has done surprisingly well chasing down Victorio and keeping him on the run."

"What of General Treviño, sir?" asked Sergeant Kingman. He peered down at the map, his eyes not quite focused, as if none of this mattered. That attitude angered Boynton more than words could ever express. They all needed to focus on the mission.

"What of him? His bugler has a fine time sounding the charge and the troops rush on in straight lines, attacking deserted camps. He is more interested in his own glory than doing his job."

"Catching Victorio," supplied Kincaid. "If Lieutenant Baylor or Treviño captures the Apache, can we leave the field, sir?"

"If Victorio's raiding career is truly ended."

"Reckon you might want to hunt down his ghost, if he's killed," came a whisper caught on the wind and poured into Boynton's ear like burning vitriol. He spun, his knee tearing the map. Charles Kingman, Sergeant Kingman's brother, stood some distance away. He had been Colonel Magee's striker and had learned insolence after his commanding officer's death. Ruth Magee had been too lenient with him.

"Private Kingman," Boynton said coldly, "we are on the trail of an outlaw, a criminal, a man who has left the reservation set aside for him by the United States government."

"Sir, it's obvious this is more to you than that," spoke up Kincaid. "None of us mind that it's personal with you. It's just that we might not be the ones who catch Victorio. Sir."

Boynton seethed but said nothing more. He stared at

the torn map but did not see the printing. He saw the real land stretching to the dusty, storm-racked horizon. He saw real movement as Victorio and his Warm Springs band sneaked across the border, riding ahead of Baylor and his Rangers like a cork bobbing on a rising wave. The more the Rangers reached for him, the more likely Victorio was to slip away.

"He will come across here. If we stretch half our force along this ridge and put the other down near the Rio Grande, we can catch him in a cross fire."

"That's taking a risk to the men along the river, Captain," said Sergeant Kingman. "If Victorio keeps ridin', then he'll be cut down from both halves of our force. If he stands and fights, either on the bank of the river or up on the ridge, our other half can't reinforce easily."

"We need to cover as much terrain as possible with a single company, Sergeant. Let's concentrate on the positive aspects of this ambush."

"Yes, sir," the sergeant said, frowning. He motioned to his brother and they left, muttering between themselves so low Boynton could not overhear. Nor did he want to. He knew Victorio would escape General Treviño, and he thought Victorio would also elude Baylor. The young Ranger had been aggressive, but the Apache managed to stay a half day ahead, no matter how hard the Texans rode or how cagey they were in laying their ambushes.

The time had come for Victorio to cross the river again. Lester Boynton felt it in his bones.

He hunkered down behind the rock, shielding himself and his horse from the wind. It blew from the north and carried more than a hint of frostbite with it. Boynton shucked off one glove and rubbed the hand briskly, keeping it flexible should he need to curl his finger around the pistol still in its holster at his right hip. He had bet everything that Victorio would come across the river soon—and here. All day he and his command had suffered in the winter cold without any trace of the wily Apache.

Boynton began to doubt himself. The dispatches from Baylor were sporadic and terse. Had he misinterpreted the locations the Ranger had come across Victorio's trail? Had Treviño somehow engaged the Apache and caused Victorio to find some other place to scurry to? Or had he simply been too eager to take his revenge and had imagined movement on Victorio's part that simply did not exist?

Boynton had no answers to any of those questions, and he froze inch by inch, starting at the toes and working up his legs. He rubbed his hand again, then thrust it in the front of his uniform jacket, hoping to share heat from his chest with the numbed fingers. His nose dripped, and he wasn't sure if his ears had closed from the chilblains he suffered for the better part of a week. All he knew for certain was that he suffered alone. Not a one of his soldiers cared about him.

And why should he care about them? They were his instrument for revenge, nothing more. Hatred failed to warm him sufficiently, though, and his thoughts drifted, building up like the thin snow around the rock. Private Kingman's snide remark produced more heat, and then even this faded. Boynton did not need to be liked by his troopers.

Still, the private's brother had not reported Boynton's failure before when he had dashed across the Rio Grande and into a trap. Because of Boynton's thoughtless action, Amos Magee had died.

Wind changed pitch and seemed to come to him now in Ruth Magee's soft voice. Looking out into the swirling, dancing snow he imagined himself back at the post social with her in his arms. She wasn't Sarah. Who could be? But they shared loss. It struck Boynton as amusing that they were allied against everyone else at Fort Davis, for different reasons.

She was an outcast because she no longer fit. She was trapped by the threat of Indian depredation, though Boynton had come to wonder if Ruth tried hard enough to leave Fort Davis. Perhaps not. But he appreciated her presence since his own company had come to hate him because he saw his duty so clearly.

"Captain," came Ruth's voice on the wind. "Captain Boynton!"

He shook himself and turned, his joints half frozen. Sergeant Kingman had joined him.

"What is it, Sergeant?"

"Spotted a rider. An Apache, from the way he rides. Across the river but moving this way. You might have been right about Victorio comin' into our country."

Boynton shot to his feet and wiped wet snow from his eyes. "Where?" he demanded. "Where is he?"

"Yonder," Kingman said, pointing. Boynton tried to see what the sergeant obviously did and failed. But his heart pumped fiercely now. He threw off the lethargy he had not recognized before. Not moving, he had been freezing to death. It would not have been long before he simply drifted off to sleep—forever.

"What of the men? Are they ready?"

"Keepin' warm, much as they can," allowed Kingman.

"What of Lieutenant Kincaid? Send a messenger up to him with word that Victorio is on his way."

"I'll send my brother. I can trust him not to get it all turned 'round."

"Do so, Sergeant." Boynton thrust his hand back into his glove, then rested it on the hilt of his saber. Combat was near. He felt it. And he felt victory was going to be his also.

Victory over Victorio—and revenge for the death of his family.

Boynton tugged at his horse's reins and then swung into the saddle. It creaked under his weight, then became wet as his body heat melted the snow that had piled there. He urged his horse forward so he could join the main body of his column.

"All ready for fightin', Captain," reported Kingman.

"Very good. What about Kincaid?"

"Private Kingman's been dispatched. And I got out two scouts along the river to let us know where the Apache will cross."

"We don't want to spook them," Boynton said, but he had to see for himself. He rode into the white whirl of the storm, picking his way down to the sluggishly flowing river. If Victorio crossed that freezing water, he would be virtually helpless when he reached this side. Boynton intended to attack then.

He dismounted and cupped his hands to shield them from the snow now coming down in hard little pellets. At first he saw nothing, then caught a glimpse of a dark figure on the far side of the Rio Grande. An Apache!

Boynton restrained the urge to draw his pistol and fire at the brave. The Apache walked slowly along the far bank, studying the ground, hunting for a good ford. In a few minutes, a second Indian joined him. Boynton sucked in a deep breath as a third Apache appeared through the shifting curtain of white. Victorio's band was gathering, ready for the crossing into the U.S.

Into country where Boynton could do something!

For what seemed an eternity, the three stood shoulder to shoulder, discussing something. Not once did they look across the river. They walked slowly parallel to the Rio Grande, as if they sought a way to waste time.

"Captain!" came Kingman's worried call. "Captain Boynton!"

"Hush, Sergeant. I don't think they can hear you, not in this wind, but we must be careful. See? Your scout was right. There are three of them!"

"Sir, something's bad wrong."

"What do you mean?"

"My brother's not back. He ought to have passed along your orders to Lieutenant Kincaid and come back."

"Maybe he's riding out the storm," Boynton said, knowing the snowstorm was not that bad. In truth, he thought Charles Kingman was probably malingering. He had fallen back on slovenly ways working as Colonel Magee's servant. Ruth had been too kindhearted to break the habits the private accumulated like dust on a mantel. Too bad Charles Kingman was not more like his brother.

"No, sir, he wouldn't. I think something's gone wrong up there on the ridge. They're out of our sight."

Boynton cursed under his breath. The three Apache braves mounted, turned, and rode back into Mexican territory.

"We've lost them. Or maybe they are going to fetch the rest of their raiding party!"

"Sir, let me ride to the ridge to look after my brother. There's somethin' wrong!"

"Yes, of course, go, Sergeant. It will take a spell before Victorio crosses here." Boynton jerked around. The wind changed, blowing now from the ridge where Kincaid and half his command laid the trap for Victorio. On that cold wind came the sound of muffled gunfire.

The first shot might have been imagined, a crack of distant lightning that confused his stopped up ears. The second and third and tenth shot told the story. Lieutenant Kincaid had opened fire—on what?

"Victorio!" cried Boynton. "He crossed farther up the river and is attacking Kincaid!"

Captain and sergeant rode hard to return to the soldiers arrayed along the river. George Kingman barked out his commands, his soft drawl gone now. The buffalo soldiers hastily formed a ragged column. Boynton was already on the faint, snow-packed trail leading up to the ridge. Every step his horse took brought louder, more insistent sounds of battle to his ears. Boynton refrained from galloping along the treacherous trail. He had to have support from his company when he got to the top of the ridge.

Horse slipping and stumbling at every turn, Boynton urged the animal ever upward. From behind he heard Kingman barking out orders to the troopers, some mixed with encouragement and others with dire threats. Boynton didn't care how Kingman kept them moving, but move they must.

By the time he reached the summit, his worst fears were realized. Kincaid had been right about splitting the company, hoping to catch Victorio between positions that could not support each other.

Bright red blood still sizzled in the snowbanks where recently slain soldiers lay. The sight of rifles and pistols still clutched in dead hands told Boynton the Apache had not had time to loot the bodies of those they had just killed. The sight of a brave moving along from the battleground fifty yards away sent a thrill of outrage into Lester Boynton.

"Charge!" he yelled, whipping out his saber and waving it above his head. Swinging the sharp blade above his head cut through the whirling snow. His horse's hooves pounded on rock and crunched through the thin crust of fresh snow. From behind he heard Kingman getting the soldiers into a line to attack in good form.

His charge led nowhere. He attacked emptiness. Boynton slowed and looked around, confused and angry and frightened.

"What does it take?" he cried. "What do I have to do to kill you!"

Boynton sheathed his sword and returned to see what casualties his command had taken. He felt a coldness that had nothing to do with the rising wind and deepening storm. Sergeant Kingman cradled the body of his dead brother in his arms, rocking slowly back and forth. Tears ran down the burly man's cheeks, to drip into the snow and freeze immediately. Boynton felt a desolation beyond any he had ever felt before, even when his family had been slaughtered.

The ambush had gone well—for the Apache. Victorio had struck and faded away into the storm, leaving behind thirty-two dead and eighteen wounded soldiers.

Into Texas

January 6, 1880
Along the Rio Grande

"The Rangers are close," Lozen said. Her face was hot and her hands bright red. She turned in a full circle, coming to a halt facing due west. Victorio saw how his sister shook as if she had a fever. Her hands lifted to the sky again, reddened palms turned upward in supplication to Ussen. Even as he watched, her hands turned a bright cherry red, then faded quickly.

"Very close," Victorio said, knowing the sign all too well. For a month the Texas Rangers had dogged their steps, no matter how they turned or dodged. The Mexican general, Treviño, had been like a rabbit, popping up and poking out his head, only to duck back or run off if anything threatened. But Baylor was not Treviño, and Victorio had to be constantly alert to the danger he posed. Twice Mimbreño had fought with Ranger and twice Baylor had forced Victorio to retreat.

"There is nowhere to ambush them," Nana said. "We have ridden this patch of land until our horses' hooves flatten the grass."

"We have not found Juh, either," Victorio said. Juh and Geronimo, rumored to be raiding to the south, proved elusive. Never had he found anyone who could confirm this, in either Indian or Mexican village. Running off in search of his ally was not a reasonable tactic as long as Baylor hunted him.

"Brother, the Rangers are only minutes from our camp." Lozen rubbed her hands against the buckskin vest she wore. Bloodstains on it came from both the deer she had caught and slaughtered the day before and the human foes she had killed in the past month. The stains mingled so that Victorio was no longer able to distinguish one from the other. Looking down at his own clothing, he knew the same could be said for him.

Too much blood and too little rest. It was the warrior's way, he knew, but he wanted to rest. He had not heard from Loco about their families, nor had any rumor come to him that the Warm Springs Apache had left San Carlos Reservation. Major Morrow might be resting snugly in Fort Bayard and finding new recruits, gathering more supplies, preparing for a long springtime campaign. He would be a worthy opponent, whenever Victorio returned to New Mexico Territory.

And return he would when spring warmed the land.

"Into Texas," Victorio decided. "For a month they have chased us in circles. Now we go into Texas again." As he spoke, he considered all the possibilities. Settlers with fat cattle and horses, buffalo soldiers from Fort Davis and Fort Quitman that lacked decent leaders, yes, Victorio decided, it was time again for Texas.

"Soon, Brother, we must go soon," said Lozen. "But I have been told by Ussen there are others waiting across the Rio Bravo."

"Oh?" This surprised Victorio. He had thought his only enemies were in Mexico. "Bluecoats?"

"Probably," Lozen said. "There are as many of them—perhaps more—than in the Ranger company."

"Ammunition, also," said Nana. "I prayed to Ussen this morning. In that direction there is considerable ammunition." Nana pointed east, across the Rio Grande.

"Your Powers convince me I am right," Victorio said. He glanced around. All his warriors were mounted already and moving in a jagged line to the east, their best way from the campground. He swung onto the back of his pony and joined their line. He rode but he saw nothing of the snowy terrain or those warriors who had fought so well these past months. Most were of his Warm Springs band, but he had drawn many other Apache from Mescalero, Jicarilla, and even Chiricahua. This surprised him since Geronimo was such a powerful Chiricahua chief and could promise great wealth to any brave following him.

This swelled Victorio with pride. His band was diverse, and they were also rich. Many horses came with them as they rode toward the river. He had done well for them. If only he could do as well for his own family. As long as the White Eyes' Great Nantan insisted they remain on the Gila River at San Carlos, Victorio felt as if he wore heavy manacles. For all his success raiding, he was a failure in giving his band their own land and freedom.

His wife and children were still prisoners, just as he was prisoner to the daily need to flee from the Rangers. He took little comfort in knowing the women and children did not have to also dodge the persistent Ranger company.

"Who do we face across the river?" he asked Lozen. "An entire company of buffalo soldiers?"

She nodded, her expression distant. Every time Ussen spoke to her it took her several hours to return to the world inhabited by Victorio and the others. He considered also what Nana had found with his Power. An entire company, probably from nearby Fort Quitman, possibly from Fort Davis. The buffalo soldiers fought well, but their leaders were not up to the demands of a fiercely aggressive foe.

The snow that had fallen gently now blew into his face, driven by the strong north wind. Victorio's band never slowed their inexorable pace. They knew that the falling snow would cover their trail, should the Rangers falter in their pursuit. This idea heartened Victorio. Baylor might even choose to camp and weather out the storm. If so, the snow would completely mask the path they took. Crossing the Rio Bravo would further confuse the Rangers, if they thought Victorio intended to join Juh.

"Chief," called a brave who had gone ahead as scout. "There is an entire company of bluecoats on the far side of the river."

"They have learned," chuckled Victorio. "They won't cross the river and split their force as they did the last time." He laughed harder at the thought he faced the same commander. He might have learned one lesson, but Victorio had many more to teach.

"They *do* split their force," said the scout. This made Victorio's grin even wider. "Half cower along the river while the rest guard the ridge higher along the river."

"Can those above see the soldiers at the river?" he asked.

The scout shook his head.

"So, one half cannot see the other. How far upriver would we need to cross so those on the ridge would not see us?"

Victorio liked the scout's answer.

* * *

"How long will they wait, once they see our three warriors on the river?" asked Nana.

Victorio had no answer. He had thought of sending two men to decoy the platoons of bluecoats hiding in ambush along the river, then decided to add a third to make it seem as if the entire Apache force would cross soon.

"Ahead," Lozen said. She stared at her palms. They were pinkish but grew more purple as she turned in the direction of the ridge above the river. "Many soldiers."

"Good," Victorio said. Their crossing of the Rio Grande had cost him two horses and a warrior, swept away by unsuspected swiftness in the middle. The freezing temperatures had also worked on those making it across, forcing him to waste almost an hour to dry out their clothing. In that time, the storm had worsened, making travel difficult. It also made it easier for them to ride up to the soldiers and simply kill them where they hid.

"All our warriors are ready," said Nana. "I will lead a few in a large sweep around to the east, then come back to cut off any escape."

"Do it," Victorio said. Nana smiled, held on as his horse reared, then took off at a trot. Victorio watched the old man vanish into the whiteness, knowing no soldier would ever get past him.

"Do we kill the ones on the ridge, then wait for the others to come up? We will have them in our sights if they try to rescue their comrades."

Lozen was a good tactician. Victorio had considered this. The bluecoat commander had laid his trap poorly, unless he expected the Apache to only come across the river and straight into the jaws of the trap. Now that it could be turned against him, their captain might decide to simply retreat along the river. If he did, Victorio would do nothing. He would have slaughtered half a company and taken their supplies.

But if the officer decided to ride to the rescue, he would face the same firepower he had thought to turn on the Apache. Victorio looked forward to eliminating an entire company of soldiers.

"We will wait for them, unless the storm worsens. To fight in a blizzard is a foolish risk, not to be taken lightly. We need to know our targets."

"We should let at least one of them live," Lozen said. "So they will know fear!"

Victorio laughed, feeling better than he had since they had killed the Mexicans from Carrizal. All went smoothly for them. Today victory would be theirs.

"A line," he called in warpath language. "A line that will sweep forward and close on them. Take them from behind." He considered sending a few braves down the ridge and around to the trail to divert attention. Make the soldiers think their trap had been sprung, then hit them from behind. Victorio decided not to risk any of his brave fighters. Even sending the Chiricahua on the decoy mission, as much as this appealed to him, risked too much.

The snow hid their movement, muffled their sounds of approach. Slowly, with Lozen at his side, Victorio rode forward. Now and then the blowing wind cleared a patch and let him see the others in the attacking line. Then he forgot all about where the other Apache were. He saw two soldiers ahead, vivid in their blue uniforms against white snowbanks. As they turned their black faces toward him, he read the fear and surprise.

Both fell to his repeated rifle fire. Then he whooped and hollered and launched a full assault. Victorio fired until his rifle barrel sizzled as snow touched it and turned to steam. Then he fought with the brace of pistols he had stolen. When he had spent those rounds, he used a lance.

It broke off in the chest of a burly soldier with corporal stripes on his sleeve. Victorio whipped out his knife to continue the good fight, but no enemy was standing.

His band had won with a single sweep through the blue-coats, position.

"Take what you want!" Victorio cried. His ears rang from the repeated rifle shots. He looked up to see Nana and the handful with him come riding up.

"You fought too well," accused Nana. "No one escaped. Do we get to kill the rest?"

The words were buffeted by gusts of increasingly frigid wind. Snow pelted at Victorio's back and caught his blanket, cold fingers working to find and freeze his flesh.

He considered having his warriors replace the dead buffalo soldiers. It would not be long before the officer below attacked, uphill, into the muzzles of half a hundred rifles. But the storm!

The Mountain Gods warned him against haughtiness. Only a few of his warriors had been injured. His only death floated along the Rio Grande, with two horses lost in the crossing.

"East," Victorio decided. "We will find the other blue-coats on some other day and kill them then. Now, all I want is a place to make a fire and get warm!"

Nana, ever the warrior, shook his head at such sloth. But he rallied those around him and in minutes the entire band slipped back from the battleground. He had been the first onto the field and now was the last off. Victorio stopped when he heard sounds near the top of the trail. Through the heavy snow he saw dark figures. A silvery flash hinted at an officer starting an attack, but Victorio was not interested. His feet were cold and the storm heightened. If he dallied, a foot of snow would blow against his horse's legs.

Victorio left the field, oblivious to Captain Lester Boynton's charge. In minutes he rode alone, wrapped in an envelope of muffling snow. In an hour he joined Nana and Lozen and the others in his band around a fire set in the mouth of a cave overlooking the river, enjoying their victory and spinning tall tales.

Then they slept well that night.

Disgraced

January 9, 1880
Fort Davis

"I have no excuse, sir," Boynton said, standing rigidly at attention in front of Colonel Grierson. Grierson stared up at him, disbelief in his expression.

"Half your command killed or wounded? Captain, I've court-martialed officers for less! You let Victorio cross the river undetected and attack a portion of your command you separated deliberately from any other support. Do you have *anything* to say in your defense?"

"Sir, nothing. I have no excuse for my actions." Boynton wobbled slightly from locking his knees together like a raw recruit on his first day in the Army. Boynton kept replaying the massacre over and over in his mind. Victorio had rounded his flank and attacked from behind and he'd had no idea it was happening. He had been completely gulled by the Apache.

"You, of all officers," wondered Grierson. "You show the most promise, Captain, of any among my officers at this desolate post. I don't know what to do."

"Your duty is clear, sir."

"How the hell should you know?" snapped Grierson. "You don't have any notion of what duty is. Your actions speak eloquently of that lack." The colonel rocked back in his rickety chair, locked his ankles around the front legs, and balanced precariously. Somehow, Boynton felt his own career hung in the balance, along with the colonel tottering on his chair.

"I can save you making a decision, sir. I wanted to resign earlier. I tender my commission again."

"Damn you!" roared Grierson. "*I* have no trouble making decisions, as you do. And you serve at *my* pleasure, not yours." Grierson grumbled a few more seconds, his jaw working as if he chewed on a plug of tough tobacco. His eyes fixed Boynton like twin bayonets, stabbing through to his soul.

"I am not accepting your resignation. In spite of your obvious failings as an officer, you are still the best I have." Grierson held up his hand to cut off Boynton's protest. "You *might* learn, but how many lost lives will it take? Twice now you have committed the same error. I might say, the identical error."

"Victorio, sir," Boynton said, his mouth dry as desert sand. "I want him brought to justice."

"You want revenge. I have no problem with that, except that it blinds you to anything but one single course of action. You wrongly think you are smarter than Victorio, which has been proven untrue. If there had not been other reports in this matter, I would not have accepted your resignation, I would have stripped you of rank, broken your sword, and damn well had you in front of a firing squad!"

Boynton blinked. He had no idea what the colonel meant about another report.

"Do not take that to mean I am accepting your resignation. That would be too easy on you. You will learn, sir. I will *make* you learn, and you will become the finest damned officer I have ever had in my command. And if you don't, then I swear, as God is my witness, I will reduce you to a lump of quivering flesh no self-serving vulture will touch!"

"Yes, sir." Boynton felt weak and confused. Grierson was not cashiering him or even punishing him. Why not? "Is that all, sir?"

"No, Captain, it is not. You will pay your respects to Lieutenant Kincaid's widow and arrange for her immediate departure from her quarters. You will see that Lieutenant Morgan's family is installed in those same quarters. Let the rest of the social dust settle."

Boynton sucked in his breath. Kincaid's widow was in the same position as Ruth Magee—and both owed their widowhood to the same man. It slowly came to Boynton that Colonel Grierson knew this and had fashioned a cruel punishment to drive home his point.

"Then you shall spend more time with your troops. And you should thank your lucky stars that you have a sergeant of George Kingman's caliber in your company."

"I don't understand, sir."

"That is apparent. Although your ineptness resulted in the death of his brother, he filed a report I found to be more complete and coherent than your own. He absolved you of any guilt, a finding I do *not* share. Is that clear, Captain Boynton?"

"Sir." If possible, Boynton braced even more rigidly.

"You will continue to follow Victorio's track. You will file timely reports on your progress in bringing him to justice, and should you be in the field against him and his Warm Springs Apache band, you will either capture the lot of them or die trying. *You* will die trying, not everyone in your command. Is that clear?''

"Yes, sir.''

"Dismissed.''

Grierson's words cut like the lash of a whip. Boynton saluted, executed an about-face, and started for the door.

"One more thing,'' Grierson said. "If you filed a report detailing Private Kingman's bravery and recommending an appropriate medal, it would not be delayed crossing this desk on its way to Washington for approval. Am I clear?''

"A good idea, sir.''

"Of course it is,'' Grierson said coldly. "It's *my* idea. Come up with some on your own.''

Boynton stepped outside into the teeth of the storm intent on dropping an inch of snow an hour on Fort Davis. He found it warmer out in the blizzard than inside Grierson's office. Boynton pulled up the collar of his uniform jacket to keep out some of the wet snow trying to work its way down his neck. He considered how easy it would be to simply walk away from the post and freeze to death in this weather.

"After I do my duty,'' he said. The snowflakes fluttered into his eyes and mingled with his tears. By the time he reached the small house at the east end of the post, where Lieutenant Kincaid's widow and son lived, the tears had gone. He knocked on the door. It took only a few seconds before he heard movement inside, barely louder than the whistle of the wind outside.

"Ruth!'' he said, startled when he saw who opened the door.

"Lester, I wondered when you would come by.'' She stepped back to let him enter the narrow foyer. "I wanted to see if there was anything I could do to help. Sarah is taking it well, as well as possible under the circumstances.''

"Sarah?" The name shocked him. "You mean Mrs. Kincaid?"

"Why, yes. I thought you knew her."

Boynton started to speak, then clamped his mouth closed. He had not even known the name of his junior officer's wife. If he had, the shock would not have been so great now. Their wives shared a name, one dead and the other in grieving. And in his way, Boynton knew he was as much responsible for Sarah Kincaid's misery as he was his own wife and family's death.

"Captain Boynton, so good of you to come by." Sarah Kincaid made a fluttery gesture with her hand, a pale white bird vainly trying to escape a sticky trap.

"Serving as an officer on the frontier is not easy, ma'am," he said, hunting for the right words. He tried to remember all that had been said to him when his family had died and to use the words that had comforted him most.

A new shock hammered him. None of the words had helped. How could he possibly soothe this widow's grief now when he had no idea how to still his own?

"He was a brave man," Boynton said, choosing his words carefully, mouthing them though they burned his tongue with guilt. "He deserved a better commander. If another had been in the field, he might not be dead now."

"You are too hard on yourself, sir," said Mrs. Kincaid, sitting with her hands folded in her lap. Her eyes were down but her voice was strong. Boynton cast a sidelong look at Ruth Magee, who stood in the doorway leading into the kitchen. She watched him closely.

Boynton aimed his words as much at her as at Sarah Kincaid.

"I am not. Your husband died because of my mistakes. Please know that I will do what I can to make your situation easier, in spite of what I must say now."

"I have to move right away, don't I? Willie and I."

"Your son?"

Sarah Kincaid nodded slightly, a small strand of hair escaping to fall across her eyes. She pushed it back with an instinctive gesture. How like a beaten animal she seemed, yet there was a nobility that hinted at an iron core. Somehow, she had already come to an accommodation with the knowledge that her husband was dead, and was ready to move on.

A new shock hit Boynton when he realized, for all her frailty, she was stronger than he was.

"I have begun packing. Mrs. Magee was kind enough to offer me a portion of her quarters. Your old ones, I believe."

"That's good," Boynton said. "You'll be crowded, but it is a better solution than any I could have found."

"When this weather lifts—and the Indian threat is past—Mrs. Magee, our children, and I can travel back to Fort Concho together. It will be good having somone else along on whom to depend."

"It will. Thank you for accepting this, Mrs. Kincaid. Your husband had a bright career, and I am sorry it was ended so quickly." Boynton's mind raced. "I cannot say how this will be received, but there is the possibility of a medal for his courageous fight against Victorio."

She brightened, just for a moment. He saw pride and even dignity return. Then Sarah Kincaid lowered her head again.

"Good day," he said. "I can see myself out. If you need any help moving, please contact me directly."

He stopped in the foyer to pull on his gloves. Ruth Magee came up, drawing her shawl around her shoulders.

"Does she need you now?" Boynton asked.

"She needs to be alone for a while with her grief. Will you walk me to my quarters?"

"Of course." Boynton held out his arm. She took it, and they stepped into the fierce storm.

Heads down, struggling against the wind, they made their way to the end of the row of houses, stopping in front of the one where Boynton had meant to live with his Sarah and his boys.

"Come in, just for a moment to warm your bones," Ruth urged. Boynton hesitated. "It's all right. You are arranging for Mrs. Kincaid's residence here."

He followed her up the creaking steps, knowing there wouldn't be anyone to see him entering a widowed woman's quarters through the snowstorm. Still, he felt uneasy at risking her reputation in this fashion. Or was it more? He feared it was. He had never told her his part in her husband's death. Everything he touched died, or so it seemed. And all because of his own stupidity.

"When do you think we can travel again, for Fort Concho?" she asked without preamble.

"Not any time soon. The storm has raged for days. The road will be impassable. If it thaws, the mud might be too much for the wagon train to supply us—or take passengers back." Boynton wiped snow off his hat. "Besides, Victorio is out there. His success will make him bolder."

"He might be back over the border in Mexico," Ruth said. "Or he might be returning to New Mexico. After all, from what you've said about him, he wants to rejoin his family."

"I said that?" Boynton's eyebrows rose, sending small, cold rivers of melted snow down the sides of his head.

"Not in so many words, but why else is he raiding? It is how the Apache gains wealth, true, but it is also his way of showing his dislike for having his family on the San Carlos Reservation."

"You are right, of course," Boynton said. "I hardly think

this is any reason to believe he will leave Texas any time soon."

"He will," Ruth said with a certainty. "I would want to return to the one I loved. So will Victorio."

"He's a heathen, a savage. He doesn't act like civilized people."

"Indeed," she said in a neutral tone. Still, it echoed in Boynton's ears. He had committed still another mistake, he realized. Ruth had pointed it out to him in her gentle way.

He stepped toward her and said in a low voice, "I don't want to see you go."

"No?"

Their eyes met. He reached out and touched her cheek with his cold hand. She did not move away. Bending slightly, he started to kiss her. The sound of Caleb crashing through the back door caused Boynton to jump back guiltily.

"Hey, Ma, I got the wood you wanted. It don't fit into the box out back so I brought some of it inside. That all right?"

"Yes, dear, yes, it is all right." She stared at him, her brown eyes carrying a message Boynton failed to decipher.

"Hi, Captain Boynton," greeted Caleb, coming into the room, rubbing his hands together. "You helpin' Mrs. Kincaid and Willie move in? I can't wait for them to come on in with us. It gets kinda lonely here."

"I am," said Boynton. "And I need to draw up some papers. For medals." He touched the brim of his hat in a half salute, aware that Ruth watched him all the way out.

This time, when he stepped into the storm, the warmth he felt was one he carried with him.

Return to Warm Springs

February 23, 1880
San Mateo Mountains

"It is good being back in our own land," Victorio said. He sucked in a deep breath, then let it out in a silvery gust. The cruel wind had died down, and the day was bright and sharp. The heavy snow clouds that had followed them so doggedly from Texas had given way to the lacy, white, lizard skeleton ice clouds running swiftly across the blue sky. But it was the smell of the land that excited Victorio. He had missed this, the holy land of his people. Apacheria. Everything about it thrilled him, from the juniper and pine and piñon in the air to the crunch of dirt beneath his moccasins to the way the very land spoke to him.

It had been in these mountains he had become a man. He had scaled a nearby peak after three days of fasting, had implored the Mountain Gods for a vision, and had been granted one of surpassing power. Then and there he had seen his destiny as a leader of the Warm Springs Apache, of honor and riches and raiding, of family and contentment.

One day soon, all these *would* be his. All he needed was his family from San Carlos.

Anew, Victorio felt that power flowing through him, from the earth and rock and sky and air into his heart. How he had missed this, his homeland!

"Morrow still hunts us," Lozen said. She had returned from a scout with this important information concerning their eternal pursuer. Ranging out as far as Tularosa, she had spied on fort and trooper, on settler and their supply trains moving sluggishly along the Jornado del Muerto.

Victorio waved this off. "Morrow is a clever man, but his soldiers lack supplies. If they had little food and no horses before the snows came, what is their condition now?"

"I spied on Fort Bayard for a full day," Lozen said. "They have few horses, true, but there are more than Morrow needs for a patrol."

Victorio shrugged. He enjoyed the sensations assaulting him from all sides. He had come home. If only his family were here to share it with him. At the thought of his wife and children, one son dead, he turned somber.

"What of Loco?" he asked. "When will he join us?"

"Soon," Lozen told her brother. She moved gracefully, pulling out travel rations from her pouch and chewing on them. As she settled down to eat, she turned thoughtful. "I saw him from a distance as I came back from Fort Bayard. He rode boldly, not caring if he was seen by the buffalo soldiers on their patrols. But he rode only with other warriors. I saw none of our families."

"I feared as much. Loco did not get them away from the San Carlos." Victorio slumped, the thrill of Apacheria fading now that he had no one to share it with. Those with him, the 150 or more, were warriors. None better, but he wanted to rest. Until his family was safely settled on good land, that was not possible. He had to keep company with those who fought the White Eyes settlers.

"Wait for him to tell what he has discovered before you make rash guesses," suggested Lozen. "I have learned patience and its place in our world."

"You are right. To jump this way and that turns us all into rabbits, frightened and always seeking safe burrows." Victorio tried to settle this advice into his own world. The past weeks had been ones of rapid travel, swift raids, sharp attacks, and then quick retreat. All the way from the battle-ground along the Rio Grande he had used those tactics, deciding then to return to Warm Springs to await Loco—and their families from San Carlos Reservation.

But it was so difficult to be patient when such important news came so slowly. Had Loco been successful? Victorio knew, given the chance, Loco would dicker with the blue-coat general. What would General Pope offer in exchange for peace? What would his field commander, Colonel Hatch, suggest? From all Victorio had discerned as he dodged the soldiers sent out from the New Mexico forts, Hatch might be convinced to let the Mimbreño live on their own land, if only to avoid the further embarrassment of having his troops defeated over and over.

"Wait," Lozen cautioned again. Victorio smiled ruefully. He had let his hopes run away with him again, even as he had vowed not to allow it.

"Thank you, Sister. Without your wisdom and strong arm we all would have perished long ago."

She bowed her head, then went back to chewing on the dried beef. A scoop of snow held for a moment melted to water. She lapped at it, then, her hunger and thirst sated, turned to honing her knife to pass the time until Loco arrived.

Victorio had finished cleaning his weapons, repairing his moccasins yet again, and had started on currying his horses when Loco rode slowly into the camp. Loco rode hunched over, as if the weight of the mountains crushed him. Victorio's earlier hope faded at the sight.

"Your travels have not been happy," Victorio said.

Loco dismounted. Behind him a dozen warriors jumped to the ground, going to renew friendships with others in Victorio's camp. Before long, they would be gambling, telling tall tales, whispering of all that they would do when they found their wives again.

"The soldiers from Fort Apache patrol endlessly. Even an Apache woman could not cross the fierce desert along the Gila and return to Warm Springs without being caught. We tried to fight our way through and failed. They used their cannon on us when we hid, their cavalry when we rode, and their foot soldiers to guard all the mountain passes through the Mogollóns. San Carlos is a prison as much as any with bars."

"So?" urged Victorio. He knew Loco would never be content with a few failed forays. Loco had done more.

"I sent a message to Colonel Hatch, suggesting peace if the White Eyes allowed us to settle again at Warm Springs."

"He did not agree?"

"He did, but his general did not. Pope is as bad as Carleton. Death to any who does not willingly rot and die of diseases on their filthy reservations."

"We have no choice," Victorio said after a short silence as he considered what Loco had said. "We number more than one hundred fifty warriors now. We are Mimbreño and Mescalero and other clans. A dozen or more Chiricahua ride with us rather than with Geronimo down in Mexico. What fort fields enough soldiers, even their buffalo soldiers, to stop us?"

"They lack supplies in New Mexico," Loco said. "Not so in Arizona."

"Or in Texas," Victorio said thoughtfully. He enjoyed raiding there, but it was not home. Ojo Caliente called to him, the bond between soul and land too much to deny. "We will go to Warm Springs and drive the settlers off our land."

"Our land!" cried Loco. The cry was picked up by others and soon a hundred and a half voices rose to challenge the orders from General John Pope.

"We are being watched," Lozen said. "The hairs on my neck rise."

Victorio looked around. The land around Percha Creek was serene, untrammeled patches of snow showing they were the first to pass since the last storm. From the icy crust, that storm had been days earlier. Even the scouts he sent ranging to his flanks and ahead reported nothing. But his sister insisted someone spied on them.

He believed her above even his own sense of serenity and safety traveling this land so close to Warm Springs.

"Would you pray to Ussen and use your Power?" he asked. He was loath to camp for the night, in spite of the land's beauty. A sense of urgency again had seized him. If they did not wrest their families from the control of the Indian Agents and the Indah generals soon, they might forever be imprisoned.

But for all this need to free his people, Victorio had no sense of danger now.

"No need," Lozen said. "Ahead and to your right. Look carefully."

For five minutes Victorio rode and stared at the spot where his sister directed. Only after a considerable amount of patience had been spent did he realize the leaves on a low evergreen moved with no wind blowing. Someone watched from this green bower.

"Apache," Victorio decided. No Indah, no buffalo soldier, could match the stealth of a good Apache scout.

"One of Gatewood's?" asked Loco.

"Possibly," he said. "That means Major Morrow is not far away. How can we surprise him?"

"He thinks to trap us somewhere ahead," Lozen said. "This scout watches and waits for us to pass. Can Morrow have soldiers coming up behind us?"

As she spoke, she turned slightly on her mount. Lozen quickly stopped this betraying action. Give away their detection of the scout's hiding place or a possible ambush and they might give up the chance to survive. Morrow was clever and a hard fighter.

"Percha Creek flows to our right," Victorio said. "Morrow will be unable to cross it without slowing his soldiers. We put it to our backs, then sweep forward in a line and kill any hiding along our left. We can be out of his valley before Morrow can forge a decent attack, if his main body is on the other side of the creek."

"If it is not?" asked Loco. "We will have his main force behind us, and we will be forced toward Mescalero, away from Warm Springs."

"If we meet his main force in our attack, Warm Springs is ours again," Victorio said. "Who else is there to deny it to us? Fort MacRae? Fort Cummings? They are hollow shells."

"If we run to Mescalero, they can stop us with soldiers from Fort Stanton," said Lozen.

"True. And if they do, we curl back and sample the hospitality in Texas again. I want to clear our land at Warm Springs of the settlers, but if the Army puts as many troops against us as you suggest they might, we are better off raiding more, gaining strength, and getting more recruits.''

"Juh and Geronimo might join us. We would have twice the warriors, if they did,'' said Lozen.

"Lozen, have a few watch our back, along the Percha. Loco, find Nana and tell him what we plan. I will take care of the scout and see if there are more lurking in the woods.''

Victorio rode along, aware of more movement in the evergreens where the scout worried about watching or returning to Morrow with the change in Victorio's force. As the Warm Springs chief came even with the clump of low-growing ferns and scrubby oak, he whipped up his rifle and fired six times into the center of the vegetation. No sound other than a body falling came to him.

Riding over, Victorio picked his way carefully through the tangles until he stared down at the dead scout. Victorio spat. The scout was Mimbreño, doubly a traitor.

The gunshots alerted others to launch the attack. Victorio heard Loco and Nana and Lozen whipping the warriors into a fighting frenzy. He jerked hard on the reins and galloped off to join them. He burst into a clearing, caught sight of Percha Creek, and had to smile. Morrow was caught on the far side. Then the smile faded.

Lozen had been right. They could escape this day if they raced to Mescalero, but not if they kept on to Warm Springs. He lifted his rifle and fired expertly, bringing a buffalo soldier out of his saddle as the man tried to get his horse across the creek with its slippery rocks. Other soldiers appeared from the woods beyond. Victorio kept firing, reloading several times, then realized he had to leave. He had killed four and could have killed forty.

Morrow would not win this day. Neither would Victorio. But from Mescalero, he could plot and plan a new return to Warm Springs. Victorio and his entire band would fight again another day. This time they would be victorious, because his raiding would draw soldiers from the forts and allow those at San Carlos to escape into Mexico.

His wife and children!

He trotted off, his hot barrel burning against the crook of his left arm. Victorio did not notice. Already he planned for Warm Springs and his family.

Gathering Forces

April 1, 1880
Outside Mescalero

"Bivouac the men," Lester Boynton ordered. Sergeant Kingman turned and bellowed the commands. Boynton rode around the clearing, seeing how the other companies stationed their sentries, where they placed their campfires, and how they related to their noncoms and enlisted men. Keyes and Lebo had transferred in from Fort Sill and, although they were both captains, Boynton was still senior company commander at Fort Davis. That did not fill him with any satisfaction. He was seldom out of Colonel Grierson's sight since they had left Fort Davis a week earlier.

He dismounted and passed the reins over to a private. "Be sure to brush her down well," he said. Then Boynton stopped. "Washburn?"

"Sir?" The private turned his dark face in Boynton's direction, eyes wider than normal at the use of his name.

Until this campaign, Boynton had made no effort to learn
any of his men's names. They had all been interchangeable
to him, parts from one carbine fitting into another, some
with rough edges or slightly out of alignment, but no different.

Somehow, since recommending both Kincaid and
Charles Kingman for citations, he had watched how his
men worked more closely. And Ruth often asked how indi-
viduals were doing in his company. She knew the soldiers
better than he did—or so it had seemed.

A small smile crept to his lips. Ruth and Caleb were still
at Fort Davis, though not for any good reason. Caleb had
taken ill, running a high fever. Until he recovered it would
be dangerous for them to travel. From Fort Davis to Fort
Concho was relatively safe now, with only an occasional
Indian attack on the supply wagons. But the post doctor
said the boy's condition was delicate and required around-
the-clock care. Some nights Boynton had stayed up, watching the feverish, tossing and turning boy as he slept. Other
nights he and Ruth had stayed by the boy's bedside, talking
about this and that. Nothing important.

On those occasions he had stayed overnight, Sarah Kincaid had been present also, but she and Willie had gone
back east two weeks ago. She wanted to meet her brother
in Dallas and from there would return to Ohio and the
rest of her family. The widow's departure had placed more
of a burden on Ruth in caring for Caleb—and it had again
raised indignant comments about her taking up an entire
house. With new officers transferring in, those quarters
were needed by those on active duty.

"See to your own horse first," Boynton told the private.
The private saluted, Boynton returned it and went off in
search of Kingman. He found his sergeant supervising the
digging of trench latrines downhill from the rows of tents
being pitched.

"I am going to report to the colonel," Boynton said. "Is all in good order?"

"Yes, sir. And thank you for putting Trent in my squad."

"How's the boy doing?"

"Better. He flops like a fish out of water, goin' from insolent to scared spitless, but he's gonna work out just fine."

Boynton nodded curtly. The fourteen-year-old had lied to get into the Army. While this was not unusual, the boy had not fit in well and had tried to get out of his enlistment. Kingman had convinced Boynton that Trent had nothing to return to, his parents dead and others in his family unable or unwilling to take him in. If the boy was released from duty dishonorably, Kingman feared he would drift until he fell in with the wrong kind. Outlaws roved throughout West Texas; the cavalry chased them down with even more determination than they fought the Indians. If Boynton had reported Trent's age to Colonel Grierson, the officer would have had no choice. As it was, Boynton bore the brunt of the problem.

"Watch him. I think there's something big brewing," Boynton said. He walked toward Grierson's tent, eager to find out what had happened. They had ridden for three days, pushing men and horses to the limit to arrive outside the Mescalero Reservation. From all he could tell from the amount of shiny braid flashing in the sun all around, at least three battalions in addition to the three companies Grierson commanded had converged here.

"Glad you made it, Captain. Colonel Hatch, this is Lester Boynton, my expert on Victorio and his movement in West Texas."

"We can use all the experts we can get, Captain," said Hatch. The man fiddled with his bushy mustache, then turned. A table held a large map of the area. Hatch looked around at the others gathered there. Boynton did not know the man, but thought the major across the table might be Albert Morrow, the officer who had repeatedly engaged Victorio and lost every skirmish.

Boynton understood how Morrow must feel.

"I went to the Bureau of Indian Affairs with a request to resettle the Warm Springs Apache at their hereditary land. The request was flatly denied. Further, I have been ordered to capture Victorio, Nana, Loco, and all the others riding with the Mimbreño band and return them to San Carlos Reservation. That and that alone is the only acceptable outcome for this campaign."

Boynton wanted to ask questions, but since Hatch did not pause, he held his tongue. He saw how Morrow wanted to ask questions also. Most of the Ninth and Tenth Cavalry had to be in the field, gathered at this one site. Even if Victorio attacked with his band of over 200, he would be defeated by force of numbers. Boynton had to wonder if Victorio even knew of this gathering storm around his head. Possibly. If so, he would head due south into Mexico to camp with Juh and Geronimo until fairer weather came to New Mexico Territory.

"We have reason to believe Victorio has been given sanctuary on the Mescalero Reservation. I have three battalions of the Ninth arrayed here, here, and here. We can sweep in and block off any possible escape north, west, or south. Colonel Grierson, your companies will rove the eastern area to engage and capture Victorio should he attempt to retreat in that direction."

"When will the trap be sprung, sir?" asked Major Morrow. "Victorio always seems to know of our movement, no matter how good our scouting."

"His sister," muttered the lieutenant at Morrow's elbow.

"How's that, Lieutenant Gatewood?" asked Hatch. "What of Victorio's sister?"

"She's a warrior, sir. Better than 'bout any of them in

his band, and that might include Victorio and Nana and all the other chiefs.''

Hatch snorted. "Women cannot fight. This is a rumor intended to scare us into believing they are invincible. I have seen their women on the San Carlos. While not docile, they are not fierce warriors.''

"Lozen is. And she has Power. Enemies-against Power. She can find our soldiers whenever she prays to her god.''

"Poppycock," snorted Hatch. "You have spent too much time among them, sir. I will not countenance such gossip being passed around as truth!''

"My scouts are as good as any Victorio has," Gatewood said, standing stiffly now. "They've saved my life more'n once. And if they say Lozen has Power, I have to believe it. It certainly explains how Victorio gets out of our traps the way he does.''

"There are other explanations," Hatch said darkly, glaring at Gatewood and then at Morrow. Boynton felt a flush rising to his own face. Hatch had virtually accused Morrow of incompetence. If he knew of Boynton's double dereliction of duty, he did not turn his gaze from the officers of the Ninth.

"We will begin our troop movement in three days," Hatch went on, pointing to the eastern portion of the map. "That, Colonel, ought to provide time to position your command in this area." He tapped the map over the Guadalupe Mountains.

"Think he might swing that far south, Colonel Hatch?" asked Grierson. "Or might he plunge right on east into the Llano Estacado?''

"He knows this country, not there. Victorio is a creature of habit, I am sure you will agree. Is that not true, Captain Boynton?''

"He prefers territory he knows and where he has allies.

There wouldn't be either known country or friends straight east from Mescalero, sir.''

"I agree. So, Colonel Grierson, guard against Victorio sneaking back down toward Fort Davis.''

"That's damn near fifteen hundred miles of territory. A powerful lot of empty to patrol with only three companies. We're scattered out across most of it, running down raiders from the Mescalero reservation. Captain Viele's C Company has logged more than two thousand miles of chasing them down in past months and is still in the field.''

"I do not expect Victorio to get that far. Your Tenth provides only a line should we fail—and we will not. Now.'' Hatch rubbed his hands together as he stared at his battle map. "One battalion will be under Morrow's command, another under Captain Hooker, and the third under Captain Carroll. We have reason to believe Victorio is in Hembrillo Canyon in the San Andres Mountains, about here.'' His finger stabbed down. Hatch looked around the table.

"Morrow will command Companies H, L, and M with a detachment from the Fifteenth Infantry and their San Carlos Indian scouts. You, Major, will join forces with McClelland, Lieutenant Gatewood, and Captain Mills from the Sixth Cavalry and go to the western slope of the San Andres. Carroll, you will take Companies A, D, F, and G westward from Fort Stanton and attack from the east. Hooker and buffalo soldiers from E, I, and K, along with a few Navajo scouts, will sweep down from the north.''

"So we guard against the chance of Victorio moving south before you attack?'' asked Grierson.

"Exactly. This campaign will be executed by the Ninth, with your help, of course.''

"If we attacked northward, we could be certain of catching Victorio. He would be trapped and—''

"Major Morrow will lead the assault on Victorio's position and capture the renegade. Sunrise, three days from this date. Gentlemen, the next time we gather I intend to make the arrangements for Victorio's return to San Carlos." Colonel Hatch started to say something more, then nodded briskly to show the meeting was at an end.

Grierson and Boynton left, the bright sun making them squint.

"Seems we don't have much to do, Captain," said the colonel.

"Major Morrow has a lot to prove," Boynton said. "I think he is a good officer—but Victorio is better."

"You put any store in what Gatewood said about Victorio's sister having some mystic ability to warn of our troopers?"

"I think Victorio's eyes are all human, all posted high on hills, in the mountains he uses so well to cover his movements, in the very places only an Apache could find. There's nothing supernatural about it."

"Comforting thought, coming from you. See to your troops, Captain."

Colonel Grierson strode off, leaving Boynton alone in the middle of the bustle of an encampment being moved hither and yon. Carroll and those officers having to reach Fort Stanton before getting their troops into the field had already ridden out at a dead gallop. Morrow, Gatewood, and those who would drive deep into Hembrillo Canyon stood in a tight knot, arguing. Boynton went to them, hanging back just a moment until Major Morrow noticed him.

"Captain? What is it? We are busy."

"I wanted to wish you luck. If I wasn't with my own company, I'd be tempted to sneak off and join your soldiers in the attack."

"You and I share a run of bad luck, don't we?" Morrow said, his eyes narrowing. "This time will be different. This time Victorio will be captured and brought to justice."

"Yes, sir!" Boynton said, giving a snappy salute.

He walked away, feeling curiously adrift. Colonel Hatch had planned the largest campaign against the Apache since the days of Kit Carson and General Carleton—but Boynton had a nagging doubt about Hatch's success. Victorio was simply too wily.

Or was it he merely hoped Victorio would escape so his own dereliction of duty—twice—would not seem so terrible?

Victory!

April 8, 1880
Hembrillo Canyon

Victorio sat with his scouts at the fire. It crackled and sizzled, too green for easy burning. He had been in a hurry to camp when night fell, so they could avoid the snakes that slithered across the rocky paths. In the distance he heard Lozen's chants as she invoked Ussen to aid her, to give her Power.

> All over this earth
> Where we live
> Ussen has supreme Power.
> Let this Power be mine
> To locate the Enemy!
> I search for our Enemy
> And only Ussen the Great
> Can reveal him to me!

"We do not need her Power," one scout said, ripping at the haunch of a rabbit that had roasted over the fire. He wiped grease from his chin as he ate hungrily. "We see the bluecoats everywhere. They swarm like bees!"

"It is true," said another. "From the north and the east they come."

"And in the west," said Nana, settling down. "With my own eyes I have seen Major Morrow's troops. Hundreds now rally to his flag."

"So many? From Fort Bayard?" asked Victorio.

"From there, from San Carlos, from other forts, what does it matter? He is not a threat, however. He reached a spot south of the Tularosa Basin and found no water."

"No water!" exclaimed Loco. "How is that? Even a White Eyes can find water there. With him are our brethren from San Carlos!"

"Traitors, all traitors," said Victorio. He spat into the fire. The brief sizzle died and a thin curl of smoke rose. He watched it twist skyward, trying to find an omen in that smoke. Better to wait for Lozen and her appraisal of the situation. In the family she held more Power than any other. He was only a warrior and nothing more. Only a warrior, but one who grew increasingly uneasy about remaining in Hembrillo Canyon much longer.

"Morrow reached a water pump and could not draw water. The handle was broken!" The scout laughed. "He still works to get water from that well. He is no threat to us."

"We cannot run west," Victorio pointed out, "without colliding with Morrow's forces. What of this Carroll?"

"His men are blundering into the canyon," said Nana. "Most are sick from drinking alkali water, and they are puking out their guts. Their horses are bloated and unable to make more than a few miles a day. We can get much ammunition and rifles from them."

"If Colonel Hatch sends so many against us, he is sure to have other routes guarded," said Victorio. "What of the southern mountains?"

"We do not know about the Guadalupes," admitted Nana. "For this only Lozen can tell, unless you want to send a scouting party in that direction."

Victorio shook his head, thinking hard. "They believe we are trapped here. Morrow was to attack us, but he is unable. The Tularosa malpais slows him. This Carroll was supposed to reinforce, but has blundered onto our camp." Victorio smiled slowly. "You are right. We must attack, then retreat to the south."

"Retreat!" cried Loco. "We can kill them all! If we defeat them now, they *have* to let us return to Warm Springs!"

"You have learned nothing of their ways," Victorio chided. "Push at the water in a stream. Your hand becomes wet, but it does little to change the flow of the river. What has been done? No, we must wait for a drought. Only then can we make demands of the Indah."

"Drought?" asked Nana. "You think they will stop giving supplies to their own soldiers?"

"If they must continually send horses and cattle and rifles and recruits, even the Great Nantan must wonder eventually about the wisdom of his actions. Bleed them. Make every fight so costly they have no choice. But to smash headlong into them? We would be crushed."

"They outnumber us ten to one, all their forces taken together. But they are scattered," said Nana. The old man took a deep breath, then let it out slowly, the spirit of the air giving him strength. "You are right. To the south they have never been able to hinder us. We raid at will."

"And we will do it again. After our victory!" Victorio shot to his feet and let out a ululating war cry that echoed the length of Hembrillo Canyon. If Captain Carroll had heard it, he would have been shaken to his very soul.

* * *

"Ahead," said Lozen, eyes closed and hands out-stretched. Victorio saw no redness in her palms, but the way she pointed like an arrow told him her Power had given her the precise location of Captain Carroll's soldiers. "Many of them."

"Good," said Victorio. "We will gain great honor this day." He checked both his rifles and the two pistols he had taken from dead cavalry officers, then settled the jacket on his broad shoulders. Twitching slightly, he felt the seams beginning to part. The soldier he had taken this from, a sergeant, had been smaller. It hardly mattered, for this day he would have his choice of dozens more of their fine woolen uniforms. All he'd need to do was to patch a hole here and there and try to remove some of the blood.

On horseback they rode silently forward into the heart of Hembrillo Canyon. The sounds of soldiers ahead told Victorio Carroll had camped for the night. Apache did not attack at night. Usually. This time Victorio made an exception, his desire for glory greater than his fear of snakes and spirits and other things that crept through the night hunting for the unwary.

He chirped like a swallow and heard an answering owl hoot, telling him Nana and Loco were both in position on the far side of the buffalo soldiers' camp. Glancing at his sister, he saw she was prepared for battle. Lozen preferred to use a knife to a pistol, but her rifle, while well tended, had the worn look of long use. She had taken it from a black soldier over a year ago and had not sought new rifles, content with this one's accuracy and reliability. She held it up and shook it, signaling her complete readiness.

Victorio dismounted. Behind him in the gathering twi-light other Apache joined him on the ground. Moving like the chilly twilight breeze, they came to the perimeter of

Carroll's encampment. It took Victorio less than a minute to locate the patrols. They had been cleverly positioned with lackadaisical sentries. He heard one retching his guts out, only to return to his post.

"Sick," whispered Victorio. "They will fight well, but only for a few minutes. Then their strength will abandon them."

With those words to Lozen, he moved forward. A guard only a few feet in front of him spun and tried to bark out a warning. Victorio's rifle butt smashed the man in the face. Lozen whispered past, her knife quickly ending the guard's life. Together Victorio and his sister moved on, killing two more lookouts. Before they could find another, they were spotted and the warning cry went up, "Apache! They're attacking us from all over! To your rifles!"

Like a flood came the Warm Springs Apache into the camp. To the feckless soldiers it must have seemed they rose from the very earth as they attacked. One instant there was only silence, the next the air was filled with war cries and rifle reports and the hiss of arrows fired from only yards away. Victorio was not sure how many troopers died in the onslaught, but the attack, against a camp debilitated by drinking bad water, was not a complete success.

"To the battlements, get those rifles firing, damn you all!" came Captain Carroll s sharp commands. Somehow, he whipped his soldiers into a semblance of a defensive position. And then the mountain howitzer fired point-blank into Victorio's braves. The explosion of the fire-belching cannon shook their nerve more than it ripped their flesh.

Victorio saw some warriors retreating from the fray. He yelled at those cowards, then realized it did no good. He pressed his attack, but the tide of battle had turned. He had lost his element of surprise, and the buffalo soldiers were now hardened in resolve and fired with military precision.

"Keep attacking!" Victorio yelled. "They are sick. They cannot keep up the fight if we press them!"

Only a few heeded his orders. The cannon fired again and again, one blast launching pieces of chain instead of a cannonball. The links cut through Blue Pony like a sharp knife through fat. The young warrior died, never knowing his fate.

Victorio yielded to necessity. He retreated, hoping to reform his warriors and attack again.

"You let them run you off! We have them! We can kill them all!" he shouted at his braves. "To the attack! Again!"

He rallied enough to force Carroll to abandon part of his camp, but the officer proved more versatile than Victorio would have thought. Captain Carroll drew his men into a tight defensive circle, their mountain howitzers aimed outward like a porcupine's quills. Try as he might, Victorio was unable to break through the circle and reach the heart. If he had, he would have ripped it out and squeezed it in his own hand until all the soldiers had died.

Thrown back, Victorio tried for another attack. This time he could not marshal his forces. Many had been killed in what he had thought would be an easy fight. Worse, Lozen came to him. Blood ran down her face from a cut on her cheek. She took no notice of the freely flowing wound.

"They come for us," she said, pointing back up Hembrillo Canyon. "Enough to reinforce Carroll."

"How many?"

"Enough," she said. "I sent Long Tooth and Always Ready out to watch the trail. They say Apache scouts led by Parker are on the way."

Victorio hesitated, considering what to do next. Lieutenant Gatewood and his Coyotero were an old affront. But those under Chief of Scouts Captain Henry Parker were worse. They had spent much of their time chasing after Geronimo. They were in large part the reason Geronimo remained in Mexico with Juh rather than riding the Chiricahua land freely.

"We can reach Carroll and his men from above," Nana said, out of breath from his swift ride around the enemy line. "A half dozen warriors can work into the rocks above him and push boulders down. We can drive him out onto our war lances!"

"Too long," Victorio said. "We must win now or retreat."

"We will need an hour or longer. The darkness works against us. The snakes come out," Nana said.

"Parker," cautioned Lozen.

"We retreat. How many have we lost? I saw Blue Pony die."

"A half dozen, no more. We have killed twenty of them! And all their horses are stolen!"

"Leave the horses," Victorio said. "They are sick and will slow us. Down the canyon" He paused, staring at the pit of gloom where Captain Carroll cowered. Victorio smiled. Major Morrow could not have done better in protecting his troops. Then he sighed. It was time to ride. And ride they did until sunup when Parker's scouts caught them.

"They fight like devils," cried Loco. "How can they kill their own clansmen?"

"Traitors bought by the White Eyes," Victorio said. But he thought of how all the scouts fighting for Parker had enough to eat, had a family to tend, and a permanent home. Were they forced to huddle along the Gila at San Carlos? He doubted it. They might have been given land at Ojo Caliente, the very land Victorio fought to restore to his people.

"We cannot fight much longer, Brother," warned Lozen. "The Power given me by Ussen tells of more soldiers coming into the canyon. Possibly Morrow has moved from the Tularosa. Even if Carroll cannot fight well, his soldiers provide reinforcement we cannot overcome."

"Morrow, Parker, this Carroll," said Victorio, exasperated. He had known Colonel Hatch planned a full campaign against the Mimbreño, but had not realized its extent until this moment. If they had made quick work of a sickened command under Captain Carroll they would have won the day.

Now, failing to remove Carroll completely from the field, it was the Warm Springs Apache who was threatened with removal—from this world to the Happy Place, if they were lucky. And to San Carlos Reservation, if they were captured.

"Ah, Mangas, what would you do?" wondered Victorio. His old friend had always known when to fight and when to negotiate. Until his final mistake. The thought of Mangas Coloradas being tortured and killed, his head boiled and carried off, put the fire back into Victorio's breast.

"The canyon branches here," he said. "Going due south is yonder path."

"It leads into Texas," said Nana.

"Take half the warriors and ride that path. If possible, we will rejoin forces at Sabinal in a month."

"What are you going to do?" asked Nana. "Parker might choose to send all his troops after one or the other of us if we divide. If he does, the ones not pursued can double back, and we can catch him between our two bands of warriors. Otherwise, we weaken our forces."

"We dare not let him slow us. To attack his scouts now means Morrow will catch up, bringing the others in at their own pace. Carroll's fighters, those we scouted to the east, all will come to us like vultures seeing a fallen cow.''

"So we run and run and run?" Nana's obvious contempt for this struck a responsive chord with others gathered. They were Apache and fought. They did not run like rabbits at the mere threat of danger.

"We fight and run, staying just beyond their grasp. Dividing here forces them to make decisions which will weaken their attack."

"Where do you go? The Guadalupe Mountains?" asked Nana.

"Sanctuary there is possible," Victorio said confidently. "I know the area well. If we escape the buffalo soldiers of the Ninth, we can laugh at those in the Tenth as we have done so many times before."

Lozen frowned. Loco started to speak, then clamped his mouth shut. Even Nana refused to say anything.

"Let us go! Nana, straight south with your band. The rest will come with me." His orders were interrupted by sharp rifle fire. Loco slumped, then moaned, clutching his arm. Blood spurted from the wound inflicted by a sharpshooter.

Victorio leaped onto horseback and wheeled around, trying to find where the attack centered. He had a hint of what Carroll and his sentries must have felt when their camp was attacked the night before. It seemed as if the ground gave up its dead, who fought like the living. Here, there, everywhere came the relentless Apache under Captain Parker, their rifles barking like tubercular dogs.

"This way, this way!" cried Victorio, only to find Parker had cut off retreat toward the Palomas River. A dozen Apache fought their brethren, firing methodically. All around him dropped braves.

Lozen rallied the stunned band. Her throat must have opened to give vent to such a hideous shriek. She charged straight at the Apache blocking their path. Her rifle smoked from muzzle and barrel as it overheated. As she rode past one warrior, she swung the rifle so it grazed his cheek. The heated barrel left a nasty burn, quickly opened to a bloody gash by the front sight. And then she was past.

Victorio joined her in the attack. He fired and fired and threw away one rifle, using his second until its magazine, too, came up empty. But by this time, he and a half dozen from his Warm Springs band were out of the trap.

"How many?" he gasped as stragglers rode past, bloodied and tired and scared. "How many did Parker kill?"

"Nana got away without losing anyone," Loco said, his arm flopping bonelessly at his side. "But the rest?" He shook his head in sorrow.

Victorio tried to count, hoping many who had not found him were with Nana. If they were not, then Captain Parker and his traitorous Warm Springs Apache had killed thirty.

"Ride," Victorio ordered. "Ride hard!"

"Parker goes after Nana, not us," Lozen said, panting harshly. Her eyes saw what others did not; she did not have to use her Power to know what she told him.

"Ride!" Victorio repeated, his anger knowing no bounds. He had been cheated of triumph this day. Hatch had succeeded in driving the Mimbreño from New Mexico—for a while. After he rested, after he rejoined Nana in Texas, Victorio vowed, he would return. This time he would not leave until he regained all his band's land!

No Place to Hide

"Well, Sergeant? Are the men up to it?" asked Boynton. He studied Kingman carefully for any sign the man was going to skirt the truth. Boynton was getting better at ferreting out the man's true feelings. Sergeant Kingman had never—quite—forgiven Boynton for the death of his brother, but Boynton worked hard at making sure such tragedy never happened again to anyone in his command. That did not mean he would not push his troopers to the limit in pursuit of their mission. They had ridden over a thousand miles since getting their assignment from Colonel Hatch, and every soldier and every horse approached the point of exhaustion. Grierson had dispatched Boynton's company to patrol the Sacramento Mountains while going farther east with his own command. Word had trickled through to all three companies from Fort Davis about

Captain Parker's triumph over Victorio when the Apache least expected it. But with every victory came a small defeat.

Victorio had split his forces, and Parker had chosen to pursue the Apache plunging straight into the heart of West Texas. That was Nana's band, and Parker had allowed Victorio to escape without engaging him. Still, Parker kept after Nana and would run the old chief to ground some day soon. That left Victorio to raid and pillage at will, even as it reduced the Apache war chief's forces.

Twice Boynton had found Victorio's trail and twice the Apache had eluded him. But he felt they were close once more. The Guadalupe Mountains were the sort of place Victorio would call his own. Boynton felt it in his bones.

"Gettin' so the men sway in the saddle as they ride, sir," said Kingman in his slow drawl born as much from fatigue as habit now. "But they're all soldiers of the Tenth and proud of it. They know how important this campaign is."

"Not only to me personally," Boynton said honestly. He wondered if Kingman considered Victorio to be in the least responsible for his brother's death or did he place that entirely at Boynton's feet? "Would it help if I repeated Colonel Hatch's orders to them? Or got Colonel Grierson to tell them how they need to keep on patrol?"

"Not much in the way of supplies, but the men know this. We've been hunting a mite as we travel. Spring is a good time for these mountains. But the horses?" Kingman took off his garrison cap and scratched his head. Boynton noticed how completely gray Kingman had turned in the last month. He wondered if his own crudely self-sheared hair was similarly turning gray from worry.

"Grama is growing faster now that spring is here," Boynton said, but the horses never had the time to get their fill. That would take several days of grazing, and they did not have the luxury of such relaxation. The mountain range stretched too far with its winding canyons and tall peaks to easily patrol.

"Sir, you point the way and the men'll be there behind you," said Kingman.

"Thank you," Boynton said, meaning it. He went off to his tent, ducking as he went in. His map was pinned to the ground by four rocks. He studied the tiny Xs, the places where Victorio had been sighted or Boynton had encountered Victorio's trail. They might as well have been put on the map with a shotgun until Boynton stood, bent over under the low tent, and circled the map.

"He's heading for this canyon," Boynton said in a low whisper. Over and over he worked through Victorio's trail and it always showed the Apache chief making his way to a single canyon that curled around and came out on the prairie north of Rattlesnake Springs. The mountains would shield the fleeing renegade and yet give him freedom of movement in the direction he wanted.

"Sergeant!" bellowed Boynton. "Strike camp. Mount the men. We are going to ride like the demons from hell are nipping at our heels. Then we're going to fight." Boynton smiled when he saw the perfect location to spring the trap and catch Victorio.

"Captain, you sure this is gonna work?" asked Sergeant Kingman. He rubbed against a rock, scratching a hidden itch on his back. He kept his carbine in the crook of his arm, but the muzzle rose and fell as he moved like a cat.

"I've memorized every movement we know Victorio has made," Boynton said, no hint of doubt in him. "He will come this way. He wants to press on south, and there's no other direct way of getting down to Rattlesnake Springs."

"Why'd he want to go there? It's not far from Fort Quitman. Even if he knows most of the troops are out on patrol from Fort Davis, there'd still be a company left to guard it. Victorio would be ridin' right on into the mouth of a pair of military posts."

"He holds us in contempt," Boynton said, a hint of anger coming into his voice, but it was anger directed at himself. He had killed Ruth's husband as surely as if he had pulled the trigger himself. And Kingman's brother had died for no reason other than hubris. Kincaid might have fought harder or positioned sentries better, but he had been under Boynton's command, and the vision a commander needed had been lacking. Boynton had thought he knew Victorio's mind.

This time was different. It was. It had to be.

Boynton rose from his position and cautiously studied the tight knots of buffalo soldiers posted all over the sides of this canyon. He had again split his force, but this time one half could give covering fire to the other half. With luck, they would fire down onto the canyon floor rather than across and at their comrades. He smiled. These were all combat veterans now, including young Trent, hunkered down on Kingman's other side. The skirmishes had not been real fights, but every man in his company had tasted fire, had bullets aimed at him, known fear, and learned to deal with it.

He ducked back, settling down with his own rifle, leaning against a boulder. The hot sun baked his face. Boynton pulled down the brim of his cap to shield his eyes and unbuttoned the front of his jacket. He would rather be cool and more comfortable than adhere to strict uniform regs.

"He really comin', sir?" asked Trent. "Victorio, I mean?"

"He will. The hard part is waiting. But he will come."

Before Trent could say another word, Boynton waved him to silence. Kingman had already flashed a signal to the soldiers on the far side of the narrow canyon. Their lone scout waiting at the northern end of the canyon used a signal mirror to alert them.

"Riders," Kingman whispered. He waited another minute, watching the bright flickers of Morse code and carefully deciphering them. Boynton knew the message before Kingman passed it along to the others. His hand tightened on the rifle stock until tendons stood out on his forearm. The officer had to force himself to relax.

Sarah. Peter. Thomas. Revenge for their deaths was near.

Amos Magee. Charles Kingman. He would take revenge for them and the others who had died alongside them also. Victorio was on his way.

Boynton's heart hammered as hard as if he had run a mile up the side of the mountain. He swung his rifle around and placed it in a notch in the rock. He had told his men to establish a small angle for fire and not shoot until the order was given. Then they were to shoot at anything moving in the cone of sight until nothing more crossed their line of fire.

"Stay calm," Boynton said, not sure if he spoke to Kingman or to himself.

"Sir, what if they get away?" asked Trent.

"Shoot straight, and they won't have a chance," Boynton told the young man. Then his mind went utterly blank. A cautious Apache warrior rode into the narrow field of vision in front of him. Boynton struggled to keep from firing wildly. To have done so would have warned Victorio of the trap.

Another rider, another, and then a half dozen. Boynton counted until he got to fifty, then could restrain himself no longer. He fired even as he shouted, "Give it to 'em, men!"

Boynton jerked on the trigger and his shot went wide, striking another Apache's horse. From a quiet afternoon erupted a cacophony of frightened horses, dying horses, angry braves, Boynton's own noncoms shouting to their soldiers. And the rifle fire! It deafened him to the agony of men and animals below.

"We got 'em smack dead this time, Captain!" cried Sergeant Kingman. The burly man rose to his feet to get a better aim at the Indians. He fired easily, accurately.

"Sergeant, get down! Don't let them blow off your head!"

"I kin see jist fine, Cap'n," Kingman said, his accent thicker than ever now. He fired until his magazine emptied, then he dropped down to reload. "Reckon I killed two," the sergeant said as he fumbled for more rounds.

"I shot a pair of the bastards too!" chimed in Trent.

Boynton wasn't sure of his own marksmanship. He had probably shot more horses out from under them than he had the Apache riders. But he had sprung the trap well, and Victorio was caught in the cross fire.

Rising to duplicate Kingman's deadly shooting, Boynton quickly found the Apache were no longer confused. A flight of bullets ripped through the air just over his head, one whizzing by so close he felt its hot trail against his ear. He jerked away and his shot missed.

"That's Victorio!" he shouted. "Get him, get him, Kingman!"

Both men fired at the Apache war chief, but Victorio seemed to lead a charmed life. Their bullets missed him as if he hid behind an invisible wall. Victorio kept his bucking horse under control as he darted here and there to rally his warriors.

"Stop them, stop *him!*"

Boynton's words hung in a momentary lull in the firing. With a sinking feeling, Boynton realized his soldiers were cutting back on their firing not because of fright or injury but because they were running out of ammunition. He glanced to his side and saw Kingman drawing a pistol. He had exhausted his carbine ammo.

"Take the battle to them!" Kingman cried, swarming up on the rock he had just used as a rest for his rifle.

Boynton watched in amazement as the huge sergeant seemed to jump into the air and hang. He fell slowly, so slowly, crashing into Trent and sending the two of them tumbling backward. Shaking off his strange dipped-in-molasses feeling, Boynton laid down covering fire until the two were safely behind the rocks. From the way Kingman moved, he had been hit.

Boynton let out a whoop that bounced from one rocky wall to the other and then returned hauntingly. He drew his saber and stumbled down the hill, leading the charge Kingman had started so impetuously. Mixed emotions filled Boynton when he saw the Apache begin to run. They could not stand to his attack, but they were not going to be slaughtered. He wanted to fight; his ambush had been successful; now some got away.

"Mount, mount and after them!" he bellowed. "No quarter!" To Boynton's surprise, only a half dozen men answered his call. One rode over, looking worried.

"Sir, these are all the horses we got left. Them Injuns kilt the rest." The private looked frightened at the notion of him and his five comrades chasing down the Mimbreño by themselves.

"Six?" Boynton stood and stared in disbelief. Victorio and his band limped away, many of their horses and mules killed in the brief, fierce fight.

"Might be more. Some got loose and run from all the shootin'," spoke up another private. "I'll ride after them red devils to the ends of the earth, but I'd like some ammunition. I used all I had issued me."

Boynton slumped. It would take a spell to get the horses that had scattered, but lack of ammunition was worse. How could he fight Victorio without ammunition? Hand-to-hand combat was fine—if he could ever overtake the retreating Indian.

He came to a quick decision, one he would not have considered earlier.

"Round up the horses. Get mounted. We'll follow Victorio's trail as far as we can to determine where he's going. Then we return to Fort Davis."

"Givin' up, Captain?" asked Kingman, hobbling over with the aid of Private Trent.

"There'll be another day," Boynton said, feeling a growing sense of accomplishment. "We caught him once. We can do it again. And then we'll have plenty of ammo."

"Yes, sir," Kingman said. Boynton saw his sergeant was as disappointed as he was at not ending the threat Victorio posed, but he also felt the acceptance that this was the smartest route to travel. Losing men accomplished nothing.

Victorio would be brought to justice sooner or later. Lester Boynton was now content for it to be later, if it meant saving his men from needless, dangerous battle.

PART VI

Riding the Ghost Pony

Ruth

"You look good with the medal," Ruth Magee said. At
her side stood her son. Caleb was pale as snow and clung
to his mother for support. He shook constantly and fever
sweat beaded his forehead, but he looked stronger than
he had even a few days earlier.

Boynton glanced down at his chest. Colonel Grierson
had insisted on giving him a medal for his successful
ambush of Victorio. The Mimbreño chief had not been
stopped, but reports subsequent to the attack showed the
entire band had been slowed grievously. Boynton's men
had killed seven, wounded an undetermined number
more, and killed half of the Apache's horses.

"If I'd had the horses and more ammunition, I could
have put an end to his career of evil," Boynton said, but

his mind was a thousand miles away from Victorio. He reached out and laid his palm on Caleb's forehead.

"You're still running a fever. You ought to be in bed."

"Wanted to see the colonel pin the medal on you," the boy said, grinning. His eyes were bright. With fever? Boynton couldn't tell.

"Thank you, but others in my company deserved recognition for their valor more than I."

"You saved your sergeant and a private from certain death," Ruth said. "That counts as bravery deserving of a medal—and more." Her eyes shone, too. She stepped closer, her lips parted slightly. Boynton stiffened, fearing she might kiss him. Or was it he was afraid she would not?

Her virtue remained intact because Evan Larkin sauntered up. He smiled and threw Boynton a sloppy salute. "Good to see you're finally fittin' into the Fort Davis way of doin' things."

"Thank you," Boynton said stiffly. He wondered if the quartermaster still made his cryptic entries into a private ledger. Probably. He ought to inquire about provisions. While he'd had plenty when he had sallied from the fort with Grierson almost a month earlier, Boynton could not help wondering if Larkin had somehow diverted just a few rounds of ammunition for sale to the settlers surrounding the fort. Those few extra rounds could have meant the end of Victorio.

"Let's get together later," Larkin suggested. "For a real celebration, unless you have something better to do." The officer looked from Ruth to Boynton and back, grinning lewdly. He laughed and hurried off before Boynton could put him in his place.

"No, Lester, don't be upset."

"He was rude to you. He insulted you with—"

"Lester, please. Compared to what some of the officers' wives have been saying, this is nothing. They have to gossip, you know. There's precious little else to do, and I have overstayed my welcome."

"Caleb's been sick." Boynton looked critically at the boy. "He still is sick. I've seen men built like a bull felled by the ague. Travel is out of the question."

"I'm afraid more officers are being transferred to Fort Davis," Ruth said. "As gracious as Colonel Grierson has been allowing Caleb and me to stay here, I fear we would soon find ourselves sleeping in the hallway of the hospital."

"That's no fit place for you," he said hotly. Boynton's mind swirled and twisted and fell all over itself. To be seen talking too long to Ruth would cause tongues to wag. It was not proper behavior.

"At least we will be closer to the doctor and the medical facilities," Ruth said. "I had hoped to be on my way back east, but the raids have intensified again. You have heard how Nana is rampaging throughout all of West Texas."

"Captain Parker's a man who will never quit until he's caught his quarry," Boynton said. From all he had heard of Parker and his Apache scouts, they would likely do more than run Nana to ground. They would catch and torture him for the trouble he had put them to.

"I've heard about him." Ruth said nothing for a moment. Silently she, Caleb, and Boynton began walking. Somehow, being in motion, as if they went somewhere and simply happened to be going there at the same time, made being with her a mite easier on him.

"He is a brutal man," she finished.

"Parker? Or Victorio?"

"Both. I am sick to the heart of all this killing."

"When Victorio is captured, it will end. He is the war chief keeping the others fired up," said Boynton. "Juh stays in Mexico and Geronimo is not the chief."

"I understand Mangus rides with Geronimo."

"You are well informed, Mrs. Magee," Boynton said,

glancing at Caleb. He wanted to call her by her given name, but not with the boy around. Boynton felt as if he walked a knife edge and any slip would cut not only himself but others he cared for.

"I have little else to do but listen to the soldiers as they talk. I must admit Captain Larkin drops by often and carries on about the strangest things. He is an odd man."

"Larkin is married," Boynton said, more harshly than he intended.

"It is all perfectly innocent, sir," Ruth said primly. "I would never allow anything . . . untoward."

Boynton felt increasingly uncomfortable. His reactions were not those of a proper officer and gentleman. Even one who had been responsible for killing the woman's husband. Boynton turned bleak at the memory of that time, the Rio Grande separating him and Colonel Magee— and Victorio's band cutting the command to ribbons.

Chained with this was the memory of his other debacle along the Rio Grande that had seen half his company slaughtered, including George Kingman's brother. These were powerful mistakes to live down.

Especially when he found himself thinking more and more of Ruth Magee. How could he live with himself and not tell her he had been responsible for her husband's death? She thought he was a hero. After all, Grierson had pinned a medal on him this day. Boynton refrained from reaching down, ripping the medal and ribbon from his chest, and flinging it away as hard as he could. He had been responsible for men dying. Saving Kingman and Trent had been almost accidental.

Boynton tried to reconstruct the act of bravery for which he had received the medal, and found it was all blurred. Sergeant Kingman had his leg shot out from under him, then slid down the side of the hill. Boynton had followed, shooting and shouting and acting like a wild man as Trent protected his sergeant. Where was the bravery when Boynton didn't even remember precisely what he had done?

Like the two grievous attacks preceding it, where so many of his command had died due to his incompetence?

"I am glad you chose to return rather than continue tracking Victorio," Ruth was saying.

"What? Oh there was no way I could have pursued. Our horses were scattered. A corporal had not secured their tethers properly, and they ran when the shooting started. And then we had run out of ammunition. We would have been reduced to fighting the Apache with our teeth and precious little else."

Ruth laughed. "There was a time when you would have done just that."

"It still hurts thinking of Sarah and the boys being killed." He sucked in a breath and started to confess to her his part in her husband's death, but she interrupted him.

"Would you join Caleb and me for dinner this evening?" Ruth smiled almost shyly, but stared directly at him. "It would be an honor to dine with the most recent hero in a long list at Fort Davis."

"I . . ." Boynton's thoughts were derailed. He had not expected this. "I would be the one honored," he said. He could tell her tonight of his dereliction of duty and all those who had died. At dinner.

"We will be expecting you at seven, Captain," Ruth said. She went off, smiling. Caleb hummed to himself. Boynton watched them go, a curious mixture of dread and anticipation filling him.

He went to find Evan Larkin. The quartermaster might have set aside something special that Boynton could get from him. An extra ration, perhaps. Or even something more intimate.

Raiders

May 8, 1880
Fort Davis

Benjamin Grierson assembled his officers in the mess hall, a large map of West Texas nailed to the far wall away from the main entrance. The colonel paced back and forth like a caged animal in front of the map, as if guarding it. Boynton had seen this behavior before, heard the colonel singing to himself, watched the nervous gestures, heard his fierce bark as irritation possessed him. These were symptoms, and all meant the same thing—Grierson was anxious for action and was being held back through no fault of his own.

"We don't know who they are," he said, tapping the map to show a settlement west of Fort Davis. "They are raiding, sniping at outriders, stealing a cow here and there. Nothing serious, mind you, not yet. But I suspect they are Mimbreño, and I suspect they are pushing farther south to join Nana but taking their sweet time going about it."

Moving his finger, he stabbed down decisively at the small town of Sabinal.

"Captain Parker and his men have chased Nana from New Mexico down to this region. We know, thanks to Captain Boynton's careful study, that this area is friendlier to the Apache than others in the area and that Victorio would likely use it as a rendezvous."

"Sir," asked Captain Lebo, his wide-set eyes squinting slightly and his mustache twitching, "where is Victorio? Could he be responsible for the raiding we know west of here?"

" 'Doubtful it is Victorio," said Grierson, turning thoughtful. "Boynton chased him out of the Guadalupes with damned few horses under his warriors. It's possible Victorio headed east from the mountains, thinking to make a wide circle around Abilene and come up on Sabinal from the south. That puts the red devil well away from us."

"Sir, let me go—" Lebo was silenced by a sharp head movement from Grierson.

"We cannot make a major campaign out of this, Captain," said the colonel. He heaved a deep sigh. His shoulders slumped slightly as if new weight had been added. "I am currently trading dispatches with General Sheridan."

Boynton perked up. The heat in the closed mess hall had been putting him to sleep, in spite of his interest in Apache movement throughout their region of patrol. He turned slightly on the uncomfortable seat. Evan Larkin worked assiduously on his ledger, making entries and fingering a stack of greenbacks under the table where Grierson and other superiors could not see his self-appointed task.

"Sir, is our mission going to change?" Boynton asked. This question drew unwanted attention, as far as Larkin was concerned. He turned paler than usual as he scrambled to stuff handfuls of money into his jacket to keep from being seen.

"General Sheridan wants our force, the entire Tenth Cavalry, to join Major Morrow's detachment from the Ninth at Fort Bayard to quell possible Apache uprising in New Mexico." Grierson heaved a deep sigh. "I am resisting this order, as I feel Victorio, Nana, and the main force of renegade Mimbreño are likely to attack within the confines of the Tenth's jurisdiction."

Boynton wondered if Grierson refused to send soldiers west toward the Rio Grande so Sheridan would have no choice but allow the Tenth to remain at their post. Whatever happened, raiders or no, he knew it would be folly for the Tenth to abandon Fort Davis and go north. The Warm Springs Apache remained at San Carlos, except for a small group of about fifty that had escaped their reservation. Those women and children included most of the families of Victorio's band.

Those few raiding throughout New Mexico made up only a small segment of the total warriors. More than this, he *knew* Victorio wasn't there. If Victorio's family had reached Mexico, *there* was where the renegade would be found. Kill off Victorio and the Warm Springs Apache band would have to select another leader, one that had to be of lesser ability.

Nana, Loco, both were capable, but not of Victorio's mettle. Boynton let his mind drift, wondering if the stories he'd heard about Victorio's sister were true. If they were, she might prove as worthy an opponent as Victorio. But imagining the Apache following a woman war chief stretched likelihood to unseen limits. She might fight like ten men—like ten *Apache*—but Boynton doubted the warriors would do her bidding without Victorio's strong backing.

Nana, he decided. The old chief with the gimpy foot

was the one who would pick up where Victorio left off. With any luck, Captain Parker would have Nana corralled and under lock and key soon. That would force Victorio to reform his band before causing new trouble.

But it would be in Texas, not in New Mexico where Sheridan thought the worst of the fighting had been. For all the driving need Victorio had of returning his family to Ojo Caliente, the Apache chief had to cross hundreds of miles of West Texas to even get there. Waiting for him to return was less palatable for Boynton than stopping him here and now. He closed his eyes, picturing the ambush he had sprung on Victorio in the mountains. It had been scant payback for the two prior disasters. Only the capture of Victorio would redeem Boynton in his own eyes, and maybe make him feel he deserved the medal he had received.

Maybe then he could tell Ruth Magee what had really happened when her husband had died.

"Colonel!" came an urgent call from the door. "I have a new dispatch. Urgent, sir." The dispatch private held up the sheet of paper. Again Boynton's curiosity was piqued. This was not written on the standard flimsy yellow official dispatch stationery but on a scrap from an officer's field book.

The private handed Grierson the sheet and waited. Grierson dismissed him, then addressed his assembled officers.

"We have something more than a few cattle being stolen, it seems. Captain Carpenter's H Company tangled with a small band of Apache—Mimbreño from his description. He surmises, as I already had, that they are on their way to join Victorio." Grierson crumpled the paper and stuffed it into his pocket.

"Gentlemen," he said, "prepare your companies for

action. And Boynton, remain for a moment. I'd have a word with you.''

Boynton looked at Evan Larkin, who smiled weakly, then beat a hasty retreat from the mess hall. He dropped a greenback by the door and never noticed. That told Boynton the quartermaster was in a real hurry to return to whatever he had been doing before this meeting. Perhaps Larkin had to replace equipment or supplies he had sold to nearby settlers. It would not surprise Boynton at all, if true.

"Sir," he said, stopping in front of Grierson.

The colonel pulled the sheet of paper from his pocket and handed it to Boynton.

"Read it," ordered Grierson.

Boynton scanned the precise lines of neatly written report. Louis Carpenter had been Grierson's most reliable officer for close to twenty years of Indian fighting, and had even won a Medal of Honor for capturing Satanta, Satank, and Big Tree. Whatever he said Boynton had to consider the gospel truth. He had ridden out of Fort Quitman for the better part of a year now and knew the territory well.

"I'm surprised Captain Carpenter did not give pursuit," Boynton said.

"Eight renegades murdered two civilians, dammit, Boynton! Carpenter has his orders, and they do not include leaving the rest of the settlers at the mercy of these killers. Get your company over there. Talk to Carpenter, find out what you can, then *you* stop them."

"Yes, sir!" Boynton was pleased to be on patrol again, especially on the trail of Apache likely to join Victorio. Find out from a captive precisely where they were going to rendezvous, and Victorio would fall!

* * *

A day of hard riding brought Boynton's company to the edge of country patrolled by Carpenter's buffalo soldiers. Boynton called over his shoulder, "Sergeant Kingman, let the troops stand down. Tend to the horses, be sure all gear is in readiness."

"Sir, right away!"

Boynton rode forward, urging his horse down the steep incline toward the bottom of the ravine where Carpenter and two of his junior officers awaited him. He took longer getting to the bottom than he wanted. Boynton was eager to get on the trail of the Apache.

"Captain Boynton," greeted Carpenter. The man was fifteen years older than Boynton and had a harried expression to him. Dark circles under his eyes told of long days in the saddle with little rest. "I'm happy to meet you after all this time—and even happier to have your men reinforce us."

"I got a few details from Colonel Grierson," Boynton said. "He said you could fill me in on all I needed to know to go after the killers."

"They ambushed a party in Bass Canyon, about ten miles from here. After killing James Grant and Mrs. Graham, they tried to finish off their raid. Harry Graham and a fourth traveler, a Mr. Murphy, got into the rocks and held them off." Carpenter looked as if he had bitten into something sour. "The Indians had modern Winchester rifles, from accounts, and were more than a match for Graham and Murphy."

"Did the Apache loot the settlers' wagon?"

"They took everything, including four mules used to pull the wagon. I followed the trail to the Rio Grande but had to give up pursuit at that point. Other settlers were beginning to sight Apache behind every clump of cactus." Carpenter sounded more bitter than ever. "I could have run them down, but my orders . . ." He let the sentence trail off in resentment at having to wet-nurse civilians.

"The Apache, were they definitely Mimbreño?" asked Boynton.

"Mimbreño? No, Mescalero. Definitely Mescalero."

"Then they might not be going to join Victorio?"

"On that count, I think it is obvious they *were* on their way to find him. General Sheridan is increasingly worried over uprising on the Mescalero Reservation. The braves are leaving in small groups, but all of those leaving are coming south to join Victorio. We caught two warriors a week back who told us they would join him in killing all us White Eyes." Carpenter smiled crookedly. "They had no idea where or how they were going to join Victorio's band. They were only twelve years old."

"Bass Canyon," Boynton said, getting back to the renegades he wanted to question. "Down that way, to the southwest?"

"It opens onto the Rio Grande, where we lost them," confirmed Carpenter. "It's good you left your company on the mesa. If you cut cross-county you can reach the ambush site before sundown and be after them by sunup. Trying to follow this maze of ravines will only get you turned around and lost."

"Why are you down here?"

"Lost cattle," Carpenter said with even more bitterness. "My soldiers are little more than shepherds and cowboys, at times. This is one of those times. The deaths have stirred up sentiment—and made my presence desirable."

"You go out, and there's nothing much there to do?" Boynton understood. The settlers were isolated in this part of the country. The presence of Carpenter or a small detachment from his company could be mighty comforting, no matter the outrageous pretext for getting them out of Fort Quitman.

"You understand, Captain Boynton," said Carpenter. "I suspect you'll be wanting to move on quickly. If you want to return any captives to Fort Quitman, feel free. Otherwise, I am sure Colonel Grierson would be delighted to put them into the Fort Davis stockade."

"Thank you " Boynton said. "I'll report what happens."

"May it be nothing but success." With that, Carpenter wheeled his horse about. His lieutenants trotted behind him, still not speaking. Boynton wondered how he could keep his junior officers this silent. His always yammered like magpies unless specifically ordered to button their flaps.

Making his way back up the steep embankment proved a quicker trip than down. His horse stumbled once but seemed to take energy from Boynton's eagerness to get on the trail of the Mescalero killers.

"Bass Canyon, Sergeant," said Boynton. He quickly relayed all he had learned from Carpenter. "I see no purpose to be served by examining the site of the battle. Better to go to the mouth of the canyon and see if the trail leads across the river into Mexico."

"That won't do much, Captain," said Kingman. The sergeant furrowed his brow. "I remember the land pretty good. What if we cut smack across this mesa and went down on the south end, about where the ford is?"

"You think the Apache might come back into the U.S. there at Ransom's Ford?"

"Unless they stay on the other side of the Rio Grande, they can't get across that easily anywhere for miles and miles because of spring runoff swelling the river. Can't see them content to go all the way to the Big Bend."

"Cheeky of them if they do come back right under

Carpenter's nose," said Boynton, knowing Kingman was right. "Mount the troop. Let's ride!"

By twilight they had reached the edge of the mesa. As much as Boynton wanted to descend to the river, he ordered camp established.

"No fires," he told Kingman. "I won't give away our position if the Apache are just across the river."

"Yes, sir. Will pass that right along."

Boynton let Kingman get the soldiers settled before he wandered through the camp on an informal inspection. He greeted many by name and halted near Private Trent's bedroll.

"Is Sergeant Kingman riding you hard?" Boynton asked.

"Yes, sir, he is. I got some complaints 'bout it, too!"

"And I'd have complaints if he weren't," Boynton joked. "Don't think about winning any medals tomorrow, Private. It's hard enough riding with Kingman and all the medals clanking on his uniform."

Boynton walked to the edge of the mesa and looked down the twisting trail leading two hundred feet to the river below. The sound of the restless movement caused by spring runoff warned him of how dangerous any ford would be this year. The Mescalero—dammit, Mescalero!—had to cross here or remain inside Mexico for fifty miles or more.

Boynton stared into the darkness, listening to the soft whispers from the river below. "I'll be ready for you," Boynton said to the renegades. And he was.

"I'm wet, and this here rock's cuttin' into my ass something fierce," complained Private Trent.

"Quiet," Boynton said, his voice sharp with command. He tipped his head to one side, listening hard. Above the river's voice he heard other sounds, not natural ones. He clutched his pistol and lifted his head, chancing a quick look over the top of the wind- and water-eroded rock where he and Trent hid.

"What is it, Captain?" the young trooper asked anxiously. For all the skirmishes he had been through, Trent still got antsy. Boynton wasn't going to blame him for that. His own heart sounded like one of Grierson's drums as it beat hard in his chest.

"Apache," he mouthed. Boynton almost spoke aloud when the boy started to rise. Then it was moot. Rifles exploded all around. Boynton recognized the muffled snap of his troopers' rifles and then the sharper crack from the Apache's Winchesters. He flopped flat on the rock and leveled his pistol.

Boynton could not say who was more surprised, him or the warrior not ten feet away.

"Drop your weapon, or I'll shoot!" Boynton cried. The Apache's move was to swing his rifle around, then he sagged as he realized he had been caught fair and square. The rifle fell from his fingers to the ground.

"Trent!" Boynton got the private up to cover their captive. "Shoot him where he stands if he moves a muscle." Boynton saw from the expression on the Indian's face he understood English.

Swarming over the rock, Boynton slid down the far side, then brought his pistol up to cover his captive again. He trusted Trent, but the boy was still a tad on the wild side and did not always think about what he did until it was too late.

The firing died down, but Boynton paid no heed to the uneasy quiet. He circled his prisoner and motioned for him to move away from his rifle. Boynton scooped up the fallen weapon.

"I wish we had arms this good," he said, tossing the

rifle to young Trent. The buffalo soldier fielded it easily, smiling.

"If'n we catch 'nuff of them, we just might, Captain!"

"Captain Boynton," came Kingman's deep voice. The sergeant scrambled around in the fall of rocks closer to the riverbank, his rifle ready. "I see you got one. That's good. We had to shoot the others."

"I don't think that needs translating," Boynton said. "Where were you headed?"

He prodded the Apache with the muzzle of his pistol.

"Victorio will eat you for his dinner! You are a dog! All you bluecoats!"

"Sabinal? You were going to Sabinal to join Victorio?" The minute the question left his lips and he saw the crafty expression on the Apache's face, Boynton knew Victorio was not in Texas any longer. Nana might not be either. "No," he said slowly, covering the first question and playing on his captive's inadvertent revelation. "No, I think you are joining Victorio in Mexico. He rides with Juh again, doesn't he?"

He might as well have thrust a bayonet into the Apache's guts. The man shrank, then stiffened and denied it all. Nothing more was likely to be gained.

"Trent, get a detail and watch after our guest. Colonel Grierson will want to afford him all possible hospitality. In the stockade!"

"Sir!"

Private Trent and several others took the Apache away.

"How's it possible, sir?" asked Kingman. "Victorio was headed east when he left the Guadalupes. There's no way he could be in Mexico."

"He rode due west, right across the Rio Grande," Boynton said. "He must have taken a route through the mountains we don't know." He berated himself for not knowing of this path to safety. Fort Concho had been placed on alert because of his report. If they had sent word to Fort Quitman and had Carpenter out on constant patrol, they might have snared their elusive enemy.

"What of Nana? You reckon he's hitched up again with Victorio?"

"I do," said Boynton. "Captain Parker and his scouts are good." He took in a deep breath, then let it out slowly. "Sometimes, we all find someone who is just a bit better."

He returned to Fort Davis in triumph, although he did not share that sense of victory. Once more, the man who had killed his family had slipped away.

Tenacity

June 5, 1880
Along the Rio Grande

"We need rest, not war," Loco complained. He rubbed his arm, which refused to heal properly, then stared boldly and directly at Victorio, pinning him with the demand for a respite from the raiding and running and dying.

"We need horses," Victorio countered. "Without them, we are nothing." He stood on the bluff looking over the runoff-swollen Rio Grande. On the far side waited herds of horses begging to be plucked from their corrals. The Indah settlers did not need so many; his Apache did. His band had rifles and ammunition, thanks to Nana's Power. But they lacked horses. Without sturdy four-legged transportation, they might as well be squaws hunting for kangaroo rats on the San Carlos Reservation. Victorio clenched his hands into fists, but his anger refused to flow outward as it should have at what the White Eyes had done to him and his people. It stayed within his breast, festering and turning him bitter.

His own family had escaped, along with some others, but too many Warm Springs Apache remained at San Carlos. He owed it to his warriors to get *all* their families free.

"For too long we have been away from our families. We see them secretly, sneaking about, and always we must leave them behind because of the buffalo soldiers. They keep our women and children hostage, at San Carlos, on the Mescalero Reservation, at places we were never intended to hunt and farm. Too few of us are privileged with our wives safely hidden in Juh's stronghold. It is time to strike back."

"Free them?" asked Nana. The grizzled old warrior took a deep breath. "I don't see how this is possible without bartering peace with the White Eyes. We might rescue the rest from San Carlos, but return to Warm Springs is impossible. Morrow watches every pass over the Mogollón Rim for our braves. We could never return without destroying all the Indah."

"That will never happen," Victorio admitted. "What can happen is getting our people off the reservation and into Mexico. Juh will let us stay with his band until we are ready for a big raid."

"What of Geronimo? We still war with him. This puts Juh in the middle. What do we say to him? Choose between Chiricahua and Mimbreño?" Nana asked.

Loco winced as he rubbed his arm. Then he continued. "We can talk to Colonel Hatch," Loco suggested. "He favored our return to Warm Springs. Only General Pope prevented it."

"I do not understand the White Eyes," complained Nana. "Who is their Great Nantan, the one they call *President*? John Pope? Who is this Sheridan we hear of? Where is Crook? What of those far away in Washington? They change constantly! We never hear of the same one twice! Pah!''

"You do not understand. We must talk. Perhaps this is the time they will honor a treaty. How can we continue in this way?'' Loco stormed away, unwilling to listen to Victorio's schemes.

"We will make it worth their while to sue for peace," Victorio said, his mind hunting for the proper course to travel. "We will create such a storm of death and destruction they must agree to our terms. All we want is to return to Warm Springs with our families. Is that so bad? Can they deny us that much, in exchange for peace?''

"The bluecoats will put more and more soldiers into the field after us," said Nana. "They will never agree to peace forced upon them."

"What choice do we have? Live with Juh forever and forget our sacred lands? Would you never see the Holy Peaks again? How will Ussen recognize our young boys who would become men if they do not climb the eastern face of Say-a-Chee, which guards us against our enemies?''

"You look into Texas," Nana said. "I *see* many rifles there, much ammunition. Do the bluecoats cache against a long campaign? Or do they carry it on mules with huge battalions sent after us? They would have killed you in the Guadalupes if it had not been for their lack of ammunition and water.''

Victorio cringed at the mention of the ambush in the mountains. He had thought that route safe. Losing so many men and most of his horses and mules had been a great blow. Only quick thinking and audacity had saved the Apache raiders. If he had followed the winding canyon around to its end as he had intended, he and his warriors would have been afoot on the great prairie to the east— and at the mercy of soldiers from Fort Concho. Instead, he had forced his warriors to scale difficult peaks and flee to the west.

Flee west.

He shuddered at the notion that he was escaping perpetually now. Power had been drained from him. He led the largest band of Mimbreño ever assembled under a single leader, and what good did it do him? He had lost more than fifty fighters since Colonel Hatch had launched his massive assault at Hembrillo Canyon two months ago. And he could hardly contain his self-anger knowing it had been Boynton who had laid the ambush in the Guadalupes. The captain from Fort Davis had been an easy target before. Now even the rabbit turned and kicked accurately with its powerful back legs.

"We attack," Victorio decided. "We will cross into Texas and recover our wealth. We will return with many horses. Again, they will fear the Warm Springs Apache!"

Nana made a noncommittal sound and left Victorio standing on the butte. The war chief's eyes moved from the frothy race of the Rio Grande to the far bank, and up to the mesa. In the distance, a dust devil kicked up more than a hundred feet into the air and whirled across the dry, sandy land in its mindless frenzy to be elsewhere.

Victorio vowed to be like that miniature tornado, whipping unstoppably across the land.

"They think to ambush you there," Lozen said, pointing out the canyon leading in the direction of Eagle Springs. They had crossed the river with sixty warriors, ready to prove themselves. Victorio had seen more and more Mescalero and Chiricahua willing to join his band. That recruitment would stop if they did not return to their camp in Mexico with many horses.

"Your Power tells you this?"

Lozen nodded.

"Then we will not walk into their trap." Victorio summoned Loco and Nana. The two chiefs came to him, Loco favoring his injured arm. He held it close to his body, secured with a broad cloth colored yellow with sacred corn pollen. So much hoddentin was a powerful symbol of their triumph.

"Go straight south along the river," Victorio said to Nana. "When you can, cut inland and find settlers with too many horses and cattle."

"Cattle?" Nana laughed at this. "We could never get cattle across the river. It was all we could do crossing with our horses this morning. The current is swift, and it would take too much time herding cattle. We would be easy targets for any passing company of bluecoats—or even a settler with a good rifle."

"Find a ford farther downriver," Victorio said, irritated that the old chief questioned his plans this way. "If you cannot steal the cattle, kill them."

"This will anger the settlers. They will demand more from their cavalry," pointed out Nana.

"Keep them running. Wear them down. They do not have the endurance of the Apache. And you," Victorio said, indicating Loco, "go directly up the hill and toward Fort Davis. Engage any of their patrols, but do not stand and fight. Lead them around in circles, make them come for you. Then join Nana before he crosses the Rio Grande."

"What will you do?" asked Loco. "Go after those who would trap you?"

"No," Victorio said, smiling at his own brilliance. "I will find horses and cattle where the cavalry does not guard. We will raid and leave them looking like fools."

"Enjuh!" said Nana.

The chiefs split, Victorio going to the small group that rode with him. He waited for Nana and Loco to leave before he turned to the braves waiting for their instructions.

"We will hunt for wagon trains, supplies left unguarded, horses!" he said. "And we will dance away from the White Eyes until they are angered. Then we will go back to Mexico where we can laugh at them without fear of pursuit!"

"Why do they not chase us into Mexico?" asked Lozen. "The Rangers did until they were chased away by the Mexican general. Why not the bluecoats? Why don't they cross the river after us?"

"Loco is right questioning all they do. Little makes sense to me," Victorio admitted. "Knowing where they wait for us, thanks to Ussen and your Power, will make this raid easier."

Riding their broke down horses, they skirted the mouth of the canyon that would take them toward Eagle Springs. Although Victorio lacked his sister's Power, he felt the presence of many soldiers. He considered setting a trap of his own at the canyon mouth, sending a solitary rider into the canyon to decoy out the bluecoats. Then he pushed the notion from his mind. Horses. They needed good, strong horses. And he would get them soon!

They rode on for an hour, then turned from the Rio Grande and headed toward Fort Quitman. Surrounding the fort were hundreds of settlers, all easy pickings for a daring raider. Victorio reined back when his sister rode closer, her knee brushing his.

"Brother, wait. There is something wrong."

"Enemy?"

"I have not used my Power since this morning. But we do not ride forward with any chance of success."

"You sound like Loco. You want nothing more than to rest in Juh's camp," Victorio said angrily. Lozen's face turned impassive, and he knew he had made a grievous mistake. Who did he have in this world but his family and clan? Mescalero and Chiricahua rode with him, but they were not Warm Springs Apache.

"Eagerness to take horses caused me to speak without thinking," he apologized.

"Eagerness will get us all killed," she said primly. Lozen rode a few more minutes, eyes ahead, focused on . . . what? Victorio saw nothing. In that he drew no solace for the sores festering in his soul. Even if he returned to Mexico with an honorable number of horses, Loco and Nana and Lozen were right. What did he do to return his people to Warm Springs?

"They rode the length of the canyon, through Eagle Springs, and now come at us from behind," Lozen said, her eyes going wide. "They anticipated our move. They had another plan if we did not fall into their trap!"

Victorio hesitated. When Lozen used her Power, he believed this was a divine gift from Ussen. But now? She guessed at what the bluecoat commander might have done. Victorio wanted to press on.

"Send a scout to watch our back trail," he said, then stopped. He twisted on horseback and saw the dust kicked up by horses pursuing them.

"Back to Mexico!" he cried to his warriors. "Forget the horses. We are in a trap!"

They cut directly for the Rio Grande, knowing they might be some distance from a ford. The first shots sang through the air, seeking his warriors' deaths. They hunched down over their straining horses' necks and galloped a mile, walked a few hundred yards, then picked up the pace. He wished that the horses were in better condition—and that they had more. He was used to letting a horse die under him, then jumping to another and running it into the ground if that was what it took to escape.

But now? He had only the struggling horse under him.

"Brother, that way," urged Lozen. She headed her horse

down a steep embankment that leveled out quickly and led to a gentler slope down to the Rio Grande. The wide river flowed powerfully. Victorio hesitated crossing here. To do so would lose many horses and perhaps a few warriors.

The buzz of bullets above his head convinced him he could turn and fight or attempt to cross the dangerously rapid river.

"An entire company," Lozen said, staring to the south. Victorio looked north and saw another.

"We are caught between Boynton and Carpenter," he said. "They have learned!"

Without another word he urged his frightened horse into the Rio Grande. The rush of water staggered the animal, but Victorio put his heels to the horse's flanks. The water deepened and his horse lost its footing. Twisting away, Victorio swam powerfully away from the frightened, drowning horse. Beside him, not ten yards distant, swam his sister. Others tried to stand and fight. Victorio saw them cut down where they stood, their horses following them to the Happy Place. Marksmen from Boynton's company arrived and set up positions on the banks to prevent any escape.

Victorio stroked harder, swimming powerfully for the distant shore. The current carried him away from the battle. He fought to angle toward the Mexican side of the river and, after a half hour's struggle, pulled himself to the banks, exhausted. Cocking his head to one side, he listened for the sounds of gunfire.

Victorio, already chilled in body, felt his soul turn to ice. The gunshots came not from upriver, where he had been ambushed, but from downriver. Loco? Nana? Both? Had they fallen prey to the increasingly clever bluecoats?

"Come, Brother, we must hurry. They might follow,"

came Lozen's worried voice. He turned and saw her limping along, her left leg injured in the crossing.

"What of the others with us?"

"Half," she said. "At least half made it to safety."

Victorio felt more desolate than ever. That meant half had not escaped. Together with Lozen, they walked along the Rio Grande on Mexican land. By ones and twos, they gathered the survivors from their band. When they met Nana and Loco, his worst fears were realized.

They had lost over twenty warriors in the ill-conceived raid.

"They will pay for this," Victorio said, shaking his fist at the unseen enemy on the Texas side of the river. "You will all pay!"

With this taunt hanging in the air, he swung about and stalked off with the others who had survived this day.

Desperation

July 29, 1880
Near Eagle Springs, Texas

"He's getting bolder, sir," Boynton said to Colonel Grierson. "My scouts tell of a temporary camp somewhere around here. Victorio has abandoned his camping ground in Mexico and thinks he can do as he pleases on this side of the river."

"Bolder?" Grierson laughed. "I've been fighting Indians for well nigh twenty years, Captain. This isn't bold. This is desperation. When you chased him back with his tail between his legs like a whipped dog, he didn't have twenty horses left for all his warriors." Grierson hummed a jaunty tune as he scanned the territory. The gently rolling hills quickly changed to steeper mountains to the west of Eagle Springs. "See that, Captain?"

Boynton looked in the direction his commander pointed. All he saw was desert, scrubby mesquite, patches of prickly pear, and arid land that would kill a man in a day without adequate water.

"I don't see what you're pointing out, sir."

"The land, Captain, the land is working for us now. Victorio can walk across it. We travel faster. The Tenth is better equipped than the Ninth ever was." Grierson made a sour face. "General Sheridan is not my equal when it comes to wrangling for supplies."

"Colonel Hatch was always complaining about his lack of equipment," Boynton said, remembering the only time he had seen Hatch and met Major Morrow. Thinking on it, he wondered if some of their resentment toward the Tenth, and Sheridan's insistence that the two regiments unite, rested on the difference in supply. General Pope, and Carleton before him, had always been more interested in diverting resources toward penning up the Apache and Navajo. Colonel Grierson—Brevet Major General Grierson, he had to remind himself—had spent most of his military career after the war on the frontier, but had powerful political connections in Washington the others lacked.

They continually fought the Bureau of Indian Affairs and the Department of the Interior, wasting money and time. All Grierson had to fight was Army bullheadedness, the same as any other U.S. Army regimental commander.

"Cut off the supplies and the raider withers away," Grierson went on. "Victorio isn't mounted as he was when Hatch chased him out of New Mexico Territory. And, God willing, he never will be again."

"But he *does* have a camp on this side of the Rio Grande." Boynton was not happy with the renegade Mimbreño moving into Texas the way he had. He took it as a personal affront, even if he had settled the score with the Apache.

"Of course he does, Captain. Victorio can't travel a hundred miles a day to make a quick raid the way he used to. Not without more horses, lots more horses."

"We must see he does not steal them," Boynton finished. "What do we do to find him? I think my scouting reports are accurate enough. He might be over yonder." Boynton tried to fix landmarks in his head. Without his map, he was at a disadvantage. This was not territory he had patrolled before.

"We'll divide our force, then, Captain," said Grierson. "I'll ride due west from Eagle Springs while you swing in a wide arc to the south and rejoin me twenty miles toward the river."

"Yes, sir."

"If you find him, be sure to send word. It might just take both our companies to stop Victorio, no matter how well we stopper up his ability to travel. He has an unlimited supply of rifles and ammunition, or so it seems. Wish I could tap into his supply train." At this Colonel Grierson chuckled, then pulled on his gloves.

"Yes, sir." Boynton's mind raced ahead. He'd had the scouting reports brought from not only his own men but from Carpenter's company out of Fort Quitman. Pieced together, Boynton had a good idea of where Victorio camped.

"And Lester," said Grierson.

"Sir?"

"Don't do anything stupid out there. You've got a pretty filly hankering for you to come back alive." Grierson smiled, then rode off, whistling his tune louder than was prudent. It caught on the gentle, hot wind and carried for miles. Or so it seemed to Boynton.

Boynton swallowed hard. Did everyone know his business? What did the gossip at Fort Davis do to Ruth's reputation? He ought not to have spent so much time with her, but he felt sorry for her and Caleb. A tiny smile curled his lips when he thought of the boy. How different Caleb was from either Peter or Thomas. But he was a good boy, smart as a whip and better with book learning than any other child at the post. One day he would grow up to be a doctor or a lawyer.

Somehow Ruth had managed to get a position as Grierson's musical assistant, the commander being positively loco about the weekly symphonies he insisted on the post band performing. Ruth got room and board for herself and Caleb, though in spartan quarters compared to Boynton's old digs. He sighed, counting his lucky stars that Ruth had remained—and wondering why she had. He dared to hope, but . . .

"Ready, sir," came Kingman's deep voice. Boynton glanced over his shoulder and saw his sergeant waiting. He fought to hold down a blush as he worried that the sergeant might have overheard Grierson—or even read his mind about Ruth Magee. Kingman always seemed to know exactly what he wanted done before he even had decided what that might be.

George Kingman was a hell of a good sergeant.

"Let's get the company moving, then," Boynton said. "Split them into two columns. You take one and swing wider to the south. I'll cover the terrain between you and the colonel's company."

"What of Lieutenant Christopher?"

"Last I heard, he was still puking out his guts back in Eagle Springs. Bad water, maybe," Boynton said. In truth, he preferred Kingman at the head of the second column. The new shavetail lieutenant lacked the experience for dealing with a renegade of Victorio's caliber. Even worse, he refused to admit it.

Boynton recognized much of himself in the newly transferred lieutenant—an earlier self. But he had no time for Christopher to learn from experience now. Lives were too precious for the mistakes it might take to deal effectively with Victorio.

All day in the hot sun they rode, only speeding up when they neared a watering hole. Boynton had less than an hour at sundown to wait for Kingman to rejoin them.

Kingman gave his terse report. "Nary a sign of Apache, Captain."

"I thought we'd find them, I really did," he said glumly. Once more he had misjudged the cunning savage. This time no one had died as a result, but he had anticipated finding Apache spoor all over. He had not even found an eagle feather or bead to show Indians had passed this way within the last ten years. "Victorio's got to camp near a watering hole. The heat will dry out even an Apache's tongue."

"Sir, rider coming. Hard. From the north."

"From Grierson!" Boynton shot to his feet and swung into the saddle. His horse protested the weight again, but did not balk. The captain rode out to meet the flustered private bearing the message from Grierson.

"Sir, sir, he's bein' 'tacked!"

"Colonel Grierson? Where?"

"Yes, sir, the colonel. All our company. Victorio, sir. We almost walked into his camp unawares."

Kingman was already getting the horses watered and preparing the men for another long ride.

"How many Apache?"

"Can't tell. They got the entire company pinned down."

"Sergeant Kingman, mount the troop!" Boynton bellowed. "Lead the way back, Private," he ordered. His pulse raced. He had another chance to gain revenge on Victorio.

With any luck, this would be Victorio's last fight.

Boynton heard the rifle fire a mile away from where Grierson had blundered onto the Apache camp. He held up his hand, letting the command filter down the column.

They rode in almost complete darkness. It had taken the messenger half an hour to cover the distance from Grierson's position to the watering hole.

Already Boynton's company had been on the trail over an hour. The moon would not rise for another hour yet. Boynton wondered if it would be a help or a hindrance when it did. Apache did not fight at night—unless they were pushed into it.

"They might have done kilt the colonel already," the messenger moaned.

"Private," Boynton said tiredly. "Listen. What do you hear?"

"Gunfire, sir."

"Then Colonel Grierson is still fighting. From what you said, he rode into a ravine and found himself pinned down by Apache firing from along the top of a ridge. Is that so?"

"Yes, sir. He rode into the ravine, and if he tries to get out, his back would be exposed to the Apache snipers."

Boynton nodded, thinking hard. Grierson was pinned down, but relatively safe. Victorio didn't have enough men to launch an all-out charge. If Grierson stayed put, Victorio could only wait him out.

"Horses," Boynton asked. "What of Grierson's horses?"

"I don't know. Most all are in the ravine with the men, I reckon."

"That's what Victorio is after. He would settle for a swap, the soldiers' lives for their horses."

"Colonel Grierson would never do that, sir!"

"I know." Boynton smiled. The plan came together in his head. Grierson's company formed one side of the battlefield. If he came up on the far side of the ridge, Victorio would maintain the high position but find himself fired upon from opposite directions.

"Sergeant Kingman, prepare the men for an attack. We will charge straight up the hill."

"Mighty risky, sir."

"We'll make it halfway before the Apache notice us. They're occupied trying to shoot up Grierson. It's our job to get close enough to spot them in the dark."

"Sir, if you figure the colonel can hold off for another hour or so, we can have the light of a half moon helping our attack. The Apache would be outlined against the moonlit sky to the east."

"That is risky, Sergeant," Boynton said. "We don't know the condition of Grierson's soldiers. But I like the plan for what the rescue offers the colonel in the way of safety. We'll do the real fighting. All the colonel need do is stand tall. You take your column and work your way north. Try to cut off any escape along the ridge. I'll stay and if it looks necessary, I shall lead the attack earlier. Otherwise, we attack in exactly thirty minutes. That seems the best compromise we can reach between need for rescue and seeing who we are attacking."

"Sir!" With that Kingman took off, his horse's hooves making dull thudding noises against the sun-baked ground. Then even this vanished when Kingman reached a sandier patch. The only sound reaching Boynton was the snap of rifles from above and the soft whinnying of his command's nervous horses.

He played the attack over and over in his mind as the minute hand on his pocket watch moved with exasperating slowness. If he began his attack before Kingman got into position, both groups would be at risk from the Apache marksmen. But he longed to finish the private war he had embarked on so long ago when he took the solemn vow to stop Victorio and his barbarous killing.

Sarah and the boys.

Boynton swallowed hard, peered into the darkness, and

saw the pale sliver of the moon poking above the ridge. Clouds blew like cobwebs across it, dimming the pale light for a moment before sweeping away briskly to reveal hints of the Apache positions.

Ruth and her son. Amos Magee.

He realized he had more than Victorio to blame for the roster of deaths. Without the Mimbreño chief's rampage, his family would not have died, but Boynton had committed serious mistakes that had caused unnecessary death and misery.

Charles Kingman and Lieutenant Kincaid and most of his command.

The half hour was up.

Boynton lifted his saber so it caught the moonlight and shone like a frozen lightning bolt in the West Texas darkness. He dropped the saber, pointing in the direction of the Apache. Slowly, slowly, slowly the line of mounted soldiers started up the hill. Boynton felt every nerve in his body scream out in protest at the deliberate advance, but he wanted to get as close as possible before ordering the full charge.

Almost at the crest, Boynton watched the moon rise enough to cast its silvery half radiance on the inky terrain. While not as bright as day, their targets showed clearly now. He had gotten close enough for the occasional tongue of orange-white flame licking from Apache muzzles to blind him.

He glanced left and right and saw his line was intact. Not a one of his soldiers hesitated. All were seasoned veterans he could count on to do the right thing in the heat of battle. He had never felt prouder.

Some extra sense caused Boynton to nod to the bugler to sound the charge. As the first notes ripped through the night air, an Apache yelped out a warning about the rear attack.

"Charge!" Boynton screamed over the discordant notes of the bugle command. His horse struggled up the steep slope. One by one the Apache turned their rifles from Grierson's command and aimed them at Boynton's.

Then the captain gained the ridge and got his horse under control. His argent saber flashed brightly, savagely, came away clouded with blood. Boynton rode past the falling warrior, already intent on another. A sharp sting on his shoulder, hardly a bee sting, rocked him and then he was swinging his deadly blade again. This time he missed his intended victim and fell heavily from his horse.

Abandoning his saber, he fumbled at the flap over the pistol holstered at his right hip. He fired as the Apache rose high above him, momentarily blotting out the moon. In the instant he fired, Boynton saw a halo form above the warrior's head. Then the dead man fell and revealed the half moon in its lustrous gray-white glory. The sounds of battle all around, Boynton rolled and came to his knees, pistol ready for action.

He cocked and fired point-blank at another Apache, taking the man from his feet. The Indian scrabbled in the dirt, trying to pull himself along. A second shot from Boynton's smoking pistol ended the attempt.

Another bee sting forced Boynton to take a step back. He ignored the pinprick of pain and waded into the fight, emptying his pistol's cylinder quickly. Then he fought hand-to-hand. Sudden pain rocked him back from an opponent. He turned and fell, unable to make his legs respond. But his senses were acute. He knew everything happening around him as if he could see in the dark and hear sounds privy to only a jackrabbit. He simply could not stand to join the action.

"You hurt bad, Captain?" came a familiar voice. Boynton twisted about to see Private Trent kneeling near him. "Your uniform's soaked in blood."

"Not all is mine," he said, wondering if this was true. He remembered only bits of the fight. He had ridden up the hill, then the infamous West Texas dust storms blew across his mind, erasing memories that ought to be fresh and bright.

Another dark silhouette came up behind Trent. Boynton came to his knees, fighting. His arms thrashed about and he connected. He drew back his fist for another punch but a stronger hand clamped on his wrist, restraining him.

"Fight's over, Captain," Kingman said.

It took Boynton a few seconds to focus his eyes. He sank to the ground and felt pain in three distinct parts of his body. A hip—which one? He was too confused to tell. His left shoulder, along the joint. Low down in his back.

"You got stabbed real good," Kingman said, chuckling. "Ridin' is gonna be a chore for you for a spell."

"What happened? Victorio?"

"Captain Boynton!" Grierson's voice came through the night as clear as a clarion. "You took your time reaching us."

"Sorry, sir. I thought it best to—"

"I'm joking, man!" Grierson knelt on Boynton's other side. "You pulled our fat from the fire. We couldn't run and we couldn't stay pinned down long after sunup. You saved half the soldiers at Fort Davis."

"Victorio?" he asked.

"He saw he was caught between my company down in the ravine and yours charging up behind. He started north along the ridge and ran into Sergeant Kingman's squad. I'm not sure what he did, but he got back through the worst of the fight and headed south."

"South? Through the cactus?" Boynton remembered the mounds of prickly pear, Spanish bayonet, ocotillo, and mesquite. Victorio would have been ripped to bloody ribbons heading that way. But it was better than dying.

Or being captured.

"Reckon that's where he went. I've got trackers after him now, following the blood trail he's leaving. From the look of it, he is making a beeline for the river and Mexico."

"I can overtake him. He can't have that many horses. How many men did he lose? How many escaped?"

"Whoa, hold your horses, Lester," Grierson said in a gentle voice. "He took a real drubbing, thanks to you. But he'll be out of reach before we can resupply. It doesn't do any good chasing him down if we have to throw rocks at him. Our ammunition's exhausted."

"But we're so close!"

"We need to regroup, return to Fort Davis, resupply."

"I'll get him on my own. All I need . . ." Boynton sat up and turned pale with shock. He hastily rolled onto his side, the hard ground and sharp rocks gouging into him preferable to the torture he felt in his left buttock.

"You need to heal. Where you got wounded is more embarrassing than serious." Grierson almost broke out laughing. This did nothing to buoy Boynton's spirits.

Twitching his muscles, Boynton figured out he had been stabbed or shot in the rump. His other bullet wounds seemed hardly more than scratches, though they bled freely. But he had somehow been knifed in the buttocks.

"We'll get you patched up and even find a blanket to pad your saddle for the trip back to the post," Grierson promised. "Young Trent here seems a good man to do the doctoring until the post sawbones can work on you."

"But Victorio! He's still so close! If he gets across the Rio Grande, we can't go after him!"

"You hush up now," said Grierson, rising. In the moonlight Boynton saw the wide grin on the colonel's dirty, blood-smeared face. "I had time to think on this while he was shooting at us in the arroyo. I know exactly how to catch Victorio. When you're patched up, that's exactly what we're going to do!''

Boynton prayed for a miracle to rush the healing of his injuries. He wanted Victorio. Badly.

The Last Invasion

August 6, 1880
Rattlesnake Canyon

"Where do you think, Captain?" Colonel Grierson asked. "Will he come across at Van Horn's Wells?"

Boynton studied the map spread on the stained mess hall table. Spots of grease came through to turn the map almost transparent in places, but Boynton had eyes only for Rattlesnake Springs, sixty-five miles northwest. That was where Victorio would reenter Texas. Mexican Colonel Valle, with four hundred soldiers, had been running Victorio ragged on the other side of the Rio Grande—or was it the other way around?

From the way Valle depended so heavily on supplies from Fort Quitman, Boynton was not willing to place a bet on it. Valle had crossed Victorio's trail after the fight near Eagle Springs, but had been unable to stop the Apache.

"You think my plan is working?" asked Grierson.

"Yes, sir, it is better than Colonel Hatch's attempt at attrition. There's no way to wear down Victorio. He's too adept at living off the land. Even now, after all his defeats, he is still getting new recruits from off the New Mexico reservations."

"I reckon he has to get water, he has to find supplies and, most of all, he has to steal more horses. I have 'bout every company in the Tenth strung out over West Texas to trap him when he comes back. There's not a pass he can sneak through or a watering hole he can drink at without me knowing."

"Colonel Valle doesn't seem up to the chore," Boynton observed. Grierson snorted in disgust.

"They've got some fine officers, son," said Grierson. "It's unfortunate Valle isn't one of them."

"He's taking supplies we can better use," Boynton said, holding down a flash of annoyance, thinking of how those supplies being drained south could support two or three entire companies on this side of the river.

"Won't matter," Grierson said, studying the map. "We'll have Victorio in the wink of an eye. Count on it."

"I am, sir."

"Your men ready for a hard ride?" Grierson asked. "If word comes in, we'll have to get to Van Horn's Wells fast." He studied Boynton a moment, then began whistling a tune. Boynton recognized it as one Ruth had written for the colonel to use as a regimental marching song.

A courier arrived at three A.M. In twenty-one hours, Boynton and Grierson had moved their troops sixty-five miles, in time to prepare an ambush.

"Company H, Twenty-fourth Infantry," Boynton explained to the small group of his officers and noncoms.

"They will accompany the wagon train through Rattlesnake Canyon."

"What are they guarding, sir?" asked Lieutenant Christopher. The young officer looked as sick as when he was vomiting out his guts the week before. Everyone stared at him as if he had just crawled out of a coffin.

"Nothing," said Boynton. "The tarps cover another squad of soldiers. Colonel Grierson is laying a trap for Victorio. The wagon train has a lot of horses, more than they need, as added bait."

"We protect them?" asked the shavetail.

"They can take care of themselves, Lieutenant," Boynton said, annoyed. "It is our duty to capture Victorio and his renegades. That is the purpose of this entire campaign. Are your troopers in position?" Boynton looked not to Christopher but to Sergeant Kingman for the answer.

Seeing that all was well, he continued. "We hang back and do not fire until either Colonel Grierson or Captain Viele of Company C signal us. We remain mounted and ready to go after Victorio, no matter where he runs. Above all else, we do not let him get back across the Rio Grande. Understood?"

Heads bobbed. Boynton wanted to say more but could not find the right words. He felt so close to success after such a long time. All he had to do was reach out and catch Victorio by the throat. If only someone did not make a critical mistake and let him escape yet again. Crossing into Mexico might stir up Colonel Valle and his troopers, but Boynton held out no chance for the inept officer ever to catch Victorio, even if the Apache was on foot.

"Any water holes not being watched, sir?" asked Kingman.

"The colonel has more troops out for this campaign than you know, Sergeant," Boynton said. "Victorio won't be able to spit without someone reporting it."

A signal mirror from eight miles away flashed. Once, twice, a third quick blink and then a long one.

"That's code for the letter V. Victorio's on his way!" With that Boynton swung into the saddle and scattered his officers, again worrying one of them would blunder at a critical moment of the attack. Rattlesnake Canyon was narrow but provided ample hiding places on either side in the jagged tumble of rocks.

"Wagon train, sir," came Kingman's baritone warning.

"Silence," cried Boynton. "Silence along the line!"

He sat astraddle his horse, his own hindquarters hurting as if a million ants had taken up residence in his flesh. The two bullet wounds had begun healing; he hardly noticed them. But his rump alternately throbbed and sent sharp jabs of pain into his back. Boynton shifted in the saddle, standing, as much for a better view as to take the pressure off his embarrassing injury.

His breath came faster when the wagons rattled into view. The four wagons moved slowly, trailing a dozen fresh horses. He tried to find any hint of the ambush and couldn't. Sergeant Kingman had placed the men well. Deeper in the canyon Captain Carpenter waited, but Boynton could not see any of the men from Fort Quitman, either. The heat was oppressive and caused rivers of sweat to run down his face and chest and back, stinging his bandaged wounds.

This pain kept him alert for the first sign of Victorio's band.

Boynton had to restrain himself from yelling out when he saw a solitary Apache riding parallel to the wagon train, sporadically hidden in shadow. Then he spotted another and another as they moved from the shelter of the scrubby trees and towering rock and came toward the rutted road. Victorio had taken the bait!

Hand signs readied the soldiers nearest Boynton to support the infantrymen riding with the wagon train. The four wagons passed his hidden position, heading deeper into the canyon toward Captain Carpenter's company.

Then all hell broke loose. Boynton never knew what happened, but bullets began flying. Shrieks of agony and fear from under the tarps told of Victorio's warriors firing point-blank. The wounded soldiers threw off the tarps and got their own muskets firing. It took Victorio's raiders a few seconds to realize they were being tricked.

"Carpenter's troops!" shouted Boynton, hearing echoes bouncing from farther into the canyon. "They've opened fire. That'll drive Victorio back toward us. Fire, fire, fire!"

Boynton lifted his saber and put his heels to his horse. The sturdy pony snorted and took off at a dead gallop. Boynton did not care if the rest of his men joined the attack. If they fired into Victorio's warriors, that was good enough.

He blinked when he saw how many warriors he faced. He had spotted a few. More than sixty appeared to take shape from shadows and, seemingly, from the ground itself. Victorio had planned well for the attack. He needed the horses, and this desperate need had betrayed him.

Boynton lifted his saber, ready to slash at one warrior rushing on foot toward the rear supply wagon. He brought back his arm, sword heavy and ready, and then found himself flying through the air. His horse had been shot from under him. Boynton landed hard, rolled, and came to his feet, shaken. He stood, sword in hand, too shaken to do anything for a few seconds.

The thunder of hooves brought Boynton around. He faced a warrior on horseback. In a split second, with some preternatural insight, Boynton recognized his foe. Victorio!

Victorio lowered a rifle and fired less than ten feet from Boynton. The rifle misfired. A puff of white smoke came from its muzzle and the rifle jerked in Victorio's hand. Boynton took all this in and reacted without conscious thought. His sword whistled through the air and caught the Apache chief's horse squarely in the chest.

A fountain of blood geysered out and momentarily blinded Boynton. He staggered away, and Victorio swung his rifle, missing Boynton's head by inches. By the time he wiped the blood from his eyes, he saw Victorio pulling himself to his feet not a dozen paces away.

Sword clutched in his hand, Boynton rushed forward. Victorio whipped out a knife and let out a screech. Sword swinging more like a club, Boynton brought it down as hard as he could. Victorio caught the blade and held it— for an instant. His knife blade snapped. But the sudden disarming of his enemy did Boynton no good.

Victorio grabbed his wrists and pulled him forward. A moccasined foot jammed into his belly, and Boynton found himself flying through the air. He landed hard flat on his back, his saber falling from his grip.

"You are the one who killed my nephew," Victorio said, swarming all over Boynton. The Apache pinned Boynton's shoulder to the ground in a schoolboy pin, then throttled him.

Boynton could not curse his enemy. He could not counter with mindless recitation of all those Victorio had killed. Sarah and Thomas and Peter and Amos Magee and Charles Kingman and so many, many more. So many dead. Boynton felt the air leaking from his nostrils and the world turned black. His vision collapsed to a narrow tunnel— and at the end of that tunnel hovered Victorio, squeezing the life from him.

With a convulsive jerk, Boynton unseated Victorio. He scrambled away and came to his feet, warily facing his longtime enemy. Then Boynton stopped letting his anger dictate his actions and started thinking. He drew his pistol, cocked it, and pointed it at Victorio.

"Surrender!" Boynton cried. He wanted to pull the trigger and get his revenge, but in that moment he knew vengeance was not meant for him. He was a soldier, not a judge, jury, and executioner.

Victorio remained in a fighting crouch, his hands clenching into fists and relaxing.

"To-dah!" he cried. Boynton wasn't sure what this meant. Victorio circled, making no move to surrender. *"Nuest-chee-shee!"*

"Hands in the air. You are being taken into custody by the U.S. Army, Tenth Regiment," Boynton said, beginning to feel uneasy. He might have to shoot Victorio to make him give up.

As he aimed, a whistling sound came toward him from the left side. Boynton jerked around and caught a war club on the forehead that knocked him down. He clung to his pistol, got off a shot. But he could not move. He had reached the end of his endurance, even if it meant his death at Victorio's hands.

Around him the battle raged, then a silence fell that was louder than any gunfire.

The battle was over.

"Sir, are you hurt?" Kingman rode up and reined in.

"Victorio," Boynton said, struggling to sit up. The world spun in wild circles and a painful lump formed on his forehead. He touched it gingerly and winced as new pain hammered into his skull. "What happened to Victorio? I had him, but a warrior came up and hit me."

"He hightailed it back down the canyon. Captain Carpenter's not able to give chase."

"A horse, get me a horse." Boynton experienced a moment of panic realizing the brief, fierce battle had passed him by. Two Apache braves lay dead near him. He saw a half dozen buffalo soldiers bandaging one another, but he saw no serious casualties.

"Here, sir." Private Trent tossed the reins of a sorrel to Boynton. Boynton did not ask what had happened to the horse's assigned rider. He vaulted into the saddle and almost passed out from pain as he settled down. He shot the private a sour look, then smiled crookedly, aware of his predicament. "They might have hit my head, but they missed my other buttock this time."

Private Trent didn't know how to react, but Kingman laughed.

"Sir, they took off in that direction. From the way they hightailed it, they might be heading for a water hole, then back across the border."

"Stop them from reaching water," Boynton ordered. He formed his company and took off after Victorio.

Lester Boynton had a constant pain in his ass—and he shared this with Victorio. For five days he hounded the Mimbreño chief across West Texas, never able to engage Victorio directly but always preventing him from reaching water or replenishing his supplies.

Sanctuary

August 6, 1880
Rattlesnake Canyon

"They have many horses," said Loco, grinning like a hungry wolf. "I watched them leave the main road with four supply wagons."

"How soon before they enter the canyon?" asked Victorio. He held down his eagerness. The earlier foray into Texas had ended in disaster. He had Grierson's command in the palm of his hand and had opened his fist for a moment only and the fly had escaped. Worse, the buzzing fly had turned into a wasp, intent on stinging the hand clutching it. Only luck and considerable mobility had allowed Victorio and those with him to escape back into Mexico.

He had lost most of the horses that constituted the wealth of the Apache. Swimming across the Rio Bravo and approaching Juh—and Geronimo—on foot was a shame he could never bear. Better to die in battle than suffer such humiliation. Worse, his family and a few others would arrive any day. How could he face his wife and children with no horses, no victories?

Victorio swelled at the thought of how those Mimbreño warriors with him had readily agreed to another quick raid into Texas. They were brave warriors and deserved only the best hunting and booty.

"What do the wagons carry?" asked Lozen. She frowned, as if trying to remember some distant whisper and failing at it.

Loco shrugged. He rubbed his arm, though it had begun to mend now. "Four wagons might mean ammunition, rifles, heavy supplies other than food. We do not need their white dust or maggoty meat. We can steal cattle and eat better than any of the bluecoats."

"They go to Fort Quitman," Victorio said, beginning to warm to this raid as he worked out what the Indah intended. As always, they made foolish mistakes. "Replacement mounts for Carpenter's company. Who cares about the rest? We have plenty of rifles and ammunition, thanks to Nana."

"There is little ammunition with this supply train," the grizzled old warrior said. "My Power shows some, but not cases stacked upon cases in the wagons."

"Food," said Victorio. "We could use some of their wretched food to give to Mexican peasants in exchange for sanctuary. Our squaws might use cloth and other dry goods also."

"You forget something, Brother," said Lozen.

"Water? How can I ever forget the water needed for our horses?" He swept his arm across the mountains, then pointed in the direction of Rattlesnake Canyon, where the feckless wagon train headed. Better for them to skirt the mountain passes than allow a dozen ambush points along the way as they did. Victorio took this recklessness on their part, in spite of a slightly heavier guard with the train, to mean Fort Quitman had become desperate for supplies.

"After the attack, we go directly to the watering hole to the south, then take our new horses back across the river."

"Something is wrong with this supply train," Lozen said. "We need to be careful approaching it."

"You forget Colonel Valle and how his *soldados* took so many supplies from Fort Quitman. The Indah troopers might be starving now, having given all their food to Valle."

"He blunders around on the other side of the river," Nana said, making a fluttering motion with his hand as if shooing away an annoying insect. "Colonel Valle is not a threat."

"To us, no," said Victorio. "To the buffalo soldiers, he is a great menace. He eats their food. He takes their ammunition. He might even be outfitted with their horses. That might be the reason for this hurried supply train."

In his mind he worked over the route and picked a half dozen places where an ambush would succeed. Victorio knew the territory well, and heeded his sister's advice about water after the raid. They had gone two days between waterings already, and their horses were suffering. His warriors could go another day without water, but to fight tenaciously they too needed water soon.

After the raid. They would kill those soldiers guarding the wagons, steal what they needed, then find the water hole to the south.

It was perfect. He would score a victory to again give those in his band the taste of a successful raid, and they would get horses. Within a handful of days they would be back in Mexico, out of the reach of the buffalo soldiers and greeting their families. Victorio would have restored his reputation as a great war chief and could hold council with Juh and Geronimo with his head high.

"Into Rattlesnake Canyon," he ordered. "We will melt into the eastern side of the canyon a mile into the mountains. As the wagon train passes, we attack all four wagons at the same time." Victorio looked at Nana, Loco, and Lozen. He saw no disagreement with his plan, though Lozen still seemed worried because of her misgivings.

He heaved a deep sigh. If Ussen had spoken to her, he would have reconsidered this raid. But the White Eyes grew impatient—and careless. He had to strike, to show them the error of their ways, to show them his greatness.

They rode for the canyon, entered, and took their positions to await the arrival of so many sturdy horses.

"They come," Nana said softly. "I count twenty-five horses in addition to those pulling the wagons."

"What do those wagons carry?" asked Lozen.

"Who knows?" Nana said. "Who cares? We will take their horses. The wagons would never travel where we must to get to water."

"We take what ammunition and rifles we can," Victorio said, "and anything in the wagons that we might use, but Nana is right. We must travel fast." He went to spit and found he could not. The moisture in his mouth had vanished. In one respect Grierson was smarter than Hatch. He had spread out his soldiers through the area to guard both Rattlesnake Springs and Eagle Springs, cutting off easy watering. What the officer did not know were all the smaller spots furnishing the Apache with sweet water.

"Strike fast, my brother," cautioned Lozen. "We are in dangerous country."

"You remember our last defeat, and do not think on our newest victory," said Victorio with some disdain. "Look, look upon the horses!"

The first wagon rattled past, not twenty yards away.

Behind it on a long rope trotted five horses. The next wagon sported ten, as did the third. The last wagon had none, apparently because of its more ponderous load and more erratic jerking and lurching. One wheel wobbled under the weight and threatened to fall off.

Victorio signaled. The first of his warriors rode out. Then another and another and still more. He was not sure what happened next.

"They're shooting into the wagons! Our braves see something wrong!" cried Lozen. "It's a trap!"

By the time his sister had shouted the warning, all of Victorio's warriors had ridden into the battle. The tarpaulins covering the wagon beds flew up like giant brown-winged birds, flapping and fluttering in the mild canyon breeze. Beneath those tarps hid dozens of buffalo soldiers. Their rifles cracked and snapped and exploded as they fired into the attacking Apache ranks.

Victorio yelled and rocketed forward, his rifle high in the air. His sister had been right. A trap! He had to turn his warriors and get them away safely. As he rode he saw the sun glint off the upraised saber of an officer leading his men into the fracas from the far side of the canyon.

Victorio jerked around as rifle fire from deeper in the canyon told of the fullness of the trap. This was no casual ambuscade. It had been carefully planned—and he had thrust his leg fully into the steely jaws of the trap.

"Anah-zout-tee!" he shouted. "Begone! Flee! We cannot fight this many!"

Ahead of him, Victorio saw the officer readying himself to take a cut at an Apache on the ground. Without thought, Victorio raised his rifle and fired. The instant his gun barked, Victorio knew he had missed. But still he saved a life. His bullet struck the captain's horse in the head, killing the animal instantly. The White Eyes warrior tumbled through the air, still clinging to his sword.

"Hie, yah!" screeched Victorio, riding down on his enemy. He levered a new round into the chamber and tried to aim as he galloped forward. The captain—was this Boynton, the one who had sorely defeated him twice?—widened his stance and swung his sword. Victorio's finger came back. The round misfired, causing a blowout on the side of the rifle that jerked the weapon from his hand and did nothing to end Boynton's life.

The next thing Victorio knew, he, too, was on the ground, next to the officer. The saber slash had cut deeply into his horse's valiant chest, killing the animal by degrees as it bled to death. Victorio whipped out his knife and raced for Boynton before he could recover.

Boynton saw his enemy and began flailing about with his sword as he raced to join battle. Victorio anticipated the overhead cut, lifting his knife to deflect the thick saber blade. He staggered and was driven to one knee as his knife blade broke under the onslaught.

He instinctively grabbed the cavalry officer's wrists and fell away, getting a foot into the man's belly. A swift tug downward, a roll, and a straightened leg sent Boynton cartwheeling through the air to land heavily. Victorio kept a grip on one of his enemy's arms and rolled over, coming to sit heavily on the man's chest.

"You killed my nephew," Victorio grated out between clenched teeth. He gave Boynton no chance to deny it. The death of the young boy had burned in Victorio's breast for too long. He gripped the exposed throat and began to strangle the officer, to drive out the spirit living within him.

As he thought he had killed Boynton, Victorio found himself unseated and knocked to one side. He rolled in the thin dirt and sharp rock and came to his feet, reaching out to grapple again. The Apache chief went cold inside when he saw Boynton draw his pistol, cock it, and aim it straight at his face.

Victorio was not going to surrender. Better to die at the hands of this White Eyes than to be disgraced by capture. Victorio had seen what the soldiers did to their enemies. How could he ever forget the torture they had inflicted on Mangas Coloradas? They had killed him and taken his head and boiled off the flesh.

Never would this happen to Victorio. And he quickly saw he did not have to die this day. From the corner of his eye he saw his sister riding hard to reach him.

"No!" he shouted, causing a moment's hesitation in Boynton. The officer had to be distracted until Lozen narrowed the distance. "Come here!" he cried hoping to urge Lozen to greater speed. He need not have worried. She gauged distance and target well. Swinging her rifle like a club, she caught Boynton in the head as he finally heard her approach and turned to defend himself.

"You arrived when I needed you most," Victorio said, staring at Boynton. The captain moaned and thrashed about, not yet dead. The Mimbreño chief searched for his knife but it was ruined. "Kill him," Victorio commanded his sister.

"We must ride, Brother. An entire company of buffalo soldiers rides down on us from farther up the canyon. Nana says they might be Carpenter's company from Fort Quitman."

"And this one is from Fort Davis. What of the soldiers in the wagons?"

"Infantry," called Loco. "From Fort Concho."

Victorio held his anger in check. He was furious with himself for springing such a trap. Colonel Grierson had brought in soldiers from all over West Texas for this ambush—and it had worked.

He swung up behind his sister. Lozen got her reluctant

pony trotting away. Victorio glanced down at the fallen Boynton. Another day they might meet. He and Boynton would have a reckoning. It just would not be this day.

"Pull closer to that horse," Victorio ordered his sister. Lozen guided her horse near the riderless one. Victorio jumped across, wincing as he landed on the split McClellan saddle. "No wonder they fight poorly," he said as he joined others in retreat. "Their asses hurt all the time riding with these saddles."

A hail of bullets forced him lower on the horse as the survivors of Grierson's ambush fought their way south, heading toward a watering hole.

"Grierson is more clever than I thought," Victorio admitted grudgingly. At every turn the wily colonel had stationed soldiers in sufficient number to block mountain passes and to guard water holes, even those Victorio was certain the Army knew nothing of. He rolled a small pebble about in his mouth to force some moisture to form. It worked, as it had for the past four days, but such craft did not help their horses. The animals wobbled as they walked. Victorio had ordered his men off their backs.

He could not even ride the horses into the ground and switch to fresher mounts. They had no other horses. Grierson had been *very* clever in guarding against theft of additional horses.

"Captain Boynton follows us like a bad odor," Nana said. "If only he had fewer buffalo soldiers with him. An entire company is beyond our ability to defeat."

"I misjudged him," Victorio said. "I thought he was only able to kill women and children from ambush. He has shown himself a better fighter than the others." He hiked along, reins dangling from his fingers. They were less than a day's travel from the river. Cross it and they would again evade their pursuers. But the cost!

Thirty warriors had died and, more telling, seventy-five horses had been destroyed. His temporary camp had been overrun by the soldiers and his supplies destroyed. All Victorio had left was his pride. Boynton intended to rob him of even this.

"How close are they?" he asked Loco, who had gone scouting.

"They move slowly, but they have water," the chief reported. "If we wait for them, they will be here within two hours."

"If we keep on the trail, we will cross the river before they catch us, although they ride faster." Victorio considered a last fight, then discarded the idea as suicidal. He had lost too many warriors, too many horses, most of his ammunition. He had thrown away the rifle that had misfired on him. The defective round had blown out the side of the firing chamber. His backup rifle held only eight rounds. He had no more ammunition.

And few of those still riding with him had more.

They could not fight. They had to run.

"Another day," Victorio said. "We will return another day and show them our greatness. We will take all that we deserve."

"We need to rest," Nana said. "I am old and raiding tires me quickly." Victorio looked at his friend and almost laughed. Old Nana might be old, but he could ride even the strongest and youngest of warriors into the ground.

"We will join Juh's band, rest, and then gather enough horses to return to New Mexico," Victorio said. Never was his family far from his mind. It had been so long since he had seen his wife and children.

"The river, Brother. I smell the river!"

"We can drink," he said, Nana's professed tiredness

settling on him. "We will drink, cross, and then concoct a new way of fighting Colonel Grierson, Colonel Hatch—and Captain Boynton."

Victorio and the Warm Springs Apache forded the Rio Grande into Mexico on August 11. Never again would the war chief set foot on U.S. soil.

No Revenge

"This is unusual, Captain. I trust you appreciate my position." Colonel Grierson frowned, then stared across the Rio Grande into Mexican territory.

"I won't do anything but observe, sir." Boynton's heart hammered. He wanted to be in on the kill, but simply to be present he would agree to any condition. He had spent a few weeks healing and could ride without constant pain, even if he had a long pink scar on his posterior. The head wound he had received during the skirmish that had finally driven Victorio off U.S. soil had been more vexing. Double vision had gone away after a few days, but the crushing headaches had lasted, even after Ruth laid cool compresses and her healing hands on his forehead.

"I don't expect that, Captain. I do expect you not to

step on your pecker when shooting does start. Don't get in the way."

"Yes, sir."

"Get on over there. I expect a full report on how this Colonel Terrazas works in the field. He's come up from Mexico City, and we've never seen him in action." Grierson spat grit from his mouth. "He's got to be better than Treviño."

"I've heard he is a bit more tenacious than former Mexican commanders." Boynton phrased the criticism of Treviño as carefully as he could, although he knew Grierson had no respect for the man. He didn't want to do anything to jeopardize the decision to let him reenter Mexico and be present when Victorio was brought to justice. If luck rode with him, he would see not only Victorio, Loco, and Nana captured, but their families that had escaped from San Carlos also.

"They still take a siesta in the afternoon when they could be marching and fighting." Grierson took a deep breath, then let it out. "There's your guide. Good luck, Boynton." Grierson leaned over, shook Boynton's hand, then returned the captain's salute.

Boynton wheeled his horse and entered the bone-chilling Rio Grande. The rushing river struggled over a sandbar here, ever shifting and always treacherous. Boynton navigated the way to the other side. He looked back, a sense of isolation overwhelming him. Grierson already had trotted off to rejoin the column on patrol. Although they rode constantly, they had not found any sign of Victorio or any Apache band since August 11. Now, the Tenth was part of a combined American-Mexican campaign to end Victorio's raiding days forever.

Ten companies under Grierson patrolled the Rio Grande to make certain Victorio never crossed back into the U.S. while Colonels George Buell and Eugene Carr from General Pope's Ninth Regiment swept down to support the new Mexican commander, Joaquin Terrazas.

"Captain, it is a pleasure to greet you. Come with me, please, and we will join Colonel Terrazas in time for the evening meal."

The Mexican officer had more braids and medals and brass buttons on his uniform than Boynton had seen at the last full dress parade at Fort Davis. And all of it was on one *capitán*.

"I'm anxious to get on the trail. Are you sure you've found Victorio?"

"Ah, you impatient *norteamericanos*," the man said, flashing a wide white smile. "All in good time."

"He's at Tres Castillos?"

"*Sí*, he is. But Colonel Terrazas is only an hour's ride away, and he is anxious to hear of your campaigns against this noted renegade. He has great desire to do only what has been successful and to avoid the mistakes so many others have made tracking down this *indio*."

Boynton rode to dinner that evening and into the Tres Castillos Mountains seven days later.

"We will not tolerate this interference," Joaquin Terrazas said hotly. He was a small man with a pencil-thin mustache. His dark eyes flashed, and he pounded on the shaky table. Boynton stood at the rear of the tent, watching the two American colonels' reactions.

"Colonel Terrazas," spoke up Carr, a burly man with a florid face, "we all want the same thing. We need to stop Victorio quickly. When he got his women and children away from the reservation, we knew we had a real fight on our hands."

"The one called Loco was responsible for arranging their escape south of the border," Colonel Terrazas said, looking mildly bored with such discussion. "This is not my problem. Victorio is. He camps in my country, and this affront will not be tolerated—any more than *your* presence will."

"You cannot get rid of us like that, you strutting little peacock!' " raged Buell. "Our troopers have chased Victorio for years. We must be there when he is brought down!"

Boynton stepped forward and cleared his throat. He had spent considerable time with Colonel Terrazas and knew the man's vanity soared higher than any eagle.

"Colonel, perhaps there is a way for all of us to participate. Your troops are second to none," Boynton said, glancing in the two American colonels' direction, hoping they would hold their anger in check. "Allow the soldiers from the Ninth to take part and learn from you. Where else can they appreciate your genius in the field?"

"No! I find *their* presence on Mexican soil objectionable. They will leave immediately." Terrazas stamped his brightly polished boot like a petulant child. "You allow his people to slip past you and come to *my* country, then you think to do as you please? No! Return to your country now!" Colonel Terrazas struck a dramatic pose, left hand over his heart and right hand thrust out like the blade of a knife, pointing north to New Mexico.

Buell and Carr sputtered and ranted a bit, but left the command tent. Boynton felt as if he had grasped an icicle and now it was melting. Nothing could hold on to the promise of capturing or killing Victorio. He did not know the American officers, but if they fought on a par with Major Morrow, they would definitely succeed against Victorio. Terrazas was throwing away an asset that would insure his success.

"Sir, please reconsider."

"So, Captain Boynton, you do not think my men capable of stopping this Apache renegade?"

"Not at all. We all want the same end."

"Good. Then you may watch and take the word of *our* success to your Colonel Grierson. We attack at dawn tomorrow!"

"Their camp, it is a large one," Terrazas said. "They have not chosen wisely its position, however. My troops surround them and will attack on my command."

"Are you certain Victorio is there?" asked Boynton. "I saw a small raiding party leave, heading to the west, almost an hour ago."

"We could not challenge them without alerting those in the camp," Terrazas said. "We will win a great victory this day. Take careful notes, Captain Boynton. Record for all history my magnificent triumph! My actions on this day of October 14 will be remembered as the pinnacle of military achievement!"

Strutting, the banty rooster–sized colonel paced as he boasted, occasionally opening a pocket watch and staring at it. He finally snapped the cover shut and cried, "To our horses! We attack!"

The sun lacked minutes of rising, but Boynton felt as if he had already been awake for long hours. He was exhausted trying to persuade Colonel Terrazas to accept aid from the Ninth Regiment. Those pleas fell on deaf ears. Terrazas wanted this fight for his own and to hell with dividing the honor.

Boynton quickly had reached the conclusion that he could not press the Mexican commander or he would be sent packing also. The need to see Victorio brought to justice overrode petty squabbling between senior officers.

He had grappled hand-to-hand with Victorio once, with

no definitive conclusion. This time Boynton looked for the fight to be final. And he, of all those with Colonel Terrazas, knew Victorio by sight rather than reputation. Boynton felt as if he had been born knowing what the renegade Mimbreño chief looked like.

"Scouts tell us their camp is stirring, preparing for their morning breakfast," Terrazas said, scanning the note he had been handed by his aide-de-camp. "We ride up the trail, we attack, we conquer!"

Boynton's horse had a difficult time climbing the steep trail. The Mexican horses were better acclimated to the altitude, and ascended faster and with less strain. By the time Boynton got to the mesa where Victorio and his Warm Springs Apache band had camped, the battle had begun.

He scanned the camp for any sign of Victorio. The confusion made it difficult to identify anyone. From all sides came the Mexican troopers, firing and shouting, fixed bayonets stabbing at running women and children. Boynton watched for several minutes before any defense formed in the Apache encampment. By then Terrazas had gained the advantage and ordered his men inward, ever inward, firing and stabbing as they went, tightening the noose around the entire encampment until a staunch defense formed in the middle.

Boynton stood in his stirrups. A catch came to his throat when he spotted Victorio. The Apache war chief stumbled along, his right leg dragging from a wound. Victorio swung about and lashed out with his knife, cutting a Mexican trooper trying to overtake him and gut him with a bayonet. Boynton put his heels to his horse and rocketed across the mesa, intent on Victorio's capture.

As fast as he rode, he saw he would never reach Victorio in time. A half dozen Mexicans surrounded the chief. The leveled rifles insured Victorio could never escape. The

Indian rose from his fighting crouch, favoring his injured leg, his knife held loosely in his hand.

"No, stop him, no!" cried Boynton. His warning was swallowed by the melee around him.

Victorio lifted his knife, turned it inward, and jerked hard. The sharp blade vanished into his chest. For a moment, time hung suspended. Victorio stood with his face upturned, as if he beseeched his gods for an answer to a futile prayer. Then he dropped to his knees, twisted, and fell onto his side. From the way Victorio lay still, Boynton knew the Mimbreño chief was dead.

It was over fast, and the emptiness he felt stunned him. Never again would this renegade kill women and children, steal horses and cattle, or threaten order on the frontier. Even so, Lester Boynton felt no triumph in Victorio's death.

The Final Battle

October 14, 1880
Tres Castillos Mountains

"You worry over nothing," Nana said. "She will bring your wife and children here soon. The few others separated from the main group, also, will come along with her."

Victorio still fretted. Of all those in his band, he trusted Lozen above all. If he could not personally guide his family to join the rest of the Warm Springs Apache families at this hideout in the Mexican mountains, no one other than Lozen would be his emissary. He watched as she and a half dozen others rode slowly from the camp, making their way down the winding path leading to the west, then curling north toward New Mexico. Soon his wife and children would be in this camp and then Victorio could rejoice.

"Loco has done well getting them off the San Carlos Reservation," Victorio said. He saw Loco across the camp, playing with two of his nephews. Victorio felt a sadness at the sight. His own nephew had died—and he had failed to kill the Indah officer responsible. With his own hands he could have ended Boynton's life, and had failed.

He looked around and heard the happy sounds of families reunited. They had heard how Colonel Hatch shifted his patrols to pursue Geronimo and keep his savage incursions in check. The instant the soldiers from Fort Apache near the San Carlos Reservation were drawn away, his stalwart friends had ridden hard and hurried dozens of families away from the deadly water and terrible land.

Only bad luck had prevented Loco from getting Victorio's family also. But now Lozen would fetch them. Victorio hardly believed it possible that he would again share the bed of the woman he loved. To see and hear his children—how they must have grown!—would be an added thrill. Many Apache warriors took several wives. Victorio could have also, but chose to remain faithful to only one.

She would be here, and he could not wait.

"The sun rises soon," he said, stretching. "You should gather Loco and some of the others so we can plan a new raid."

"Not into Texas," cautioned Nana. "Grierson is no rabbit to run from us. Unlike Hatch, he understands how to fight."

"Not into Texas," Victorio agreed. "Not right away. If trouble boils around Warm Springs, perhaps we can return to our own land."

"A dream, nothing more," scoffed Nana. "The only way we will return to our land is to kill all the White Eyes. And how can we do this when they pour into our country like swarms of locusts?"

"A dream, but don't we need that to survive? Ussen gives us power. We must supply the hope." Victorio stopped and cocked his head to one side. "What is that sound?"

As he spoke came a loud cry from the top of the trail Lozen had taken earlier.

"Mexicans!" Victorio cried. "Soldiers!"

Nana bolted and ran as fast as he could, hobbling on his broken foot, heading toward Loco. Victorio looked about for his rifle, but saw soldiers charging from directly behind him, cutting him off from his tipi. A single shot sounded, to Victorio as clear as a coyote's mournful howl. Sudden pain caused him to stumble. Then the sharpness of the pain blasted throughout his right leg. Clutching at his wound, red oozed between his fingers. No bone was broken by the bullet but, walking was difficult. Muscle had been torn deep inside.

Whipping out his knife, he gave throat to a furious war cry and lurched forward to fall on the soldier struggling to reload his musket after his first shot did not end Victorio's life. The soldier died swiftly, the Apache's knife digging into his throat. Victorio jerked away, only to find himself facing a short, stocky Mexican trooper with bayonet fixed. The soldier advanced warily.

Victorio saw Nana and Loco trying to rouse warriors and put up a defense. They were mounted. This gave mobility, but there were so many Mexicans! Too many.

"Die on my knife," Victorio said. The soldier lunged, missing as Victorio sidestepped agilely. Another soldier died, but in the killing, Victorio had miscalculated. Five soldiers circled him. They were joined by another and yet another. He remained crouched. He saw a man—a bluecoat—racing across the mesa. Victorio sucked in a lungful of the clean mountain air and knew he could never permit himself to be captured. Not by Mexicans, not by the U.S. Army.

He stood, the knife hanging at his side. The soldiers advanced warily. Victorio turned the knife and shoved its point into his belly. Another deep breath, then a convulsive move. The blade sank into his muscular body.

"Good-bye, my dear wife, my children, good-bye my sister."

He dropped to his knees, then fell to his side. The world clouded. He blinked at the dusty boots shuffling toward him. One soldier kicked him in the back. Victorio scarcely felt it. Horse's hooves came closer and perhaps he saw his old enemy Boynton through the gathering darkness in his eyes. Or maybe it was the Ghost Pony come to take him away. Too many times before he had refused to mount and ride to the Happy Place. Now he gratefully rose, leaving his body behind on the ground, and his spirit soared faster and farther than any earthly horse could gallop. At last he would join Mangas Coloradas, Blue Pony, and all the others in the Happy Place.

Victory

October 20, 1880
Fort Davis

Lester Boynton hesitated before going into Colonel Grierson's office. He had ridden like the wind to return with his report, only to find the curious emptiness at seeing Victorio killed remained. They had won. Where was the thrill of victory?

"Enter!" barked Grierson. The post commander curled his legs around his chair in a Gordian knot. He almost fell from the chair when Boynton came to a halt in front of the desk, snapped to attention, and saluted.

"Captain Boynton, reporting as ordered, sir!"

"Didn't know you had returned, Captain. I've received dispatches from Hatch and even General Pope. Touchy situation. Since it took you this long to return, I assume Colonel Terrazas allowed you to remain with his troops."

"Yes, sir. His attack at Tres Castillos was successful."

"Indeed?" Grierson arched an eyebrow. "This is good news. From what Carr and Buell reported, they thought he would have trouble finding his own—well, never mind that. Tell me about it." He rocked back in the chair and fixed his gaze on Boynton. Again the captain felt as if he was a bird being watched by a hungry snake. The colonel's gaze was almost hypnotic.

"We attacked at sunrise. By nine o'clock that morning the entire Apache camp was subdued."

"So quickly. He planned this well?"

"Yes, sir. For all of Colonel Terrazas's boasting and bragging and posturing, he executed the attack well. His men fought bravely and sustained few casualties. The same could not be said of Victorio's band."

"Victorio?"

"Dead, sir. I saw him die." Boynton hesitated to mention the Mimbreño chief had killed himself rather than be taken prisoner. "He fought well, too, until almost a dozen Mexicans surrounded him."

"Expected no less from him," said Grierson, stroking his mustaches. "Quite a fighter, Victorio. Go on."

"I was unaware that so many of his clan's women and children had been rescued from San Carlos. Casualties among them were awful."

"Rescued?"

"That's not exactly what I meant, sir. They *escaped* from San Carlos, possibly aided by chiefs Nana and Loco. Sixty warriors and eighteen women were killed at Tres Castillos. Another sixty-eight women and children captured. The remainder of Victorio's warriors escaped, including Victorio's sister."

"You sound upset over this, Captain. No need to be. No operation of this scale is ever completely successful."

"Well, sir, Colonel Terrazas felt he had to allow Lozen to escape."

"Beg pardon?"

"She and a handful of warriors rode out before the attack, heading north into New Mexico. Terrazas felt trying to capture her and the others presented a risk to tipping our hand about the attack."

"Quite so. This Terrazas is a good thinker."

"She escaped, as did Nana and Loco. Victorio might be dead, but his ablest assistants escaped."

"Can't be helped. Victorio was a clever one. He won't be stealing our horses—or killing our families—any more. Anything else to report, Captain?"

"Just that Colonel Terrazas also took a hundred and eighty horses and other animals. That will force the survivors of the attack to reckless raiding, or so thinks the colonel."

"I agree. With a significant defeat like this, it might even persuade Geronimo to surrender. I doubt Juh cares, one way or the other. He is a cold one, Juh is. With the Warm Springs Apache done for, I am sure the Chiricahua will not be long in coming around to accepting surrender terms."

"They'd have to go to San Carlos Reservation, too, sir," Boynton said.

"You think they will take heart from Victorio's refusal to leave Warm Springs for Arizona? Nonsense. They cherish raiding more than anything else. But we need only watch for Geronimo now, and he has never been as interested in Texas as Victorio was. I am sure Terrazas—and Hatch—can deal with the Chiricahua. There is some gossip about Gatewood, under General Crook, being sent after Geronimo." Grierson hummed a tune to himself for a moment, then smiled broadly. "Good work, Captain."

"Thank you, sir. Anything else?"

Grierson pursed his lips, then tented his fingers under his chin. He thought for what seemed an eternity, letting

Boynton squirm. Then he asked, "Victorio's death doesn't make the hurt go away, does it?"

"I still miss my family, sir."

"It is good that you do, Captain. Remember them and know what would happen to others if we were ever to cease our vigilance on this frontier. Now get out of here. I'm putting you in for a week's furlough. What with your time in the saddle and your prior, uh, injury, you deserve the time off."

"Thank you, sir." Boynton saluted but before he was dismissed Grierson spoke again.

"One other thing. If you see Larkin, send him in. I have a few questions to ask of that young man."

"Yes, sir."

Boynton left the office filled with a mixture of relief and the same exhaustion, not of the body but of the soul, that he had felt seeing Victorio die. Purpose had left his life. Sarah and the boys would never be properly avenged.

"Ruth!" he said, almost walking into her. She hurried along bent over, a shawl pulled around her sturdy shoulders against the sharp wind blowing down the canyon to the northwest of the post.

"Lester, how good to see you again," she said. Ruth smiled and some of the emptiness within him filled. "Are you on your way somewhere?"

"Why, no," he said, momentarily at a loss. "I reported and Colonel Grierson gave me a week's furlough."

They walked side by side into the teeth of the wind. He noticed they headed for the hospital.

"Caleb?" he asked, suddenly worried. "He's not sick again, is he?"

"No, thank you for asking," she said in her soft voice. "We were moved from the little house Colonel Grierson had arranged for us when new officers reported for duty last week. As popular as my arrangements are for the colonel's band, the officers on active duty come first. The doctor has been good enough to let Caleb and me stay in one of the unused wards. It is nice having a bed, and the number of injured has declined since you defeated Victorio. I remember one post where we had to sleep on the bare ground." She sighed.

"I will see if I can't find better accommodations."

"That's all right, Lester. Now that the Indian threat has died down and Caleb is fit enough to travel, we'll be going on the next wagon to Fort Concho. I enjoy working for the colonel, doing all kinds of music for the post band, but it is no way to spend my life. I'm not sure exactly why I remained this long."

The desolation almost overwhelmed him.

"You can't go. Stay, Ruth."

"Stay? For what reason?" She stared up at him, her brown eyes wide and innocent.

"I don't want you to go."

"Many do." She nudged him in the ribs and tilted her head in the direction of Evan Larkin, hurrying to Colonel Grierson's office. "There's one whose bed will soon be empty. Colonel Grierson had me compile an alternate inventory of supplies for him to compare with the official list Larkin submitted. I am sure there were considerable differences."

"The colonel asked me to have Larkin report to him. It's never been much of a secret how Larkin always had wads of greenbacks."

"The supplies have been turning up missing more and more, and stories of Larkin's gambling abound. Unless Larkin spins a better tale than he keeps the post supplies, I'd say a court-martial is in the works."

Boynton felt no need to go to Larkin's aid. Stealing from the troopers was criminal, and he ought to be punished for it. Somehow, it had never seemed such a matter for concern.

"Are you getting your bandages changed?" Ruth asked as they climbed the steps of the hospital. "Or have you healed?" The corners of her mouth curled into a smile. "I'd not mind aiding the doctor in this endeavor."

"For my head injury?"

"For all of them, Lester." Her eyes dipped devilishly, then locked again with his.

He stood uncomfortably, the words trying to force themselves from his throat but indecision holding him back from speaking.

"Yes?" she asked.

"I'd miss Caleb. He's a good boy," Boynton said.

"He is that. I am sure he will miss you too."

"There's no need for that," he said, still unable to speak what his heart was telling him.

"We have to leave Fort Davis. There's no place for us. Unless—"

"Unless your husband desired your presence?" Boynton asked.

"Why, yes."

"I'm only a captain, not a colonel," he said, still awkward. It had been this way when he had spoken to Sarah about marriage. Was this what he was doing now with Ruth Magee?

"You are a quick study. You've learned well."

Boynton went pale with shock as he realized what he must say, what he must confess, and the woman's likely reaction. "You don't know *all* my mistakes, Ruth. I—"

"I know, Lester," she said, putting her finger against his lips. "Amos was not a great soldier, but he was a brave man. He tried to save you and your squad, didn't he?"

"If it hadn't been for me chasing Victorio into Mexico,

your husband would not have died. Because of me, he died!"

"Your men speak better of you than they do of other company commanders. You've grown from your errors of judgment. I know. I've listened. And I do not think ill of you."

"But your husband died!"

"Yes," Ruth said softly. "Do you think my luck will improve with a new husband? A captain?"

He saw tears in her eyes and longed to kiss her. Boynton held back.

"We will need Colonel Grierson's permission," he said.

"He is a fair man. He would never refuse. After all, he has allowed me to stay far longer at Fort Davis than another commander might have. I cannot believe he needed someone to write and arrange music for him. He is a capable man in that area."

"If he refuses, I will resign my commission!"

"What would we do then? You'd have a wife and son to feed." Ruth smiled broadly now.

"What's the difference, if we are together?"

"As a family," she said.

"Colonel Grierson won't deny us permission."

Nor did he.

Epilogue

Nana, now seventy years old, assumed leadership and raided on with Lozen's help. Nana promised her many deaths in revenge for Victorio's death. He was successful in this threat. Until General George Crook's campaign, Nana raided with skill and daring. He was captured in 1886 and sent to Fort Marion, Florida, as a prisoner of war. After Nana's capture, Lozen remained with Geronimo until his capture by General Crook. Lozen died of tuberculosis in late 1888 at the Mount Vernon Barracks in Alabama, like Geronimo and Nana, a prisoner of war.

HELL-FOR-LEATHER, RAWBONED ENTERTAINMENT FROM THE MASTER OF FRONTIER FICTION, FREDERIC BEAN

BLOOD TRAIL   (0-8217-4369-4, $3.50)
His wife and child brutally murdered, his Texas ranch in ashes, John Vilalobo finds himself back in a role he thought he'd left behind: that of a lawless pistolero on a trail of danger. He won't rest until he gets bloody revenge against the men who've destroyed all he's held dear.

CRY OF THE WOLF   (0-8217-3667-1, $3.50)
U.S. Marshal Sam Ault has a tough mission—rescue a 14-year-old girl seized by a war party of Comanches in the Texas panhandle. But will his green-as-grass deputy have the grit and guts to stare down death when the bullets start flying?

SANTA FE SHOWDOWN   (0-8217-4065-2, $3.50)
A beautiful woman, a chest full of Mexican gold, and the bloodiest range war west of the Pecos are among the hazards and enticements facing Colonel Trey Marsh, a Civil War veteran riding the dusty road to Santa Fe. His amazing skill with a .44 will soon be tested against the quickest gun in the territory.